ICED
out

LEIGHTON U BOOK ONE

CE RICCI

Editing: Zainab of Heart Full of Reads Editing Services

Proofreading: Amanda Mili of Amandanomaly

Cover Design: Emily Wittig Designs

Michaela,

Fight me, baby.

♡ CE Ricci

To the ones who broke the mold and wrote their own stories:

Continue chasing your most authentic self.

And to Taco Bell:

This manuscript would have never been finished

if it weren't for you and your Baja Blasts.

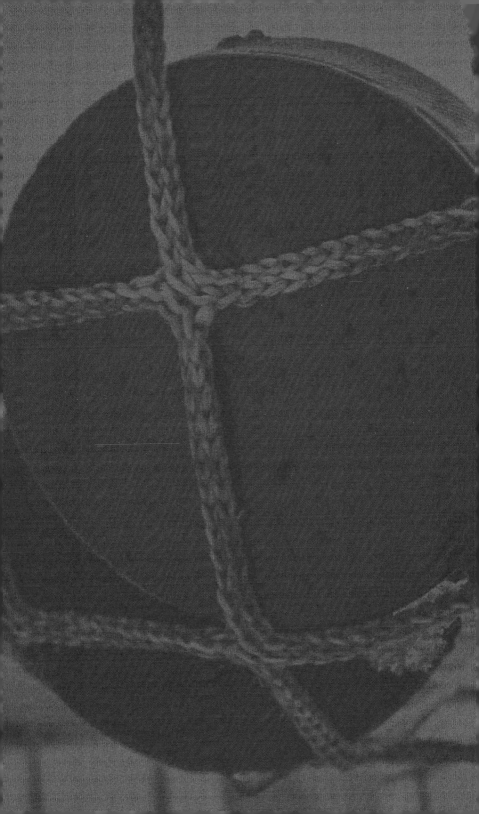

"THE WORLD'S PERCEPTION OF YOU
EXISTS ONLY IN MEMORIES.
GIVE THEM NEW ONES."

— ATTICUS

Theme Song

Antisocialist—Asking Alexandria

Playlist

Bite My Tongue—You Me At Six, Oli Sykes
Agree to Disagree—Sleeping With Sirens
Straight to My Head—You Me At Six
It's Over When It's Over—Falling In Reverse
Enemy—Nerv
Limits—Bad Omens
medicine—Bring Me The Horizon
Underdog—You Me At Six
Harder To Breathe—Letdown.
MANTRA—Bring Me The Horizon
Personal—Palisades
Light it Up—From Ashes To New
Anthem For The Underdog—12 Stones
RISE—I Prevail
Temporary Bliss—The Cab
Not Enough—Outline In Color
Colors—Crossfade
Carnivore—STARSET
True Colors—Wage War
What's It Like—You Me At Six
Less Of Me—Until I Wake
Your Misery—Palisades
FWYTYK—I Prevail
Blackout—Breathe Carolina
THE DEATH OF PEACE OF MIND—Bad Omens
Animals—Ice Nine Kills
Rise Above It—I Prevail
Sink—Remember the Monsters
Like A Villain—Bad Omens
Cutthroat—blessthefall
Fall—Palisades
Glass Houses—Bad Omens

Listen to the playlist on Spotify

Disclaimer

As a dedicated sports enthusiast, I've done my best to portray all aspects of the NCAA and NHL hockey rules and regulations as accurately as possible. However, sometimes rules when applied in a fictional setting need to be bent to fit within the narrative, so some creative freedoms and liberties were taken for plot purposes of this book.

Leighton University, along with any other university within this work and series, is completely made up, fabricated so as not to misrepresent the policies and values, curriculum, or facilities of real institutions. The views in this book in no way reflect the views and principles of the NCAA or NHL, as it is a work of fiction.

PROLOGUE

Oakley

Senior Year—Eighteen Years Old

One of the few times I ever let myself feel free and at ease is with blades on; ice beneath my feet. It's difficult to describe, considering how fast-paced hockey can be, but a sense of peace takes over every inch of my being, and it's like I become one with my team and the puck.

It's a sense of belonging. Of purpose, going back to the first time I ever put on a pair of skates, and it only continues to grow with time.

It's a feeling, deep in the marrow of my bones, confirming this is what I was called to do. Not because of the legacy my name carries, but because of the unchecked joy vibrating through my body every second I'm on the ice.

That feeling…it's everything I could ask for.

And I want nothing more than to chase it to the ends of the earth.

This fact solidifies in my bones every time I fly up and down the ice after a loose puck, or score a shot on goal, seeing the lamp light up before my eyes. When every accomplishment and milestone I reach sets me further apart from my predecessors, letting me finally be seen outside the shadow they cast.

And it's in the adrenaline rush, the intoxicating high, the all-consuming pride that comes from bringing home a hard-fought and well-earned win.

Which is why it's understandable that I'm still on cloud nine when I'm on my way to board the bus after not only playing the best game of my high school career, but also winning Chicago's city championship game against our biggest rival, Centre Prep. Even though the title is not nearly as prestigious as state champions—one Centre managed to snatch from our grasp last month—it still feels amazing to not only up the ante with a rematch, but to come home with the win.

Makes the victory all the sweeter.

Their star forward for the past four years, Quinton de Haas, leans against the wall about ten yards down the hallway. His gaze lifts to collide with mine, finally noticing me as I'm about to pass by.

"Good game tonight," I tell him, because he did play well. Minus the parts where he was tossed in the sin bin for blatant penalties, playing more like a youth player than a top-tier recruit for numerous collegiate hockey programs. But I'm not about to hand him a backward compliment and cause a blow up, seeing as once his fuse is lit, it's only a matter of time before it explodes.

Too bad for me; he detonates anyway.

A hand is fisted in my shirt and I'm being slammed against the wall before I have a chance to blink, let alone react. Once my brain registers what just happened, I lock eyes with him.

"Don't start with that bullshit, Reed." He's seething, fury written all over his face. Bubbling below the surface, waiting to be unleashed.

His rage is nothing new, especially on the ice. He's one of the most ruthless opponents I've played against in the past thirteen years. Hell, I've seen that fury come to life firsthand a few times; the anger he plays with building and building inside him until there's no room left.

And then he snaps.

Just like right now.

My hand wraps around his wrist, and I try to break free of his hold. It's no use, so I just dig my fingers into the tendons there and glare at him. "What the hell's your problem?"

His forearm presses against my sternum as he crowds me more, ice-blue eyes full of unchecked rage. "You're my fucking problem. Hockey's little golden boy, coming out here with your *good game tonight,* acting like you own the sport."

He's trying to get under my skin, but it won't work.

Unlike him, I don't let my temper control me, and I definitely don't toss hands at the drop of a hat whenever I can't rein in my feelings.

Which is why he doesn't get the reaction he was hoping for, and I snort out a laugh. "Seriously? It was a compliment. One I meant, so just take it and move the fuck on."

"Move the fuck on?" he echoes, the incredulity in his voice apparent. Dark brows, the same color as his hair, slash down, and the frown on his face shifts into a snarl. "You want me to *move the fuck on* when we both know that win belonged to Centre?"

This time, I really can't help the sharp laugh that bursts past my lips. Because, seriously? That's the hill he wants to die on?

Aware that I'm tempting fate by taunting a loose cannon like de Haas, I lean in closer. "A win only belongs to the team that earns it."

"Or it goes to the team that pays off the refs."

His comment takes me aback. "What?"

"Yeah, you heard me," he continues. "Bet Daddy made a little donation to the pockets of those officials. Just make sure you didn't completely tarnish the Reed family name this season by losing to us at State *and* here."

My spine stiffens as his words fall between us like a damn guillotine.

Nepotism is real, but damn if I've ever been on the receiving end. In any capacity, but certainly not in the way he's implying.

There have been plenty of times in my life where I wish I wasn't a legacy to not one but two hockey legends. Being taught the game from two greats was amazing. But sharing a last name with them causes complications when you're only trying to make a name for *yourself*.

Finding a way to shine on my own seems impossible most days. Forever being labeled as the son of ten-time all-star forward Travis Reed or the nephew of Trevor Reed—record holder for the most shut-outs in a single season by a goalie—isn't all it's cracked up to be.

I'd much rather be *me*. Oakley Reed. Future forward to the Leighton University Timberwolves. And whatever else comes after that.

Quinton running his mouth about my family only proves the point.

"Unbelievable," I mutter. "If that's what you need to believe to sleep tonight, fine. Think what you will. Nothing I say is gonna change that."

"Oh, is that an admission?"

"No, it's you pulling some bullshit out of your ass and reaching for a reason for the loss when it's simple." I pause, sure to staccato every word for emphasis. "You. Didn't. Play. To. Win."

If he wants to try digging under my skin, two can play at that. And by my count, I'm up, as I watch the flames in his eyes ignite at my barb.

"Or our team played the better game, meanwhile yours got lucky with a bunch of bullshit penalty calls against us."

And just like that, I see right through him.

"Against your team, or against *you?* Because I think the real problem here is that you were too busy playing dirty to actually *play the game.* And that cost your team the championship."

It's true. I think we had five total power plays in the second period alone, and two were because of Quinton either running his mouth or taking cheap shots at my teammates, landing him in the sin bin to sit and watch.

Sure, there were a few calls that could've gone either way; I'll give him that much. But the same thing happened to our team. Doesn't mean we paid off the refs to make it happen.

"Oh, that's right, because you've never been tossed in the penalty box before, right, Oakley? Tell me, what's it like, being perfect all the time?"

He hits his mark with that one, and my irritation sparks.

"It's got nothing to do with being perfect and everything to do with playing the game the way it's meant to be played. *That's* how you win. Now, would you just give it a rest already?" I give him an exasperated shove, tired of the crap he's spewing about not just me, but my family too. "Take your participation trophy and go home. Listening to your sore loser nonsense is pathetic."

"I'm pathetic?" He bares his teeth, stepping into me again, so close his nose brushes mine. "What's pathetic is getting everywhere in life because of your last name rather than your own merit."

There it is again, the twitchy, burning sensation from his accusation. It radiates from my core, twisting and curling all the way down my extremities until I'm wound so tight, I might burst at the seams.

A vise that tightens around my self-control with every mention of my last name or family.

Because I am not my uncle, nor my father.

And I'm fucking sick of the world playing this little comparison game.

"*I* was the one out on that ice tonight, de Haas. Not any other Reed."

"He's still the reason you're out there playing at all. Still the trailblazer for your path to success," he growls, voice nothing more than a vicious whisper. "Which is a path most of us are forced to carve out for ourselves."

He's right about one thing. My roots in hockey made it an easy path to follow, but I'll be damned if it makes the blood, sweat, and tears to get to where I am any less real. The grueling practices any less tiresome. Plus, I'm also forging my own identity while attempting to carry a legacy. Finding my place within an industry and world that's already slapped a label on me.

Which is a lot fucking harder than it might seem without assholes like Quinton thinking I've been handed a throne and crown with no idea how to rule a kingdom.

"I've worked just as hard as you have," I grit, my jaw ticked with effort as his words claw at my carefully crafted facade of the hockey god he claims me to be.

But even solid gold can scratch and dent. Tarnish in the wrong hands, or even break.

"I'm sure you have, just like I'm sure you'll get the pick of the litter when it comes to hockey programs next year." He pauses, a venomous sneer on his face. "Right after Daddy signs a blank check to the university, of course."

On a dime, all the tension coiled inside me just…snaps.

I knew there was a chance this conversation would start with words and end with fists. With Quinton, the odds are always high.

I just never bet on being the one to throw the first punch.

ONE

Quinton

October—Four Years Later

"D e Haas. You're late."

Coach's penetrating stare is aimed at me the second I burst through the locker room doors, having just dashed across campus like a madman to avoid this very scenario from playing out. But hopes that I'd be able to sneak in unnoticed rather than be a dead man walking right into my own funeral seem to be in vain.

Well, shit.

"It won't happen again," I murmur, meeting his gaze with the appropriate amount of remorse he's looking for. Just enough to not get a verbal smackdown unleashed on me before the first game of the season.

As the team's captain and the person expected to set an example for the rest of the team, I'd be lying if I wasn't anticipating a full-out reaming regardless. Even if I've been a lot better about managing my time this season.

Until today, that is.

Today, the hockey gods decided I would oversleep by an hour, making me the run-across-campus-like-crazy-to-not-miss-faceoff kind of late. Which is just a fan-fucking-tastic way to start my morning. It's the only reason I wait, ever so patiently, to get chewed a new asshole. Yet I'm surprised when all I get is a firm nod and a *see that it doesn't* grumbled back at me.

Not one to look a gift horse in the mouth, I scoot by him and head toward my stall to suit up. After all, being late means I've got only five minutes to dress before we're due out on the ice for warm ups.

The locker room is bustling, a buzz vibrating in the air the way it always does before a game. Something I attribute to all the nervous excitement radiating off everyone inside. But the buzz only makes me anxious, and that's why I'm doing my best to zone in mentally as I dress in the bottom half of my uniform.

Until a voice startles me.

"I don't think I've ever been more jacked for a game in my fucking life."

My eyes lift from where I'm lacing up my skates to find a fully-dressed McGowan, one of our sophomore defensemen, taking a seat on the bench in front of me. He's still green as shit, not getting a lot of ice time his first season on the team. But he's on my line this year after really proving himself these last few weeks, earning a starting spot on the ice. Something he's never experienced before.

So *jacked* could mean a couple things in this situation.

Arching a brow, I ask, "In a good way, or…"

He gives a sheepish sorta grin, his blond hair flopping down on his forehead. "I mean, I feel like I'm David, ready to pound the shit outta Goliath. But I also wanna upchuck everything I've eaten in the past twelve hours. So…both?"

I let out a bark of laughter, not at all surprised. "Let's not barf on the ice, unless you wanna be the one to clean it up." I pause. "But the David-pounding-Goliath-to-a pulp bit, I'm a fan of. Channel that shit, Danny."

He nods, but I swear the guy gets even paler as he does it. "Channel it. Right. I can do that."

Let the record show that he definitely *does not* sound like he can. But I smile, placing my hand on his shoulder pad and giving him a few pats.

McGowan's been under my wing since he came in as a freshman last season. It's the way Leighton University runs a lot of their athletic programs; sort of how frats have Bigs and Littles, only spaced out two years instead of one. It's supposed to help the team bond more and let the younger guys have an upperclassman that can help keep them on the straight and narrow. Help give them the tools they need to succeed at the collegiate level.

So Danny is…well, my Little, I guess.

Why the hell anyone would ever trust me to keep someone else's head firmly on their shoulders when I can barely manage that on my best day? I have no clue. Yet, here I am anyway, with Danny looking to me for support.

And while I don't think I'm all that good at it—I'm more of a tough-love kinda guy than the nurturing type—I can't help the feeling of *wanting* to help him keep his shit together instead of losing his lunch. So I give out the only piece of reassurance I can.

"I've got your back out there, D-man. We all do."

Diverting his gaze to the floor, he nods. "Thanks, Cap."

And just like that, he's gone. Probably embarrassed, though I don't know why he would be, considering he's one of the few members of the team who actually likes me.

Maybe he's left to vomit in one of the toilets instead.

I'm banking on the latter as I chuckle and shake my head, all the while something he said makes my stomach feel all warm and fuzzy inside.

Cap.

As in *captain.*

It's been months since I was selected as captain at the end of last season, but the title hasn't sunk in. Maybe because I've tried not to let the title go to my head too much, but I can't help it. And honestly, there's no real reason I shouldn't, at least today.

Because this is it.

My last first-game-of-the-season as a member of Leighton's hockey program. And more than anything, I want this to be the season the Timberwolves bring home a Frozen Four trophy. A championship title for the first time in five seasons, and with me leading the team to victory.

While we've had our share of hiccups in practices and scrims, I'm feeling confident about our chances this year. Hopeful, even.

But all my hopes come screeching to a halt the moment I look up to find Oakley fucking Reed walking right toward me. Also known as the one person on this damn team I *really* don't get along with.

Though, as much as I hate to admit it, the fault of this beef rests squarely on my shoulders.

Even if he is the one who decked me first—an extremely out-of-character reaction from him—I was still the one to start our little squabble after the city championships senior year. And that moment would forever etch me into Oakley Reed's mind as his biggest rival. Maybe even a straight-up enemy.

At the time, we didn't know the unthinkable would happen.

That we'd both stay in Chicago and end up here.

At Leighton.

For four fucking years.

Together.

"De Haas," he mutters, already suited up like the rest of the team, save for his helmet. "Seems you decided to join us after all."

I try not to let his voice get my hackles to rise, but when Oakley takes opportunities like this to toss out little barbs, it's hard to keep from reacting. It seems like no amount of self-work and reeling in my anger seems to help with him around. It still seeps through the cracks to get the best of me, no matter how hard I try to garner some sense of control.

But can I be blamed when he eggs me on just as much as I do him?

"As if I'd be anywhere else right now?" I bite out, shoving my duffle into my stall before rising to stand.

A fake smile is plastered on his lips. "Never know with you, especially when you're the last one to show up on game day."

I grit my teeth as I grab for my chest and shoulder pads, not daring to walk straight into the trap he's baiting for me. But man, it's hard. He's the most infuriating person I've ever met.

"Don't you have better things to worry about?" My eyes take a second to evaluate him, running from his head of golden-brown hair all the way to his toes before returning to his legs. Then I make a show of leaning down and staring at his shins, even tapping against them. "Like maybe the fact that your stupid lucky socks are showing through your team-issued ones? Are those…kittens? Pretty sure that goes against regulation."

Truthfully, I can't see jack shit other than the white fabric, and even if I could, the shin guards would be in the way from seeing whatever pair of wacky socks he's wearing beneath them. But it doesn't make it any less fun to poke the bear.

I think I even catch his eye twitch as he does his best not to look down and double check.

"Hilarious," he deadpans, not a hint of amusement in those chocolate-colored eyes. "But you should know better than to make fun of someone else's juju. It's bad luck on you."

That *is* true.

Plenty of athletes are superstitious as hell during the season—myself included, though that is confidential information no other living soul knows about. And it's an unwritten rule that you don't fuck with a teammate's ritual, superstition, juju, whatever. Throws the entire fucking vibe outta whack.

Just ask Justin Parsons, our goalie from my freshman year. One of the starting wingers that season tried catching his lucky stick as it was falling over in the locker room after a morning skate.

But Justin had a rule. No one touched the lucky stick unless he handed it to you.

It sounds hilarious to someone who doesn't get athletes and their superstitions, but I'm not kidding when I tell you eighty percent of the team got the stomach flu a couple days later, causing us to forfeit not one, but two games.

And I can honestly say I've never been more sick in my entire life. I shudder just remembering it.

"I'll take my chances," I tell him, sliding the pads over my head and going back to minding my own business. Except the jackass is still right here, looking to pick a fight.

"Why am I not surprised? You clearly don't give a flying fuck about anything at this rate if you're showing up an hour late."

I stop what I'm doing, tilting my head as I stare at him. "You seem awfully concerned about my whereabouts, Reed. Trying to keep tabs on me? Miss me too much when I'm not around?"

Oakley's nostrils flare with anger, dark brows drawn down over narrowed eyes. His typical death glare. A look I've been on the receiving end of far too many times for it to instill fear anymore.

"Hardly, *Captain.* I just figured, since you're in charge now, you might make some effort to act like you care about this team. Make us a priority. But I can see I was mistaken. Instead, you're planning to lead us right into the damn ground."

The venom behind the word *captain* doesn't hit the mark, though I can tell he's hoping it would. But the sensitivity toward that topic is his issue, not mine.

I never asked to be considered for captain; I was just chosen. But again, not one to look a gift horse in the mouth, I graciously thanked Coach for naming me, took on the damn title, and ran with it. Shit, maybe it would actually be enough for some guys on the team to stop looking at me like a fucking leper half the time just because hockey's golden boy doesn't like me.

Of course, naming me as captain only added more fuel to the fire already blazing between myself and said golden boy that started all the way back in high school. And then growing more at the end of last season, when Oakley got taken out with a broken collarbone from a hit that was meant for me.

And then there's also every other combative conversation in between, continuously stoking the flames.

Hell, I'm surprised Coach didn't just give Oakley the damn title to *prevent* this very thing from happening. And I'm sure Oakley did too, seeing as he's Coach's nephew. Plus, he was pretty much a shoo-in for the position.

But it's not my fault Oakley thought nepotism would secure the spot for him.

Stick and helmet in hand, I give him an exaggerated sigh. "Yeah, well, at least I'm leading."

Fire burns in his eyes, his jaw ticking with effort to keep his temper reined in. And that's how I know I won tonight's little pissing match. When he's so fucking pissed, he can't even come up with another witty, dickish retort.

It's actually a fun little game I like to play—see how many digs it takes for him to shut down. Sometimes, I even try to beat my own record.

Going for a low score, like in golf.

Right now, I'd say I'm two under par.

Arching a brow, I give the jackass a winning, plastic smile. "See you on the ice, Reed."

TWO

Oakley

I stare after Quinton's retreating form, still fuming from the verbal sparring match he coaxed me into having. Or maybe I started it this time. Honestly, it's hard to tell anymore with every single shitty encounter leading into the next.

For the life of me, I wish I knew how to let his crap just roll off my back. Yet somehow, he bends and twists me in all kinds of knots every time he opens his damn mouth, forcing me to engage.

He's the only person who's ever been able to get a rise out of me.

You'd think after four years of playing together, I'd be immune to it by now. The taunts and the jokes and the straight-up insults. But nope, it still works to his benefit. Maybe even easier now, with having to spend so much time around each other.

No part of me wants to spend more time than necessary with him.

Ending up on the same team with him was so far outside my plans for college, it's laughable. So imagine my fucking horror when I was getting suited up for my first day of practice freshman year and he walked in.

If I was the violent type, heads would have rolled.

But we've reached the point in this stupid beef where the only thing I truly want is one day where we aren't at each other's throats.

Who knows, today might be that day. Starting…now.

Here's to hoping, right?

Needing to channel this frustration into something a lot more useful, I head out to the rink after the dickhead, knowing one thing's for certain.

I'll feel better once I'm on the ice. I always do.

As far as the first game of the season goes, I can't complain about how the team is performing as a whole. The chemistry is there, most lines working together seamlessly, both offensively and defensively.

The problem is Quinton…and me.

We don't mesh on the ice. Never seem to be on the same page, and sometimes, it feels like we don't even play on the same team. Then again, with all that time we spent as opponents rather than teammates, I guess it's a little hard to train out of us.

All I can do is hope that the kinks get worked out as the season goes. Or we figure out how to stay out of each other's way while being on the ice at the same time. And that appears to be working well, actually.

Except that Quinton's version of staying out of my way entails acting like I don't exist altogether. And by doing so, he also ignores me when I'm open to take a shot on goal, instead taking it himself—which only ends up being blocked by the goalie—or turning the puck over to the other team before he gets the chance. Either way, we miss out on a chance to score. Something kinda important to, I don't know, win a game.

And it doesn't just happen once, either. There are multiple occasions over the initial forty minutes of game play, and by the time we're skating our way off the ice for a second intermission, I'm frustrated beyond belief.

And here I thought hockey players outgrew being a puck hog by now.

He goes to skate by me after the rest of the team, and in my irritated state, I make an irrational move, grabbing his arm to stop him in his tracks.

"What?" he snaps, harsh blue eyes locking with mine.

Deep, calm breaths. Don't bite his head off, just offer a suggestion.

It would work except the suggestion comes off a little bit more like an insult.

"You're not the only player on the team who can score, de Haas. You do know that, right?"

His nose wrinkles, giving me a look that reads a little something like *are you fucking stupid.* "Obviously. I'm not a child, Reed. I know how to share."

I almost laugh at that. *We'll have to agree to disagree, I guess.*

"Okay, well, pass the damn puck if you see I'm open."

He continues staring at me for a moment, then just skates off to where the rest of the team is heading to the locker room without another word.

Okay then...

There's no use getting into it with him here and now, so I just keep my trap shut and follow him to the locker room. But much to my pleasure, I overheard Coach pull him to the side on our way back out for the third period and rip him a new one for not passing the puck when Rossi and I are open.

"You're a leader, now," Coach bit out. "And leaders know sometimes you need to let others step in."

While hearing Coach's snappy comment made me preen a little, considering I had told de Haas the same fucking thing fifteen minutes ago, it also gut-punched me in the most unexpected way.

I've always done my best to embody what it means to be a leader and team player, not just playing well and doing my part on the ice but being someone the rest of the team could look to as an example. Something a captain *should* be.

And clearly, everything Quinton is not.

The guy's talented, as much as I hate to admit it. He could make it big—I'm talking NHL big—if he wasn't such a hothead. Or a raging douche canoe. But his habit for using his fists on the ice as much as his stick makes him more of a liability than an asset. Which is something I *thought* my uncle might've realized isn't the makings of a good captain.

Guess I was wrong.

If it wasn't for the hit I took at the end of last season—resulting in a broken collarbone and tear in my rotator cuff—I'd probably be the one leading this team. Hell, every person on the damn team knows it should be me. Yet here we are, with the title I've coveted for myself in the hands of the one person who shouldn't have it.

My sworn enemy.

But at least Quinton seems to take Coach's demands at face value, playing a lot more like a team player than a solo act to start off the third period. Even passes the puck off to me on a breakaway, allowing me to run with it and—

Out of nowhere, I'm slammed into the boards by one of their defensemen, and the impact sends a jolt of pain lancing through my shoulder. I freeze on impact, the defender taking the puck with ease, leaving me empty-handed and in a panic as the dull ache continues to spread through the entire limb. It takes a couple minutes for the throbbing to subside, so I know the hit probably tweaked a muscle or something, but it's not any less nerve-wracking.

The last thing I need is a re-injury during the most important season of my career.

"Pass you the puck, only for you to pull that shit?" Quinton snarls. "Nice. Jackass."

I watch as he takes off down the ice, attempting to stop Trenton College from scoring while irritation vibrates through my chest.

Quinton's inability to keep his fucking mouth shut on the ice is the same reason I was injured. Instead of focusing on his game, he was too busy running his damn mouth to one of the defensemen from Waylon during the playoffs last season. All game. Until he finally had enough of Quinton's crap. Unfortunately, that happened in the middle of a change on the fly, and instead of slamming *Quinton* into the boards and breaking *his* collarbone, it was me.

The fucking guy even told me he was going for de Haas, but the shuffling of all our players caused him to lose sight for one second and… well, the rest is history.

I went in for surgery a couple days later and spent my summer months going to PT multiple times a week, only barely feeling like I was at a hundred percent a couple weeks before practices started this season.

And none of that would have happened if de Haas knew how to keep his mouth shut. Yet another thing on the ever-growing list of reasons why this guy is the bane of my fucking existence.

I'm about to skate back toward where the rest of the guys are helping Cam defend the net, the forwards for Trenton on an aggressive offensive attack.

That's when Trenton's center, named Adams, checks Quinton into the wall. Hard. A lot harder than necessary. Meanwhile, the puck is sent sailing to the other end of the rink. Instincts tell me to skate after it, but the whistle blowing catches my attention and drags it back to where Quinton is crumpled to the ground.

A hush falls over the arena as everyone holds their breath, something that always happens when a player goes down.

Shit.

"Give him some room," one of the officials commands, creating space around Quinton as he pulls his helmet off.

When Quinton raises his head, I catch it. The fire in his eyes burning brighter and hotter, just like when he's about to—

Quinton lunges from the ground, grabbing Adams around the waist. They both go tumbling back to the ice, and de Haas rips the helmet right from Adams's head as he's pinned beneath him. I know what's coming, and from the look on Adams's face, he does too.

And with the first punch thrown by Quinton, the hockey arena has turned into a boxing ring.

Utter pandemonium breaks out as Quinton continues to land blows on Adams. The team boxes clear, everyone moving to the ice to either help break up the fight or start one of their own. The officials do their best to block anyone from getting closer, meanwhile a couple of our guys attempt to stop de Haas from using Trenton's center as a punching bag.

Adams must get a shot in on Quinton too, because when Cam and Rossi pull Quinton away, his eyebrow is split, blood starting to spill down the side of his face.

That doesn't seem to faze him though, because he shoves our guys away from him and surges toward Adams all over again, who's only just gotten to his feet.

Okay, that's enough.

I skate toward the hot-headed idiot, grabbing him by the collar yanking him away from Adams.

"What the fuck are you doing?" I snap, my teeth bared as I back him against the glass.

From the corner of my eye, I catch Rossi and one of the wingers for Trenton both holding back Adams, doing their best to keep the two from going in for a third round. Meanwhile, Quinton's still seething in my grip. Foaming at the mouth like a rabid dog, looking to take a massive bite out of Adams.

"He had it coming," Quinton bites, his eyes still two furious balls of blue fire. The hottest flame there is.

"That might be, but you don't need to escalate the situation," I hiss, pushing against the boards harder as he fights against my hold. "You might've just cost us the damn game with this shit."

A sneer paints his face. "Nah, Reed. You're the one who doesn't want to play like a team, needing to be the star of the show. Telling Coach I never pass you the puck? Turning it over when I finally do? That's not a team player." He scoffs. "If we walk away tonight with a loss, that falls on your shoulders. Not mine."

He's kidding me, right? *I'm* the one not wanting to play as a team? *I'm* the one costing us this win?

"You're delusional."

He arches his brow as if to ask *but am I?*

My voice comes out in a snarl. "You're the one in charge on this ice. Not me. So instead of worrying about what *I'm* doing, why don't you start showing some qualities of an actual leader?"

His brows clash together, nose wrinkling back in disgust. "I think it's time you get over the fact that your last name wasn't enough to get this position for yourself."

Wow. He actually went there. Again.

"You're unbelievable, de Haas. Classy as fucking ever." I nod over toward the penalty box. "Enjoy watching me lead this team to victory while you're in time out."

He glares at me, wiping away the blood from his eyebrow with the back of his hand.

I'd hope getting punched in the face might teach him a lesson, but if history has proven anything, it won't make a damn bit of difference.

"Captain material, my ass," I mutter under my breath as I watch him skate his ass over to the sin bin and plop his temperamental ass down on the wooden bench.

Unfortunately, I'm full of shit by saying I'd lead the team to victory.

It's actually the complete opposite of what happens when we get smoked during the five-minute power play, thanks to Quinton's temper. And to make it worse, his absence on the ice makes it possible for Trenton College to score not one, but two goals.

Giving them the win.

The atmosphere in the locker room afterward is somewhere between abysmal and depressed, especially since we haven't lost a home opener in years. Since well before any of us came to play at Leighton.

After the dressing down we get from Coach in our post-game meeting, most of us keep to ourselves, either jumping in the shower or ice baths to get cleaned up, as if that's enough to wash away the stench of loss.

Braxton, who is one of my roommates, sidles up beside me as I redress. Both of us are aware of the way de Haas is banging around at his stall like the petulant child he is, still unable to get ahold of his rage, though we do our best to ignore it.

It's embarrassing.

"Am I actually seeing this?" I mutter more to myself than anyone, but from the way Braxton nods in agreement, I know he heard me.

"I wish we weren't." He pauses, and we trade a quick glance. "We gotta do something about this, man. Or we're gonna be in for a long season."

"Like what? It's not like we can just impeach him or something. Hockey isn't a democracy."

"It fucking should be."

He makes a point.

I'm at a complete loss here, just like I bet half the team is. Because this sure as hell isn't the way a captain should act or perform on the ice. Or off it.

"If we were still in high school, we'd just have to plant some weed or booze in his locker and he'd be done for." I sigh, slipping into my shoes. "If only it were that easy now."

"You're telling me," Braxton grumbles, falling in step beside me as we head for home. "But we'll get him outta here. One way or another."

THREE

Quinton

Helmets and pads bang and clack against wooden stalls as the team strips down after practice. We've been gearing up for our first away game series at none other than our rival school—also in the Chicago area—Blackmore University, and despite the hiccups in our first two games at home, I'm feeling good about how the team is meshing.

At least, for the most part.

The exception is when I'm on the ice with Oakley. The rhythm between the two of us is still shaky at best, usually looking more like Bambi on ice than two top-tier college athletes who have been on the same team for years. But it's better than it was a few weeks ago, so I'll take all the progress I can get.

Honestly, I don't think Coach thought this whole thing through. While tossing us out on the ice together might be a good idea in theory, it's clearly not working well in practice. Figuratively and literally.

There's a reason we've spent most of our college careers on two different lines. It just works better that way. Causing less issues between us, since we both have our time to shine. We don't have to cross paths more than necessary, and we work better with different people. Only problem is, those people graduated last season, and for the time being, we're all each other has.

Most of the guys undress quickly, ready to rush off to the shower before heading out. But then Coach steps out of his office, and almost immediately, the team comes to a halt.

"All right, guys," Coach booms, authority and respect demanded by his tone alone. And it does, because silence falls over everyone, every set of eyes in the place fixated on him. "It seems there's been some concern at the administrative level about steroids and other performance enhancing drugs at the collegiate level. Two other schools in the NCAA had multiple players testing positive on either their hockey and football teams. I'm sure the lot of you are clean, but we have to be sure. So"—he holds up a sterile plastic container we'd have to be blind to not recognize—"let's make this quick and get about the rest of our day."

I heard about this last week. Both Lincoln Center's hockey team and Blackmore's football team had players who tested positive for PEDs. I almost didn't believe it at first, but one of my high school friends who's a student at Blackmore confirmed it's true.

Supposedly, a lot of the players are looking to appeal, claiming false positives, but the jury's still out on that being the truth.

But if this is what we all need to do to prove none of us are cheaters, fine by me. So I do exactly what Coach requested. I shower, do my business, drop off my sample to the lab tech waiting by the door, and go about the rest of my day.

"De Haas, my office. Now."

Coach's call echoes through the locker room as I start dressing for the Blackmore game later that week. I'm not even out of my street clothes yet, so I shuffle my way through countless half-dressed athletes until I reach the door of Coach's office.

I knock twice before opening it as a courtesy, and when the door swings open to reveal all three coaches, I realize there must be some information about the team we're about to face that he needs to share with me.

Or someone died, but I'm banking on the former.

"You wanted to see me?" I ask, leaning against the frame.

"Yes. Close the door and sit."

Cryptic. Okay, then.

My brows furrow, but I follow his instructions despite my confusion, sliding into the seat across from him. He leans back in his own chair, steepling his fingers as he stares at me. Not saying a damn word to let me know why the hell I'm in here when I should be getting dressed, zoning in on my pregame routine.

Thirty seconds pass, the silence already close to unbearable, so I break the ice. "Did you just want to look at my pretty face before we go out to kick some ass?"

His hands drop, and he leans forward over the desk, grabbing the top paper out of the file folder I hadn't noticed when I first came in.

"On the contrary. You're in here because you failed your drug test."

I don't think I heard him right, because it sounds like he said—

"*What?* That's impossible."

Coach slides a piece of paper across the desk. "Then how do you explain this?"

I glance down at the paper, where my drug test shows a positive result for—

"Opioids?" I ask, dumbfounded. "Coach, I've never touched that shit. Even when I got my wisdom teeth out back in high school and they gave me God knows what kind of narcotic for the pain, I still didn't take anything stronger than Tylenol."

But from the wary look he gives me before glancing between both the assistant coaches, my rebuttal won't matter. Results are results, and none of us can do anything to change them.

My stomach sinks, the contents in it threatening to make a reappearance.

"This can't be right. It's not mine, I swear, Coach. The lab must've gotten it mixed up with someone else."

He nods once. "I want to believe you, Quinton. You're a lot of things—including the biggest hothead I've ever coached—but I'd never peg you for something like this. You care too much about your future career to pull this kind of stunt."

"Which is why I didn't do it!" I say with earnest, rising to my feet in panic. My attention darts between the three men before falling back to Coach. "I swear on my life, I didn't do this. There has to be some kind of mistake. Tell me there's something you can do."

The look Coach gives me, paired with the creases running through his forehead, tell me he's already tried working though solutions. Probably long before he called me in here. And the only reason to have called me in here is if he came up empty.

"This isn't something I can just take your word for and hide it, de Haas. Of course, we had the lab check for *which* opioid it was, seeing as one drug that falls in that category is heroin—"

"Heroin?" I almost screech.

"—but it came back as hydrocodone. Vicodin."

Oh.

Well, I guess it could have been a lot worse.

"Look, Quinton. Vicodin might not be heroin or coke or meth, but prescription narcotics are still classified as banned substances without a medical exception filed with the NCAA..." He continues on, droning about the policies and bylaws enacted by both the school and the NCAA—ones I'm perfectly fucking aware of, because unlike some, I'm not one to waste an opportunity I worked my ass off to earn—while I try my best to figure out how the hell this could've happened.

The more I think about it, the only possibility besides the lab results getting mislabeled or swapped somehow, would be that I took something without knowing it.

Could there be something in the medicine cabinet back at my apartment that was mislabeled?

It's a long shot, considering I don't even have any narcotics prescribed to me currently. Never have, apart from the one time years ago I just mentioned to him. I doubt Hayes, my roommate, does either. He's as straightlaced as they come, but I still make note to ask him about it when—

"...and because of it, I have no other option than to suspend you."

His statement snaps me back to reality as the floor seems to fall from beneath my feet.

This is exactly the kind of thing I was hoping to *avoid.* But here we are, my heart crawling into my throat at hearing the consequences all the same.

"Suspend me for something I didn't do?"

His lips form a tight line, and then he sighs. "I have to until I can prove you aren't using, de Haas. My hands are tied. You have to realize it's my ass on the line too, especially with the way the NCAA is cracking down after the shit that happened with Blackmore and Lincoln Center."

I look between the three of them again, unsure where to go from here. But from the solemn expressions aimed at me, there's nothing to do but accept the punishment.

There has to be something that can be done. Anything.

I'm damn near close to getting on my knees and begging at this point. Because this *can't* be the way my hockey career ends. No team in the NHL would dare touch me if this catches wind and I'm suspended for drug use. Drugs I didn't even *fucking use* to begin with.

That won't matter to them, though. This would be a black mark on the resume I've been building since the first time I put on skates as a kid.

Dejected and defeated, I cradle my head in my hands.

"But…" he says, trailing off.

That one word breathes new life into me, and I lift my head. "Please tell me that's the good kind of *but* and not the kind that will make this even worse."

Coach lets out a bark of laughter, eyes softening around the edges. "We can get you retested. Today, before we start talks of complete ineligibility. After all, if you were a habitual user, the drugs would still be in your system. And if that doesn't work, we'll submit an appeal on your behalf. Like I said, I don't think you did this. The last thing I want to see is you being punished for someone else's mistake, if that's truly what this is."

"None of us do," Coach Davis—one of the assistants—cuts in.

"That's good," I breathe, letting out a sigh of relief. "That's really good."

Coach nods. "We still can't let you play until the second set of tests come back—hopefully, negative—at the very least. Which could very well be another week. But it's better than nothing."

"Better than nothing," I repeat, feeling a small amount of hope blossoming in my chest.

It's all gonna be fine. I'll test negative and the appeal will go through and everything will be back to the way it was before I pissed in that damn cup.

I'm too busy chanting silent prayers to listen in on what the three discuss among themselves. After all, if this has been my luck lately, I'm gonna need all the help I can get. Especially from the hockey gods.

But something Coach says snags my attention, causing my hair to stand on end.

"Get Reed in here for me, will you?" Coach says to Coach Jacobson, who nods and exits the office silently.

"Reed?" The dread in my gut returns. He's the last person I want to see or talk to right now. "What's he got to do with this?"

Coach sighs, like he always does when Oakley and I are involved. It's not like we've made it easy on him these last few years, and honestly, I'm sure he's ready to be rid of us. Even if Oakley's his own flesh and blood.

"We need another captain on the ice while you're on temporary suspension," he says just as the door opens again, revealing Oakley and Coach Jacobson.

"Suspension?" Oakley says, clearly catching the tail end of his uncle's sentence. His eyes land on me while the door clicks shut behind him. "What's going on?"

"You'll be taking over as captain, Oakley. Effective immediately," Coach says gruffly, and I flick my attention back to him to find his attention still locked on me.

Another rush of embarrassment floods me, even though I know Coach is on my side in this—and more importantly—I did nothing wrong. There's absolutely no circumstance where I'd ever think of using any kind of drugs.

Oakley steps further into the room, and I feel his stare burning the side of my face like a white-hot brand. Penetrating, even. Like I'm as transparent as glass.

When I maintain my silence, keeping my stare directly on Coach—who is watching us like a hawk—Oakley lets out a bark of laughter.

"What'd you do this time?"

I try not to give him my attention or let him get under my skin, but the freedom in his laugh and taunting tone ignites a fuse inside me. Hard not to, when this jackass is being handed everything I've worked for, and for no *real* reason.

But I cave, letting my gaze collide with his, boring into each other. I know mine have to be showcasing every bit of rage and defeat coursing through my veins, because Oakley's eyes narrow, like he's reading the silence between us to figure out just why—

"You tested positive," he says. Not a question; just an incredulous statement. When I don't respond, a shit-eating grin slides across his face. "Damn, de Haas. I knew you were reckless, but I didn't know you were stupid too."

"Bite me," I snap between clenched teeth.

"I'm good, thanks," he retorts before letting out another laugh. "I just wanna know why. Because even you have to be smart enough to know PEDs shrink your dick."

My lips curl up in what has to be a sneer. "It's actually your balls that shrink, Reed, but regardless, your concern for what I'm packing is duly noted."

Oakley goes to open his mouth again, a flare of red tinting his cheeks at my inadvertent comment about his sexuality. Which…I'll admit, was tacky.

But it's too late to take it back now.

"Can it. The both of you," Coach bites out, for which I'm grateful.

This entire situation already has me on edge, and Oakley running his mouth like the jackass he is, antagonizing me for sport, will only make things worse. Which could lead me into even more trouble if I let my temper get the best of me.

Biting my tongue is the safest option, so I do just that. To the point of blood filling my mouth. And though it kills me, I don't use the moment of silence granted by Coach to correct Oakley's assumptions. He doesn't need the specifics as it is.

Nor does he deserve them.

Coach's eyes drift between us, studying and analyzing in a way that makes me feel almost naked. And again, transparent.

Guess that's a Reed family trait.

"The two of you need to get it together. I haven't said anything until now because I was hopeful that putting you on the same line this season would help you find some common ground. Apparently that's not working, so I need the two of you to *actively* find a way to fix your shit. Am I clear?"

He doesn't even have to leave a threat hanging over our heads like an executioner's blade. Simply getting chewed out for our little spats is enough to make both of us straighten our spines and hear what he has to say.

"Crystal," I murmur at the same time a quick "Yes, sir" comes from Oakley.

I fight the impulse to roll my eyes at him calling his own uncle *sir*, no doubt to garner more favor with him. Shit, I don't think I've ever heard him refer to Coach as anything other than just that. Coach.

Damn suck-up.

"Are we done, then?" I ask, looking between the three coaches. When I get the nod, I make a move to get up, ready to get the hell out of here as quickly as possible.

"Okay, great. Well, I'm gonna go get dressed, and then—"

"You can't suit up, kid," he tells me, a look of remorse on his face. "You'll have to watch from the stands. As a spectator."

A poorly disguised laugh comes from Oakley, and I roll my lips inward before clamping my teeth around them to keep from screaming.

Because this day just gets better and better, right?

FOUR

Oakley

When I pull my car up outside the rental townhouse I share with a few of my friends, I can already tell I'm gonna find the place in its usual state of semi-controlled chaos when I walk through the door. Unfortunate for me, considering we lost tonight—again—and all I want to do is crawl under my covers and sulk.

Of course, a house of controlled chaos is exactly what happens when a group of very social student-athletes—not including myself in that category—decide to become roommates. It becomes a literal cluster-fuck when all the extra bodies of friends, girlfriends, and teammates come over and hang out at all hours of the day and night.

Not that I blame them, since we have a pretty sweet set up in the basement with a massive television, pool table, and insanely large sectional to make the perfect chill space. But it also drives me bonkers that the place is rarely quiet when I want it to be.

And right now, I sure as fuck want it to be.

When I open the door and faintly hear the surround sound from the basement, I know there's some sort of…something happening down there. God only knows what, but I'm willing to bet my fucking life it has something to do with Holden—also known as roommate number one. After all, Leighton U's star quarterback loves to have a good time.

Theo, roomie number two and the shortstop for LU's baseball team, is in the kitchen with a couple of his teammates when I walk a little further into the house. I think Phoenix and Keegan are their names, but with the house packed full of guys who play for one of the LU athletic teams these days, it's so hard to know who is who.

Camden, our team's goalie, and his current flavor of the week are heading up the stairs, probably to his bedroom. I don't even bother learning the names of the girls since they don't last long enough to bother with it.

But the one roommate I'm actually looking for is Braxton, because we have things we need to talk about. Most important being the shit that went down at practice today with de Haas being pegged for using fucking drugs.

I don't know what the odds are for Quinton to be using, let alone getting caught with them, but it can't be high. No doubt around the same probability as my ability to comprehend quantum physics.

Really. Fucking. Low.

Thankfully, I find Braxton, beer in hand, on the living room sectional with a few girls I know to be jersey chasers—Kinsley, Ashton, and Mikayla. And I say jersey chasers rather than puck bunnies because these three aren't picky on the sport. They just want to bang athletes in general. Apparently, as many as possible before the end of college.

I know for a fact that Kinsley, the blonde currently draped over

Braxton's lap, has slept with every guy in the house. This week. Apart from myself, though not for her lack of trying. My being gay and having zero sexual attraction toward women throws a little kink in her plans—and not the good kind.

And from the way she's blatantly eye-fucking me as I cross the room to where the four of them are sitting, she's ready to make yet another pass at me.

Fantastic.

"There he is, the man of the hour!" Braxton says the second I take a seat on the other half of the sectional beside Ashton.

Not sure why he's calling me the man of the hour, though. We lost tonight.

"Hey, man." I glance between him and the three girls watching with the eyes of hawks. "You think we can chat real quick? Alone?"

A crease lines his forehead. "Why? You know the girls won't repeat the shit said between us."

No, actually, I don't know that. In fact, I'm sure anything secret or confidential Mikayla hears is instantly spread to all her little harpy friends via social media moments after she learns it. So I'm not looking to discuss team matters with her—or any of them—around.

"I just think we should get Cam and talk. About what happened at practice."

"You mean about Quinton de Haas getting nailed for using PEDs?" Mikayla asks. I glance up and find her studying nails that might as well be talons like they're the most interesting thing in the world, all in an effort to act as nonchalant as she can muster.

I move my attention back to Braxton. "You told them?"

He shrugs. "It was going to be all over the school by tomorrow anyway. You know the NCAA is cracking down on this crap. I'm sure they're happy to make an example out of him."

Unfortunately, I know what Braxton's saying is the truth. Quinton's bound to be all over hockey headlines by this time tomorrow. News like this always spreads like wildfire, especially when it's someone with his reputation.

Worst part is, even if he fights it for an appeal—which I'm sure he plans to—and wins, the stain will already be left on his name once it's out in the open. There's not many people who come back from that.

Brax shifts, tossing his free arm around Kinsley. "We wanted him out, and now he's out. Who knows how long it'll last, but for the time being, he's not a problem anymore. Let's focus on racking up some wins instead."

Again, he's right. So maybe I should be thankful fate landed us here, and now I can lead this team to victory for the rest of the season.

It's just all a little too…convenient.

Contrary to what I told Quinton in the Coach's office, I don't think he's stupid. Sure, I was spot-on about him being reckless as hell, but if I know anything about the guy, it's his dedication to hockey. Even if I act like I've never noticed, I've seen it for years. It's actually one of his few qualities I *like*; I just don't particularly care for some ways he proves it. Like throwing fists on the ice, even if it was in defense of his teammates or himself. So I'm supposed to believe he would go use drugs to give himself an edge in the game?

He's reckless, but not *that* reckless.

"Look, I'm just glad the captainship is in the hands of someone who actually fucking deserves it now. Think about that instead of a shithead who might not even see ice time for the rest of the season," Braxton says, finishing off the beer and setting the empty can on the table behind the couch.

I glance between him and the three girls, all of whom are nodding in agreement.

"Okay." I blow out a long breath. "Okay, thanks."

He waves me off. "No need to thank me. You know I got your back."

And there it is again. The nagging feeling that I'm missing something. Though I was ready to put the subject to rest and enjoy the rest of the evening, there's something about his words and the tone he says them with.

It doesn't sit right. Like he knows something I don't.

"What're you talking about? This was all on Quinton. How did you have my back?"

A sly smile creeps onto his face, but he simply shrugs and plays with a lock of Kinsley's hair.

But my nerves are set completely on edge; a cool prickling feeling taking over every inch of my skin as dread fills my gut. Because he *definitely* knows something. Or worse, maybe even played a part in this whole fucking mess.

"Brax. Spill," I demand slowly. "Did you do something?"

His eyes lift to meet mine. "I didn't do shit."

The thing about being friends with Braxton as long as I have—I know when he's being a bold-faced liar. And I'm damn near positive he's being one right now.

"Braxton," I hiss, this time a little more harshly. "What. Did. You. *Do?*"

"Look, man. You're captain now. You need to keep your hands clean."

Oh, Jesus Christ. Keep my hands clean?

"How is it possible the more you talk, the less you actually say?"

He keeps grinning. "God given talent, obviously."

My teeth grit, the sinking feeling in my gut stirring and swirling unpleasantly. Because I'm pretty sure I know what happened.

Braxton somehow fucked with Quinton's test to get him suspended. Maybe even kicked from the program. And I'm willing to bet Braxton didn't think about that being *his* fate if this gets out.

It could too, depending on what de Haas's second test results are. My bet is they'll come back clean this time, because why would anyone who is guilty ask to prove they're more guilty?

Which leads to a whole new problem. Him coming back after all this happened.

Shit.

I didn't think about it when Coach told me about Quinton's second test, but now it's the only thing in my brain. Which means I need to see where his head is, if only to make sure when he comes back after this garbage, he's not even more explosively violent than he is now.

That's the last thing the team needs.

Braxton's stare is hard as he watches me mentally work through all the loose ends of this hairbrained plan he *probably* set into motion. I can tell the moment he sees I've caught on to enough, because he removes his arm from behind Kinsley and leans toward me, clapping me on the shoulder. He holds my gaze as he does, a warning look in his eyes. The kind telling me to stop asking questions before I find something out that I can't unlearn.

Which is all the confirmation I need.

I don't need the words, and I sure as hell don't need the details of how he pulled it off. All it does is make me more of an accessory than I am right now.

"I took care of you, bro. That's all you gotta know."

FIVE

Quinton

November

"Quinton!"

The booming voice of my father catches my attention as I'm about to round the corner toward the player exit of the arena after my first game back from my suspension. My *undeserved* suspension, since the second one came back negative because—in a shocking turn of events—I don't use drugs. Of any kind.

Like. I. Said.

Though my test came back negative, Coach said the likelihood of me having to provide random drug testing for the rest of the season is high. And while I guess I can understand the reasoning—the NCAA needs to make sure we're running a clean program here—it doesn't make the entire situation suck any less.

My name's called again with a stern authority I know better than to ignore, no matter how much I want to.

Fucking hell. I don't need this right now.

I already played like a heaping pile of garbage tonight. There's no need to add to the shit storm with a visit from good ole Dad.

Too bad there's no escaping it now, so I paint a smile on my face as I turn to see not just my father, but my mother too. Both dressed impeccably—as expected when out in public representing the de Haas family name—and looking more out of place than a nun at a brothel.

"Mom. Dad. I didn't expect you to be here," I say in a way of greeting as I approach them, stopping short a few feet away.

I do my best to keep my hackles from rising the second I catch a whiff of my father's Tom Ford cologne, but it doesn't work.

"Of course we're here, darling," Mom says, though from the almost pained expression on her face, she'd rather be anywhere but. She's completely void of emotion; just a hint of a fake smile on her lips.

Then again, it could be all the Botox.

But my father's stone-cold expression? Well, that's just his face.

"Yes, of course. We wouldn't miss a chance to watch you throw down in a controlled setting. Remind me again why you didn't just take up boxing if you're so interested in using your fists for sport?"

My jaw ticks at his dig, not wanting to feed into his appraisal by letting my temper take over.

After all the years I've been playing, I should come to expect some sort of comment after a game he attends. Even one we win, since my love for hockey is the thing he despises most. To the point where I don't know why he let me start playing in the first place.

I can't fault him for his assessment, though. Not when I was tossed in the sin bin twice tonight. Once for a hit that—I'll be honest—was a little harder than necessary, and sent one of the defensemen for the other team crashing to the ground face-first.

Half the officials in the league wouldn't have called anything on it, but luck wasn't on my side with the set we had tonight.

The other time was for a fight, and hell if I'll apologize either. Not when a winger checked me straight into McGowan, sending us both to the ground. Under normal circumstances, that'd be enough to get my temper boiling, but when he skated past me after scoring the winning goal and spat the words *cheating juicer* at me, I was done. I don't regret a single punch I threw at him after that. Fucker deserved the bloody nose. Honestly, part of me even hopes it's broken. It'd serve him right for running his mouth about shit he has no business in.

Plastering a plastic smile on my face, I reply, "You know me, always the over-achiever. Why play one sport when you can combine them?"

"Why play any at all when it's just a childish game and a waste of time?" he counters, stony eyes narrowed on me.

And there it is again. His never-ending disapproval for my decision to play hockey.

"I guess knowing it makes me happy isn't reason enough?"

"Really? Because you don't look very happy right now."

Observant as ever, Dad.

"Hard to be when we racked up another loss," I snap, momentarily forgetting myself. But I'm already on edge from missing out on the two games last week against Blackmore, and adding this loss tonight isn't helping.

"Losses happen all the time, son. In any aspect of life. They shouldn't make you look this miserable."

It almost sounds like he understands where I'm coming from, but I know him. I can tell he's working out ways to use my words against me.

Twist them to fit his version of how this conversation should go, all to make his point.

"Maybe this loss is meant to be a wake-up call. One saying it's time to focus on a real career path, rather than skating around chasing after a rubber disk."

And there it is.

"Not like you have to come watch me do it."

"No, I don't," he murmurs, his tone low and measured. "But I do have a business. One you're meant to be groomed to take over down the line. Preparing yourself for when the time comes would be much more appropriate."

My teeth clamp together tightly, somehow knowing this would, once again, be the subject of discussion. Lately, it's about the *only* thing my father wants to talk about. When I'm planning to call it quits on my own dreams and aspirations to make it to the NHL, all so I can follow the life plan *he* wants for me.

If being sidelined for almost a week, not even able to step on the ice for practice, has taught me anything? It's that I'm miserable without hockey in my life. And doing whatever he does would only make it worse.

Watching my team get their asses handed to them in two more consecutive losses—both of which were complete shut-outs—and not being able to do anything about it was maddening. The worst of it is I can't help but feel it's partly my fault for being benched. Even when none of the blame actually falls on my shoulders, because I didn't do anything wrong, I still feel the pang of guilt.

"It's one more season. My team needs me," I grind, teeth still clenched.

I don't miss the subtle arch of his brow. "Didn't seem like it tonight."

It's a low blow, but unfortunately for me, he's not entirely off base. Because the loss tonight is one that can't be blamed on my lack of appearance on the ice, but rather *because* I was on it.

Something was just *off* with the energy in the locker room when Coach told the team I was able to suit up—clearing the air about my test actually being negative. I thought that'd make it so nothing ever happened, and we could get back in the groove of things as a team.

Unfortunately, I was wrong.

I could feel it when anyone would look at me tonight—teammate or opponent. The judgment and the disbelief. That I'd be so careless to have ruined the namesake of Leighton's program. Like my reputation—what little good there is of it—has been tarnished by what happened. Doesn't seem to matter much to anyone that the results were actually negative and I was proven innocent; I'm still stuck with the stigma.

In their eyes, I'll always be guilty of a crime I never committed. One I'd never *dream* of committing.

And now I'm being iced out for it. Like a fucking pariah.

Surprisingly, the only one who seems to give me any benefit of the doubt is fucking Oakley. Though, I must admit, it's probably just because he got my title as captain when there was no actual reason for it to be taken. Which only makes me feel like I've lost pretty much everything I've earned. The captain spot and the respect of my team.

The last thing I need right now is my father digging the knives in deeper.

"Is that all you needed? To let me know, once again, of your disapproval in my decision-making? Remind me I'm not necessary?" I hiss, willing my temper to ease off. "Because if it is, I'm gonna go."

I don't stick around to hear what either of them have to say, hauling my bag over my shoulder and moving toward the exit. Continuing even after I hear both my parents call after me.

With a glance over my shoulder, I catch my father furiously pacing in place, which is far better than him chasing after me to continue this pointless conversation. I've got nothing left to say, no more fight left in me. Not for them, not for anyone. So I'll take the easy way out and let another set of people think I'm sucking air where I don't belong.

Even if they are my parents.

When I turn the corner, I'm met with a sight even more unfortunate than my parents waiting for me a few minutes earlier.

Because there's Oakley, plastered against the wall, looking like he was caught with his hand in the proverbial cookie jar.

The second he registers my face, his complexion goes sheet-white, and I don't even have to ask how much of my father's crap he heard. All that matters is he heard enough to look at me in a way I'd never dreamed he would. Not with anger or disdain or irritation.

Instead, all I see etched in his features is…pity.

"Quinton."

It's my name. Only my fucking name leaving his lips. But it's the way he says it, the softness of his tone, that gets me. He's never spoken to me that way before.

I fucking hate it.

I hate everything about this entire day, and I'm ready for it to be over.

Moving to shove past him works, but he falls into step beside me.

"Quinton," he says again, this time with a little more conviction. But I still don't stop, nor do I look at him. I just keep my eyes locked on the door ahead of me. My only means of escape.

He grabs for my arm, and I do my best to brush him off. But this fucker isn't anything but persistent, wrapping his hand around my wrist.

The feel of his skin against mine instantly makes me volatile, and I rip my arm from his grip before shoving him up against the wall. I pin him there, forearm across his throat, and snarl in his face. "Don't fuck with me right now, Reed."

"Too bad, I need to talk to you."

It's at this moment I realize they're the same; my father and Oakley. Not in looks or stature, but the way they carry themselves. Like they're kings in this world, and the rest of us, mere peasants. Lowly servants who should lap up their attention, or come with the drop of a hat at beck and call.

And then there's the way they look at me. Like I'm nothing more than scum of the Earth. A problem in need of fixing. A disappointment that only manages to get in the way.

Until five minutes ago, Oakley's never looked at me any differently.

But then he overheard things he had no business hearing. And the sympathy written on his face right now because of it does nothing more than piss me off.

I don't need his pity, and I sure as fuck don't want it.

"Whatever you have to say doesn't matter."

"Look—"

"What did I just fucking say?" I growl, pushing away from him. "I'm leaving. Don't fucking follow me."

The lack of footsteps other than my own as I hustle down the hall lets me know he can actually listen to what I say; something that sets him apart from my father.

Gold star for the golden boy.

"Quinton!"

My teeth sink into the inside of my cheek, tasting the faint hint of copper as I ignore him. And no matter how many times he shouts my name, I'll continue to ignore him.

All the way to the exit doors.

Without looking back.

SIX

Oakley

Why I'm at a frat party after the ass-kicking we just received on the ice—for the fifth time this season—is beyond me. I sure as hell don't want to be here with the way I played like absolute trash tonight, and especially when I know I *shouldn't* be here at all. Not when we have another game tomorrow night, where we can hopefully get our heads out of our asses long enough to bring home the first win of the season.

But the thing about being best friends with a guy like Holden is that he's always down to party—even on a Thursday night, apparently—and will rarely take no for an answer when he wants you to come along for the ride. Tonight is the perfect example of that, because instead of letting me go home and crash in bed, he's dragged me out here.

To let loose and have some fun, he'd said.

He's not the one with a game tomorrow, though.

It wouldn't matter if he did. He always wants to party his damn ass off at every available opportunity, no matter if he's in the middle of football season or not…and still plays like the first-round draft prospect he is every Saturday.

I'd be in awe of him if it wasn't so irritating.

"Drink this," he orders, handing me a red solo cup full of foam. And I do mean full of it, because whoever poured this beer has no fucking clue how to do it correctly.

Just as well, though. I don't have to drink the damn thing once Holden finds his conquest for the evening. Hopefully, I can sneak out of here as soon as he disappears to some dark corner of the house to fuck around with whichever lucky girl—or guy—he chooses.

My gaze collides with his golden honey one, and I grimace. "Why do you insist on torturing me?"

He laughs before clapping me on the shoulder. "Because you make it so fucking easy, Oak. Now drink up. Decompress a little. We'll leave before eleven, I promise." His smirk is devilish when he adds, "I know you need your beauty rest."

"Oh, fuck off." I chuckle and shove his shoulder playfully. "Now go get laid so I can go home and sleep. I have a game tomorrow."

"Ah, see," he says, pointing at me. "Your little omission proves my theory to be correct! But who said I'm here to get laid?"

My brows raise as I give him an incredulous look. "You expect me to believe you *aren't* here looking to get some? Really, Hold? Did you forget I've lived with you for the past three years?"

At least he has the decency to look a little sheepish, if only for a second. "Okay, okay, you got me. Lucky for you, I've already laid all the groundwork with this one. Shouldn't be more than an hour."

I snort out a laugh, watching his golden head bob and weave through the crowd as I take a swig from my cup of foam. Tracking him through the crowd, I'm surprised to see him stop beside none other than Kason Fuller. A good ole semi-closeted southern boy built like a brick shithouse with more muscle than should be legal. Also one of the best tight ends this school has seen in a long time.

But he's also Holden's teammate.

Cue my endless sigh of disapproval.

He might be my best friend, but I've never said he was smart. Call it too many hits to the head, or a general lack of giving a fuck, but it doesn't matter. Messing around with a teammate will only lead to issues later, especially when shit goes south. Which it always does with Holden, seeing as monogamy is a word he doesn't seem to know the definition of. But that's something he has to figure out on his own, no matter how many times I could tell him not to.

Removing my eyes from Holden, I watch the bodies on the make-shift dance floor moving and grinding to the beat of Breathe Carolina's "Blackout" pounding through the speakers. Everyone's having a great time, not a care in the world as beer sloshes out of solo cups, coating the dance floor in a slippery sheen of liquid and foam.

My gaze drifts over them all, taking in a scene straight out of *American Pie*. I'm surprised to find several teammates here tonight, either looking for a pretty girl to lick their wounds from our loss or maybe even trying to drink away the memory of it altogether. I can't blame them, but it makes me a little uneasy all the same, what with another game against Lakewood Heights tomorrow night.

All I want for this season is to see the Timberwolves bring home a

Frozen Four victory…and I'm not sure how we'll achieve it if half the team is out at all hours the night before a game.

But the last thing I want to be after this loss is more of a buzzkill. So rather than say a damn thing to any of them, I head up the stairs to keep an eye on them. Make sure they don't do anything more stupid than they already are. Like get in a drunken brawl.

I start typing out a text to Holden, letting him know where I'll be when he's ready to dip, and make my way to the loft overlooking the living room. There are far fewer people up here, at least compared to the chaos downstairs. Mostly ones smoking weed or looking for a place to shamelessly dry hump each other before finding a bedroom for some actual privacy. Not at all my scene, but from this spot looking over the railing, I have the perfect view of everything happening below.

I'm about to hit send on the text when someone bumps into my shoulder, causing the foamy beer in my cup to slosh over the rim and onto my hand.

Fucking great.

Irritation seeps through me as I wipe my hand dry on my jeans and pocket my phone. It's what happens at gatherings like this; people bumping and brushing into each other due to so many bodies being jam packed in a single, confined space. But it's not hard to apologize either.

Only, when I glance to my left and see *who* bumped me, understanding hits me like a Mack truck.

Quinton.

He's leaning against the railing, eyes locked on the scene taking place below. But I know he saw me. That's why he bumped me. Anything to get under my fucking skin.

Dressed in his signature jeans, tee, and leather jacket makes it obvious he brought his bike tonight. As if drinking and driving isn't bad enough as it is. Which he's clearly planning to do, if the solo cup in his own hand is any indication.

He's the last person I expected to see here. Not just because I assumed he would lay low with the PEDs drama still following him around like a stench that won't go away.

But then there's the shit with his dad earlier tonight.

If it were me, and my father spoke to me the way his did? I'd be buried in my bed for weeks. Absolutely destroyed by the lack of support coming from the most important person in my life.

Yet here he is, beer in hand, partying it up without a care in the world.

Rather than letting him win this little game he's trying to start by popping off at him, I go another route and ignore him. The same way he did me when I tried to talk to him a few hours ago after the game.

Thoughts of his brush off stir the idea of restarting the conversation I wanted to have, but this is hardly the time or place. The last thing I want is to be overheard. Sure, the entire school is well aware of Quinton being pegged for drugs, but they don't know what I know.

Well, what I'm *pretty sure* I know.

The real question here is, does Quinton know? Which is exactly what I wanted to find out earlier tonight, before he shoved me against the wall and bit my head off. But if he had any suspicions, he would have aired them by now. Made some snide comment in passing. And Braxton would be long gone from the hockey program if Quinton suspected his involvement.

So instead of bringing it up and risk planting a seed, I just keep my trap shut, take another swig of the disgusting foam in my solo cup, and throw away the worry altogether.

But my refusal to acknowledge him quickly becomes something of a frustration to him. I can tell by the way he keeps tapping his cup against the railing restlessly. It's why I'm not at all surprised he's the first one to break the silence.

"Shouldn't you be at home, golden boy?"

Ignoring the golden boy comment, I mutter, "Babysitting duty." Motioning my hand toward where Holden and Kason are all over each other on the dance floor, I continue, "Roommate needed to get his dick wet."

For the first time since he sidled up by my side, I feel his eyes on me, narrowing in as he reads my features. It's irritating.

"What?" I ask, my gaze colliding with his.

"Leave it to you for judging the very people you call your friends." He scoffs, running his fingers through dark hair. "With friends like you, who fucking needs 'em?"

"I'm not judging him."

It's not exactly a lie. I'm not judging Holden for wanting to get laid. I'm judging his choice of people to do it with.

The look on Quinton's face is dubious at best. "Oh, please. Save the bullshit for someone who actually cares."

"Well, you don't care about anything, so…"

He rolls his eyes. "So because my entire existence doesn't revolve around a puck and a pair of skates, it means I don't care about anything?"

This I can do. Tossing words with him until something gets him to bite back. And from the hellish look in his eyes, I can tell he's close to doing just that.

"No, but it does explain why Coach didn't give the captain spot back to you after your little suspension."

A snort comes from him. "Please, the only reason that happened is because you share the same last name as him, and we both know it."

"Or it's because I actually know how to be a leader. Which means dedicating everything I have to the sport and the team. Something we both know *you* can't say."

His nostrils flare. "I give this team everything I have and more."

"Really?" I pause, canting my head to the side. "Because it sure didn't seem like it tonight on the ice."

I must've made the winning blow, because Quinton's arm flashes out, grabbing the front of my shirt in a vise-like grip. The sudden movement sends both our cups tumbling over the railing and into the crowd below.

"Someone's getting testy," I taunt. It feels good to be the one getting under his skin.

"And someone's pretending like he played the best game of his life tonight when you couldn't find the net if it crawled up your ass and made a home there."

A bark of laughter burst from me. "Again with the gay jokes, huh, de Haas? Couldn't come up with something to make you sound any more like a bigot?"

His lips curl back into a sneer. "Oh, suck my dick. Fucking douche."

I smirk and lean into him, allowing our proximity to work in my favor. "Whip it out. I'll drop to my knees right here and now. Best head you'll ever get, guaranteed."

Quinton's blue eyes flare, scorching me as the fist holding the front of my shirt tightens. Then he narrows in on me, again, like he can see right through me.

And I don't like it.

"Best head *ever*? You're quite sure of yourself there, Reed."

My stomach coils itself into knots, his response throwing me off, but I do my best to keep my voice confident and steady. "Who'd suck dick better than someone who has one?"

He scoffs. "Plenty of people, I'm sure. I could do it easily."

I chuckle, because *really?* That's how far he wants to take this? Saying he—a straight guy—could suck dick better than someone like me, who's been doing it for years?

It makes absolutely no sense.

Which is why the words, "I'll believe it when I see it," slip out of my mouth before I can stop them.

He wets his lower lip before running his teeth over it. "I could, but I think you'd like it too much."

Yeah, that's probably true.

I might hate the guy on principle, but he's a sexy motherfucker if I've ever seen one. Believe me, I've done my best not to notice too. Being openly gay on an athletic team means I already keep to myself more in the locker room than I did while I was still closeted. I'd never want to make any of my teammates uncomfortable, and thankfully, they don't do it for me anyway.

Of course, because God hates me, the one exception would be Quinton.

My eyes avoid him as much as they can, above everyone else, because of it. Like they'll continue to, because he is straight and the world's biggest asshole.

But I have to admit, seeing him deep-throat my cock would be—

Stop thinking about it. Stop, stop, stop.

Thankfully, my brain gets the memo and halts all immediate thought about the jackass in front of me. All *sexual* thoughts, at least. And it's quickly replaced, yet again, with a flicker of fury when I notice a glimmer of amusement in his eyes.

"I severely doubt I'd enjoy it," I bite out.

The way his brow arches signals his surprise at my response. Almost as if he's in disbelief I wouldn't be jumping at the opportunity to have him on his knees, mouth wrapped around my dick.

Abruptly, Quinton's fist leaves its place on my shirt and latches onto my shoulder. My *bad* shoulder, and I barely have the chance to register the pain shooting through the joint before I'm being hauled from our spot against the railing.

A slight fear that he's about to do something insanely reckless—like maybe tossing me over the damn bannister and into the mass of bodies below—zips through me.

But fortunately for me, he makes a quick detour about halfway to the stairs, yanking me through a door after him.

SEVEN

Oakley

"What're you do—"

The sudden shove he gives me after the door falls closed behind us sends me stumbling backward blindly. My heart damn near leaps out of my chest while I try to stabilize myself in the dark, nameless room. Which becomes infinitely harder to do when the light is flicked on, blinding me altogether while I grab on to the edge of something.

A sink.

Bathroom. We're in the fucking bathroom.

Fantastic.

"What the hell, de Haas?" I snap, blinking to help my eyes adjust. When I look over toward the door, I'm even more irritated to find him leaning against it with a smug smile on his face. He says nothing, just keeps on fucking grinning. Like he's enjoying this.

But that can't be right, because Quinton doesn't enjoy anything unless it involves a fist fight, puck bunnies, or his stupid fucking motorcycle.

None of those things are involved while he's locked in a bathroom with me.

Unless…

"This isn't about to turn into a bathroom brawl, is it?"

His brow quirks slightly, his head cocking to the side while he studies me. "Just how hammered *are you* right now?"

I frown. "I've had less than one beer."

He continues staring for a second, those damn eyes as incinerating as ever. "Then why the hell would you think we're about to brawl in a goddamn bathroom? Quality party entertainment should happen"—he taps the door behind him—"out there. You know, so everyone can cheer me on while I kick your ass."

The argument is solid enough to believe. Even the part of him kicking my ass, since the douchewaffle never seems to back down from solving his problems with his fists. But it doesn't explain why…

"Want to tell me why we're locked in here, then?"

The grin on Quinton's face turns devious. Predatory even, as he pushes off the door and stalks toward me. And he doesn't stop until he's—quite literally—backed me into a corner. Like a hunter after his prey.

His icy gaze turns liquid. Molten even, as he places his palms on either side of my hips on the sink. The proximity has my heart ricocheting off my ribs, pounding hard enough I swear one might crack. A feeling that only gets worse when he leans in closer, the scent of his cologne wafting over me sending a lightning zap straight to my balls.

Fuck, what is he doing?

Like the guy can read my mind, he whispers against my neck, "You're saying it's not obvious? We're here to silence your doubts."

His lips brush against the shell of my ear at the same moment his chest presses into mine. A thrill rushes through me at the feel of his firm, sculpted pecs, and my dick twitches behind my zipper.

"You're joking," I breathe, hoping the tremble in my voice is only apparent to my own ears.

"I'm joking?" he taunts, one hand leaving the counter to cup my cock behind my jeans. "I think the only one joking is you, telling me you're not interested in what I'm offering."

Shit.

My body betraying me before my sworn enemy isn't the way I thought this night would go.

"Get the fuck out, de Haas. This isn't happen—"

The rest of my dismissal is cut off somewhere in the back of my throat when he rubs the crown of my cock through the denim. Pair it with the way his lips are now trailing down my throat, and I doubt I could remember what I was in the middle of saying.

All I can focus on is the zap of electricity coursing between us, sparking where our bodies are in contact.

And *fuck*, it feels good. Too good.

My fingers form fists in the fabric of his shirt, and I do my best to shove him away, no matter how much my body is begging for him to keep touching me. But every ounce of fight and willpower I have left in me isn't enough. Hell, even brute force wouldn't be enough.

I'm trapped, completely at his mercy.

And he knows it.

"Fight me, baby. There's nothing I want more."

The deep rasp in his voice sounds like *he's* the one being touched, and…fuck. It does something stupid to my brain. So much, I let desire outweigh common sense and allow him to unbutton my jeans. Tug the zipper down. Shove the denim and my underwear past my ass so he can take me in hand.

The second his fingers wrap around me, I swear I could come on the spot.

Quinton doesn't waste time, stroking my length until I'm painfully hard as his lips explore the skin of my neck some more. Teasing and taunting; two things I'm more than used to when it comes to him. But never like this.

Truth be told, this is the first time I've wanted more of his torment, though I'd ever let him in on that little secret.

"I thought the plan was to *suck* it?"

Goading him is a tried-and-true way of getting under his skin, maybe even letting the hot-headed side out to play, but it's a chance I'm willing to take to call his bluff. Because there's no way in hell he's actually going to—

A sharp hiss escapes between my clenched teeth when he suddenly bites into the muscle between my shoulder and neck, sucking like he's Edward fucking Cullen or something. Though, with his nearly-black hair and those ice blue eyes, he gives off more of a Damon Salvatore vibe.

Yet as sexy as it might be, it doesn't mean I want to play vampire.

"What the fuck?" I ask, shoving at his chest until he releases me.

He pulls back to meet my glare, and I swear to God, bats his eyelashes like he's the picture of fucking innocence. But the hint of a smirk at the corner of his lips gives him away.

"You said suck. I was listening."

Oh, that's fucking it.

My fingers latch on to his shoulder, and I attempt to push him down.

"My dick, not my throat, de Haas. It's time to put your money where your mouth is."

His nostrils flare slightly in challenge as two rows of white teeth come out in a hellish grin. Then he drops to his knees on the tile floor and leans forward, not a flinch or pause in sight as his tongue flicks out against the blunt head of my cock, giving him his first taste of me.

But instead of easing into it, he goes all Quinton on me and dives in without a second thought of what he's doing or the repercussions of his actions. And for once, I'm not at all upset about it.

"Holy shit," I groan, counting backward from ten to keep my shit together. It works, but only just, because he's using the perfect amount of pressure and technique to have me primed and ready to explode in less than a minute flat.

Which begs the question, has he done this before?

For whatever reason, the thought doesn't sit right with me.

I'm not able to linger on it for long, though, because my mind circles immediately back to one thing while Quinton continues to lick and suck at my cock.

Release.

He runs his tongue along the underside of my shaft, his eyes flicking up to my face while he does. The sight is intoxicating. One of the most erotic things I've ever experienced.

"Fuck, this is a pretty sight," I mutter, my hips giving small thrusts every time his mouth descends over my length. "Had I known this was the best way to get you to shut up, I would have suggested it years ago."

The comment must spur something inside him, because he works me harder, taking me all the way to the back of his throat until he gags. The sensation of smooth, wet muscle constricting around my length shoots rockets of desire straight to my balls.

"Ohmyfuck," I breathe harshly, my grip white-knuckled on the vanity top behind me.

In the back of my mind, I know I should stop this before it goes further than it already has. And with *Quinton*, no less. I'd never be able to live this down if I don't stop him from making me co—

Ah, fuck it. This can't get much worse.

So I give in to the primal desire barreling down my spine, one hand leaving the cool porcelain for the longer hair on top of his head. My grip on the dark brown strands serves as an anchor, allowing me to hold him exactly where I want him as I take what I need.

Control falls from him back into my hands, exactly where I like it, and I waste no time putting it to use. I guide him up and down over my dick as my hips snap forward with a fast, relentless pace. Pressure builds at the base of my spine, and I let myself become consumed by the need for the release.

The ragged sound of my panting and the wet, sloppy noises Quinton makes while keeping up with what I'm feeding him bounce off the walls, serving as the soundtrack to a filthy fantasy I never knew I had.

And it's fucking perfect.

Thrust after thrust inches me to the edge of impending ecstasy, right there for the taking. And when his hand reaches up and cups my balls, the pressure is enough to send me shooting without warning into the back of his throat.

Stars explode behind my eyes, and I continue to roll my hips forward while he milks my orgasm from me, swallowing down my cum like he's greedy for it. He makes no signs of stopping, either, only pulling off long after I've been wrung dry.

Spit drips from my cock to the tile between my feet, and I focus on the spot as I try to calm my erratic heartbeat after what can only be classified as a mind-blowing orgasm.

But the thing about being shot high into space to the point of being weightless?

There's always the crash back to Earth after.

And this one...it's devastating. Probably enough to send the human race into extinction, like the goddamn dinosaurs.

Because the second my breathing evens out, the high wears off enough for me to recall *who* I just let blow me sky-high in a frat house bathroom.

How the fuck did this happen? Why didn't I stop it?

Well, I know *how*.

It's because *I* had to be the antagonistic asshole who just couldn't let him win another round of this messed up beef between us. Instead of shutting my mouth and walking away, I let him get to me. Allowed him to see the cracks in my armor, giving him an opening to take his best shot at me.

One he took without hesitation.

As for the why...well, I'm still trying to figure it out.

My throat constricts as I stare down at him, all swollen-lipped and sex-mussed before me. And though I was the one who was just fucking his mouth, I'm smart enough to realize *I'm* the one about to be fucked.

Because there's no going back from this. I'll never regain the upper hand.

His thumb brushes over the corner of his lips, collecting a stray bit of cum—*my fucking cum*—before sucking it into his mouth. The sight has my dick twitching, stirring back to life against my brain's better judgment. Which is horrifying enough without adding the fact that it's still out and shiny from his spit, right there for him to see.

This actually might be my worst nightmare.

His eyes lock with mine as he rises to full height before me. When he does, I'm reminded of just how small this bathroom is, especially with a couple six foot plus hockey players inside it.

He steps forward, keeping me crowded against the sink the way he did earlier. Nowhere to go but through him. Which is what I should do, considering the amount of ammunition he has now. Garner some much needed space between us and get the hell out of here.

Too bad my brain is firmly locked on the feeling of his erection against my thigh, begging me to return to favor. And God, how I want to.

Fuck, no. Stop that shit.

The heat from his body radiates through his clothes and mine, only getting worse when I press my palm to his chest to push him away. Animosity licks at my skin like scorching flames until I'm enveloped in them.

But what's simmering beneath the surface is something far more dangerous.

Attraction.

One I've never allowed myself to place on him before, or at least notice. But now it's at the forefront of my mind, and I can't unsee it.

Clearing my throat, I say the four most important words I've ever said to him.

"This never fucking happened."

His tongue swipes out over his bottom lip, a small smirk curling into place there. "At least we can agree on something, Reed."

While I'm sure this'll be the end of it and he'll back away to leave, my world is flipped further on axis when he leans in, mouth mere centimeters from mine, and whispers, "But get your head on straight for tomorrow's game, and maybe you'll get a repeat."

And though I know I shouldn't, I want his taunt to be an offer for another round of the best head I've ever received.

EIGHT

Quinton

There are days I really wish I was less of a manwhore.

It's not often, seeing as the benefits far outweigh the drawbacks when everyone involved is on the same page.

But today?

As I'm shoving my way out the door of the frat house?

Well, let's just say I wish I would've mastered the art of self-control. And willpower.

My only saving grace in this whole scenario is that I bolted before Oakley had a chance to: A, make himself presentable again. And B, follow me. Not that I think he'd follow me, necessarily. From the way he stared at me—somewhere between pure bliss and abject horror—when I told him he could get a repeat if he played well tomorrow, I don't think following me would've been high on his list of things to do.

Unless it were to kick my ass for the stunt I just pulled. Either way, I wasn't about to stick around and find out once his orgasm high wore off.

Fuck, what the hell was I thinking?

I wasn't. That's the problem.

My brain was all over the goddamn place. The shit with my parents after the game hung over me like a storm cloud, souring my mood, even when I was doing my best to let loose before heading home and sleeping the shitty day off.

But then finding Oakley at the party after he'd bore witness to it all only made it worse.

The verbal smackdown between us was the fucking cherry on top of a shit sundae.

And that only led my instincts in the exact wrong direction. The one where the obsessive need to prove him wrong took over, feeding this stupid competitiveness I have with him. Building inside me more and more until I just...snapped.

Or blew, considering the circumstance.

I don't know whether I'm proud of the way I got him to lose his mind with my mouth or if I'm terrified about what this means going forward in this so-called rivalry we have. Because I can only imagine that licking him like a lollipop will make things much, much worse between us.

I round the corner of the house and take off at a jog down a couple blocks, making a beeline for my Indian Scout. Not bothering to throw my helmet on, I bring the bike's engine roaring to life and hightail it toward my apartment.

Normally the wind whipping around me while I ride is enough to cool any building anger or tension within me, but nothing is enough to get me out of my head right now. Not for more than a minute or two at a time. All my brain seems to want to do is replay what happened in the bathroom.

My dick twitches at the thought of tasting him again, and I'm floored by the realization I wasn't kidding when I offered a repeat. I mean, sure, it was said as a taunt—half the things I say to him are—but I'd do it again without thinking twice.

And I'm not even into dudes.

Right?

After pulling into the garage at my apartment, I burst through the front door, so caught up in my tormented thought process, I don't even notice Hayes sitting on the couch in our living room.

"Jesus, where's the fire, Q?"

The sound of my roommate's voice momentarily causes me to halt in my path toward my bedroom, and I turn to him. "What?"

His dark brows hitch up, and he motions to me with his chin. "You seem a little out of sorts. Everything good?"

Hayes knows me better than pretty much anyone in the world.

We've been friends a long time, an entire decade between our time at Centre Prep and here. I'd tag along on vacations with him to the beach or the mountains, seeing as my parents never took us anywhere during the holidays. We'd stay up at all hours of the night, binge watch horror movies or trash talk to each other while playing video games. Hell, I even helped him sneak out of his parents' house so he could get laid for the first time.

If all that doesn't make him my best friend, I don't know what would.

So this is something I should be able to trust him with, right? To talk about with him while I try to get my head on straight?

Or not-so-straight?

Scrubbing my hand over my face, I decide to keep this to myself. For now, at least. There's no use in telling Hayes I got on my knees for the one guy in the world I can't stand and blew him—to completion—when I doubt it'll ever happen again.

With Oakley, or with anyone else.

"I'm good, yeah. Sorry. Just realized it's late, and I need to get some shut eye so I don't play like garbage again tomorrow night."

His blue eyes—more royal blue compared to my icy ones—narrow on me, searching for my lie. But thankfully, if he finds it, he chooses not to call me out.

"Okay. I'll still be out here for a while, as long as that's cool."

I nod, seeing as he's such a quiet roommate, he might as well be a mouse, and start for my room again. As I've reached the door, he hollers for me again.

"Hey, Q?" When I turn, I find him looking at me from over the back of the couch. "Don't be so hard on yourself about the game tonight. You're fucking good at what you do, no matter what anyone says."

Hayes doesn't know a ton about hockey, even if he is my best friend. He's got just enough knowledge to come to games whenever he's not busy being the wicked smart, always studying, lives-in-the-library nerd he usually is. And I say those things with all the love in the world.

But the knowledge he lacks when it comes to hockey, he makes up for with knowing *me*. My life, my history, my family. Hell, *Hayes* is my family more than the two people who brought me into this world.

Which is why, when he says anything like that, I know I should take it at face value.

"Thanks, man," I tell him. "Have a good night."

Once I'm locked inside my room, I strip down to my underwear and slide between my sheets, ready for this day to be over. But while my body is exhausted, my brain is wired. Under normal circumstances and it being the night before a game, I'd be able to crash immediately once my head hit the pillow. Yet tonight, the only thing I can do is stare at the goddamn ceiling and contemplate what made me lose all sense of reason the second Oakley said, *"I'll believe it when I see it."*

I love to prove him wrong and make him eat his words, all in the name of this damn rivalry he won't let go of. But blowing him has to be taking it a step or eighty-four further than normal.

So, what? Am I bi now? Does sucking one dick make me bi?

I let out a tortured sigh, because in reality, I know that's not how sexuality works. Like if I would've kissed him, it wouldn't make me bi either.

Sexuality is about so many other things, but most of all, it's want. Desire. Attraction.

So…am I attracted to Oakley? Do I want and desire him the way I've only ever wanted females in the past?

From the tent pitching my briefs just thinking about this, I'd say yes.

"Fucking hell," I groan absently, because this is the last thing I need. Literally dicking around with Oakley is the dumbest idea I've *ever* had. Which is saying something, because I love to think up stupid shit. And follow through on it, apparently.

First with letting him shove his dick down my throat and swallowing his cum like it's a fucking Slurpee. Then again, as I yank my dick free from my underwear, spit in my palm, and start stroking.

All with two brown eyes full of hatred rolling around in my mind, the star of the show.

My fist shuttles faster as images of tonight come flooding back to the forefront of my mind, this time, without me trying to stop them.

The closeness in the bathroom, the anger in his eyes. The breathy sounds, the bites of pain from him gripping my hair tight enough to yank it right from my skull. The ruthless way he held himself deep in the back of my throat. The intoxicating scent of his woodsy body soap in my nostrils as he filled my throat with his length, then again with his cum.

 I welcome each and every thought; their presence bringing me closer and closer to a desperately needed release.

But then they take a turn, and just like that, Oakley and I have traded places.

He's the one on his knees, taking my cock all the way to the back of his throat.

He's the one swallowing down my cum, milking me for all I'm worth.

He's the one who's left a panting, breathless mess on the floor.

He's the one who can't get enough.

He's the one destroyed by what we just did.

Him.

My feet dig into the mattress below me, a mixture of memory and fantasy swirling and blending in my mind. Building my climax until the only thing left to do is to fall over the edge…and I come.

I come harder than I have in my entire fucking life.

I come with the taste of his still on my lips.

Not allowing myself to linger in a blissful, post-orgasmic state, I make a move to clean up the remnants of my release still coating my hand and stomach, all the while a low, churning feeling settles low in my stomach. One I recognize as frustration.

Climbing back into bed, I yank the sheets over me and slam my head against my pillow with enough force, I'm able to feel something hard beneath it.

My lucky puck.

My superstition.

I shift, shoving my arm beneath my pillow until I find it. My fingers travel along the cool, smooth rubber disk, allowing the texture to calm the countless overwhelming emotions ebbing and flowing through me.

Taking a deep breath, I fiddle with it more until my racing heart subsides into slow, steady beats. And it works. Soon enough, I'm relaxed again. As much as I can be, focusing on the things I know and have control over rather than all the unanswered questions lingering in my brain to torment me.

What I don't know is if my dick likes all dudes, some dudes, or what.

But I *do* know he definitely likes the one person he really fucking shouldn't.

And I don't think a dump truck full of lucky pucks would be enough to help me work through that unfortunate fact.

The last thing I needed this morning was to be running late. Again.

But here I am, barreling my way across campus to one of my economics classes when I almost run smack dab into the last person I thought I'd see. And probably the last person who wants to see *me*.

"Jesus Christ," Oakley grumbles, a glare aimed my way as he steps out of my way and continues down the path the opposite way. "Watch where you walk much?"

At first, I don't think he notices it's me. Hell, I know I would've completely missed him if I didn't recognize his voice. But I'd know the sound of pure contempt anywhere.

"Good morning to you too, Oakley," I call after him in a sugar-sweet voice.

I expect him to turn around and say something—even a grumpy, smart-ass comment—but instead, he keeps walking away from me.

There's a brief second where I think I might've imagined it to be him, and it was some other random student. But the navy-blue duffle bag over his shoulder—an exact replica of my own—clearly emblazoned with a huge, white #33 is a dead giveaway.

So I do the only logical thing.

I follow him.

Why is it logical in my messed up, sleep-deprived brain? I don't have the slightest clue. Which is a real fucking problem when I grab his shoulder, spin him around to face me, and get a vicious *what?* snarled in my face.

I pause for a second, and for once in my life, I'm at a loss for words. Because I've seen Oakley mad. Hell, I've made Oakley so fucking angry, he might as well have been steaming out his ears.

I made the guy *punch me,* for fuck's sake, and he claims to be a pacifist.

But I've never seen him as ragey as he is while glaring at me right now. The kind of glare capable of making lesser men drop dead on the spot if only to escape it.

"I…just wanted to make sure you got home okay last night." I wince as soon as the words come out.

Jesus Christ, really, Quinton? That's all you could come up with?

If the way the crease between Oakley's brow deepens is any indication, now all I've managed to do is piss him off *and* make myself look like a fucking idiot.

And even more late for class, on top of it all.

"Seriously?" he seethes, stepping toward me. "That's what was so important you had to chase after me in the quad? You wanted to *make sure I got home okay last night?*"

Once again, I have nothing to say.

He continues to glare at me for a second before turning his head, as if to look around to see if anyone caught us speaking to each other. That's when I catch the edge of a hickey just barely peeking out over the collar of his shirt. In the exact same spot where I bit him last night.

Instantly, all thoughts of getting to class on time are out the damn window. In its place is the sound of his pants as I took his cock down my throat and groans of pleasure as I brought him to release.

Even though those things supposedly *didn't* happen. Something he's quick to point out.

"What happened to you agreeing with *this never fucking happened*?"

And now I'm the one who's getting all raged up.

"There's a difference between acting like something never happened and avoiding someone like the fucking plague. Which is exactly what you were doing by acting like I don't exist."

He steps back, crossing his arm over his chest and tilting his head to the side. "Would we be having this conversation any other day of the week? If last night had truly never happened, would we even be speaking to each other outside the confines of the arena?"

"No, probably not, but—"

"Exactly. So just drop the shit and get on with your day."

Another wave of irritation ripples through me, and I let out a heavy sigh. "I'm just saying us ignoring each other isn't exactly good for team morale."

"Oh, and us hashing out the details of our hook-up is?"

That makes me smirk. "I never mentioned anything about the details. But if you wanna go into them, be my guest."

He glares even harder at me, if it's even possible. "Cut the fucking shit, Quinton."

I raise my hands in surrender. "I'm not doing anything but attempting to have a civil conversation with you."

His nostrils flare and his eyes lift to the sky, as if to say a silent prayer to the heavens for strength not to murder me right here for the whole student body to see. Even a pacifist has their limits. As we both know.

When his gaze collides with mine again, it's hard and unyielding.

"Fine. You wanna talk about it? Get the stroke your ego so desperately needs? Make sure I can never forget it happened? Great. It fucking happened."

For the sake of this conversation, I choose to leave the whole *stroking* thing untouched.

"That's not—"

"But let's get one thing crystal clear, de Haas. No matter how good it was, it will never. Happen. Again." He bridges the gap between us, clearly using his proximity as an intimidation tactic.

Too bad all it does is remind me more of last night.

His body pressed to mine as I pinned him to the sink. Which lead to his strong, powerful thighs beneath my palms as I took his cock deeper down my th—

"Quinton," he snaps, pulling me from my thoughts. The frustration on his face tells me I missed something he said while I was off daydreaming about his dick.

"What?"

The way his jaw ticks lets me know he's just about at his wit's end with me. "I asked if you understand what I'm saying."

Oh. "Absolutely."

"Good," he mutters, and I think I watch a hint of relief cross over his features for the briefest moment. Stepping back, he puts a bit of much-needed distance between us and glances around the quad. "Now why don't you channel your energy into something more useful? Like being on top of your game tonight."

I raise my arm and give him a mock salute. "Can do, Cappy."

A shake of his head is all I get in response before he brushes past me to continue wherever he's going. I'm about to do the same and turn back toward my class, but my brain won't allow my feet to move, instead latching onto a tiny little detail he let slip.

One very tiny, *important* detail.

"So you thought it was good, huh?"

He doesn't turn around; just flips the bird over his shoulder and keeps walking away.

NINE

Quinton

There ain't no rest for the wicked, even coming off the high of winning for the first time this season. Then again, how can there be?

We took five losses before we finally tasted victory, and in my book, five losses are too many. We have a long-ass way to go to turn our season and record around in order to make the playoffs. Which is why Coach has us back in the weight room on Monday morning before we hit the ice this afternoon for a regular practice.

Most of the team is still riding the high from our win, and I'd include myself in that category too. But unlike the rest of the team, I seem to be the only one with my mind focused on something other than pumping iron or making sure I don't drop dumb bells on my own damn feet.

Which I've almost done. Twice.

I could say it was something like jitters, adrenaline, or excitement.

But in reality, I'm on edge being in the same room as Oakley. Because the stupid, insane, and obscenely superstitious side of myself thinks our goddamn hookup with him in the frat house on Thursday night was the key to our success during Friday's game.

My success, because it was by far the best I've played all season.

Maybe even last season too.

And the only thing that changed before the game? The only shift in my otherwise standard routine for nights before a game?

Blowing his goddamn dick from the dirty floor of a frat house bathroom.

As much as I wish it's coincidence alone, I'm the kind of athlete—along with plenty of other guys around here, Oakley included—who just doesn't believe in those kinds of things.

As the saying goes, if something ain't broke, don't go trying to fix it.

And more importantly, if something causes you to play the best game you've ever played? You do not, under any circumstance, change, alter, or breathe differently until the streak is broken.

It sounds insane, I know. Even to my own ears, it's nuts.

But come postseason, I'm not the only one around here who takes them seriously. There will be a range of guys who do things from not shaving until we lose to wearing the same *unwashed* pairs of underwear or socks for each game. Some go as far as eating the exact same meal at the exact same time every single day until the season is over.

Athletes are a rare sort of breed.

Which is why I catch myself staring over at Oakley far more than I should, trying to figure out if I'm going fucking insane by having these thoughts in my head. Because I might be, and I'm sure the second I approach him to tell him my theory, and then my solution?

Well, he'll either laugh in my face and tell me to fuck right off.

Or…

He'll agree to go along with my idiotic plan.

And let's be clear, it's without a doubt the dumbest, stupidest, most hairbrained idea I've ever had. I know it is.

Truthfully, I don't know which would be worse, but after I spend about ten minutes watching him doing his squats with Braxton, finding out where he'll fall with my idea is starting to seem like the only option. So my feet carry me toward him when his partner steps away to grab some water.

He watches me approach, brown eyes giving absolutely nothing away. Which is unsettling. Normally, the guy's easier to read than a picture book, at least when I'm pissing him off.

"We need to talk," I tell him as I come up beside him, fiddling with a twenty-pound plate to keep my hands occupied.

He looks amused as he watches me, a stupid little smirk on his lips. "Don't sound so ominous. I might piss myself."

I roll my eyes. *Why would he make anything simple?*

Of course, Braxton has to make it even more difficult by choosing that moment to start walking back toward us, cutting this conversation off before it can even begin.

Goddamnit.

My attention flashes back to Oakley, and I give him the most imploring look I can muster. "Just meet me outside the back doors to the locker room once you're done here, okay?"

He blinks, flattening his lips into a thin line. And he stays like that for a few seconds, clearly in debate as Braxton reaches us.

"All good, Reed?" Braxton asks, a frown creasing his forehead when he notices me. Ever since the whole debacle with the damn drug tests went down—and I came out of the whole thing clean as a whistle—he's been leery of me.

"We're good," I answer for Oakley, still pinning him with my stare.

Five minutes, I tell him with my eyes. *Just give me five fucking minutes.*

Finally, after what feels like an eternity and the world's most uncomfortable silence, he nods before giving me a clipped *fine.* Then he just walks away, Braxton in tow, like the whole thing never happened.

God, he's such a fucking asshole.

Even if he does have a major lapse in judgment by saying yes to this, one of us is sure to end up dead before it's all over.

Following his lead, I head in the exact opposite direction and do my best to garner some focus for the rest of our training session to work off some of my irritation, along with the new sense of anxiety floating through my nervous system.

From Ashes to New's "Light It Up" blares through my AirPods as I grab a seat in front of the cable row machine, going through the last of my reps for the day. The muscles in my back are on fire with every pull of the bar, but it's nothing compared to the searing sensation I feel on the back of my head from Oakley's eyes burning a hole right through me.

I'm still feeling them until the moment he leaves for the locker room over an hour later.

TEN

Quinton

This is so stupid.

Those four words are stuck on repeat inside my brain as I pace the hall near the locker room's back entrance. I've been waiting for Oakley for twenty minutes now, and now I'm wondering if he agreed to meet me and then ditched out because it'd be funny.

Newsflash, it's not.

He was still in there after I'd showered, though. Talking to Coach in his office. So there's still a chance he's being kept by whatever they need to discuss. So I keep waiting for another half an hour before he finally appears from the locker room.

He glances up, and the curious yet weary expression on his face lets me know he wasn't expecting me to still be hanging around this late.

"Wow, you're still here," he muses before brushing right past me toward the exit.

"I told you we needed to talk," I say, falling in step right beside him.

"So talk."

Be nice. If you bite his head off, he'll never even consider it.

It would be a lot easier to say if I knew he was actually listening. Looking me in the eye to know just how serious I'm being about this, no matter how crazy it might sound.

Grabbing his arm before he reaches the set of double doors to the parking lot, I drag him in the other direction.

"What the—"

"Somewhere private," I hiss, pulling him down a deserted hallway leading to who knows where. But we're sure as hell less likely to be overheard by some random person down here than by the main exit.

Once we're about halfway down the vacant corridor, I come to a halt and face him.

"Private enough for you?" he asks, a fair amount of snark in his tone.

My jaw ticks, another bolt of irritation zapping through me, and I realize this will be a lot more difficult than I thought. Maybe even impossible with the way we constantly take digs at each other.

Plus, I don't know how to broach this other than blurting my theory out and hoping for the best. Which, with my track record, won't do much good.

"God, this is insane," I mutter more to myself than him.

He shifts, leaning back against the wall, and I look up to find a frown line creasing his forehead. "Not exactly the way you wanna lead into something, de Haas."

"We need to start hooking up more."

I wince at the words tumbling out of my mouth in a spectacular display of word vomit before I have the chance to figure out the right way to phrase it. And believe me, I've spent every minute since he walked into the weight room this morning trying to piece my thoughts together well enough to pitch this idea to Oakley.

And this was not the execution I was hoping for.

Fucking smooth. How can he resist that offer?

Oakley blinks a couple times, studying my face. I do my best not to let my confidence falter under his stare, but it's hard not to feel completely transparent right about now.

After a few more seconds of watching me, he smirks and shakes his head. "You almost had me there, de Haas."

Well, fuck. I'd imagined him laughing in my face, but because he thought the idea was as insane as it truly is. Or because he can't stand me on my best day.

But I never imagined he'd think the offer was anything less than genuine. It kind of pisses me off.

"I'm not kidding about this. It wasn't exactly the way I planned to ask you, but I guess—"

"Hold the fucking phone," he says, cutting me off with a raise of his hand. "What happened to our agreement about *this never happened?*"

I close my eyes and sigh. "I agreed at the time. But it was before we won our first game all season."

The confusion written in his expression lifts, and I see the second he realizes what I'm clearly struggling to put into words. "You think…us hooking up has something to do with us winning?"

Yeah, I do.

"I'm not exactly sure," I hedge, sinking my teeth into my lip. "All I know is we were looking like the *Bad News Bears* of hockey until then. You and I were on two completely different pages on and off the ice, and I swear some of those guys were playing like it was the first time they'd ever held a stick. And then the bathroom happened and everything's suddenly taken a complete one-eighty."

He's silent for a second before coming back with, "What happened wouldn't contribute to the way everyone else is playing."

"No, but the way *we* play would," I point out. "You know as well as I do, when one person on the line is having an off game, the rest of us feel the effect too. Well, you and I were having an off *season* until I wrapped my lips around your dick. Completely out of sync on the ice, and the rest of the guys notice shit like that."

He scoffs out a laugh. "So that automatically means we just keep doing it? Fucking around? Sucking each other off in semi-public places until the season is over?"

"Yeah, I guess it does."

"You're delusional."

My teeth sink into my cheek to keep from snapping back at him, but it still doesn't keep the iciness out of my tone.

"No, Reed. I'm superstitious. Just like plenty of the guys on the team are. Like *you* are," I remind him. "We hooked up the night before a game, then we won. For the first time all season, we tasted victory. And you and I both know you don't fuck around with what's working when it comes to routine before games. So that's why I think we need to keep doing it."

A long, awful silence falls over us as Oakley continues to stare at me like I've grown two heads and he doesn't know which he wants to chop off first. That alone tells me this is a lost cause, and I'll just have to find a new way to keep playing well the rest of the season.

I know when to cut my losses, and I can tell this is one of those times.

Running my hand through my hair, I sigh. "Look, it's fine. Just forget

I said anything, okay? I knew the chances of you saying yes were slim, so let's just…" I trail off with a shake of my head. "Let's just stick with *this never fucking happened.*"

I make a move to turn and walk away—already trying to figure out if there's some other way to keep my game going well without my off-the-wall idea about Oakley and I jumping into bed together—when a firm grip on my wrist halts me.

He doesn't use any force to stop me, doesn't even tighten his hold on me. Like he knows the heat of his skin touching mine is more than enough to keep me here. I fucking wish it wasn't, but it's like tasting him the other night was the key to awakening this stupid, hot, achy feeling I get around him.

When I turn and meet his gaze, I catch a glimpse of something similar written in his expression. Just not enough of it to completely erase the wariness also present.

He narrows his eyes at me into near slits. "You're being serious."

I blink, nodding once. "Superstitions are pretty much the only thing I take as seriously as hockey. And this could be my last season. Yours too. I just wanna come out on top."

Or bottom. If he'd prefer it that way.

He gives me a measured look, then lets out a short laugh of disbelief. "You have to understand, this is the craziest thing I've ever heard. Especially when we"—he motions between us—"basically hate each other."

That's putting it mildly.

"I wouldn't say hate," I object, weighing my words. "More like severely dislike."

"Because that's so much better," he mutters, releasing me and crossing his arms.

I shrug. "Who knows. Could be fun."

A whole lotta naked *fun, to be exact.*

"I think we have different definitions of fun, de Haas." He pauses, another laugh bubbling out of him before turning into an uncomfortable cough. "And also, it might not really be my place, but I…I thought you were straight."

It's on the tip of my tongue to say *I am*, but something inside makes me rethink it. Holds me back from saying the words that have defined my sexuality for the last almost twenty-two years of my life. Now, they seem inaccurate. Yet, so does saying I'm anything else.

I shake my head, a low chuckle slipping past my lips at this ridiculous situation I've found myself in. Of course it'd be him—the one person I generally can't stand on my best day—that my dick would have to suddenly take an interest in. Or be the reason we played like all-stars this past weekend.

Better to be honest, I guess.

"I, uh…" I clear my throat, not sure how to put this into words. "I thought so too. But now, I guess I'm not so sure."

I'm surprised to find his eyes actually soften around the edges, if even for a split second. Almost like he gets it, not knowing where I stand with my attraction toward men.

Some people might know from the start where they fall in terms of sexuality. The label comes as easy as breathing, and there's no point in second-guessing it. Not everyone has that luck, though, and the understanding in his eyes screams he's been here before.

And despite all the animosity still flowing between us, I feel a weird sort of kinship with him forming because of it. Which only has me hoping he might not think this is as crazy as it sounds.

That he might say yes.

"Fucking hell, man." He blows out a harsh breath. "I'm gonna regret ever saying this, but I enjoyed you, ah, *servicing* me at the frat house. It was great—"

I snort. "Servicing? Is this the 1950s, or are you just too afraid to say I sucked you off?"

Ignoring my jab, he continues like I never even spoke.

"—but there's more to this whole proposition of yours than you've taken into account. It's a recipe for disaster, for one, and breaks just about every rule I put in place for myself."

My skin tingles at the thought of getting Oakley to let loose. It might be even more fun than digging under his skin.

"Rules are made to be broken," I remind him, earning a glare in return. One that says he's still uncertain of my asinine idea.

"You would see it that way, but I don't." Oakley crosses his arms before leaning back against the wall behind him again. "I don't fuck around with teammates, de Haas. Or baby bi's. Too messy for my tastes. And seeing as our relationship is already a shit storm…"

He lets the thought hang in the air between us, adding to the stifling awkwardness already clouding the hall.

As much as I hate admitting it, I get it. The two of us together is probably equivalent to throwing a ticking time bomb down on center ice and expecting it not to blow the whole arena to smithereens.

I'm still brimming with irritation even as I stare at him, silently begging him to say yes.

Doesn't stop me from wanting him to say it though.

"Your points are valid, and while I respect them, this is bigger than just you and me."

One dark brow lifts, the corner of his mouth quirking into a smile. "Why am I not surprised you aren't taking no for an answer?"

Because my brain refuses to register the word. It's not in my damn programming. Which is something I'm sure Oakley's had to have noticed in the years we've known each other.

Just like I know him well enough to realize I'm never gonna live this shit down. He might not be mad or popping off at me for suggesting this, but I know he'll use this as ammo in what's sure to be another six months of torment, bickering, and fights between the two of us.

Remember the time you tried to hit on me and I said no?

I can hear it now.

But if there's one thing I can count on, it's that he wouldn't do it publicly. He'd never out someone. He's a dickish asshole, but he's not fucking heartless.

I scratch my neck before mirroring his pose against the wall opposite him. "You and I both know this could go sideways and blow up in our faces. I guess I just figured what's the harm in trying? If we hook up and keep winning, it's a literal win-win situation. Getting off and getting the W."

"And losing every ounce of self-respect I have by sleeping with you."

So that's what this is about? That's *why he's so leery of this?*

My blood flares at his dig, and I have half a mind to call him on his bullshit about not fucking around with teammates or *baby bi's,* when really, *I'm* the issue. I'd bet if I was any other guy on the team offering this up, he'd jump at the chance.

I grit my teeth and rein in the temper fighting to break free. "You didn't seem to care too much when I was on my knees for you the other night."

He rubs his thumb over his bottom lip and smirks. "Call it a lapse in judgment."

Goddamnit.

I can't help the glare I aim his way. "Still the best blowjob you've ever had if I had to bet my last dollar on it. I'd double down and say it was the hardest you've ever come too."

His grin only widens. "The answer's still no."

Fucking hell.

Pushing off the wall, I close the distance between us until I'm standing right in front of him. My hands land on either side of his shoulders, flattening against the wall as I look him dead in the eye, and press in close enough so our thighs brush against each other.

That's all it takes—that tiny bit of contact—to get the first waver in his resolve.

A sharp inhale causes his pecs to brush against mine, and even through the thin fabric of our shirts, the heat from his skin still sets my entire body on fire.

And in his eyes, I see it. Exactly what I'm feeling.

Want. Need. Desire.

Lust.

It's all plain as day in those deep brown irises.

My voice comes out grated when I ask, "You sure about that?"

Oakley's head sinks back against the wall behind him, and I catch the subtle shake of his head. But I also notice the thrumming pulse in his throat and feel his heart racing against my chest, both of which tell another story.

Then there's the way his cock is thickening in his jeans against mine, and I'm pleased to find what he's claiming is nothing but a lie.

Knowing he's as affected by my proximity as I am by his is exhilarating. Intoxicating, even. It makes me want more.

More what? I'm not entirely sure.

More of his time? His attention? The look in his eyes he's giving me right now?

Maybe just more of this feeling humming in my veins.

"Not even for the good of the team? To get to the Frozen Four? To hold that trophy over our heads and bring home a championship I know we *both* want? Because that's what's at stake right now, Reed."

His teeth sink into his pouty, pink lower lip, and damn if my dick doesn't take notice too.

Calm the fuck down. He hasn't said yes yet.

But those three letters are right there. I know it. They're sitting on the tip of his damn tongue, so close, I can almost taste them.

If there's anything Oakley and I can agree on, it's that this team is one of the most important things in our lives. It might be for different reasons and we might have different goals down the line, but those things don't matter right now. What we should be worried about is the next game. Then the one after. And each and every one until we're holding that trophy over our heads.

Which is more than possible. The only thing needing to happen for us to get there is Oakley saying one simple word.

Yes.

I'm fucking sure of it.

I need to get him there. To see things from my point of view, and going off our track record, I'm gonna need every weapon in my arsenal to get through to him.

My tongue darts out, and Oakley's eyes track it as I wet my lips.

Say yes, Reed. C'mon.

I lean in even closer. As close as I dare.

"I can tell you're frustrated. Believe me, I am too. You drive me fucking insane, and most of the time, not in a good way. But what better way than to work it out on each other? I'll even let you go first. Whatever you want."

I run my lips over the pulse point on his throat, just below his jaw as I work my way over to his ear. "I bet you'd like to fuck my face, for real this time. And you can. I'll get down on my knees for you, here and now, if you say yes."

My mouth glides along his skin until it hovers against his lips, only a sliver of air separating us. Still too far apart, but close enough to brush when I whisper, "Just say yes, Oak."

His breath comes out hot against my lips, in harsh pants, like he's just run a marathon. I feel the same, but also keyed up and ready to go. Ready for him and whatever he's willing to give me. Which I'm hoping starts with him closing the gap between his lips and mine.

When he grabs the back of my neck, I'm sure he's about to do just that.

But instead, he uses the grip to switch our positions, pushing me back against the wall. Crowding into me the way I was him, overwhelming me with his presence. And something about the way he just man-handled me…makes me itch for another taste of him. Has my blood humming with need and want like I've never felt before.

He doesn't even have to roll his hips into me for me to feel his cock rubbing against mine, and it makes me want to get both of us naked. Fast.

But as soon as it's there—the heat and friction I'm desperately seeking—it's gone.

In its place is a bucket of cold water delivered by the man I now wish I didn't lust after.

"Not happening, de Haas," he mutters, leaning back to meet my gaze before stepping back. "Not in this fucking lifetime."

ELEVEN

Oakley

My body thrums with anticipation as I slide the key card into the slot on the hotel room's door after our loss against Fall River earlier tonight. It's not unlike any other night for an away game, but I'm on edge. And the reason is clear as day, seeing as Quinton is the one standing behind me, patiently waiting for me to let him into *our* room.

An unfortunate circumstance I have no control over.

When Coach called out our rooming assignments at the beginning of the season, sticking me with Quinton instead of Braxton like it'd been all last year, I was beyond pissed. Not only for the obvious reasons of de Haas and I not getting along, but because being an openly gay player sleeping in a room with another dude can cause discomfort for some guys. Every year since freshman, I've been paired up with either Braxton or Camden. So why the fuck he changed shit up on me this season is beyond me.

Maybe it was another tactic of trying to get us to bond and get past our rivalry on the ice, as misguided as it would be.

Since he's my uncle, it should've been easy enough to ask for a reassignment, get Brax back—or even Cam—and call it a day. But the last thing I want is for all those nepotism murmurings to become true. So I just suck it up and deal with rooming with my mortal enemy.

The door slams closed behind us once we're both inside, and I toss the key onto the dresser next to the television. The room is standard for our away games, two queen beds, a bathroom, and an adjoining door to one of our other teammates. Camden and Rossi, if I remember right.

Maybe I'll just pop over there and hang out for a while if things get a little too stifling in here to survive.

Dropping my bag onto one of the beds, I strip out of my suit in favor of something a little more comfortable. Movement in my peripheral snags my attention, and I find Quinton silently rifling through his bag to do the same. He pulls out a pair of gray sweats a second later, tossing them on the bed before working his belt out of the loops on his pants.

The back of my neck grows warmer, and I quickly turn away to give him some privacy.

Again, no straight guy wants their gay teammate checking them out while they change. Especially when it's just the two of them. Only, after what happened at the frat house, I'm not so sure *straight* is the right label for Quinton. Just like he said himself.

Still, I grab my own pair of black sweats and my toiletry bag before heading into the bathroom to give him a little extra privacy. And to hopefully get my stray thoughts under control before I have to sleep five feet away from the object of all my hate…and unfortunately, my desire.

A few minutes later, I exit the bathroom to the distinct sound of Sleeping With Sirens playing from his phone speaker, and when I round the corner, I find him repacking his bag after changing.

His posture is rigid, the way it's been since we left the ice after the game, along with the solemn expression painted across his features. Two things I'm not used to seeing on him. And call it the leader in me, but I hate seeing my teammates down in the dumps after a loss. Especially a rough one.

All of us could feel how close we were to victory, or at least to a tie, only to have Fall River's right wing, Johnson, slip past Quinton and slap the puck beneath Camden for a goal during the last minute of play. The only thing they needed to secure a win.

It was nothing we did wrong, really. Just a lucky shot and great timing on Johnson's part. Something we all know, Cam and Quinton included.

At least, Quinton *should* know.

"You…" I start, then clear my throat. "You played well tonight."

I don't miss how the phrase takes me all the way back to high school. To the night he pinned me to the wall and I decked him in the face.

Here's to hoping it doesn't happen again, though, considering the way he freezes where he stands. And I wait to see if I've only pissed him off more.

I don't know why I broke the silence with that statement. It's not like he needs my approval or praise. Hell, he's gone three freaking years without it, and he's been just fine, so what's the point of giving it to him now?

But when the tension lining his shoulders melts away rather than getting worse, I take a silent sigh of relief.

"Thanks," he says softly. "You did too."

"Thanks," I mutter back, just as quietly.

He leaves the conversation at that, and I crawl into my bed while he finishes what he's doing. Before long, he's strewn across his own bed with his phone in hand, enraptured in whatever he's doing. And more importantly, oblivious to me staring at him.

A pair of black, square frames now sit on the bridge of his nose—the kind Henry Cavill looks ridiculously hot in as Clark Kent—and I realize I never knew Quinton wore glasses when he's not on the ice. Probably because he and I are never around each other unless we're at the rink, and he must wear contacts when he plays.

Part of me hates myself for realizing how much more attractive it makes him.

My eyes leave his face and track down the length of his body, noting the way his tee rides up slightly on his stomach; a bare strip of smooth, tan skin peeking out between the hem and waistline of his gray sweats. And damn, those sweats. They cling to his muscular thighs like they were tailor-made for him.

Hell, knowing the kind of money he comes from? I wouldn't doubt they were.

The tattoos on his arms peek out from beneath the sleeves of his shirt, the dark ink swirling around his biceps and down the tops of his forearms. It's ink I've seen before countless times, having shared a locker room with the guy for the past three years. But again, I've never taken the time to look or notice them.

The fact that he's a complete and total dickhead made it very, *very* easy to ignore all the things I'm now realizing make him hot as fucking hell. Truly the sexy, bad boy of hockey he makes himself out to be.

Coming to this realization makes it a lot harder to not think about the ridiculous idea he threw into my lap about us hooking up to win games.

Which is what it is. Fucking ridiculous.

Right?

Not to mention, bringing it up again would only make things more weird between us. Heighten the strange mixture of animosity and sexual tension floating between us whenever we're in the same room. But as I keep staring at him, I realize this might be the perfect solution to work out some of the tension we have toward each other *and* hopefully help the team.

It would be a win-win situation, especially if it works, like he said.

Am I really about to reconsider this ridiculous idea of his?

Yes. Yes, I am.

I can't keep going down this damn road of loss after loss. We're only a quarter of the way through the season, and if this shit keeps up, I'd rather slit my wrist with my skates than lace them up on my feet to play.

And I sure as hell don't want to continue feeling like I'm walking on eggshells around him, either. Which is exactly what's been happening since the night in the bathroom. There's nothing to lose, and that's what I keep telling myself as I open my big, fat mouth to repeat a conversation I never would've thought of having a couple weeks ago.

"I think we should…" I trail off, scrubbing my hand over my face.

Fuck, this is so much harder than I thought.

Quinton's eyebrow raises as he drops his phone to his lap. "You think we should what, Reed?"

My eyes meet his as I sit on the edge of my bed across from him. The nerves I was feeling before have only multiplied in the passing minutes, and I can't see them going away anytime soon.

I hate it.

This lack of control is new, and I'm not at all comfortable with the way he ties my stomach in knots for no reason at all lately.

"We should do it."

His lips twitch, clearly amused. "Do what, exactly?"

Oh, Jesus fucking Christ.

I aim a glare his way. "Don't play coy with me, de Haas. You know exactly what I'm trying to say."

"No, I don't think I do. Because it sounds an awful lot like you're wanting to put some stock in this superstition after all. Which would be crazy, considering you said it would…" He trails off, tapping his hand on his leg. "Oh, that's right. *Never happen in this lifetime,* I think you said?"

"Quinton."

"Oakley."

The shit-eating grin on his face is more than pissing me off. Then again, I can't blame him for tossing this back in my face when I literally told him it would never happen. Now, here I am, crawling back to him and asking to revisit his offer.

My eyes sink closed, and I sigh. "I think we should do it, meaning I think at least trying out your theory wouldn't hurt any more than we're already hurting."

When he doesn't respond right away, I blink open to find him staring, a hint of amusement in his eyes while he waits for me to spell it out for him. Which I do.

If only for the good of the team.

"Us hooking up, being your theory," I grind out through clenched teeth. "So if you're still in, we can try it."

One corner of his lips curls into a sinful smirk, popping a dimple out on one side of his mouth I never knew he had. It seems so out of place on him. So innocent and cute for a person who's as short-fused as he is.

He lifts his body into a sitting position before scooting over to the edge of his bed until he's directly in front of me too.

"Be real for a second. Are you fucking with me right now?"

I shake my head. "No. I might've lost my damn mind, but I'm not fucking with you."

His smirk turns into a full-blown grin then. "What made you change your mind?"

My brow lifts. "It's not obvious?"

"We've lost two games since we hooked-up at the frat house." He shrugs. "I just figured you didn't care enough to do anything about it."

"You know that's not true. I'm the captain. Of course I care if we win or lose. It's why…" I sigh, rubbing the back of my neck. "It's why I think we need to try this. I feel like I owe it to the team to do whatever it takes to turn our season around, like you'd said."

"Even if it means sleeping with me?" he notes, a slight lilt of amusement in his tone. "A teammate and a *baby bi*? Doesn't that break these rules you're so fond of?"

I pin him with a glare. "Don't make me fucking regret this, de Haas. Call this an exception to the rule. They still stand in general, and the second this doesn't work out and we lose, there won't be an exception anymore. I'm not looking to get you into bed; only to win some games this season."

A low chuckle, smooth like whiskey, comes from him, and he grins. "Everyone always comes back for more, even when they say they won't. So, fair warning."

"Highly unlikely."

The smile on his face grows. "Anything else you'd like to add?"

"What?"

"What other rules do you have for us?" he prompts, motioning with his hand. "You know, since you're so hell-bent on making this a business transaction rather than a good time."

"Oh, fuck off. Despite what you might think, I know how to have fun. I just think it's better for us to have some…guidelines."

"Like I said. Fun-sucker."

I swear, every time I glare at the asshole, it only gives him more joy.

"Next rule," I grind out, rather than letting him bait me into retaliation. "No one can know about this. Especially not Coach or the team."

He nods, his grin erased in a heartbeat with a more serious topic on the table. "Yeah, I'm fine with that. I don't know if this attraction I have for you is just a phase—like my big gay college experiment—or if I'm actually into dudes." There's a quick pause and he runs his hand through his hair before adding, "And until I know for sure, I'm not exactly jumping to do the whole *coming out* thing."

Understanding washes through me. I get it, all too well, not wanting to say it out loud or let anyone know until you know it to be true yourself.

As much as I hate admitting it, it took me a few years to be comfortable enough to admit it out loud, even just to myself in the mirror. And even longer to tell anyone else, like my family or closest friends. Especially not knowing how their reactions would be. After all, I never gave off any vibes that I'm into guys. It took everyone by complete surprise, though they were supportive in the end.

I can only imagine it would be the same kinda thing for Quinton, even if he's not the type to be worried by much. But seeing him with his parents after his first game back…I can't imagine it would be an easy conversation for him to have on top of everything else he's dealing with when it comes to them.

"Is that it?" he asks, and it's then I realize I've been staring at him like an idiot without saying anything.

Well, shit.

"Um," I start, wracking my brain for anything else I might've missed. "I think, since we're going at this like a superstition, we only do it on the nights before a game. Just like it was the night at the frat house. Keep it as true to the first time as we can."

He snorts, and I hear a flare of annoyance in his tone. "So let me guess, me sucking your dick is the only thing allowed?"

"No, no." If I'm doing this, I wanna enjoy it too. And I like giving as much as I like receiving, at least when it comes to foreplay. "I was just thinking about what worked before. Besides, I have to put my money where my mouth is and outperform you with my superior oral skills."

His mood lightens again almost on an instant.

"Superior oral skills?" He laughs, shaking his head. "Again, you can just call it a blow job. There's no need to make it sound so…clinical. And two, like you've so aptly put it…" He leans forward, resting both elbows on his knees. "I'll believe it when I see it."

I give him a shove, sending him to his back on the mattress. "I've been sucking dick a lot longer than you have, de Haas. You'll see soon enough that I'm not lying about my skill set."

A playful smirk rests on his lips, and there's fire flicking in his eyes when he sits back up, both of which get my cock stirring behind my sweats. But a heated look alone has nothing on the lust dripping in his words. "Believe me, Reed. I'm looking forward to it."

Just like that, I feel like I'm drowning in the sexual tension clouding the room. The hairs on my arms are standing on end, and suddenly, it feels like the temperature's spiked to somewhere between Hell and the surface of the sun.

And from the look on his face, I can tell I'm not the only one being scorched alive.

"Good, okay." I clear my throat awkwardly. "What else?"

He's silent for a second before asking, "Think hand jobs would be okay too?"

"I think we'd be safe with anything that isn't anal." I roll my teeth over my lip and glance up at him. "Plus, I don't even know if it'd be on the table for you as it is."

A thoughtful look crosses his expression before he nods. "Okay, anything but anal goes for the hook-ups."

His quick agreement with me doesn't settle right. Which is insane, because this whole fucking plan is about as cockamamie as putting a pig in a tutu and teaching it ballet. I shouldn't be upset when a guy I don't even like on my best day won't let me fuck him.

Yet…I kind of am.

Make it make sense.

Rather than voicing my disappointment, I just nod. "That's everything I can think of, unless you have anything else you wanna add?"

"I think you covered it all, Reed." He laughs again, icy eyes filled with humor. "Just make sure you don't go falling in love with me."

I scoff. "A little hard when I'm already in hate with you."

"Wouldn't want it any other way."

I hold my hand out for him to shake. The warmth of his fingers wrapped firmly around my hand immediately reminds me of the way it felt to have them around my cock instead, and another bout of lust surges through me.

But then the idiot goes and opens his damn mouth.

"Shouldn't we seal the deal with a kiss instead?"

His words heat my blood with both irritation and desire, and the latter only annoys me more. I shouldn't want him when I can't stand him. And

I definitely shouldn't be as excited as I am to get down and dirty with him since it's a fucking recipe for disaster.

Yet here we are.

"I'd rather lick the shower tiles in the locker room."

His laughter rings out as he leans in, his lips brushing against my ear as he whispers, "Really? Cause I'd love to get a taste of your animosity."

I push him away on instinct, now more annoyed than turned on at the cavalier way he carries himself. Cocky bastard.

Pulling at the sheets on my bed, I slide in without looking at him and mutter, "Just shut up and go to bed."

I hear his deep chuckle from behind my back when I roll over, setting another round of irritating lust through me before he clicks off the light.

"Aye, aye, Cappy."

TWELVE

Quinton

Anticipation has been churning inside me at an all-time high this week, and not just because of the games against Fall River the next two days. It should be the main reason for my intestines doing somersaults as I lace up my skates for practice this afternoon, but nope.

It's the stare I feel firmly fixated on my ass as I bend over that's got my blood thrumming in my veins.

Lifting my shoulder slightly, I peek behind me from under my arm in time to catch Oakley's gaze locked on my back side. No doubt thinking about all the dirty things he plans to do to me later tonight, the same way I am with him.

A smirk sits on my lips when he realizes I've seen him checking me out, and a slight blush colors his cheeks before he quickly looks away.

That just won't do.

I wanna see the embarrassment tinting his face after being caught eye-fucking me in the locker room with all of our teammates around. It adds another layer to this rivalry between us, at least in my mind. Instead of how much I can piss him off, I'll see how red I can make him turn.

Don't get me wrong, I can still feel the hatred from him when he looks at me, along with what's sure to be an unhealthy dose of animosity. But now, there's something else too.

Interest, maybe.

Sexual tension, definitely.

Whatever else besides that is only making this newfound *thing* between us much more complicated. Even if it's a friends-with-benefits situation. Or enemies.

That's why I know this could end one of two ways.

This might be the best idea I've ever had, and we could keep riding this wave—and each other's faces—all the way to the Frozen Four. Or this could cause shit between us to get even worse, possibly more awkward, and could implode.

Either way, the anticipation is higher than a pothead on 420.

A hand lands on my shoulder as I attempt to dig my keys out from where they've played hide and seek in my duffle. It startles me, almost making me jump out of my skin since I thought I was the last one here.

I was counting on it to give Oakley some time to drop off his shit at his apartment before coming over so I wouldn't be pacing around while I waited for him to show up.

Anticipation has turned out to be a real fucking bitch.

But as I spin around to find him standing here scaring the shit out of me instead, I realize my plan is screwed—and not in a fun way.

Once my heart stops pounding a mile a minute, I raise my brow at him. "I thought you were meeting me at my place?"

Shoving his hands in the pockets of his sweatshirt, he shrugs. All sheepish-like, matching the guilty expression he has painted on his face. It has my hackles rising. Spidey-senses tingling. Aggravation surging through me.

My arms fold over each other. "Just say it."

Two brown eyes sink closed, and he sighs. "I don't think this is a good idea."

I shouldn't be surprised. On some level, I knew this was coming. That this would never make it past the planning stages. But it doesn't lessen my disappointment…or frustration. Neither of which make any fucking sense, but they're there nonetheless.

My jaw ticks with clear irritation as I hike the duffle strap over my shoulder. "You're backing out."

I don't ask it as a question, because it's not one. It's simply the truth, and it's written clear as day on his face. In the hesitancy in his eyes, the way his lips curl down into a frown.

Whatever tension, sexual or otherwise, radiating off him in waves earlier, is gone now, leaving behind…whatever the hell this is.

Regret, maybe?

But regret for what? For cutting this thing short? Or for even letting it get as far as it has? Either way, I don't need to know.

"Look, I—"

"Just save it." I sigh, pinching the bridge of my nose to keep from flipping a lid on him. "I really don't wanna hear it."

He doesn't listen, though. Of course. Because this is fucking Oakley, and heaven forbid he listens to a damn thing I say.

"It's better this way. For everyone involved."

"Nah, Oak. The only person this is better for is you. Because you don't have to break any of your stupid fucking rules." The anger's blazing at full force now, and instead of backing off, I feed the flames. "That's what it is, right? What it's all gonna come back to? Your incessant need to control the situation?"

His eyes harden, going from melted chocolate to cold, hard stone.

"Fuck you, Quinton."

"That was the plan." I shrug, scoffing. "Then you decided to bitch out."

The comment lights a fire under his ass too, and soon he's right in front of me, in my face, and pissed to hell.

"It's not bitching out; it's called thinking something through. Weighing consequences." He seethes, baring his teeth at me. "Something I know you don't do very well, Mr. Throw Fists First."

A quick shove against his chest has him stepping back a few paces, giving me some much-needed distance. Because yeah, the nickname he gave me is more than accurate. My short temper has gotten me into shit more times than I can count, and yeah, it's because I hit first and think later.

But this isn't some bullshit call on the ice or a dirty hit I'm retaliating against.

It's so much more than any of that.

And him insinuating this is remotely close is fucking bullshit.

"How can you say I haven't thought this through?" I shout, tossing my arms out. "You think I just up and decided to go gay for a little bit? See if I like the grass on this side of the pasture instead? Figured it might be fun to bat for the same team for a while? Do you have any idea how ridiculous that sounds?" My fingers rake through my hair haphazardly. "Jesus Christ, I think I've thought about what this means more than I thought about what college to go to or what I want to major in, which was a path in life basically decided *for me*."

His lips form a tight line as he measures my words and their value. Like he has the right to determine if they're the truth or not. Again, a bunch of bullshit, but after a few seconds, he concedes.

"Maybe, but have you thought about what happens when this doesn't go according to your perfect little plan?" He steps back into my space, and I swear he's asking me to deck him. "Because plenty of things can go wrong here. Like, what if you hate having another guy touch you? What if you realize you're not into it? What if people find out?" he asks, listing off the questions at a rapid-fire pace while ticking off his fingers. "What if we have no chemistry?"

I could laugh at the last one, but him using that as a point is only pissing me off more.

"Not possible," I growl out, my tone low and angry. "And you know it's not. Because you've felt it, just like I have. In the hotel room when you agreed to this. Outside the locker room where I could *feel* what I did to you. And let's not forget the night that started this whole mess to begin with."

His face is a mask, unreadable when he cuts me deeper still. "I wish I could forget."

It's not even a blow to my ego, his words. It's more like he's cutting me at the knees before ever giving this a chance.

Because, even though I rationalized this entire plan to make it about hockey and *for the good of the team*, it's not just about that. Doing this—us messing around together—was also for all the things I could learn about myself. My sexual preferences, being one of them.

And it fucking sucks, seeing the answers to your questions at the end of a path standing right in front of you, but you can't take it.

"I don't doubt it, seeing as you can't really stand the sight of me. But since that's not the way the world works, you decide to pull this shit instead." My lip curls back into a sneer. "Out of spite, no less. Because pretending it didn't happen and like this doesn't exist is better than admitting you liked it. Or worse, that you might actually like m—"

I don't have a chance to finish my thought before the unthinkable happens, and Oakley grabs the back of my neck, slamming his mouth to mine.

A mixture of surprise and excitement courses through me, and it takes a moment for his kiss to register in my frustrated, lust-fogged brain. And once it does?

Hell.

My fingers grip at the collar of his hoodie, wrapping the strings around my fist and yanking him in closer. His tongue spears between my lips to find mine, and the second it does, every little bit of pent-up lust and aggression I've been feeling for him ignites.

Because this is it. What I've been waiting for. What I've been fucking craving since the bathroom at the party.

Him, giving in to me and this *chemistry* he denied us having.

Admitting to whatever this is between us is real. Tangible.

But admission through action only goes so far. I wanna hear it too, because now? There's no denying this.

I rip my mouth from his—about to ask for just that—when he cuts me off before I can even start.

"You win," he half pants, half snarls into my mouth. "Now, shut the fuck up, Quinton."

Rather than argue, I take a page from his playbook and answer him with another scorching kiss. One to show him there's no holding back.

Now, there's only war.

The kind with lips and tongues, rather than shots fired from a gun, but a war nonetheless.

One I intend to win.

He's not making it easy on me, though, and as we fight for dominance over each other—starting with whose tongue is in the other's mouth—I'm quickly realizing I might've met my match. Hands grip harder than necessary as they slide under shirts, seeking the heat of skin on skin like it's enough to keep us from annihilating each other. He's grinding into me, and I'm pressing into him, and we're clawing at each other like two raging animals.

Pure, carnal need fuels this battle, and it's one neither of us are prepared to lose.

It's messy and brutal and fucking addictive, taking all the pent-up aggression and giving him mine in return.

I feel like I could kiss the hatred right out of him.

Crowding further into him, I push and push some more until he's pressed against the door leading to Coach's office. He doesn't let me have the upper hand for long, though, swapping our positions and slamming me back against the wood. Hard enough to leave me breathless.

"Like it a little rough there, Reed?" I murmur, licking at the seam of his lips before he tears them away from mine. "Because I know I do."

Teeth sink into the line of my jaw as his hips roll into me, eliciting a primal growl from deep within my chest when I feel just *how* much he likes getting rough with me. The ridge of his erection rubbing against mine sends bursts of adrenaline coursing through my veins, and I could care less about the rivalry, the team, the wins, or this stupid deal we made. All I care about is—

"Don't fucking stop."

It comes out as a plea, but it doesn't matter. Because Oakley presses his hips into me again and again, grinding his dick against mine with the perfect amount of pressure to light my entire body on fire. Or so I thought, but then he slides one of his thighs between my legs, parting them enough so when he lifts my leg to wrap his hip, it—

"Oh, *fuck*," I moan on a rough sigh, because this new angle adds friction *everywhere*. My cock is in filthy heaven as it ruts against his thigh, my balls drawn up tight since they've joined the fun.

Not even five minutes, and he's already made my body sing for him.

"What did I say about shutting up, de Haas?" he growls into my neck, the raspy cadence mixed with the heat of his breath sending goosebumps across my skin. The hand holding my thigh skates over the fabric of my sweats, up and up until he's palming my ass.

"Mmm, then you better make—"

His mouth slams back to mine with bruising force, cutting off my taunt. Hot and hungry, he slips his tongue between my lips and devours me whole. Commanding, yet still in control, the way he is on the ice.

But I wanna see his control slip. Even a little.

My hands slip under his hoodie, tracing over the smooth, defined abs hiding beneath the baggy material. I'm well aware his body is carved to perfection, showcasing the dedication he has to staying in top shape. Hard not to, since we've shared a locker room going on four years now while walking around in just towels on the regular.

But fuck me, I wanna explore every curve and line and indent on his body. Learn it with my lips and tongue while it follows the paths my hands have already taken.

The hand cupping my ass tightens with another grinding thrust, and I swear from the rumble I feel rippling through his chest, he's reading my mind right now. Hearing every dirty thought running rampant through my brain while he fucks my mouth with his talented tongue.

We go on like that, touching, tasting, and teasing each other for God knows how long. Could be minutes or hours, but it feels like only seconds before he tears his mouth from mine again, leaving us both a panting mess.

"We need to stop." It's more a request than a demand, and in a tone much lower than normal. More broken and grated too. "I'm gonna come if we don't."

I smile into his mouth before taking his bottom lip between my teeth and tugging at it. It's already swollen, probably bruised from how rough we've been with each other.

And it's only the beginning.

I can't think of anything I'd love more than Oakley coming apart right here and now from some heated kissing and fan-fucking-tastic dry humping. But I want to see it, feel it, and hell…maybe even taste it again. Whatever he'll let me have, I'll lap up greedily and probably come back asking the asshole for more.

Which means we need to move this little party to somewhere *a lot* more private.

"Hold that thought," I murmur, the rasp in my voice giving away all the filthy things I plan to do to him soon. "At least, until we get back to my place."

Which won't be soon enough.

THIRTEEN

Oakley

I'm not one to get nervous about something like sex, but as Quinton pushes open the door to his apartment, my stomach rolls with the same nerves it was earlier when I tried to back out of this whole plan. Only now, it's churning with a mixture of anticipation *and* anxiety.

I don't know what it is about him that's got me all out of sorts.

Maybe it's because whenever I hook up with a guy, most of the time, I'm the one doing the chasing. Coming onto him, picking him up at the bar or club. The first message online if I'm looking to find a quick lay on Toppr, this hook-up app for the gay community.

It's where I'm most comfortable. In charge and in control. Taking the lead.

But this? Planning out sex? The when and where, and all of it being on someone else's terms? Someone else doing the chasing for a change? And to top it off, having that person be *Quinton?*

It's got me off-balance. And not in the fun, new, exciting way either. It's more in the weird way you get when you're about to have sex for the first time. More anticipation than is healthy, and even when you know what you're doing—thanks to the extensive amount of porn you've watched—it all goes out the window the second the two of you are alone.

"Hayes is gone for the weekend," Quinton says, cutting into my thoughts.

"Hayes?" My eyes flick to where his hand is clicking the deadbolt into place, and my body hums even more.

"My roommate."

Oh, right.

I thought he'd live alone, seeing as the de Haas family has more money than God and might as well own Chicago. So why would anyone *want* a roommate in college if they can afford to live on their own?

Add it to the list of things I clearly had wrong about Quinton de Haas.

My throat works with difficulty as I lift my gaze to meet his eyes. The heat in them is searing, the same way it was before practice, as he crosses over to stand in front of me. His lips are still red and swollen from my kiss back in the locker room, and from the way he's got his stare locked on my mouth, mine isn't faring much better.

"Okay, well I don't…" I trail off, clearing my throat. "I don't think we need the whole weekend."

His lips lifts in a lopsided grin, popping a dimple out on one side. "All-weekend sexcapades aren't your style? Good to know."

"It's not what we agreed to."

"And you're always a stickler for the rules, aren't you?"

Compared to you? Always.

"I—"

His grin grows, and paired with the mischief dancing in his eyes, I realize he's just giving me shit. At least, I think that's what he's doing, because while Quinton joking around is nothing new, having him do it with *me* must mean I've been tossed into some sort of alternate reality.

Or I've gone insane.

Then again, this deal we've agreed to might be a sign we've both lost our goddamn minds. No matter how good it might make us feel in the moment.

"You're nervous," he murmurs. A statement, not a question, as he steps further into my personal space. "That's why you tried to chicken out after practice."

Once again, just like the night in the bathroom, I find my feet taking me backward. Away from him and the intoxicating aura he casts until I can't go any further. The backs of my thighs hit the couch, my ass settling onto the cool leather arm. Quinton boxes me in against it. One hand rests on either side of me—so close to my hips—and the heat of his almost-touch sends my pulse skyrocketing.

I hate myself for wanting them to be touching me instead of the leather. To push me onto my back and cover my body with his, naked or not, while we devour each other all over again.

Jesus, I need to slow my roll.

Because, despite how ready my body is for whatever we're about to do, it doesn't take away from how much I can't stand him. It only adds to the nerves he's picking up on.

I swallow, looking into his eyes and do my best to deflect. "I take it you're not?"

He blinks at me, slanting his head. That damn dimple pops even more, and *shit*, why do dimples have to be so fucking attractive?

"You *are* nervous."

My teeth sink into my lip as I try to figure out some sort of plausible deniability. The last thing I want is to be an emotional open book when I can barely get a read on him. Unfortunately, I come up with nothing.

"Yeah, I am," I admit, however begrudgingly. "Guess I'm alone in that sentiment, though."

He leans back slightly, his eyes darting between mine. "You're kidding, right?"

"I'm really not. This? You and me? It's fucking crazy." I let out a deep breath. "Part of me feels like I've gone off the deep end by even agreeing to this in the first place. And you being so comfortable with this whole thing is—"

"You're wrong," he cuts in. His hands move from the leather to find my thighs, and I look down to watch his long fingers splay out over my jeans as he steps between my thighs. Heat seeps through the denim where he touches me, and instinctually, I reach out for more.

My fingers dip into the waistband of his sweats, and I pull him in closer. He towers over me now, still standing at full height, and for the first time, I actually feel small. Not just in stature, either. Quinton's presence alone is larger than life, and he's sucked me into his orbit.

Fuck, what am I even thinking right now?

I crane my neck up to meet his stare. "Wrong how?"

"I'm gonna let you in on a little secret," he whispers, tracing his fingers up and down the denim. "And if you tell a soul, I'd deny it to my dying day. But, Reed…I'm the furthest thing from comfortable right now."

My brow arches at his attempt to placate me, because he must be lying. He's practically oozing ease and confidence, not to mention a ridiculous amount of sex appeal. The last one is far too tempting to get lost in, especially with the recent memory of his body pressed against me, the planes of hard muscle and smooth skin I can touch freely and—

"I know you might not believe me, seeing as this whole thing is my idea," he murmurs, one hand moving from my thigh to skitter up my side, "but I can assure you, I'm just as nervous about this as you are."

"You're right," I rasp, my voice coming out far more graveled than I'd like. "I don't believe you."

Not by a fucking long shot.

He shakes his head. "At least you've done this before. With another guy, I mean. My level of experience with a dick other than my own is everything we've done together."

"Plenty more than most baby bi's have."

"There's that fucking term again." He chuckles, and the sound sends a zip of electricity through my body. "Doesn't make me feel any less like a born-again virgin."

I crack a smile, finally matching the one he's been wearing for the past few minutes. "Have you ever kissed a guy before? Besides, uh…"

Besides me?

Quinton's confidence falters slightly at my question, and I watch him work to swallow before he shakes his head.

"Are you okay with it?" I ask, my eyes moving to his mouth too. "I probably should've asked *before,* but…"

I expected words. A simple yes or no to be his answer. But instead, he leans down, closing the gap between us with a single move until our lips meet for the second time tonight.

The action alone surprises me, but not as much as the soft, sweeping pressure of his mouth. It's slow and tentative, his kiss, when I was expecting something more brash to match the recklessness I've come to associate with Quinton.

It's the complete opposite of the way we went at each other back in the locker room.

But sweet and gentle don't last longer than thirty seconds before he asks for more.

One hand anchors in my hair, tilting my head back before tracing the tip of his tongue along the seam of my lips. They part automatically, and the first swipe of his tongue against mine is a taser to the balls, sending me into action.

All nerves gone thanks to the taste of his tongue, my arm wraps around his waist as I pull him into me more. Closer and closer, until not an inch of space separates our bodies. Until my back lands against the leather cushion, dragging him down with me and giving my earlier fantasy life.

Until I'm consumed by his touch, his taste. Just him.

My hands work their way beneath his shirt, dancing up and down the smooth expanse of his back. He shudders under the touch, goosebumps rising along his skin, and for whatever reason, I find the slight sign of vulnerability even sexier.

Quinton's tongue rolls against mine in time with his hips while his thumb runs the line of my jaw in a feather-light touch. Still keeping a touch of sweetness amidst the ferocity he kisses me with, and I realize it's the very thing putting me more at ease. I have no idea how he knows it'll help keep me from losing my shit and bolting, or if maybe it's a coincidence.

Either way, it makes my heart pound harder in my chest.

Our mouths stay damn near glued together as we pick up where we left off earlier tonight. Clothes make it harder, forcing us to settle for sneaking under waistbands, groping asses, and shamelessly exploring each other as best we can.

But it's not enough for me.

From the way Quinton's eyes smolder like two balls of blue fire when he rips his mouth away, it's not enough for him either. Not even close.

"If that didn't make my answer obvious, I'm okay with kissing," he pants against my lips. "So fucking okay with it."

We both groan when he presses his hips into me, the thick ridge of his cock rubbing against my own erection. The pressure combined with the heat of his mouth lingering a breath away has me burning from the inside out.

"And from the feel of it" —he rolls his hips into mine again— "so are you."

Okay with it?

Um, yeah. To repeat his sentiment, I'm so fucking okay with it.

"You're ridiculously good at that," I murmur, nipping at his throat because I'm *obsessed* with it. "Like, how? You've been into dudes for all of five minutes."

"Mmm, yes, that you know of," he teases, fingers tweaking one nipple beneath my shirt. And again, that one little action goes straight to my balls. "But sex is sex, Reed. I don't need experience with a dude to know how to dry-hump one. I know what feels good to me, so it's a safe bet it'll feel good to you too."

I pull back enough to meet his gaze, floored by what he just said. "And you just applied the same theory to blow jobs?"

He gives me a sheepish look. "Yeah, am I wrong?"

I laugh and shake my head, pulling him back in for another searing kiss and slipping my hands back into his sweats. Gripping at the firm muscle in each palm, I let my fingers drift in closer to his crease while he fucks my mouth with his tongue some more. I expect him to flinch or shy away when my middle finger brushes against his rim, but he just moans with pleasure and kisses me harder.

So, I push further.

We said no anal, which is fine. As someone who tops ninety percent of the time, I can respect that. But maybe he's down for some backdoor play not involving my cock. Slowly, I press my finger against the tight ring, massaging the opening lightly as I thrust up into him.

"Fuck," he groans, ripping his mouth away from mine. His eyes burn with lust as he pants out, "You. Me. Bedroom. Now."

I lick my lips and smirk, kneading his ass in my palm. "You think you're the one in charge here, de Haas?"

Our gazes lock in challenge, the way they usually do when we're about to enter one of our verbal sparring matches. The grin on his face is filthy, full of delicious, sinful promises.

"Until you show me differently? Yeah, I think I am."

He doesn't give me a second to form a rebuttal, grabbing my wrist and pulling me down the hall toward his room.

"Someone doesn't know patience."

Once we're through the door, he kicks it closed behind him and shoves me down onto the bed. His lips are raw from our kiss, neck red from where my stubble and teeth have been scraping at his skin, and hair on the top of his head a mess from my fingers knotting in the long, silky strands.

I don't think he's ever looked sexier in his life.

"Never claimed it to be one of my virtues, Reed. Now strip."

My stomach flips when he pulls his shirt over his head, tossing it in the hamper in his closet. Hard muscle and smooth skin covered in ink are exposed, and instantly, what little remains of my nerves are completely gone. In its place is a shot of adrenaline zipping straight to my dick at the sight of him half-naked.

My eyes trace and map over every inch of his body, taking in the ink covering his back and the length of his arms, trying to figure out which I want to explore first. Something I've never dreamed of doing with him, nor the number of filthy images currently in my head right now.

But while we're within the parameters of this deal, there's nothing stopping me from doing all those things to my heart's desire.

Shedding my shirt, I toss it to the ground at the end of the bed. My hands quickly move to my belt, desire coursing through me as I struggle threading the leather out of the loops. Quinton's already stripped down to his boxers, watching me in amusement as I fumble miserably.

"Need some help?"

The amusement in his tone sets me on edge, and my teeth sink into the fleshy wall of my cheek on instinct, trying not to let him set me off when I'm sure he means nothing by it.

The deep timbre of his laugh floats through the room as he knocks my hands away to undo my belt, ignoring the slight irritation I shoot his way. But he doesn't care, and doesn't dare let it faze him.

He's slow yet methodical in his movements, and Jesus Christ, I didn't realize someone could make taking clothes off *me* seductive. But the way his eyes trail over me flicks fire and lust across my bare skin, and by the time he's got me naked and on display before him, I'm consumed in flames.

Then he strips off the last layer of his own decency, revealing his long, thick, gorgeous cock, and I combust into an inferno.

"Get over here," I demand gruffly.

My hand anchors at the back of his neck, dragging his mouth back to mine. We're all teeth and tongue as he layers his body over mine across the mattress. With each grinding roll of his pelvis and harsh pants against my lips, I'm driven to the brink of insanity with want.

I can't remember a time where I wanted anyone as much as I want

Quinton right now.

Digging the ends of my fingers into his ass, I yank him closer before flipping our positions so I'm on top. In control. Exactly where I like to be.

"Mmm, there he is," he rasps into my mouth before taking my lip between his teeth. "I knew a fighter was inside there somewhere."

Quinton chooses that moment to press his hips up into mine again, his bare cock rubbing against my own.

"Lube?" I rasp out the word, already leaning away toward the nightstand before he can confirm it's in there. It is, and I quickly flip the cap open and douse my aching length with the liquid. His attention latches on to my hand working myself over, and where I expect to find fear, regret, or uncertainty, all I see is desire.

Desire, and a whole lot of curiosity.

When my hand wraps around his shaft, lube sliding between my fingers and over his length, he inhales sharply.

"God, your hand feels amazing."

A smirk makes its way across my face as I reposition myself over him, knowing if this feels good, what's about to happen next will be other-worldly to him.

But hell if I won't drive him to begging first.

I take my time coating his shaft, taunting and teasing him with every stroke. Learning exactly how he likes and wants to be touched. I catalog every hitched breath and tortured moan to memory, as if they won't be permanently seared there by the time this is over.

"You're a noisy fucker," I murmur, leaning down to nip at his collarbone when he lets out another groan of pleasure.

"Observant as ever."

"Mmm," I hum, rolling my aching cock into his hip as I continue to jack him. "Why am I not surprised?"

His head turns, lips skimming against my skin as he pants out, "Is that gonna be an issue?"

An issue? Abso-fucking-lutely not.

My favorite kind of partner in bed is someone who's vocal. About what feels good and what doesn't, of course. But what I really like is hearing how good I'm making the guy feel. It's powerful and invigorating, having enough control to make them completely lose theirs. I literally get off on it.

So no, I don't care if he's loud in bed. This might be one of the few times I actually *enjoy* Quinton's constant need to yammer and babble like an idiot.

I shake my head, moving to his mouth and letting my lips brush against his. "Not at all. Just wanted you to be aware."

"Oh, I am." He laughs, his hand sinking into the hair at the nape of my neck. "Why do you think I brought you here? I knew Hayes was gone and I could be as loud as I wanted."

Rather than answering, I continue exploring his body as my fist works him over, my own dick continuing to grind against the crease of his hip like an animal in heat.

"Oh, fucking hell." His moan comes out breathy and needy, already as keyed up and turned on as I am.

Right now, there's no rivalry. No hatred or animosity between us. Every awful thing we've ever said to each other doesn't exist in the confines of this room when we're both hot, naked, and sweaty, seeking a high only the other can provide.

And chase, we fucking do.

His hands are everywhere; on my back, clenching my ass, locked in my hair so tight, he might pull it out. They move around, scraping against my skin, grappling for hold as I stroke him from root to tip. He doesn't stop clawing at me for a single second as he loses himself.

In me. In my touch. In us, together like this.

And I don't blame him, because I'm doing the exact same thing.

But as high as he might take me with his body against mine, it's not enough. I need more. I need him writhing beneath me, begging me to come as I edge him closer and closer. I need his breath against my lips and his tongue warring with mine.

I need friction. Pressure. Aggression and anger, even. Just *more* than this.

So I take it.

I shift to wrap my fist around us both, the heat of his cock searing against my own as I stroke both our lengths before squeezing my fist a little tighter. It's exactly what I was looking for, the friction I was seeking, and the pressure sends bolts of lust shooting through my extremities.

"OhholyJesusfuckingGod," he moans in a single breath. One I'm quick to cut off, stealing oxygen straight from his lungs. It only makes him groan into my mouth again, and I swallow it whole.

His tongue spears between my lips, warring with mine as I take us higher and higher. Edging our way toward impending release.

I twist my palm around the heads on the upstroke, gathering the precum leaking from the tips and smearing it down our lengths. His hips move on reflex, fucking into my palm as I jack us from root to tip and back again. Rutting and chasing his own release as I lose myself in the sensation of his cock gliding against mine.

I roll and rock my pelvis into his, meeting him thrust for thrust as he pants against my lips.

"I'm so…I'm so close," he utters. "I'm gonna come."

I am too, lingering right on the edge of peaceful oblivion as I dip down and lick my way up the column of this throat.

"Then come," I whisper into his ear before nipping at the lobe.

I feel his dick pulse in my palm and against my own, and without warning, his teeth clamp down on my shoulder. He lets out a low groan, and they sink deeper into my flesh. Hard enough to probably draw blood, but for sure enough to brand me yet again.

But I don't care, because the sounds he makes when he comes is worth it. Those filthy, erotic moans are sure to live rent-free in my head for all the days between these hook-ups.

His release spreads down my fingers, mixing with the lube on our cocks as I keep shuttling my fist over the both of us, bringing myself close to climax. It doesn't take long before I'm right there behind him, the pain radiating from his bite catapulting me off a damn cliff. I spiral and flail on the way down as my orgasm takes hold, coming harder than I ever have in my life.

Releasing my shoulder from his grip, he sinks back against the mattress in a sated, exhausted heap. My head burrows into the crook of his shoulder, and I follow, my body slumping down against his until we're connected from head to toe with the mess of sticky cum caught between us.

"I'm not crushing you, am I?" I murmur. The question is more to be polite than anything, because I doubt I could move right now even if I was.

"Nope," he pants. A breathy, airless laugh comes out of him. "Fuck, and that wasn't even real sex, but you're already—without a doubt—the hottest lay of my life."

Yeah, I'd have to agree with him. Which is problematic. As much as I enjoyed what just happened, I know there's a good chance the whole reason we're messing around—for a damn superstition—isn't gonna last.

Meaning I don't wanna take the chance of getting too used to it.

I clear my throat, the sudden constriction on my airway making it hard to come up with a response. Simply responding with *you too* should be easy enough—especially because he was spot-on about the chemistry we have—but the words won't come out of my mouth.

Instead, I say something else.

Something worse.

"I gotta go."

I bolt up after saying it, immediately moving to redress. But I'm halted when Quinton's expression snags my attention. The brief flash of hurt crossing his face is enough to make my regret instant. But I just keep digging my hole, driving the knife in deeper as I do.

"We, uh…fulfilled the superstition or whatever. At least, I think that should've covered it. So I'm gonna go home. Sleep. Big game tomorrow, you know?" I trip and stumble over the words, wanting to kick myself as each one comes out with a bitter taste. Even more when I watch as the post-orgasmic haze leaves his face and a mask of indifference takes its place.

God, I'm such a jackass.

The worst part of this entire situation is I'm still butt-ass naked and covered in our cum, only adding to the vulnerability I'm feeling. So I grab my underwear from where they'd been discarded on the floor, slipping them on before finding the rest of my clothes.

"Yeah," Quinton says slowly, and I hear a mix of irritation and disappointment in his tone. His eyes burn with them as I toss my shirt on over my head and slide into my jeans, watching with a silence capable of making me feel like I'm still stark naked before him.

"Okay, great." I pause, searching for my shoes…only to realize they're in the obvious location. Out by the door. Where I took them off when I got here.

For the love of God, just hold it together for another five seconds.

Get your shoes and get out the door.

"Oakley," he says, cutting into my thoughts.

My spine stiffens, but I ignore him, moving for his bedroom door instead. I've got my fingers wrapped around the knob when a hand lands on my shoulder, causing me to freeze. The grip I've got on the handle tightens enough to rip the damn thing off, but I'm powerless to move. To breathe. To do fucking anything other than sit and wait for him to speak.

His hand releases me a moment later, and the cool air licking at my skin where his touch is no longer present causes me to look at him.

Instantly, I wish I didn't.

Because instead of the anger I was expecting, I find the pain of rejection lingering on his face.

He must know it's there too, because he looks away when I meet his gaze.

"Good luck tomorrow," he whispers before stepping away from me. "Not that you'll need it."

FOURTEEN

Oakley

December

So, despite the way I bolted like a dickhead after our first hook-up... Quinton's theory actually works.

I shouldn't be surprised, seeing as I'm also a firm believer in superstitions—at least when it pertains to hockey. But I'm still in complete shock when the scoreboard at the end of the game against Fall River shows we won. In a shutout.

And then later the same night, after I apologized quite a bit for my hasty exit the night before, we went for another round testing this superstition. Only this time, I took my turn learning every inch of Quinton's dick with my tongue.

We won the game the next day, four to one, and I got a fucking hat trick out of it.

At first, I thought it was coincidental—maybe the team was finally starting to form into a cohesive unit and play well together—and had nothing to do with this little arrangement Quinton and I created. But as more time passes and we keep winning, I know it's time to put some stock in this little superstition.

We've racked up six more wins in the past three weeks, and it's safe to say our plan has turned the entire season around. We even have the eyes of the entire NCAA on us, and thankfully, it's got nothing to do with PED or steroid use anymore. Nope, we're being called *the comeback kids,* and the whole team is eating it up, using it as a driving force to continue competing at an elite level.

Now we're to the point in the season where we only have a few more games before winter break starts, and it might be strange to admit, but I'm kind of worried about it. With the roll we've been on, I'm terrified we might lose this momentum going into the new year and the second half of our season.

But we still have another week and a half of classes, practices, and games to go, so I'm refusing to let my thoughts linger on it.

Instead, I shift my focus to the present and the naked man in front of me, about to redress after our latest roll in his sheets. My eyes trace over the sculpted muscles of his back, covered in intricate artwork, until I reach his smooth, bare ass. I can still see the faint imprint of my palm from where I was squeezing one cheek earlier while he fucked my face.

Yeah, I'm definitely gonna miss this view.

A classic side effect of really good sex. The top-tier, mind blowing kind of sex that can only happen when the chemistry between two people hits just right. Everything about the person becomes addicting.

Plus, this little theory has made us a lot more fluid with each other—both on and off the ice. It's like we thought; we're literally fucking out our aggression with each other, and now we can sort of get along.

But only sort of.

"I can feel you staring at me like a piece of meat," Quinton chides, not even sparing me a glance as he slides a pair of athletic shorts on, sans underwear. Something he does a lot, and it's far sexier than it should be. Or is fair, when he turns, and I catch the way the waistband hangs low on his hips, revealing the damn V that never fails to get my dick stirring.

And the tattoos.

Those. Fucking. Tattoos.

I've never been into tatted guys, at least to the extent Quinton has covering his body. In fact, I used to think they made him look like a delinquent, only adding to his reckless attitude and persona. Now, after getting to see each piece of art up close and running my tongue over each line inking his skin, I realize I was wrong, and tattoos are now my new kink. At least with him.

The ram's skull across the top of his back and shoulders is sexy as hell. It's more of a sketched style of artwork, the linework messy but the shading and depth created in it is impeccable. And as for why a ram…well, it's because he's an Aries.

Sometimes it really is that simple.

Maybe it's why I like them, though. Because I can see little pieces of who he is through the artwork painted across his body. Tiny snippets into who he is inked on his skin for the world to see.

Out of them all, my favorite is the piece on his thigh. It's a fractured old-fashioned clock—the kind with Roman numerals for the numbers. All the inner workings, the gears and mechanics hidden within, peek through the gaps of broken pieces, and the little shards were made to look like they're piercing his skin.

I've never asked him about it, but I can tell there's a meaning to it every time I touch or trace over it.

A sock hits me in the face out of nowhere, interrupting my eye-fucking session.

"I'm not a piece of meat," he says again, but the playfulness in his voice tells me he doesn't give two shits about me ogling him. From the way I see him flex his ass, he's actually enjoying it.

"Mmm," I hum, the rumble coming from deep within my chest. "Disappointing because you look good enough to eat."

"Glad to know you really are attracted to me." He chuckles. "I was worried there for a second."

My brows knit as I continue to watch him move around the room. "What? Of course I am. Why would you think I wasn't?"

He glances up at me from where he was bending to grab a shirt off the floor, giving me one of those *get real, Reed* looks. Brows raised and all.

"It's not like you made this whole"—he waves his arms around—"situationship easy. If anything, the roles should have been reversed and you should've been the one chasing me, since you knew you were into dudes. At least, that's the way it happens in the movies and shit. The gay guy falling for his straight friend—"

"No one's falling and we're not friends."

His face hardens slightly before the snark comes out. "Ah, yes. See, this is exactly what I mean. Why would you ever give me something like affection when you can keep being hostile?"

I smirk and give a single nod. "Now you're catching on."

That earns me an eye roll. "As I was saying…I had to practically beg you to get in bed with me, and even when you agreed, you *still* almost bitched out at the last minute." He pauses, shrugging his tee on over his head, leaving his hair a tousled, sexy mess. "I thought maybe you weren't attracted to me. You know, the whole *he's just not that into you* thing."

"Definitely not." I lean back against the wall, grinning. "Guess I just needed a bit more convincing."

A returning grin appears on his lips, and it's filthy. His eyes are heated as he stalks over to where I'm sprawled on his bed, not stopping until he's climbed over me and straddling my waist. My dick takes immediate notice of this new positioning, and even though it hasn't been more than twenty minutes since he came all over Quinton's chest, he's definitely a fan of getting a round two in before going home.

Too bad it's probably against the rules. *My* rules, but still.

"Or," he says, palms landing against the wall on either side of my head, "you just wanted me to work for it."

"Oh, absolutely. I wasn't about to be one of those puck bunnies that just jumped into bed with you on a whim, looking for a good time."

"Why do you continue to make me out to be a total manwhore?"

My brows furrow. "Uh, because you kind of are? Exhibit A being the way you're currently grinding down on my cock like a stripper giving a lap dance."

And he is. I didn't notice when he first straddled me, but somewhere between now and then, he must've felt my dick perk up and decided to play games. The devilish smirk on his face only proves it.

"I have no idea what you're talking about."

"Mhmm, sure you don't," I mutter before shoving him off me to adjust my erection. "Now I have to wait for this to go away so I can leave."

He laughs, his stupid dimples peeking out in his cheeks as he leans against the wall beside me.

"Tell me something real, then. To pass the time 'til he decides to behave."

My brows crash together. "What do you mean?"

"You say I'm all fun and sex and surface level, but it's not like you've shown me anything deeper either." He lifts his shoulder in a shrug. "So if you're gonna talk the talk, you better—"

It's my turn to roll my eyes. "Yeah, yeah. I got it."

But the thing is, I'm not sure I want to.

This is supposed to be just sex. Not sharing feelings and all that crap. Hell, I probably shouldn't have gotten in the habit of hanging around afterward. Yet I did because the way he looked at me when I rushed out of here after the first time made me feel all kinds of disgusting.

"Earth to Oakley?"

I shake my head free from the thoughts plaguing me, flicking my gaze to him. "Yeah?"

"Pick something to tell me."

Ugh. "What's the point? My dick's calmed down, now I can go."

He ignores me, maintaining his focus on wiggling some information out of me instead. "Pick something easy. Like…why did you care about being captain so much?"

My brows arch. "Why did *you?*"

"Because it pissed you off," he says, a wry smirk sitting on his lips. "Nice deflection, though. Your turn. Why'd you want to be captain so bad?"

Goddamnit.

I have no interest in doing this. It's not why I'm here. And I'm about to say that too, to make my point known that it's useless for us to get to know each other on this level when we're just…enemies with benefits.

But then that expression crosses his face. The same one he had the first night when I was leaving, and it hits me square in the chest all over again.

Rejection.

And I just can't let him feel it. Not anymore, and not because of me. *Fucking hell.*

"I…" I trail off, not knowing where to start. "I guess it was just something I expected from myself."

"Because you're Coach's nephew?"

There's no hate or inflection behind the question, but it still pricks at my nerves the same.

"Not in the way you might think. He and my dad have been grooming me to take the place as a role model and captain since I was a kid. It's literally in my blood, a legacy I wanted to continue."

"So it was for them, not for you?"

"It was still for me, because it's *in* me. I've built my career on being the teammate who picks up everyone else, to put our success as a whole above my own." I shake my head. "It sounds stupid—"

"It doesn't," he says, cutting in. When I meet his gaze, I find honesty in it. "I swear, it doesn't."

His understanding keeps me talking, diving in a little deeper.

"I just want to build on it, I guess. I don't want to keep being the son of Travis Reed or the nephew of Trevor Reed. I want to make my own name, put my mark on the league as Oakley Reed, badass hockey player. With whatever accolades and titles I earn on my own."

He stares at me like I've grown a third eyeball in the middle of my forehead, and it puts me on edge.

"What?"

"I'm just trying to figure you out." He licks his lips, clearly piecing together what he wants to say in his head first. Something I've noticed him do a lot more lately, and I think it's to keep from saying something that'll irritate me.

"Continue," I try coaxing, albeit begrudgingly.

"It's just…" He pauses. "You say you don't want all these things because of your family, but it's the exact same reason you do want them too. And it's confusing."

"I want them if I've earned them," I correct him. "I want to feel like everything happening in my career is because *I've* made it happen for myself, not my last name."

Suddenly, it's like a lightbulb turns on in his brain, and he sits up straighter.

"Oh my God. That's why you decked me when we were back in high school, isn't it? Because I was talking trash about you only getting places because of your name when it's actually the last thing you want."

Bingo.

"Pretty much, yeah," I say with a sigh. "Wasn't too hard to keep adding fuel to the fire after that."

"Well, shit." He shakes his head before letting out a wry laugh. "My mouth really does cause more problems than it should sometimes."

"You're just figuring this out now?"

He nods. "How's the saying go? The first step to change is awareness?"

"And you expect me to believe you wanna change? Really? You?"

"Hey, I haven't gotten in a fight since we started following through on this superstition," he protests.

It's true; he's reined in his temper a lot in the past month, though I'd chalk it up to regularly getting laid and tasting victory, not because he's a changed man. But I still give him the benefit of the doubt, if only to placate him.

"Yeah, yeah. You're a real pacifist now, de Haas."

"Takes one to know one, right?"

I can't stop my eyes from rolling. "Sure."

I swear he gets off on me giving him a clipped or sarcastic response, because he always grins at me like an idiot whenever it happens. Dimples and all.

Probably because I'm feeding him exactly the reaction he's hoping for. Always looking to get under my skin.

But his grin slowly fades as he continues staring, studying me the way he would a playbook. I'm not sure what he's looking for when he does it, only that he must find it when a solemn expression crosses his features.

"Oak?"

I try not to let the nickname burrow its way into my chest the way it wants to, but it manages anyway, nestling up behind my ribs. "Yeah?"

"I just want you to know…I'm sorry." He pauses and clears his throat. "You know, for all the shit I said back then."

The sincere tone he uses is enough to set me on edge. Because this isn't how we act together, all soft-spoken apologies and deep, meaningful conversations. Which is exactly why I shift the energy back to teasing.

Where it's comfortable. Where we're *supposed* to keep it.

"Just back then?" I ask, raising a brow. "Not for the past three years on top of it?"

A smirk plays on his lips, breaking through the heaviness. "I mean, we both know you had some of it coming."

Just like that, we're back to our regularly scheduled programming as I shove his shoulder, almost causing him to fall off the edge of the bed. It makes us both burst out into laughter.

"And there goes your chance of me apologizing for decking you. Because you *definitely* had it coming."

FIFTEEN

Quinton

"There's no way in hell we don't win tomorrow. Not after that," Oakley pants, dropping to his back across my mattress.

I'm still on top of him, cum leaking from my dick and onto his chest from what might be our hottest hook-up yet, and I have to agree. But Cornwall has been undefeated so far this season, so it will be the first real test of our team.

And how well this superstition actually works.

"Honestly, we're doing it again, even if we don't."

He chuckles, his hands resting on my thighs giving a little squeeze. "Deal."

Sliding off his body, I wipe myself clean with a dirty shirt and toss it in my hamper. I can feel his eyes on me as I drag a pair of sweats up my hips, studying me the way he tends to. He's been doing it a lot more lately, though I refuse to point it out. The last thing I want is to inadvertently piss him off when we've just started getting along.

"You mind if I hang here for a bit?"

"Not at all."

I've realized having him around isn't so bad. And not just for the sex part, though I'm not complaining about that either.

Take the other day for example. We were on our way out off the ice after practice when he pulled me to the side and asked if I wanted to grab dinner and study at my place. He needed someone to quiz him on some philosophy crap for a class he's taking, and even with a ton of roommates who could help him, their townhouse is far too rowdy—even on weeknights—to actually be beneficial.

So…I said sure. And to my surprise, it wasn't weird. We ordered a pizza, I quizzed him with his flashcards, and I learned a disturbing amount about Kant, Hume, and Marx in the process.

No arguing or bickering, and also no hooking-up, per the rules we agreed on. Which was fine with me…until Oakley stretched out and I got a peek at his abs. Then I had to rein my dick in from getting too many ideas.

But honestly, the best part of the night was when Hayes walked in after his night class to find us on the living room floor—notebooks, flashcards, and pencils strewn out around us—only to ask us who died.

We both got a good laugh out of it, though I understand why he'd ask that. He's been privy to this little feud Oakley and I have longer than just about anyone.

But it was nice to see we could spend time together fully clothed and still not want to rip each other's heads off. It's progress.

"At least get dressed though," I tell him, throwing his underwear at him. "In case Hayes decides to make an unexpected appearance."

"True," he says, and not even two minutes later, he's cleaned up and fully dressed.

I'm at my desk on the other side of the room, reading through another chapter of this damn economics book, when he collapses back on my bed, stomach first, and shoves his arms beneath my pillow.

I shake my head and go back to reading; a comment something along the lines of *"make yourself at home, why don't you?"* on the tip of my tongue.

I don't get to say it, though, because he breaks the silence.

"What the hell?"

When I look up again, I find Oakley pulling the familiar disk out from under my pillow. Holding the puck in the air between us, he asks, "Were you missing this?"

I smirk and join him on the bed before plucking it from his grip. Rolling to my back beside him, I turn it over in my hand a few times. "No, it's where it's supposed to be."

"What?" He laughs. "You're being serious?"

I nod, still fiddling with the rubber, flicking it between my fingers like one of those fidget spinners a few times, wondering why I didn't just lie and say it made it there by mistake. It'd save me from giving him more ammunition to use against me, should this whole thing between us end poorly.

Yet instead, I end up giving him the truth.

"It's my version of socks," I reply before placing the puck into his waiting hands.

"Socks?"

His eyes flash to my cheeks when I grin, popping my dimples. "You know, your crazy sock thing? The ones you wear every game under your uniform socks?"

A look of surprise flashes over his face for a moment. "You have a superstition too?"

"Seems so, doesn't it?" When he says nothing, I roll to my side, propping myself on an elbow. "You think I would've brought up us sleeping together if I didn't believe in superstitions too?"

"I figured you did, especially after the whole debacle with Justin freshman year. I just didn't realize you had your own."

The pinch between his brows is kind of cute, and it takes a good amount of self-control—an amount I didn't know I possessed—to keep my thumb from smoothing it back out.

"Because no one knows," I murmur. His eyes flick to me, and I continue, "Apart from you, I guess."

His attention moves back to the puck in his hands before giving it back to me. I roll my body over his, trying to place it beneath my pillow again while his head's still on it. My chest brushes his as I do, causing every nerve of my body to stand on end. Which is why I shift to move away again as soon as it's back where it belongs.

Only Oakley's hands catch my waist and hold me against him, locking me in place.

"So how does it work?"

Our proximity is too much for me to handle, and a lie catches in my throat, begging to fall from my tongue. If only to save myself from giving away a secret part of me in a moment far too intimate for enemies-with-benefits to share.

But the truth still slips free.

"I sleep with it under my pillow for the entire season. Every single night, no matter what. It goes with me on the road and it's the first thing I unpack when we get to the hotel when you're not looking. And it's the first thing I pack again in the morning before you notice it's there."

"You take it for away games?"

I nod.

"So it's going with us tomorrow night?"

I nod again.

"Okay," he says slowly, clearly working through the information I'm throwing at him. "And what's so special about it?"

"It's the puck I scored my first goal with. All the way back when I was a kid and just discovering my love for hockey. Scoring that goal…I guess it cemented the love for me more. Putting it under my pillow turned into a superstition pretty quickly after that, thinking it was good luck. My team lost, or I had bad games, obviously. Plenty, over the course of my career so far. This season being the perfect example."

His brows furrow. "So then…why keep using it if it doesn't work?"

"There's two actually," I say slowly, measuring my words. "One, because it's a habit at this point. I doubt I'd get much sleep knowing it's *not* there, you know?"

The corners of his lips lift. "And the other?"

I hesitate before more secrets spill, darker ones this time. But no matter how much I might want to, I'm helpless to stop them.

He's carving out chunks of who I am and taking those tiny pieces for himself.

"I…know you overheard that shit with my dad earlier this season. After the first game I was back after the drug test shit."

Oakley stiffens beneath me, so slightly, it wouldn't have been noticeable if my body wasn't plastered to his at every point. His head turns away, something like embarrassment written on his face until I tilt it back and force him to meet my eyes.

Once again, sympathy is etched into them as he meets my gaze. "I didn't—"

"It's fine," I assure him. "I'm not mad about it or anything."

He opens his mouth to object, and I retract my statement.

"Okay, I'm not mad about it *now*. When it happened, I guess I was embarrassed or pissed. Or both, honestly. Knowing you heard him lay into me, especially after I played like garbage and had to appeal my suspension for something I truly didn't do." I sigh and rest my chin on his chest. "I wouldn't have wanted anyone to hear that conversation with him, let alone my pain-in-the-ass rival. And I didn't know how much you heard of what he said either, which only made it worse."

"I think I caught the gist of it," he murmurs. His hands leave my hips, fingers moving to glide through my hair instead. Two brown irises soften even more as he searches my face. "So this has to deal with the puck because he doesn't want you playing hockey?"

I nod, my jaw ticking with effort not to lean into Oakley's touch while the countless times my father's attempted to remove hockey from my life over the years run through my thoughts. And believe me, there are plenty.

"Ever since I started college, it's become more of a reminder of why I started playing in the first place. For the love of the game and the thrill that comes with it." Pausing, I roll my teeth over my bottom lip and offer yet another secret. "I can list only a few things in the world I love as much as being out on the ice. It's something I wanna hold on to as long as I can, even though I know the odds are stacked against me."

He nods, a wave of understanding passing over his expression. "I get what you mean. Though I don't think the odds are at all stacked against you."

"You say that, but…"

He studies my expression before rolling me to my back, his turn to hover over me. "But what?"

But do you actually mean it?

I don't say it though. For once, I keep something to myself rather than spilling my guts to him, lifting my shoulder in a shrug instead.

Oakley's expression hardens fractionally, and he leans away from me into a sitting position. I follow suit, sliding up to rest against the headboard. My fingers slip beneath the pillow, rubbing against the rubber puck in a way of comfort while he continues eyeing me.

"How is it possible for you to have so much confidence all the time, yet you don't seem to grasp just how talented you are?"

"I know I'm talented—"

"*Do* you?" His brow arches in challenge…and I relent.

"It's like…I know I have the talent and the skill to make this something I could do for a long time. I've worked my ass off to get here, and I'm determined to make it happen. But I still constantly feel like the team's black sheep. Normally it doesn't get to me, but then there are moments where those doubts worm their way in, and I just feel like an imposter."

The look of sympathy he's giving me grows, if it's even possible.

I should not have said that.

"We make you feel that way, or your dad does when he tries to force you into his version of you?"

Both.

I just give him another shrug and pull the puck out to play with it some more, wishing we could just end this conversation. Or better yet, go back in time before I offered the information up when I knew I shouldn't have.

He lets out a sigh at my lack of engagement. "Look, you're good at what you do, Quinton. Don't let your dad, or anyone else, convince you otherwise."

My eyes flick to his face, and I give a mock salute. "Aye, aye, Captain."

"I'm being serious." His gaze takes on a more imploring look, and it makes me sit up a little straighter. "I'll deny ever saying this, but you've got far more raw talent than I do."

I snort. "You're born to hockey royalty. That's not even possible."

"Maybe I am, but I also know we grew up loving the same game in two different ways. You excel on the ice because you were born to be out there. Whereas my talent was trained into me since I could walk. It wasn't something I was just gifted through genetics. It took a lot of work and coaching to get me here."

"For real?"

He nods. "Yeah. You can ask Coach. He and my dad made me run drills every day for three straight summers when I was in elementary school to get better control on the ice. Something…I'm sure you never had to do." When I don't immediately negate his point, he continues, "See. You fit in a lot better than you think you do, and you're only the black sheep because of your temper. Now, if you'd just learn to keep your head on straight—"

"—I have a real shot of making it to the NHL?" I supply, my brow arched.

From the way his lips part and brows rise, he's taken by surprise at my ability to literally take the words right outta his mouth. "Uh, yeah. That."

I nod as I fiddle with the rubber disk. "It's nothing I haven't heard from every coach I've trained with, your uncle included."

"Then don't you think it's something worth taking to heart?"

And as much as I hate to admit it, he has a point.

"I'm working on it."

He shifts on the bed, moving to sit beside me again, our shoulders touching against the headboard. "We've noticed. Ever since getting back after the whole…" He trails off, clearly not wanting to bring up the suspension again. "The team, Coach, everyone has noticed your attitude shift."

"Yeah, because no agent is gonna pick up an athlete with a short temper *and* a history of substance abuse."

"I'd hardly call a false positive drug test *substance abuse*."

"It still made a black mark on my reputation. One a lot harder to change than being a bit temperamental. So I figured, why risk it, you know?"

My attention drifts back to him in time to catch his nod.

"And to think, we've uncovered all this deep shit because of a fucking puck," he muses, lifting it from my palm.

I motion at it in his hand. "Guess it's more unlucky than lucky after all."

"Just be happy I don't make fun of you for cuddling with it every night the way you do my socks. Especially in front of the guys. That'd really make you a black sheep."

He's got a point there.

"Ah, see, but then they'd wonder how you got that information. Which would only lead to them inquiring why you're in my bedroom at all, let alone in my bed."

A small smirk slides on his lips, and the temptation to kiss it right off is high. But I don't because the hook-up is over, and the rules are back in place.

"We definitely can't have that, can we?"

All of a sudden, he freezes and drops the puck back in my palm. "Wait, this isn't like the stick incident, right? I can touch it and the team won't be blowing chunks before the game tomorrow?"

A laugh burst from my chest. "You think I would have let you go on fucking with it this long if that were the case?"

"I don't know what kind of witchy voodoo you could be trying to work on me."

"Must already be working if I'm getting you in bed with me."

He lets out a laugh. "Touché, de Haas. Tou-fucking-ché."

SIXTEEN

Oakley

onight's game against Cornwall ends in another win, and at this rate, I know whatever is happening between myself and a certain teammate has to be part of the equation. We've been playing like stars on the rink these past few weeks, working together seamlessly like never before. Which is fantastic for team morale, on the one hand.

And it also means the sex keeps happening.

The hot, dirty, and downright addictive sex that often leaves us panting harder than any run out on the ice does. But if hopping into bed together is the thing keeping us on this winning streak we're riding, I'm all for it.

We've got another game against Cornwall tomorrow, and if we can take this win back to Leighton, we're on track to get a solid seeding for tournament play. Something we both desperately want if we're planning to get to the Frozen Four in Indianapolis this year.

The door to our hotel room barely has time to swing shut before Quinton's dropping his duffle to the ground and is on me like white on fucking rice.

"You fucking killed it tonight," he says, grabbing the arm of my suit jacket and hauling me to him until we're chest to chest. "I think we're gonna be celebrating more than anything tonight."

"Oh, really?" I counter, setting my duffle on the desk.

He gives me a *you're kidding me* look, brows arched so high, they might as well be in his hairline. "You don't think your third hat trick of the season is something to celebrate?"

"It definitely is." My blood heats as he helps me out of my jacket and tosses it to the bed. "But it's awfully forward to think I'd want to celebrate with you."

A smirk sits on his lips as he works to open my shirt buttons. "Wouldn't be me if I wasn't a little too sure of myself, right, Reed?"

He's got me there.

Hell, he's been unruffled by this entire thing between us, which is more than I can say for most baby bi's I've known through the years. The couple I've been with in the past—and the reason I made it a rule not to get with them anymore—were always hesitant in making moves or acting on instinct, the whole "is this too gay for me" thought usually causing them to falter. And not that I can blame them, but it usually takes away from the whole hook-up.

It's never happened with Quinton. Not once.

He's taken everything I've thrown at him in stride, unfazed at each turn, and usually ends up asking for more when it's all over. Which only adds to his ridiculous amount of sex appeal.

"You might have a point."

He tosses my shirt to the bed with my jacket before starting on his own clothes. "I know I do. Just like it's something you like about me."

Nail on the head.

"I wouldn't go that far with it," I say, trying to play off his comment.

Disbelief crosses his features. "The tent pitched in your pants begs to differ."

And would you look at that, he's right. The traitorous appendage between my legs made me a liar.

"I'm gay and you're an attractive man currently stripping in front of me. Of course I'm going to get hard."

"The only reason?" he counters, now shirtless and working the belt free from the loops. "Pure, carnal instinct? Nothing else?"

My cock throbs behind the zipper of my slacks, and not just because Quinton is now down to only his underwear. Apparently, his taunting is yet another thing capable of turning me on.

"Nope. Nothing el—"

"Just shut up, Oakley."

Without any preamble, he hauls me in from the back of my neck until our lips collide. His tongue teases along the seam, coaxing me to open. The second I do, it's an all-out war.

He fucks his talented tongue against mine, and my dick grows impossibly harder in my pants. Aching to be released from its confines and have its own turn with Quinton's mouth.

"Fuck," I mutter, anchoring my fist in his hair as I explore his throat. "What the hell are you doing to me?"

"I don't know, but believe me, the feeling's mutual." His hands coast down my back, and he arches his neck into where my lips are brushing against his skin. "Is it weird to say I've missed you?"

I grin before moving to capture his bottom lip between my teeth. "You've been with me almost all day."

Though I have to admit, I understand completely. The time we've been spending together has become this weird security blanket, and it's becoming a bit of a problem.

I guess it's more than just the sex that's addictive. He is too.

"I've missed *you*." His arm snakes between us, palming my cock through my pants. With a naughty smirk resting on his lips, he lifts his gaze to meet mine. "I'm planning to fucking worship this tonight."

I hum, my hips seeking more friction from his hand. "Using me for sex, de Haas?"

He chuckles, a dimple popping in his cheek, and I nip at it. "Could be using you for a lot worse things."

Another scorching kiss is pressed on my lips, tongue once again diving in for more, kneading and twisting with mine while he works to open my pants.

I break away to catch my breath, helping him shove the fabric and my underwear to my feet. "You're in quite the rush."

"Mmm," he hums, wrapping his hand around my shaft. "Worshiping properly takes time. I'm not looking to waste any."

I almost drag him to one of the beds with that comment, ready to get this little celebration kicked off in the best way. His mouth wrapped around my dick.

But a new side of Quinton came out to play tonight, becoming more apparent when he shoves me back onto the mattress, strips out of his briefs, and climbs up to straddle my waist. His ass bumps and grinds down on my aching length as he dives in for another kiss and pillages my mouth some more, the combination of sensations driving me crazy.

God, I wasn't wrong when I said his mouth would be my undoing. But

I didn't consider the way the rest of him does too. His taste and scent, the sinful dimples I just can't get enough of. The way his fingers coast over my skin, light as a feather, before gripping on to me for dear life.

Everything he does unravels me a little more.

He reaches beneath him, wrapping his palm around me and gives an expert stroke. My eyes roll back in my head, lost in the blissful nirvana of his touch. It's not long before I begin rocking up into his hand—seeking more friction as my desire builds—and the movement causes his cock to bob in front of him. Hard, glistening with precum, and ready to get in on the action.

It's then I realize, as much as I want to feel his exceptionally enthusiastic mouth wrapped around my dick, I want my turn at his too. After all, going down on him seems to be a common thing with scoring hat tricks, and I'm looking to test this theory again for tomorrow's game.

"Lemme taste you."

He laughs. "And what if I wanted to go first?"

I can't believe I'm about to suggest this, but... "Then turn around."

His brows furrow, hand faltering on my cock. "What?"

"Just do it, or I'll make you," I tell him, already grabbing at his hips to do it myself. Thankfully, he helps me out, flipping us into the perfect—

"Sixty-nine?" Quinton says, eyeing me from over his shoulder. "Now who's in a rush?"

I hike a brow up. "It's better than arguing about who has to wait their turn sucking dick."

A disgruntled expression crosses his face, his nose wrinkling up a little when he figures I'm right. Or he just doesn't want to argue with me.

Either way, it's a win-win for me.

"Good. Now give me my reward."

"Your reward?" he asks with a laugh.

I flick the tip of my tongue over his crown. "I said what I said."

A low rumble comes from deep within his chest, and it might be the sexiest sound I've heard from him yet.

"Keep licking it like that and your turn is gonna be over way before you want it to be."

I smirk before I take a long, languid suck on his dick and give a measured thrust up so my cock brushes his lips. "Less talking, de Haas. More sucking."

Despite my demand, Quinton takes a slower approach than I do, licking and teasing along my shaft until I'm practically panting for more around him. I even attempt to thrust up into his mouth when he starts sucking on the head, forcing him to take more, but his hand quickly holds my hip in place.

It's pure, agonizing torture, but he keeps at it, refusing me the one thing I'm desperate for.

And then it happens. He hollows out his cheeks and takes me into the back of his throat on the first go.

I moan around his length and take him deeper too, my hands grasping either side of his ass and pulling him down toward me. When the tip of his dick inches its way down my throat, I swallow, giving him the same care and attention he's showing me—gagging around his shaft until I can't fucking breathe.

"Fuck, baby," he growls, licking up and down the length of my shaft more. "I love the sound of you choking on my cock."

My eyes roll to the back of my head, his words going straight to my dick that twitches against his lips. He wraps them around my length again, plunging deep until I hit the back of his throat. The soft, smooth flesh constricts around my crown, and stars form behind my eyelids.

We keep going at each other, licking and sucking like our fucking lives depend on it. And they very well might, at this point. If I don't come soon, I might actually end up six feet under.

I adjust my grip on his ass, trying to coax him into a steady thrusting rhythm when my middle finger accidentally gets closer to his crease than I intended. The touch causes him to moan, loud and needy, like a fucking porn star, and the vibrations around my cock go straight to my balls.

Releasing him, I pop a finger into my mouth to wet it before bringing it back to his crease. Another moan comes from him as I tease the digit over the tight little bud.

"Have you ever been introduced to your prostate?" I ask, swirling the pad of my finger against his hole. I've played with his ass a couple times prior to this, but never broached the topic of penetration before now.

He nods, popping off my dick and taking over with his hand. "A few times."

My brows arch in surprise. "Really?"

"I mean, it wasn't something I was seeking out. But this one girl would get really into giving head, and her fingers started straying, and—"

"Okay, yeah. I got it," I mutter, cutting it off before he spills details I don't need to hear while we're naked and going at each other's dicks like they're popsicles.

Or ever, really.

He bites his lip, and the sight does something to me. Something wicked and animalistic. Until he opens his mouth and words come out.

"Are you jealous right now?"

"Just shut up and go grab the lube."

Quinton listens, making quick work of grabbing the bottle from where I keep it in my bag, and tossing it at me. Then he's climbing back over me in the same position like he'd never even left.

"It's okay if you're jealous, you know," he continues, and if he wasn't already leaning down and licking at my cock again, I would push him off me for the hell of it.

I roll my eyes in response as I apply a generous amount of lube to my first two fingers. Mostly because, yes, I'm a little jealous of some random girl he probably doesn't even remember the name of. Which is the last thing he needs to know, considering this is no-strings and only to benefit the team.

My fingers are at his crease again, swiping the cool liquid up and down over his ass. And just like before, he's already rocking up into my touch, seeking more pressure against his hole.

"Just tell me to stop if it gets to be too much," I say in warning before pushing into the tight heat of his body.

I take my time working him open, giving shallow pumps of my hand while swirling my tongue around the head of his cock. Lavishing it with attention while priming him for the orgasm of his life.

"Fuck," he bites out, his teeth sinking into the fleshy part of my thigh the moment my finger swipes against his prostate the first time. "Oh, my fucking Jesus God."

The sharp pain from his bite makes my cock twitch in response, and he's quick to dive back in, taking my entire length in a single pull.

Fuck, he's good at that. To the point where his ass clenching around my finger and the heat of his mouth might send me over the edge far sooner than I'd like.

My hips take on a life of their own, pumping up into his mouth as I pay extra attention to the tip of his dick, lapping at the precum continuing to leak from it. More and more of it escapes with every brush my finger makes against the little pleasure button inside him, and I'm greedy for it.

Desperate, even.

Another moan comes from him, and I can tell he's close. I am too, my balls drawing up from the way his throat contracts around my length, pulling me impossibly deeper.

He's getting sloppy now, the excess spit dripping down from my shaft onto my balls adding another layer of torture to this heavenly experience. Priming me to be launched into another dimension.

Soon enough, Quinton's thrusting down my throat and then back up into my hand at a rapid pace. Taking me from both sides as I inch him closer and closer to ecstasy. Using me the way I'm using him without a care in the world.

His cock pulses against my tongue, the telltale sign of release, and I fuck him harder. Faster. Until I've got nothing left to give.

I'm the first to go at the gentle scrape of his teeth along the bottom edge of my cock. Cum spurts free, and he swallows it like a champ, all the while rocking between my mouth and hand. Taking what he needs to find his own climax.

Another groan—this one from deep within my chest—breaks free, and it's enough to send him into his own downward spiral. His ass clamps down on my finger, squeezing it tighter than a vise as he fucks my face like it's the last thing he'll ever do. Going deeper and deeper until my chin brushes along his pelvis.

He's shoved off the cliff into freefall the moment I peg his prostate, the salty tang of his cum hitting my tongue until it fills my mouth.

"OhfuckingChrist," he utters, all breathless and airy, as I swallow down his release. I keep rubbing against that button inside him, coaxing him through the orgasm until he's milked completely dry.

After he's finished, I lick him clean, my tongue swirling around his softening cock before popping off. But I'm not done with him yet.

When he goes to lift off me, I grab his wrist and drag him until he's facing the same direction I am. His body now layered to my side, I spear my tongue between his lips, tasting my own cum along with his.

The mixture of our essence is intoxicating. Fucking euphoric.

"Holy fucking shit," he mutters into my mouth. "That was..."

He doesn't even have to finish the thought for me to know what he's trying to say.

"I know," I whisper back, doing my best to catch my breath as we break the kiss.

Shifting, he curls into my side, his forehead pressing against the side of my throat as we take our time coming down from the orgasm high that launched us straight into the stratosphere.

"I think I'm addicted to the taste of your cum," he says on a heavy exhale.

I laugh. "Not something I've ever been told before."

"Hmm. Well, all those other guys are either stupid or tasteless. Literally."

Another chuckle leaves me, and I wrap my arm around his shoulder, holding him against me. "You're the most ridiculous person I've ever met."

He yawns then, nestling his entire body against mine as our heart rates return to normal.

My arm slides beneath his pillow, and I'm surprised to find nothing beneath it. No lucky puck, and I realize it's because we went at each other the second we entered the room. He never had a chance to put it there.

I try to slip out from under him, but the arm he draped over my stomach tightens in protest.

"Where are you going?"

"Your puck," is all I say.

Bleary eyes meet mine, a softness around the edges, almost childlike, and he releases his hold on me. "My duffle. Inside pocket, on the right."

I shift out from under him and find his duffle, redressing in my underwear along the way. The puck's exactly where he said it'd be, and I grab it before bringing it back to where he's sprawled across the mattress.

Doing my best not to startle him, I shift the pillow until I'm able to slide the puck into place, exactly where it belongs.

"Thanks," he says, his voice all cracked and graveled from exhaustion, and I must admit, even that's sexy.

"No problem," I murmur back, the little knot in my throat keeping me from speaking much louder.

"Are you coming back?"

I know I shouldn't. Just like I'm positive *he* knows I shouldn't either. Post-sex cuddling isn't something we've ever done before. Basking in the glow beside each other, sure. But this is uncharted territory we're about to cross into.

Yet with every inch of my brain telling me this is a bad idea, I still crawl back into the space beside him.

He nuzzles back into the crook of my shoulder, our bodies plastered to each other from shoulder to our knees. The heat from his forehead radiates against my throat, causing my pulse to race beneath the surface.

Not to mention what this little encounter does to the slab of muscle struggling to beat evenly within my chest cavity.

He falls asleep like that, naked as the day he was born, with an arm draped over my chest. I let him stay there for a while, allowing him to fall into a deeper slumber while I study the patterns in his breathing.

It's my every intention to move to my own bed once I know he won't wake again.

But my intentions are damned to hell when the warmth of his body pressed to mine sends me off to sleep too.

SEVENTEEN

Quinton

Break started last week, but the hockey schedule kept us on campus until a couple days before Christmas, per usual. Not that I mind, since going home for the holidays isn't something I'm ever excited for.

Christmas at the de Haas house is more like another one of Dad's board meetings. Plenty of business executives present, and there's usually more talk about work than any fun holiday or vacation plans. Honestly, I don't remember the last time we had a Christmas with just the three of us, or if it ever happened at all.

Needless to say, it's not my favorite holiday. But I did get a smidge into the Christmas cheer when it comes to Oakley. Only because it was an opportunity I just couldn't pass up. Or more, a gift I couldn't not buy for him.

The only issue now is I've been waiting for him to get over to my apartment to give the damn thing to him. He said he'd be over soon, but that was almost an hour—

A knock on the door has me bolting from where I was sitting on the couch, my anticipation almost immediately turning into anxiety. Which is new for me.

Ever since I woke up with my arm slung over Oakley's stomach in our hotel room the morning of our second Cornwall game, I've had a lot of anxiety when it comes to him, and that was over a week ago.

Opening the door reveals Oakley on the other side, dressed in a knit beanie and winter coat with bits of snow on the shoulders.

"Hey," I say, opening the door further for him to come inside. "I didn't realize it was snowing."

"Yeah, a storm's blowing in and the roads are already a mess." He removes his jacket and hat, pieces of his hair sticking up haphazardly, and the urge to run my fingers through it ignites inside me. "Gonna make for a fun drive over to my parents today. Even if it is just forty minutes."

The thought is immediately on my tongue; he should just stay here with me. Go tonight or tomorrow morning once the storm passes and the plows go through. Hayes is already gone for the holidays, so we'd have the place to ourselves. Completely uninterrupted.

Except...it's against the rules.

But maybe with it being the holidays, he might make an exception. At least, that's what I tell myself as I open my mouth to mention it.

But then he plops down onto the couch and gives me a curious look, cutting the words off before they even form on my tongue.

"What's up? You said you needed me to come over."

"Yeah," I say, crossing the distance to where he is. I drop down beside him and grab his gift off the coffee table, handing it over to him. His brows furrow, and he takes it carefully. Like there might be a live grenade wrapped inside or something.

"What's this?" he asks, turning the box wrapped in festive Christmas paper over in his hands. Done as a favor by Hayes because I can't wrap for shit, and weirdly enough, he happens to be a damn professional at it.

I blink at him and cock my head. "Most people would call it a present, Oakley."

"I understand it's a present. But what I don't understand is why you're giving one to me."

Sometimes I think he's the most obtuse person I know. This is one of those moments.

"The decorations and ridiculous amount of terrible music playing since freaking Halloween didn't give it away?"

"The snark's not appreciated, de Haas," he snaps right back, flipping it in his hand once more and setting it across his thighs.

"Neither is your ungratefulness, but you don't see me—"

He aims a glare my way, one capable of scaring Lucifer shitless, and I shut right up.

"Answer the question, Quinton," he says in a low tone. "Because I didn't get you anything, since normally it's reserved for...dating and shit. Or friends, which we're barely classified as."

His analysis of the situation makes me feel paper-thin. Completely transparent, and even a bit vulnerable, splayed out before him.

"I know that. But it's not a big deal, okay? I just thought of you when I saw—"

A grin takes over his face, erasing all seriousness from moments before. "You thought of me, huh?"

Oh, Jesus. "Yeah, I—"

"Well, in that case…" He trails off, holding the box to his ear and shaking it. "Is it a sex toy? Glow-in-the-dark lube? A silicone cast dildo kit?"

My brows furrow. "A *what?*"

"You know, the thing where you make a mold of your dick and turn it into a dildo."

That sounds like the kind of gag gift I'd get someone—especially Oakley—so I can't even be offended by his assumption.

"No, it's not sex shit. It's…" I sigh, shaking my head. "Would you just fucking open it already?"

He rolls his eyes and peels the paper off the box. "Way to spoil the fun of *my* gift."

"I'm about tempted to take it back altogether," I mumble under my breath in indignation, crossing my arms across my chest and digging myself further into the couch cushions. Leave it to him to make a nice gesture into something I regret doing. "Jackass."

He's down to the box now, ripping off the lid and clearing the little tissue paper crap out of the way.

"Oh, don't be like that. I—" he cuts off, clearing his throat and looking up at me. Two big, brown eyes peer straight into my soul when he does, and it gives me an uncomfortable ache in my chest. One I don't fucking like, making me think maybe this was a really bad idea.

No. Actually, it definitely was a bad idea.

Shit.

"Look, if it's stupid or whatever, just return them. There's a receipt in there. I was just trying to be funny."

He glances back down at the box and whispers, "You got me socks."

The way he says it, with reverence almost, makes it sound like I got him something far more…meaningful than three pairs of fucking socks.

Of course, these aren't just any socks. They're the funny, crazy kind he wears under his official uniform.

Lucky socks, per his superstition.

I'd seen them a couple weeks back online when I was scrolling through one of my socials. Apparently, my phone did that creepy thing it does, listening in on one too many of my conversations with Oakley about his damn socks. So lo and behold, I had ads for socks plastered across my feed. When I found these on the site, they were too perfect to pass them up.

One pair is all black with white writing on it reading, "00 FUCKS GIVEN", with the zeros looking like the timed out clock of a scoreboard. The second pair are white with a ton of eggplants on them and says, "I give the best blow jobs" down the sides.

The last pair is covered in suns and rainbows. Near the top in bold letters, it reads, "It's a beautiful day" and then "Don't fuck it up" on the bottom of the foot.

They're my favorite.

"You…got me socks," he says again, and this time, it hits me square in the chest.

"Yeah." My shoulder lifts in a shrug when he looks at me again. "It's not a big deal. Like I said, I just thought of you when I saw them."

He doesn't say anything, instead tearing my favorites out of the package and holding them up in front of him.

"If you don't like 'em—"

"They're perfect," he cuts me off, his voice ragged like he's just run a marathon.

A sense of awkwardness falls over us, and I'm not sure why. Maybe because I wasn't expecting a couple goofy sets of socks to get him all in his feels, or maybe because he feels guilty for not getting me anything.

Whatever it is, it sticks to the air like cling-wrap, and it's stifling.

Enough to remind me why I rarely do things like this for people.

He lifts the other two pairs up, turning them over in his hands and reading them again before a small smile forms on his lips. "These all seem like they're meant for you."

He's got a point there. Because I laughed my ass off when I picked every pair out.

"Maybe, but I don't wear lucky socks. It's your thing."

"My lucky socks don't have profanity on them," he counters. "Just like…ducks and donuts and shit."

I give him my winningest grin. "Perfect time for an upgrade."

An eye roll is aimed at me. "We'll have to see how well they work before we can call them an upgrade." He pauses, then adds, "But…thank you."

The temptation to blast this moment to smithereens—ruining any emotion still lingering between us—hits me like a ton of bricks. But for once, I choose not to give into the self-destructive part of my nature and just smile.

"You're welcome, Oak."

He holds up the eggplant pair for me to read. "And at least you can finally admit I give the best blow jobs."

I wrinkle my nose up at the sentiment. "Absolutely not. They were just funny, so I got them."

"Uh-huh," he says, not at all believing me, while setting the box back on the coffee table.

His eyes heat as he crawls toward me, forcing me to lean until my back hits the leather seat cushions of the couch. Dipping his head toward my neck, he peppers kiss after kiss to my throat before rocking his hips into mine.

I'm hard instantly.

His lips trail up to my ear, and he nips at the lobe. "Maybe I need to take some time and remind you before our next game."

God, I want that. I want to say fuck the rules and do it right now, actually. But it's not what we agreed to. Sure, I could bring up altering the rules, like I was ready to before. After all, he's become far more physically affectionate with me as of late.

But something inside me…can't be the one to broach the topic. Not anymore.

Maybe because I'm wanting more than the steamy hook-ups and stolen moments neither of us want to end.

I want more moments like today. Seeing a different side of him—one more open and vulnerable with his emotions—only creates a hunger for more. I'm yearning for more pieces and layers of him I never knew existed, still waiting for me to discover, unwrap, and learn.

And it's terrifying, wanting that.

But what scares me more is how much I want him to see those parts of me too.

Christmas passes quickly in typical de Haas fashion.

An obscene amount of cash stuffed in a generic Christmas card, not even signed by either of my parents, was left on the table for me Christmas morning. They were both already gone or busy by the time I made it down there; Dad at work, Mom overseeing our staff in preparing for when the caterers arrived. Then the opulently decorated house was filled with loads of people, all gathered in our massive living room, none of which were family. And as promised, most of Christmas dinner was spent talking business. Mostly about this new deal made with some Key whatever Holdings company out of New York.

I don't think I said more than five words the entire time, unless it was to Marta, who used to be my au pair, but my parents kept her on the staff as a cleaning lady after I was old enough to take care of myself.

When I go up to my room to escape, I find a small package and card waiting on my bed. Inside is a note from Marta, along with a keychain of a little hockey player she had personalized with Leighton's school colors, my last name, and the number 19 on the back.

I hastily added it to my BMW keys, trying to keep the knot in my throat from growing any larger as I did, and after thanking her, I spent most of my time in my room to avoid any conversation with my father.

Who, at Christmas dinner, announced I'd be working under him next year. Something I don't remember agreeing to, but then again, it's never stopped him before.

When I brought this up with him after everyone had left, it turned into what might be our biggest blowout yet. Resulting in him threatening to cut me off. And if there's anything I know about my father, it's that no threat coming from him is idle.

This was my final warning.

Locking myself away in my ivory tower seemed like the only logical thing to do afterward, if only to escape reality down the mindless rabbit hole of TikTok.

It's close to midnight and I'm in my third hour of doing just that when a text notification pops up at the top of my screen.

Oakley: Merry Christmas.

I haven't heard from him since he left my apartment a couple days ago, and I've been doing my best not to think about what it might mean. Especially since he left us both hard up and aching when he pulled his body off mine and drove home to his parents.

I didn't ask him to stay, and from the way seeing his name on my phone screen makes me grin like an idiot, it's probably a good thing.

I'm falling into this a little deeper than I should allow myself to.

Me: Same to you.

His response is almost immediate.

Oakley: How's it going with your parents?

Me: Exactly as expected.

Oakley: That bad?

Me: Well, apparently, I start working with Dad in June, though I have no recollection of making any agreement with him.

Oakley: So it is that bad?

Yep, sure fucking is. But I don't really feel like vomiting all my feelings about Dad's ultimatum to him via text, so I turn the conversation on him.

Me: It's fine. How's it been with yours?

Oakley: The usual. A lot of extended family came over, since we usually host Christmas. Logan being an absolute terror any time hockey was mentioned. Which is often when Dad and Coach are in the same room.

I frown, reading the name I don't recognize over again. But no matter how hard I think on it, I can't seem to place it.

Me: Logan?

Oakley: My younger brother.

Wait, he has a brother?

He's never once mentioned him in passing. Talking about families isn't something we've done until very recently, but I feel like it's a topic that would've come up by now.

Me: Why did I think you were an only child too?

Oakley: Because I might as well be. When your family has generations of hockey players, but you have no interest in the sport despite years of being coaxed into giving it a shot, you tend to disassociate yourself from said family.

I wince, knowing exactly how it feels. Trade hockey for the de Haas family business, and it's the exact same thing I'm going through at home.

But at least Logan's family gives him a choice in how he wants his life to go.

Me: Ouch. I feel for him. Black sheep unite.

Oakley: LOL you would probably get along. He's as moody as you are. Too bad he would also hate you on principle for being a hockey player.

Me: Moody? I think you have me confused with someone else. I've been a ray of fucking sunshine lately.

It's true. I've been a lot less cranky lately, and in part, it's thanks to him. But information like that is best kept to myself.

Oakley: Yeah, you're right. I'm probably thinking of the other teammate I've been messing around with who loves to make my life hell.

Me: Don't lie, you enjoy it.

I'm expecting some witty retort or straight-up denial. This is Oakley we're talking about; he'd probably deny enjoying spending time with me until his dying day.

But I get an unexpected response instead.

Oakley: It's been weird not seeing you.

My heart hammers against my rib cage a little harder as I reread the text a couple times, hating how much it's making me smile.

I know exactly what he means, though, because I've been feeling it too.

Me: Missing me already, Reed? At this rate, I'm not sure you'll be able to survive ten days without me.

Oakley: It doesn't have to be ten days.

My blood heats and my stomach rolls as anticipation courses through me. Because he's not saying what I think he's saying. There's no fucking way.

But I type out my response, just to be sure.

Me: What do you mean?

I wait for what feels like an eternity while the three little dots start and stop on the bottom of the screen, my mind racing all the while.

Finally, a reply pops up.

Oakley: I was thinking we should meet up. Gives you an excuse to get out of the house for a while at the very least.

A smirk spreads across my face.

I was planning on going back to my apartment tomorrow as it is, not wanting to spend any more time here than necessary and risk the chance of Dad bringing up quitting hockey again.

But I'm not about to tell Oakley that.

Me: You do miss me.

Oakley: Not at all.

Me: Liar.

Oakley: Think what you want. I was only taking pity on someone in need. You know, in the spirit of the holidays.

Well, that's a bunch of bullshit if I've ever heard it.

Me: Nice try. Christmas is over.

Oakley: Not for another 23 minutes.

A glance at the corner of my phone screen reveals he's right. It's still Christmas Day, but only by technicality.

Me: Semantics.

The little dots pop up in the corner before disappearing. Then they keep doing it, back and forth, for a couple minutes, and finally stopping altogether.

Two minutes pass, then five, and still no response.

A slight twinge of disappointment hits me square in the chest as I set my phone down on the bed beside me, realizing I might've played this game with him a little too well.

But then my phone dings with another text notification.

Oakley: So is that a no?

An invisible coil constricts around my heart and lungs, and I do my best to sound casual as I type out my response.

Me: What did you have in mind?

EIGHTEEN

Oakley

January

Five past noon on New Year's Day, two hands cover my eyes, blocking my view of Millennium Park and scaring the absolute fucking shit outta me. But the second I hear the smooth cadence of Quinton's laugh, the fear turns quickly into…irritation.

"Why are you like this?" I snap, yanking at his wrists so I can see again.

When I turn around to face him, I become even more irritated to find he looks fucking edible in a beanie, jeans, and long black jacket. A sexy-as-hell look he can pull off any day of the week, but even more so today with his glasses on.

He smirks in his signature way, a dimple popping in one cheek. "You're gonna have to be a little more specific. Why am I so ruggedly handsome? Why am I always late? Why—"

"Why do you get off on being such a gigantic pain in my ass?" I finish, pointing a glare at him.

"You'd know a lot about what gets me off, wouldn't you?"

Oh, I do. But it's not something I need to be thinking about in public. Around children, no less.

"Unbelievable," I mutter under my breath.

He laughs, a sound that used to grate on my nerves, but now I want to hear it more. "You make it so easy sometimes."

Both dimples make their appearance now. They seem to do more and more around me lately, and every time I see them, it does this weird thing to my chest. A sort of…fluttering.

"I'm already regretting asking you to hang out."

"Wouldn't be you if you didn't," he points out, crossing his arms. "Truth be told, I was more surprised you did in the first place."

"Like I said, it was purely out of charity. I didn't want you to suffer any more than you already were."

A grin the Cheshire Cat would be envious of spreads over his face. "Except I've been back at my apartment on campus since the day after Christmas."

"What?"

"I only told you I was busy to see how long you could hold out without begging me to move things around. Props to you, by the way. I thought for sure you'd cave before now."

I bite the inside of my cheek to keep the expletives from spilling free around all these impressionable ears. Mostly because he's right. I almost caved plenty of times, hoping to find a way to see him before today.

But there's no fucking way I'm letting it slip now.

Why does he have to ruin everything?

"Not at all. Like I said, I just wanted to get you out of the house. But now that I know you're perfectly fine and also a liar, I'm leaving."

I move to walk away, but he grabs my arm and pulls me back. Right into his chest, with our mouths only inches apart.

"You're not going anywhere anytime soon," he murmurs. The heat of his breath sends shivers down my spine and goosebumps breaking out across my skin. "Because I know you missed me."

"Only in your dreams."

Another sinful, dimpled smile curves his lips. "There's plenty of things we do in my dreams, but that's not one of them."

The filthy, seductive tone of his voice sets my blood to a boil. Not in anger, but with desire. And paired with the way he's holding me against him, the proximity of his lips to mine, makes it all the harder to resist him.

"There are kids around," I hiss, already trying to tamp down my cock thickening against his thigh. Something he's all too aware of from the way he discreetly presses against it.

"And here I thought you were a master of self-control." Another shift of his thigh sends a zap of lust straight to my balls. "Better get a grip on that libido, Reed."

The sexual tension zapping between us is palpable, though he seems unaffected. But that won't do for me. I want—no, I *need*—him just as hot and bothered as I am right now. So I do what makes sense when it comes to a showdown with Quinton de Haas.

I fight fire with fire.

"I hope you know how much you're going to regret this the next time I get you in bed."

His nostrils flare, the heat in his gaze magnified in intensity as he stares at me through his lenses. Enough to make me think I've won this little battle of wills he's started.

But then he takes it a step further, letting his lips brush against mine as he speaks. "Oh, believe me. I'm counting on it."

My teeth sink into my lower lip to keep from biting into his, and I step away. "You win this round, de Haas."

A shit-eating grin spreads across his face, almost breaking it in two.

"A fantastic way to start the day." He claps his hands together, child-like giddiness and excitement radiating off him. "Now what do you have planned for us?"

A quick five-minute walk from where I met Quinton brings us to Maggie Daley Park, home of the Ice Skating Ribbon. One of my favorite Reed family holiday pastimes as a kid was to come skating either here or at the one directly below the Bean. We'd come almost every year if Dad wasn't gone on a stint of away games. Well, until Logan threw a fit about hating it and we stopped some time in my late middle school years.

I haven't been back since, but I figured there's no time like the present.

"I'm pretty sure this is the first time I've ever put skates on for something other than hockey," Quinton says as he laces up the pair of rentals we got from the stand beside the rink.

My head snaps up from where I was tying my own skates to look at him. "You're telling me you've never gone ice skating before? Just for the hell of it?"

Still working on his laces, Quinton shakes his head. "Nope. Never had anyone take me. First time I ever put skates on was the day my dad took me to my first youth league practice when I was eight. And the only reason he even took me was because he wanted me to shut the hell up about it."

"Seriously?"

"Seriously," he replies before rising to his full height. "I'm sure he thought I'd suck at it immediately and quit within the first couple weeks. But much to his displeasure, I picked it up really quick…and it's been the bane of his existence ever since."

Understanding floods me as we make our way over to the rink and step out onto the smooth surface. The moment we do, like nothing else exists. Sure, there are people milling about—though not as many as I'd expect during winter break—but I don't even notice them.

It's just us, and I wouldn't have it any other way.

Side by side, we take a slow lap around the amoeba-shaped rink, gliding over the ice like the seasoned pros we've worked hard to become. Silence lingers between us, but it feels comfortable, not stifling or awkward the way it would have a couple months ago.

Hell, a couple months ago, I would have laughed at the idea of us spending any time together. Yet here we are, two sworn enemies, ice skating together on New Year's Day like some kind of…couple.

The realization makes my stomach churn in a weird, unexpected way.

Shoving the feeling down, I recall something he said earlier, letting my mind take hold of that thought instead. "When you say you picked it up quick, how quick are we talking? Like a couple months?"

"I mean…" He skates out ahead of me and spins around, skating backward in front of me. "I was comfortable enough to skate with a stick in my hand by the end of the second day. But obviously I wasn't doing a whole lot with it at that point. Just…skating."

I roll my eyes. "Show off."

I knew I was right when I told him he had natural talent. It even took me a few months to become a master at skating *without* a stick. Meanwhile Quinton just said he went and did both together in the first week of ever being on the ice.

Granted, he started playing a few years after me when he probably had a lot more stability and balance, but still.

He bites back a smile, teeth sinking into his lower lip. Like he knows exactly what I'm thinking.

"I think you like it when I'm a show-off."

My brow kicks up. "Oh, really?"

"Yeah. I think it turns you on, being around someone just as good as you. Someone who might actually be…better."

The arrogance of this man astounds me. But he's right about one thing. The quiet air of confidence surrounding him on the ice when he's zoned in is beyond sexy. He knows he's good—yeah, maybe even better than me—but it's proven by the way he performs. It's when he starts showboating that he pisses me off.

"You're a lot of things, de Haas. But better than me isn't one of them."

"Care to put your money where your mouth is?"

This time, I'm the one to smirk. "I think I've more than done that already. The socks you got me prove it."

Heat flares in his eyes. "We're talking about things happening on the ice, Reed. Not between the sheets."

I'm not one to back down from a challenge, and certainly not one coming from Quinton. He's still my rival, even if we've become this weird friends-adjacent thing since we started following through on his superstition theory.

"What were you thinking?"

"A race. First one to complete a lap around the rink wins."

I glance around, noting there's far too many people and not nearly enough room for us to get as competitive as we are. We could easily turn a corner and plow a little kid over, and that's the last thing I want to start the new year with.

"I don't think it's a good idea."

His brow raises. "You scared to lose?"

"No, I—"

"Oh, you definitely are," he says, continuing to taunt me.

"There's too many people, and I'm not looking to ruin anyone else's time by being some psychotic—"

"God, you're such a stick in the mud sometimes," he cuts in, humor dancing in those ice blue eyes. "Live a little. Smile. Laugh. The world isn't gonna end if you do, I promise."

I know it won't. That's half the problem, though. Because Quinton has this air about him, making it almost impossible to *not* smile or laugh in his presence. He's like...fucking sunshine sometimes. Or whatever other bullshit people wax poetic about. Which is hilarious considering he looks like every father's worst nightmare with the ink and the leather and the *I don't give a fuck* attitude he usually has plastered around him like a shield.

But he's shown me another piece of himself I doubt many others have seen. The part that, despite his persona, *does* give a fuck. About a lot of things. About people.

Maybe even about me.

And maybe that's why I agree to yet another one of his cockamamie ideas.

Letting out a long sigh, I mutter, "And what does the winner get from this little display of masculinity?"

Dimples pop some more. "Winner can decide."

"Those are some high stakes."

He licks his lips. "Then don't lose."

Too bad for Quinton, losing isn't in my nature. A fact I prove when I win our little race by a landslide, skating past our makeshift finish line a good two seconds before him. He's caught up by a group of little kids who serve as the perfect roadblock, but still, victory is victory. And when I get one over Quinton, it always tastes that much sweeter.

"Damn kids," he mutters as we skate off toward the side, getting out of the way for everyone else passing by. "I would've won if it weren't for them getting in the way."

"Whatever helps you sleep tonight knowing I'm better than you, both on the ice and between the sheets."

He leans back against the railing in front of me, a sly little smirk sits on his lips. "I'm still winning the day, though. You know that, right?"

"Care to elaborate?"

"You're having fun."

I don't even bother trying to lie, instead shrugging in confirmation. "I'm having fun."

His smile is instant. "Why does it feel like you're surprised? I'm pretty much the master at having fun."

It takes everything I have to not roll my eyes. "It's more like I was expecting you to annoy me eighty percent of the day and end up wishing I never asked you to meet up."

There's a slight nod before he raises his brow. "But…"

"Like I said," I mutter. "I'm having fun. So, I guess…thanks for agreeing to hang out."

He grins more. "Eh, you're not so bad. Most of the time, at least."

God, those fucking dimples. They do something stupid to my brain. Short circuit it or something. Plus, his smile and laugh, a killer combination not many people could withstand.

Or maybe it's just…*him*.

Everything about him.

To the point where the urge to kiss him is overwhelming. Stupidly so. And even though I know there's no reason to act on the urge other than pure desire, I still want to.

I ache to.

And that's all it takes.

"Fuck it," I mutter.

My hand slides around the back of his neck, and I haul his mouth to mine in a scorching kiss. One that...fuck, it makes me want him all the more. And in all the ways I know I shouldn't.

His tongue slides past my lips, warring with mine in a way that makes my toes curl inside my skates. My body crowds against his, crushing him to the wall of the rink so our bodies align. Even through our jackets and clothes, I feel the strong, powerful lines of his muscles pressed against mine.

His arms weave their way up, wrapping around my neck, my hands moving to cup his face, tilting his chin for better access. Deeper, because nothing seems like enough.

I'm drowning in him. So much so, I don't care if it might go against the rules we've set out. Nor do I give a flying fuck about kissing him in public, where anyone can watch or judge or feel forced to shield their children's eyes.

It's not like we're fucking it out right here on the rink. It's a kiss.

One I couldn't not steal while the opportunity presented itself.

And if any of them knew Quinton de Haas the way I'm starting to, they'd understand exactly why.

I pull back before too long, not wanting things to get so heated we can't skate out of here without putting on a show for everyone more than we already have. His forehead presses against mine, the puffs of air leaving our lips intertwining in a single cloud.

"What was that for?" he asks, slightly breathless. When he pulls back, his blue eyes shimmer with a mixture of amusement and desire. "And how the hell do I get more of it?"

"It was…a thank you," I whisper, deciding that would be the best way to label it.

"For letting you win?"

A soft laugh escapes from me, because I won fair and square. "For making me live a little. Let loose. All the crap you seem to think is so important."

A small smile tilts the corners of his lips. "Well, I'm just glad we discovered you know how to."

Boy have we ever discovered. I don't think I've smiled or laughed as much as I have today, and it's only just begun. It's almost as if spending time with him outside the arena has lightened my soul somehow, allowing me to step back and breathe. Enjoy myself, if only for a moment, instead of being weighed down by the pressures I've put myself under.

So we keep skating and laughing and having fun, letting ourselves just exist in a circumstance where we're not enemies or rivals or teammates. We're not in this thing way deeper than we should be.

For one afternoon, we're just two guys doing their best to live a little.

As our time comes to an end, the sun's already set and the cool night's air fills our lungs, and I discover I'm not ready for this to be over. I'm not ready to say goodbye.

From the look in his eyes as we leave the park, neither is he.

I open my mouth, about to offer the option of grabbing dinner and prolonging the inevitable for a little while longer, but he says something first.

"You probably need to get back to your parents, but…thank you. I needed this more than I realized."

Quinton shoves his hands into his jacket pockets and rocks back on his feet, awkwardness settling between us for the first time all day. Which is a surprise, considering how easy things have been between us all day.

But then I recognize the swirling in my gut as anticipation. The same kind I had the first time we hooked up after the frat house bathroom.

The same kind you get at the end of a first date, and you know you're supposed to go in for a kiss, but you're not sure if the other person wants you to. So then, you just flounder.

And floundering is exactly what I'm doing.

Except…after earlier today, I don't know why.

"Yeah, uh, it's no problem. Like I said, I had a good time too." I clear my throat before awkwardly adding, "Drive back to campus safe."

He nods before asking, "I will. And I'll see you tomorrow?"

I'm about to say no when I realize he's right. We have a late practice tomorrow night to get back in the zone for the two games falling over break. The first of which is in two days.

The anticipation from earlier quickly takes a turn straight toward desire, knowing this time tomorrow, we'll be in his bed doing ridiculously filthy things to each other's bodies. And I can't fucking wait.

"Yeah," I murmur, offering a small smile. "See you then."

I try not to focus too much on the slight disappointment forming in my chest as I head off in the other direction. After all, going off to dinner or a goodnight kiss is asking for more, and I already fucked up by kissing him earlier today.

Besides, *more* isn't what we agreed to. *More* will only complicate things further than we already have by simply following through with this superstition. And *more* could lead us to a place where hearts get involved; something I doubt either of us wants or is ready for.

But knowing this still isn't enough to stop the disappointment.

I'm about to cross Michigan Avenue when a hand lands on my forearm, halting me in my tracks. There's not even a second for me to register what is happening when Quinton reels me back into him, and without hesitation, drags me in for a kiss.

The second kiss of the day, but this is entirely different than the first.

Soft and gentle, lighting my heart on fire with a single press of his lips. It's a kiss I'd never think him capable of giving, and yet, it's somehow the best of all the ones we've shared so far.

And the way it makes my stomach flip and hurdle like a damn gymnast tells me I'm in a shit ton of trouble.

NINETEEN

Quinton

We won the first winter break game by a landslide, and the second one tonight is no different. I'm running on an adrenaline high, having gotten my first hat trick all season, and to top it off, Coach called me into his office to talk after the game about agents.

Specifically, ones asking about me. Something I hoped would happen eventually, but now that it actually is…I honestly can't even believe it.

By the time I'm out of Coach's office, my head's so high in the damn clouds, I don't even notice the locker room is close to being abandoned.

Well, shit.

My eyes automatically search for Oakley—they always seem to lately— but I come up empty.

Double shit.

I have no idea what his plans are tonight, let alone for the next few days until the new semester starts, but I'd like to find out. The only issue is Coach pulled me in the office to chat before I could mention meeting up over the rest of our break.

And I wanna see him. Tonight, especially. Celebrate another well-earned win. Grab a couple drinks at a bar or something. Maybe even tell him about the meeting with Coach, where he mentioned the agents asking about me.

Pulling my phone from my stall, I send him a quick text.

Me: Wanna see you. You still here?

A couple minutes pass while I finish undressing, but when I check my phone again, there's no response.

He could be driving, sure, but I doubt he was able to shower, change, and get out of here in the time I was in Coach's office. It couldn't have been more than ten minutes.

Then again, half the team is already gone—probably ready to get back to their families for the rest of the break.

I wrap my towel around my waist, ready to head toward the showers when Camden rounds the corner and starts packing his stuff in his duffle on the bench across from me. Pretty sure he's the last one in here besides me.

And while it might be risky, if there's anyone I could ask about Oakley to, it'd be him.

Hopefully.

Only one way to find out…

Clearing my throat, I look up at the goalie and do my best to act casual. "Hey, Cam?"

He glances up at me from his spot on the bench, dark blond hair flopping into his eyes. "Hey, man. What's up?"

"Did you happen to see if Reed left already?"

His brows furrow for a second, but he schools his expression quickly. "Don't think so. Last I saw, he was walking into the showers. That was maybe…five minutes ago. Why?"

"Just need to talk to him about something before we go back on break. Nothing serious."

Lies, lies, lies.

He takes a moment, measuring my words before he rises to stand, responding when he tosses the duffle strap over his shoulder. "Pretty sure he went to the last stall. If he's not there anymore, he can't be further than the parking lot."

"Okay, cool. Thanks," I say awkwardly.

"Course. Have a good one. And great game tonight, by the way."

I give him a nod. "Yeah, you too, man."

And with that, he grabs his keys and heads out the door.

I make a discreet sweep of the locker room as I walk toward the showers, noting there's more guys here than I originally thought. Maybe four or five.

And when I notice the only shower running is the one at the very end—the one Camden mentioned seeing Oak go into—I might as well be shot up with adrenaline.

I don't even have to see the guy. Just picturing him naked, surrounded by steam. Dripping wet and covered in soap, and Jesus, I need get ahold of myself before I do something stupid. Like get in there with him. Run my hands all over his sinful body.

That's what I want, though.

I want it so much, I don't even think of the repercussions of someone seeing me going into his stall, or worse, having it not be his stall at all.

It takes me all of two seconds to decide the odds are in my favor, glance around to see the coast is clear, and pull the handle on the frosted glass door.

Thank God they didn't put locks on these damn things.

Luck is on my side, because as I slip in and silently close the door behind me, I find Oakley standing under the spray of water. Even with his back facing me, I know it's him. At this point, I'd recognize that ass anywhere, complete with a little dimpled indent above each cheek.

Hanging my towel on the hook next to his, I step under the spray behind him.

"Wha—"

My palm clasps over his mouth to silence the *what the fuck* about to leave it. Loudly. And I didn't make this whole effort to not be seen, only for him to blow our cover.

"Shh," I murmur into his ear. "It's just me."

Releasing my hand from over his mouth, I let it slide down over his shoulder before stepping away. He spins around to face me, eyes wide, and a look falling somewhere between stern and pissed off crosses his face.

"Are you insane? What're you doing in here?"

Not exactly the response I was hoping for, though I don't know why I expected anything less.

"Being reckless," I surmise with a playful smirk.

He wipes the water from his face and shakes his head, a mixture of irritation and panic painting his expression. "Someone could've seen you."

"Just relax," I soothe, keeping my voice low. "I checked to make sure no one saw. Most of them are gone already as it is, and by the time I'm nice and squeaky clean, they all will be."

He gives me a wary look, one clearly stating he doesn't believe me.

"I promise, it'll be fine. Just keep your voice down and no one will be the wiser."

It takes a second, but for once, he nods. The tension in his shoulders melts away before my eyes, and he lets out a sigh.

"You scared the crap outta me," he says, his voice a gruff whisper.

I let out a soft laugh and step into his space, my hands itching to touch him. "I had no idea."

"Okay, smartass."

I grin more as he grabs the body wash, handing it over to me. He watches for a second as I lather the soap in my palms before he steps out from under the spray. Thinking he's about to dry off and leave—which makes little to no sense if he's concerned about blowing our cover—I pivot.

"Stay. Less likely for people to catch us," I say, not letting myself second-guess the reasoning. Because as much truth is behind it, I just want to be near him and in his presence. Feel the electricity humming between us whenever we're this close to each other.

I'm already as addicted to that feeling as I am to being on the ice.

"You think I'm about to pass up this show?" A slow smile creeps over his lips as his eyes rake up and down my naked body. "Not a chance, de Haas. I was just getting out of the way to get a better view."

My cock perks up at the want dripping in his voice, and I'm instantly filled with annoyance about the other guys still milling around the locker room.

Not that we'd be fooling around even if it was empty.

Oakley's been a stickler with this hooking up stuff, and since we don't have a game tomorrow, neither of us will be getting off. With each other, at least, because I know he won't touch me tonight. Even if I begged him to take me in his fist or his mouth, he wouldn't.

But from the way I feel him staring at me while I lather his body wash over my chest, it's clear I'm gonna have to partake in some solo action when I get home later. He's got me all kinds of keyed up from looking alone.

Watching like a voyeur.

And apparently he's into it, because his cock thickens as my hands move down to my crotch, cleaning my own dick. I fight the temptation to start stroking, but only just.

Waves of want and desire flow through me at breakneck speeds. It's so strong, I have to turn away from him to rinse off. Turn away so I can't see the need written on his face or the way his cock—hard and standing at attention—waits for me to drop to my knees.

My eyes sink closed as I try to rein myself in.

Damn him.

Damn him for being so fucking...hard to resist.

To the point where I don't even know why I'm bothering—

"I'm fucking obsessed with this," he mutters, cutting into my thoughts. His fingertips trace over the lines of the tattoo covering most of my back in a featherlight touch. "It's so sexy."

The grin taking over my face is instant, even though he can't see it.

It's not the first time I've caught Oakley looking at my ink by any means—he's asked me about plenty of them—but he's never voiced his opinion on them before. And call me vain, but it feels good.

Two large hands slide over my wet skin, down each side until they reach my hips, leaving trails of heat in their wake that have nothing to do with the temperature of the water.

"I thought you were staying in here to *watch?*" I point out.

"Couldn't without touching you."

His lips skate over my shoulder and up my neck, tongue lapping at the water pouring over my skin. Every flick is a wicked lash, lighting my body up, turning my blood to liquid fire coursing through my veins.

I've been dying to touch him whenever and however I want since our day spent downtown; kissing not once, but twice, when our arrangement didn't call for it. But it was an entirely different circumstance. It was just...a moment. The kind that presents itself and you just can't help but take it.

All of me wants this to be one too.

"God. You drive me fucking crazy," I groan when his teeth nip at the crook of my neck, soothing the bite with his tongue after.

"The feeling's more than mutual."

His mouth moves, brushing teasing kisses between my shoulder blades as he crowds into me more. The length of his cock presses against my ass, sliding right between my cheeks as his hand reaches around to grip me in his fist. I'm already harder than granite from his taunting alone, but with his hand on me and his dick right there against my ass, it's a wonder I haven't come already.

I turn slightly, just enough to get a look at his face. Which is a mistake, because as water pours down his cheeks in tiny rivulets and cascades over his jaw, I don't think I've ever seen anything more stunning.

I'm sure that's the reason my voice comes out like shattered glass.

"What happened to the rules?"

He licks the water dripping off his parted lips. "Fuck 'em."

It comes out gruff and gravelly, thickened with enough lust to drown us both as his lips come crashing into mine. His tongue slips into my mouth as he rocks into me from behind, rolling his hips in time with each pass his palm makes over my cock. Long, languid strokes, like we have all the time in the world, send zaps of pleasure rippling through my body at hyper speed.

It's a juxtaposition I've never experienced: the hunger and need he kisses me with paired with the leisure in his touch.

It ignites something inside me until I'm engulfed in flames and burning alive.

And I love every single second of it.

Reaching back, my fingers knot in the wet strands of his hair and I push for more. Our tongues war against each other, lashing and thrusting in time with his hips until we're both lost in the feel of each other. But it's not enough.

I need him inside me. And I need it right fucking now.

A groan escapes me when his thumb teases the sensitive underside of my cock, and he breaks away, returning to my skin as he continues to torture me with his hand around my dick and every seductive roll of his hips.

"Want you," I mutter when his teeth nip at the junction of my neck and shoulder. "Want you so fucking much."

I know he wants me too. I can feel it with the way he rocks into me, his cock slipping and sliding between my ass cheeks. Rutting against me with long, measured thrusts that have me begging for more.

More contact, more heat, more friction.

More lingering caresses and scorching kisses and harsh bites.

My entire body screams for it, and with every addictive taste or blistering touch, he unravels me further. Groping, grasping, driving me fucking wild with desire the way no one ever has before.

"How much? Because…fuck, Quinn." He sighs, his forehead pressing between my shoulder blades. "I'm hanging by a thread here."

"I've never needed something more in my life."

The thought of him fucking me? It scares me, yeah. Maybe more than anything else in the damn world. Yet, it also sends a thrill racing through me I've never felt before.

It's new and exciting, and I *want it*.

His breath comes out in hot pants against my skin as he rolls his hips again. He's not doing more than pressing against the tight rim, but I can feel the stretch already. Like all it would take is one smooth thrust and he'd be buried inside me.

Oakley's made me more than acquainted with my prostate over the few weeks before our break started, but only ever with his fingers. Yet all I can think about now is the head of his cock brushing against the little pleasure button while he fucks me.

I'm vibrating with anticipation, waiting for him to do just that. If he did, I can't even say I'd be mad about it, because I want him more than I want my next breath. More than I want to prove myself to my parents.

Hell, I want him more than I want that stupid trophy at the end of the season, and that's just insane.

It should be enough to make an excuse for *not* having sex with my stupidly hot teammate. The guy I'm so in lust with, I can't think straight. Or be straight, either.

But it doesn't matter.

"Please," I pant, pushing back toward him more. "Put me outta my misery. For the love of fucking God."

"No condom."

"You know we've both been cleared," I say in rebuttal, knowing there's no reason we can't go without. Especially when the situation is this dire.

"True. And I'm sure sinking into you barrier-free will be nothing short of heaven. But we don't have lube either." He brushes a kiss on the back of my neck. "I'm not about to fuck you for the first time with body wash. That shit will sting like a motherfucker."

My heart hammers in my chest, ricocheting against my ribs, and if I wasn't so stupidly turned on, I'd come to my senses enough to say anything other than what I do next.

"Just do the tip. Give me something. Fuck."

A stifled laugh comes from him, the heat of his breath against my skin sending lightning bolts down my spine. "Just the tip? Is that what you used to tell all those puck bunnies?"

I glance at him over my shoulder. "Actually, you'd be the first."

Something about my answer lights a fire in his eyes. They burn with smoldering intensity I've only ever seen from him on the ice.

"You wanna play Just the Tip with me, de Haas?" Oakley arches a brow at me as he presses the head of his cock against my ass more. Enough to feel the rim stretching again, and God, if I don't welcome the burn.

"I'll take what I can get. Unless your infamous self-control can't handle it." My pulse pounds in my throat quick enough, I think the artery might burst. "Let's put it to the test."

His teeth skate along my shoulder before sinking into the muscle. The sharp bite of pain sends a zap of desire straight to my dick, making it ache for more. His mouth, his hand. His cock inside me. Anything would be better than the sheer torture he's putting me through.

"Egging me on doesn't work. You should know that by now."

Well, that's a blatant fucking lie if I've ever heard one, but two can play at that game.

"Mmm. But a guy can dream."

And it might not be a dream at all. Because, to some extent, it's working. I'm almost positive of it when I hear the telltale sound of him spitting right before I feel his fingers rubbing where his head presses against my hole.

"We've gotta work on your priorities if getting dicked down is high up on your list of aspirations. Now relax and let me in."

He squeezes my shaft, rolling his thumb over the nerve just below the head, and it's enough to ease the tension. The burn gets worse as he gives a couple more tentative thrusts before finally easing past the rim.

My ass clenches around the head like a vise, and I hiss out a low, "Fuck me."

"Hmm," he hums softly. "Maybe another time."

"Or right now," I counter, attempting to rock back into him. But his hands land on my hips, already one step ahead of me, and preventing me from taking more of him.

"Don't move." His tone leaves no room for debate on the matter. "If you start moving, I'll pull right back out."

"Fucking sadist."

The hand around my cock squeezes again, this time hard enough to lean more toward pain than pleasure, earning him a glare. But he's already glaring right back, brown eyes burning with more than just lust.

"You want a sadist? You want me to hurt you? Torture you? Fuck you so hard, you're nothing but a bloody mess on the fucking tile floor afterward? Because that's *exactly* what would happen if I pound into you the way you're asking."

"You're already torturing me," I pant, giving another push back, only to be immediately met with the resistance of his hold.

"You're not ready," he murmurs. "But I'll make the wait worth it."

He fucks into me slowly, stretching me with the thick head before easing back again. Each time, I beg him silently to lose control and slip in a little bit deeper. Honestly, I'm not above asking him to pound me into the shower wall; I'm that keyed up.

Fuck if I care about a little blood and pain. It makes the pleasure all the better.

But true to his word, he doesn't do it. Doesn't take me the way we both want, and it's fucking infuriating. Only once does he slide in a little bit more, and the burning sensation starts all over again. Yet, it's gotta be one of the best types of pain I've ever felt.

If only he'd give me more of it.

I let out a frustrated groan, more irritated at this point than anything else. But it quickly turns into a moan when the ridge of his tip brushes over the little magic spot inside me.

My prostate.

Also known as the key to an orgasm capable of sending me to another fucking dimension.

And holy shit, it does. Every single time Oakley's touched the damn thing, I came buckets. Gallons, even, and harder and longer than I ever have with anyone else. I'm at that point already, and just from one fucking pass of his cock against it. I can't go back to his fingers after feeling this.

"Fuck, right there," I moan again when he swipes over it again, my head falling back against his shoulder. "More, Oak."

He continues sinking into me slowly while I slide through his fist, the most exquisite kind of pressure filling and constricting me at the same time. It's overwhelming, and it continues to hurtle me toward the edge of a cliff I'm desperate to jump from. One leading to pure fucking nirvana.

The noises he manages to rip straight from my chest are nothing short of animalistic. Like there's no human left in me, just pure, carnal need.

"God, listen to you," he rasps, the deep cadence of his voice strained. "So fucking needy for me, and I've barely given you anything."

He's right. If this is what he can do with only the head of his cock? I have no doubts he'll reduce me to a panting, moaning mess with the whole thing. And if my responses are any indication, I'm sure to enjoy every second of it.

"More." I turn my face, taking his bottom lip between my teeth and tugging. "Let me have it all."

"Not happening."

"Oak—"

"Ask again and I'll stop right now."

Goddamnit.

A wicked smile forms on his face at my silence before he brushes his lips against mine, and I don't know if it makes me more desperate for him to fuck me like he means it or if I'd rather slap his smug-ass grin clean off his face.

But to hell if I'll open my mouth and say a thing, because each and every pump of his hips shoots rockets of desire through my entire body, and I'm not ready for it to end.

Oakley's free hand moves from my waist to my throat before offering a light squeeze. "Taunt me about self-control again, de Haas. I dare you. Because in the end, you're gonna be the one who suffers."

I'm ready to tell him it's too late, I'm already suffering from the dire need to be fucked and filled as soon as humanly possible, but the words die on my lips as he pegs my prostate again and only a guttural groan breaks free.

My balls seize up, my cock throbbing and aching with the need to release as I pant into his mouth.

"I'm close," he murmurs against my lips, the hand wrapped around my throat tightening slightly as he pumps his hips faster.

The back of my head connects with his shoulder, and I wrap my fist around his, helping him jack me the way I need to get me there too. Impending release barrels down my spine, and when Oakley pulls out and pushes me against the wall of the shower, I lose all control.

I barely have time to take over where he left off before cum soaks through my fingers, falling to the floor and washing down the drain at my feet. Oakley's head lands in the crook of my neck, his teeth clamping onto my shoulder, and I know he's not far behind me.

"Come," I pant, my forehead pressed to the cool tile.

And he does seconds later, his release spilling across my lower back.

Marking me. Maybe even claiming me.

As much as I'd like to bask in this glow and not move for hours, I know there's a good chance of someone coming to check the showers soon before heading out for the night. And I also know there's exactly a hundred percent chance Oakley would never want them to discover us in here together.

So I peel my body away from his and turn to rinse his cum off my back.

He leans against the opposite wall to catch his breath, and I use the opportunity to ogle. Shamelessly, I might add.

"Guess we're not very good at following our own rules," I say with a laugh as the evidence of his orgasm washes down the drain at my feet. "Because I'm pretty sure we just broke every one we've set."

When I glance up, Oakley's studying me curiously.

"What?" I ask, suddenly a little more self-conscious.

"I…" He laughs. "I can't believe I'm saying this, but I wasn't kidding. Fuck the rules. We should toss them altogether."

Not what I was expecting. At all. But holy hell, am I down for more of what just happened in this damn shower. So much more, my entire body vibrates with need all over again.

Jesus, I'm such a slut for this guy's dick, it's insane.

And there's one sentence I never once saw myself thinking, but here we are.

"Even the part where we don't tell anyone?"

He bites his lip for a second, and I swear, he's about to say yes. It doesn't last long, though, before he shakes his head. "I think it's safer if that one stays. But…fucking hell, I'm fine with doing whatever, whenever.

Screw the *before game only* rule."

"I like this idea. Especially if it involves more screwing."

His eyes flare with heat, gaze tracking down my body and back up again before landing on where his teeth sank into my shoulder. Where I have no doubt he left a mark, the same way I did to him at one time.

"Now what? Admiring your handiwork?"

"No. I was actually just thinking…I definitely want inside that ass again. For real, next time." A pause, then, "As long as you're okay with it."

"Okay with it?" I echo, swapping places with him and stepping out from under the spray. I grab my towel off the hook to dry off and glance back at him, surprised to see…he's actually questioning whether or not I want more.

My arms cross over my chest. "I was literally just begging you to fuck me, and you think I'm about to call take-backs?"

He frowns, rinsing his stomach and dick off. "Really, Quinn? Take-backs? Are we five now?"

The grin that spreads out over my face when hearing the nickname can't be helped. It makes me feel…weirdly affectionate toward him. Even after he just insinuated I'm a fucking kindergartener.

And he must be taken aback too, because he's staring at me like I've sprouted two more heads.

"Why're you smiling like that?" He waves his hand in front of my face, and it only makes me grin more. "Jesus, did I break you or something? If just the tip did this, I hate to see what you're like after I fuck you for real."

I laugh and shake my head. "Trust me, I can handle it. It's just…" My brows furrow, and I lick my lips. "You called me Quinn."

He frowns deeper before slowly asking, "It's your name, isn't it?"

"Not to you. You only call me de Haas. Or Quinton, sometimes."

He's silent for a moment, then his laugh sends cool shivers running through me. "Huh, I guess you're right. Leave it to you to ruin my orgasm high by making me think about what I call you in the moment. Maybe I'll go with *asshole* next time."

I smirk, shaking out my hair. "Quinn's fine."

"No, no. I'll think of something better. Something more creative."

"I'm serious—"

"What about *dickweed*? That's a great term of endearment, right?"

I let out a sigh and repeat myself, thinking maybe he'll hear me this time. "You can call me Quinn, okay? It's just that no one really does."

"You're telling me no one shortens your name to the most obvious option? Seriously?"

I shrug as I wrap the towel around my waist. "Yeah. I've always been an athlete, so it's always been de Haas. Or some of my high school friends, like Hayes, usually call me Q."

A low chuckle comes from behind me again, followed by kiss after kiss being peppered against the top of my spine. "Good. I don't want to call you what everyone else calls you. Takes the fun out of it."

"Oh, so you know what fun is now?"

He grips both of my shoulders and spins me around. "Yeah, I do. Because I had a ton of it a few minutes ago."

"So that's fun? I thought you said it was reckless. Or was it insane?"

"I called you insane. Which you clearly are, sneaking into my shower." He pauses for a second, a smile sliding on his face before adding, "*Babe*."

I burst out laughing, letting my face fall into his shoulder. "Please, just shut up. Before I make you."

"Mmm." He chuckles more, curling his hand around the back of my neck. "Then maybe you should kiss me."

I can't stop the way my heart ratchets in my chest when he kisses me instead.

TWENTY

Quinton

I saw Oakley less than an hour ago at practice, but to an addict going through withdrawals from their drug of choice, minutes have a way of feeling like a thousand years.

That's what I am when it comes to Oakley.

Addicted, and desperately craving another fix.

The other night in the showers only cemented it into my brain, and now I'd give my left arm to have a repeat of every glorious minute.

Oakley Reed has a deeper pull on me than I realized.

And the second he knocks, I'm hit with a rush of adrenaline. To the point where I almost rip the damn door off its hinges to get to him.

"Hey," he says, a smile on his face, hauling his bag over his shoulder.

A grin creeps onto my lips too. "Hi."

God, am I fucking twelve?

He doesn't even give me the chance to open the door all the way and let him in, just grabs me by the shirt and hauls me to him. His lips are on mine a second later—slow and tantalizing sweet—then they're gone again, and he's brushing past me into the apartment.

Ever since he kissed me the day we skated downtown, it's felt like something's changed with him. With the way he sees me, the way he wants to continue acting when we're together. The way he willingly gives affection without thinking about it first.

Even when we're on the ice, something's just different.

Almost like he…

I try to shake the insane ideas rolling through my head. Because that's what they are, right? Completely fucking insane.

But is it really?

He's the one who threw the rules out; first with the kiss, and then again last week in the shower. Is it really so crazy to think things are shifting for him the way they are for me too?

He gives me a quick glance over his shoulder, that ridiculously sexy grin of his in place. "You ready to smash—"

"What are we smashing?" Hayes's voice comes out of nowhere.

Both of us turn at the sound of it, finding him leaning against the kitchen counter, dark brows arched in curiosity. He takes a long sip of the water in his hand, eyes locked on me the entire time.

I've got no idea how long he's been standing there, but there's a good chance he saw the two of us kiss in the doorway before Oakley came inside. And though I know he won't say anything in Oakley's presence, that leaves a massive tale for me to unpack with him later.

Maybe he didn't see.

"Econ," Oakley finishes his sentence before holding up his textbook.

"Quinn took it a couple semesters ago and said he could help me if I needed it. Less than a week into classes and here I am, already caving."

"Oh, I'm sure *Quinn* did." If possible, Hayes's expression becomes even more impish. He takes another drink of water before adding, "You know, since it's one of *Quinn's* major requirements."

Goddamnit, Hayes.

Oakley's eyes shift to me, clearly aware of his fuck up. Which only makes my best friend's amusement grow, and irritates me even more.

"Yeah," Oakley says slowly. "Exactly."

"Don't take this the wrong way or anything, but don't you have your own house you can do that at? Or did you move in here and I just didn't realize it?"

Yeah, he definitely fucking saw.

My teeth sink into my lower lip as I glare daggers at my best friend. "Funny, Hayes."

"I thought so." A knowing smirk rests on his lips, and he raises his half empty glass of water in mock cheers. "Well, I'll leave you to it, then."

Relief floods my body as the door to his room closes behind him, leaving me alone with Oakley again.

I have to admit; Hayes makes a solid point. Oakley's here so often now, I might as well just give him the spare key so he can come and go as he pleases. But it's not like he *sleeps* here or anything. He always goes home after hanging out or hooking up.

The only time we've ever slept in the same bed was by accident, and it was in a hotel room we were sharing anyway.

"Should I go?" Oakley asks, a hint of worry in those brown eyes.

I shake my head. "It's just Hayes being Hayes."

"So being a dick."

A smirk works its way onto my face. "He wouldn't be my best friend if he wasn't."

"Like attracts like."

"Absolutely," I confirm before pulling him into my room, the door slamming closed behind us. "Which is exactly why *you* like me so much."

His eyes roll so hard, I'm surprised they don't get stuck. "Sure. Let's go with that."

"The world wouldn't crumble around us if you admit you like me. Even just as a person. Please tell me you know that."

His expression softens then, and one hand traces up my side. I feel the heat of his skin through my shirt, and once his fingers have passed any specific spot, goosebumps are left in their wake. Another new effect he has on me.

"I think it's just safer to pretend I don't."

I know that. The problem is, I wish I didn't. Just like I know it's a problem for me to be seeing him in a completely different light than I was a couple months ago.

In fact, I'm struggling to hold on to the reason why we were even enemies in the first place.

With Hayes's senses on high alert when it comes to the two of us, sex of any kind is out of the question, at least while he knows Oakley's here. Which means he really does pull out his econ and set to work, strewing textbooks and flashcards across my bed like it's a giant desk.

Unfortunate for me, considering I was hoping to get naked and under him this evening.

Hell, I'd settle for just hanging out. Watching a movie. Listening to music. Anything other than crack open another fucking textbook and ignore each other for hours. But considering college is no joke, especially as a student athlete, it's probably a good idea for us to start getting ahead on class work for the semester.

Crawling over the mess he's made of my bed, one of my upper level econ textbooks in hand, I slip into place beside him and lean back against the wall. The bed jostling with my movement causes Oakley to shift, rolling his shoulder before settling back into place.

Which would be fine, except it's the shoulder he tore last season along with his broken collarbone. And I've noticed him messing with it a lot more lately.

"You good?"

His brows furrow. "Why wouldn't I be?"

Reaching out, I run my index and middle fingers along his collarbone over to his shoulder. "I dunno. You've been rolling this a lot during practice. And then you just did it again a minute ago. So I wanted to make sure you were okay."

"Oh," is all he says, the frown still present on his face. "I guess I didn't realize I did it."

My teeth scrape over my bottom lip, becoming increasingly aware I pay far more attention to him than I thought I did. Or probably should, for that matter.

From the way he's staring at me, confusion slowly shifting to realization, he's figuring it out too.

"What's that look for?"

His head slants to the side. "What look?"

"You tell me. You're the one giving it."

"I didn't realize I was!"

We both laugh then, the intensity of the moment broken.

It feels great to laugh and joke with him, and even exist peacefully in a way I didn't know our relationship could be. Two people who finally found common ground, and as it turns out, it's all we needed to understand each other.

Which is why I'm not at all surprised by his next words.

"It's just that you're nothing like I expected."

I feel my eyes crinkle around the edges with humor. "Uh, thanks?"

He laughs again. "I promise I don't mean it in a bad way. You're just…" He trails off and shakes his head. "I dunno how else to say it. Just unexpected."

"Try explaining it, then." I close my textbook and drop it off the edge of the bed, only to wince at the loud *thud* it makes when it hits the floor.

"Hayes is gonna think we're fucking now," he says, arching his brow.

I give him a dirty smirk as I spread out on my back. "I mean, we could be, but—"

"Not a chance in hell."

I chuckle, rolling to my side and hitching up on my elbow. "You were talking about me being different than you thought?"

His eyes roll at my less than smooth reroute of the topic, and he mirrors my position.

"I guess when we're on the ice, I've always had this picture of you in my head. The hotheaded bad-boy of the team who gets in more fights than Muhammad Ali and Rocky combined. Brash and reckless. A rebel, in a way. And so, I sorta just assumed it would extend to who you are off the ice too."

I search his brown eyes for a minute. "And now you're saying it doesn't?"

He shakes his head and sinks to his back, eyes locked on the ceiling now. "No, you are. But you're *more* than those things too. Like sure, you're still a pain in my ass ninety-eight percent of the time when you're causing chaos on the ice—"

"I don't do that anymore."

"—but over the past couple months, I've started seeing your cockiness and attitude shifting into confidence in yourself and your abilities, not letting anyone tell you otherwise. And I guess...I kinda admire that."

"Confident enough to corner you and suck your dick in the middle of a party," I muse.

He snorts. "You say it like it was in the middle of the crowd dancing downstairs when we both know it was a lot more private. Again, surprising considering your reputation as a manwhore."

I make a buzzing sound with my lips. "Ah, see. You should know by now, slut shaming doesn't work on me, baby. I embrace who I am, flaws and all."

I expect him to come back with a witty retort, but the way his eyes grow wary and distant after I stop speaking tells me I said something wrong. It only takes me a second to realize what it was.

Baby.

I've called him that before, whether it be as a taunt or in bed. But never in place of his name. Never as...an endearment.

"I—"

"It's fine," he says, his head rolling from side to side against the mattress. "I know you didn't mean anything by it."

Except, that's where he's wrong. I think...I did mean it. But instead of letting the anxiety of this revelation get to me, I play it off with a smirk on my face and change the subject.

"So tell me. Are you gonna *finally* try a new pair of socks tomorrow?"

A funny look crosses his face. A mixture of humor and confusion, I think. "I hadn't really thought about it yet. I kind of just pick a pair each day. Whatever I'm feeling."

Lame.

"What do you mean *finally?*" he asks a moment later.

"Because I've been checking to see if you've worn them yet, and you haven't." Obviously. It's not like I sneak into his room and go through his dirty laundry.

"You've been checking," he repeats.

"Hell yeah," I tell him, a grin on my face. "I try to check before every game while you're getting dressed. Gotta make sure you're still as dedicated to the cause as I am, Cappy."

"I hate when you call me that," he grumbles, rolling his head away from me to face the wall.

"Why? Chris Evans is hot as fuck."

A deeper, richer kind of laugh comes from him. "You're unbelievable." But then he pauses, turning back with a seriousness taking over as his eyes narrow in on me. Suspicion radiates off him, and for a second, I worry I did or said something wrong. "You watch me get dressed?"

My lips quirk, and I lean in closer, my mouth inches from his. "No. I watch you get *undressed.*"

He grins some more and mutters, "Wow. What a creep."

"Maybe. Or maybe you should just be flattered that you're the one guy on the team who caught my eye."

The arch of his brow tells me he begs to differ. "Flattered, huh? That's what we're going with?"

"Absolutely. Takes more than a hot piece of ass to get my attention."

He tries to fight a smile—covering his face with his forearm and everything—but fails. Miserably. At first, I think he's trying to hide embarrassment. That's when the laughter starts, and I yank his arm back down.

"Are you laughing at me?"

"I'm sorry," he says between chuckles. "But you're kidding, right? You're the guy on the team who no one would let date their daughter. Straight up fuck-boy. And now you're trying to tell me it takes more than a hot piece of ass to get your attention?"

I roll on top of him, boxing him in against the mattress with my entire body. My fingers lace with his before pinning them above his head, and I can tell the position I've got him in is setting him on edge. There's fire burning in his eyes while he looks up at me.

"Well, then, I guess I misspoke," I murmur, leaning in and brushing my lips along his jaw. "It takes more than a hot piece of ass to *keep* my attention."

It's his turn to roll us so he's the one pinning me to the mattress, slowly fucking into me with every grind of his hips. One quick move, and I'm primed and ready to go to whatever filthy place he wants to take me next.

"But don't get me wrong, you're still so fucking hot," I murmur, reaching around to squeeze his ass. "Never in my life did I imagine telling you something like that, but there it is. Don't let it go to your head."

"I think you're talking about yourself there. I know how to keep my ego in check. Unlike someone I know, who's gotten all cocky ever since he tasted dick the first time."

"What can I say? I have superior blow job skills."

"Again," he whispers against my mouth, "those socks you got me beg to differ."

I let out a groan of frustration and let my head slam back against my pillow. "I'm really starting to regret getting those for you."

His head drops against my shoulder and he lets out a soft, husky laugh that...hell. It does everything for me. Fries my nervous system, short circuiting my brain enough to make our rivalry seem like a thing of the past.

Because I wanna hear it again. Just like this.

In the crook of my neck, floating over my skin like satin.

Breathy and raspy and just for me.

And that's really fucking dangerous.

TWENTY-ONE

Oakley

My phone buzzes on the nightstand, pulling my attention from the textbooks scattered across my bed as I attempt to study for this damn economics test I have later this week. Which is insane, considering we've only been back in classes for two weeks.

That's college for you. Cramming as much crap in our brains as humanly possible before tossing us out into the world to be functioning members of society.

Like Hayes so aptly pointed out earlier this week, Quinton's already taken this class a couple years ago as one of his undergraduate requirements. Which is lucky for me. Not because he still has the notebooks or anything useful for me. It's Quinn we're talking about. But he knows the material and can still help me should I need it, which is more than enough.

And speak of the devil, that's exactly who texted me.

Quinton: What are you doing?

Me: Studying econ. Wanna come help?

Quinton: Can it take a rain check until tomorrow?

I smirk at my phone screen. Ever since the night we broke the rules for the first time, we haven't cared to go back to obeying them. Now, barely twenty-four hours can go by without Quinn or I touching each other.

Me: Is this a booty call, de Haas? Are you wanting me to put your sexual needs before my education?

Quinton: It's not a booty call, though it's comical to hear from the one who begged to come over last night so I could come all over YOU.

My dick twitches at the thoughts of Quinn and I last night. It was like a repeat of our first official hook-up, only he was the one in charge this time. It was different from what I'm used to, having someone else above me like that. Pressing me down into the mattress and stroking us both to heaven while I sank my finger inside his ass. But as strange as it was, I loved it. I loved every dirty, sweaty second of it. And from the way he kissed me afterward—all teeth and tongue and need—I'd say he was definitely a fan too.

Me: That was so hot. Remind me some more and I won't be able to leave without my dick saluting everyone I pass on the way out the door.

Quinton: Is that a yes then? Is it really that easy? You don't even know what you're agreeing to, Mr. Stick To The Plan.

Coming from the guy who's made it his life's mission to get me to loosen up and have a little fun.

Me: Do I have to know every detail? Unless you're planning to kill me, chop me into tiny pieces, and toss my parts into Lake Michigan, I think I'm good.

Quinton: ...the fuck? How the hell did you jump from booty call to dismemberment?

Quinton: No, never mind. I don't think I wanna know.

My grin is instant. Throwing him off-balance, even in the smallest ways, always makes me smile or laugh. Probably because it's not an easy task, as I've learned over the past months.

Me: Let me know when and where to meet you for the non-booty call that may or may not be my plotted murder.

Quinton: You're ridiculous. I'll pick you up out front in ten. Bring a change of clothes.

Me: Thought you said this wasn't a booty call?

Quinton: Just pack your shit, Oak. Before I turn you into fish food.

I do as he asks, and true to his word, Quinton pulls up outside our house in his flashy BMW ten minutes later. He's halfway to the door when I slip out, not wanting him to knock and risk one of my roommates answering. Especially Brax or Cam.

Or Holden.

Quinn looks edible in a dark brown, worn leather jacket, a charcoal thermal shirt, and dark wash jeans. A knit beanie sits on his head, and I try not to smile when I notice he's wearing his glasses again today. Something he's been doing a lot more lately, and part of me wonders if it's because I've mentioned liking them once or twice.

"Hey," he says, grabbing my bag from me and tossing it in the trunk beside his own. "Thanks for agreeing to come."

He seems excited. Giddy, almost bursting with energy as he moves back to the driver's side door and climbs inside.

"You're in a good mood," I say slowly, sliding my body into the luxury car beside him. "Any particular reason why?"

Both of his brows quirk up, writing his amusement all over his face. "I can't just be happy?"

"Absolutely not," I deadpan. "I prefer it when you're miserable."

Picking up on my sarcasm, a slow smile breaks out across his face, and he lets out a low, rich chuckle. It washes over me like whiskey and warm honey, and I feel it to my toes. "Touché, baby. I know the feeling."

We drive in silence for a while, the only sound coming from the roar of the engine and the low, seductive thrum of Bad Omens's "THE DEATH OF PEACE OF MIND" from the speakers.

"Where are we going?" I finally ask about fifteen minutes later, just as Quinn pulls out onto the interstate that loops around Chicago's eastern side. It runs right along the shores of Lake Michigan, the setting sun casting a glow over the relatively calm body of water.

He glances over to me for a second, tongue in cheek, before returning his attention to weaving the BMW through the traffic on the highway. "You gonna be mad if I tell you it's a surprise?"

No, but it might make me slightly more irritated. Which I'm sure he knows, no doubt.

"Why do I have a feeling you really are about to turn me into fish food?"

A grin breaks out over his face. "You tell me. You're the one who put the idea in my head to begin with."

Laughing, I shake my head and stare out across the water. Soon enough, Chicago's infamous Navy Pier comes into view. One of the main attractions for tourists visiting the city.

"Have you been here?" Quinn asks, and when I shift my focus to him, he nods toward the pier.

My brows furrow, and—

"I don't think so," I tell him, astonished by the fact. "At least, not that

I can remember, anyway. I'd have to ask my parents to be sure."

I put a pin in the thought, because with it so close to Millennium Park, I've been here a few times. At least when my brother and I were younger. I'm still lost in thought as Quinton veers off the highway and onto the exit for the pier, stopping a few minutes later when he pulls into a parking garage.

"Were you planning to come here all along? We don't need an overnight bag to walk around the pier."

"The world may never know."

"You're the most infuriatingly ridiculous person I've ever met."

His lips twitch, fighting a smile. "So you've told me once or twice."

After killing the engine, he grabs my hand and pulls me toward the garage exit leading to the main level of the pier. Though, dragging might be the more appropriate term, because, once again, I can feel the excitement radiating off him in palpable waves. It seeps into my skin where our palms touch, and soon enough, I'm feeling the same level of anticipation he is.

Right until he starts crossing the plaza to the ticket booth for the Centennial Wheel.

I stop in my tracks, damn near yanking his arm from the socket. He turns and gives me a *what the fuck* look as I glance up at the wheel. When my eyes drift back down to him, I swallow my pride and admit something very few people know.

"I'm afraid of heights."

The way his eyebrows almost jump into his hairline would be laughable…if I wasn't being dead serious.

"You're afraid of heights," he repeats, to which I nod.

"Deathly afraid might be an exaggeration, but it's close enough."

I expect him to say we can forget about it and do something else. Maybe go ice skating again, grab dinner, whatever. But instead, a devious, shit-eating grin crosses his face and he drags me straight to the ticket counter, the line empty because it's the middle of winter. In the Windy City. On a giant pier. Sticking out into a large body of water.

Panic sets in, a thin coat of sweat already gathering on my forehead beneath my hat. "You heard the part where I said I'm afraid of heights, right?"

"Sure did," he says, ordering us two tickets.

"Don't worry, honey," the middle-aged woman at the ticket counter says. "There's those little puke bags in there if you start feeling woozy."

"Is that supposed to make me feel better?" I mutter, which only makes her laugh.

"You two enjoy your evening."

Quinn thanks her, pocketing his wallet and grabbing the tickets before taking my hand too.

"You'll be fine, Oak," he says, pulling me over to where the passengers get loaded. "I promise. And I'll hold your hand the entire time."

"It's really not as bad as you think. Nothing like those ones they have at the fair," a little girl in front of us says, clearly having never heard of the whole *stranger danger* concept. Then again, I'm willing to bet the woman whose hand she's holding is her mother, so how dangerous could it really be?

She's right, though, it doesn't look nearly as scary as those sketchy ones that travel around for fairs and carnivals and shit. But it's also like eighty-five times the size.

"What she said," Quinn says, motioning to the little girl and chaperone currently loading into their gondola.

"I don't think that's enough to stop me from having a panic attack while hundreds of feet in the air on a spinning wheel of death," I say to Quinn, all the while keeping my eyes locked on the door sliding closed on the gondola.

Oh God.

My heart races, more sweat causing my hands to get all clammy as our own gondola circles around. It stops at the loading platform for us, and after the people inside it disembark—all in one piece, I note—Quinn hands over our tickets.

The attendant motions for us to board, and Quinn's eyes lock with mine.

"Trust me," he murmurs and holds out his hand.

I'm surprised to find...I do trust him. So I grab hold of his hand and let him drag me into the tiny box on the spinning wheel of death.

That's when I'm also surprised to find how big it is. With little leather benches running down two sides and a capacity to fit at least half a dozen people. Not what I was expecting.

I take a seat beside him, still clenching his hand in mine.

"This...isn't so bad."

Except the thing chooses the same moment to move, starting the upward swing into the air, and I'm about to retract my previous statement.

Quinn eyes me, looking for any signs of discomfort in my face. I'm sure there's plenty there, but he must not see enough to cause any real worry.

"Do you need me to kiss you at the top if you get too nervous?" he says, a lilt of teasing in his tone. "Like in those cheesy rom-com movies?"

"I don't even think fucking you while this things spins us silly would make me less nervous."

He leans over and his breath coasting over my neck causes me to shiver. "That could be arranged if you want." His voice is a low, husky whisper. "We'd have to be quick, though. The ride's less than fifteen minutes."

I let out a bark of laughter, his ridiculous antics helping to put me more at ease. "You would, wouldn't you?"

A knowing smirk rests on those sinful lips. "Maybe not full-blown anal. But I'd definitely suck your dick if you needed a way to relax and get your mind off it."

I have a snarky *my hero* ready to burst free from my lips, but it gets caught in the back of my throat when our gondola rises high enough for the sunset to shine through each little crack and crevice of the Chicago skyline.

"Wow," I murmur, my attention fixated out the window.

"This is my favorite spot in the whole city," he whispers, and when I glance over, I find him staring out the glass too. "I swear, it's like being on top of the world."

"I believe you're thinking of Mount Everest," I supply, though from the way my heart is still racing a little, I might as well be standing at the top of the planet's tallest mountain peak. Heights are heights.

"You're a wise guy today, aren't you?"

"It's the fear talking."

"No, it's definitely just you," he says, smiling, and I'm starting to realize I'm not strong enough to withstand the sight of those damn divots in his cheeks. It's like dimple warfare.

It's not until the wheel starts its first descent when he finally turns to face me, allowing me to see both of them in all their stupidly attractive glory.

"When I was a kid and had hockey practices or games over at the rink in Grant Park, I'd beg Marta to bring me here after. It was always my reward for playing well, getting to ride the Ferris wheel."

"Marta?" I ask, because surely he doesn't call his mother by her first name.

His smile turns a little sad. "She was my au pair growing up. Now, she just works on the staff as one of the housekeepers."

Confusion hits me. "I thought your dad took you. To hockey, I mean."

"Only in the beginning. But when it became too much of an inconvenience for him, Marta was tasked with taking me."

"And what about your mom?" I pause, a realization hitting me. "Wait, are your parents married?"

"Whether or not they should be remains to be seen, but yeah, they are."

"So why didn't she take you?" I ask slowly.

He gives me an off-handed shrug. "Not sure. Probably too busy banging whatever junior partner at the firm was suiting her fancy that week."

I almost choke on my spit. "You're kidding."

All I get is a slow shake of his head for a response.

"They didn't even go to your games at all?"

Another shake of his head as the wheel ticks upward again. "Normally, no. I remember having a parents' night for a game senior year. I'd told them about it weeks beforehand; reminding them, putting it in the phone calendars and emails. It was so important to me, I even went to their personal assistants, making sure they had all the information too." His blue eyes shimmer, and it's not just from the glow of the sunset. "I'm sure you can tell where this story is going."

A sinking feeling causes my stomach to roll, instantly making me want to vomit more than this Ferris wheel ride ever could.

"Neither of them showed," I whisper. Not a question, because I know it could only be the truth.

His teeth roll over his bottom lip and he nods. "But there was Marta in the stands, just like she always was. So I took the rose we were supposed to give to our families straight to her. She was my parent that night." A soft scoff comes from him. "*Most* nights, actually."

My chest aches for him, in no way being able to imagine being raised the way he was.

My dad was gone a lot, sure, and my mom had to raise Logan and I on her own for six months at a time, but we never lacked in love or support or just…quality time as a family. Even if it was us going to see one of Dad's games, at least we were all together.

"But your parents come now." Again, not a question, but a clear observation because of the conversation I overheard earlier this season between Quinn and his dad.

Another scoff leaves him. "Only for their own benefit. Usually to look like the doting parents they could never be, supporting their collegiate athlete son when my father despises the sport simply because it brings me joy."

"I'm sure that's not the reason why."

"It might as well be. Anything that doesn't fit into his little plan for how my life should play out should be removed immediately. There's only room in it for things like taking over the firm, the society wife. Fancy cars and houses and kids to pass stupid amounts of money on to. Even when it's never been *my* plan."

"That's…quite a different version from what you have in mind."

A solemn nod is his response, and it's then when I finally get what he's saying.

My parents have always been supportive of me and my coming out about my sexuality. It's who I am, not something I chose for myself. But I'd have to be blind or stupid to not see their vision of my life with the wife and two-point-five kids and house with a picket fence going out the window when I told them I'm attracted to guys. And I'm sure it was difficult for them to swallow at first.

But never once did they tell me what I want for myself is wrong. Never.

"You want them to see you for who you really are? Then you make them. At every turn, you take the version of you they want and you toss it out the window to get left in the dust. Because there's nothing more important than being the person *you* want to be."

He whispers, "I could say the same about you, you know, Mr. I Have To Follow My Legacy."

I smirk. "Yeah, but we're not talking about me, are we?"

That gets him to at least crack a smile, and I find myself glad to lift even an ounce of the heaviness weighing on him. Something I never thought I'd be doing when it comes to him.

Hell, if anyone would have told me I'd grow to be fond of Quinton de Haas, let alone *like* him, I would have called them a fucking liar on the spot. Yet somehow, the walls I've built to keep guys like him out of my life are crumbling down, brick by brick.

I know I don't have time for the fun, flirty heartbreaker with a heart of gold, or whatever crap people write about in romance novels to make women swoon. It's not what my time at Leighton is for. I'm here for hockey, to pass my classes and get a degree. Maybe even search for a job if I don't get any feelers from an NHL team—though Dad and Coach's old agent, Louis Spaulding, has already been harping on me about a contract.

All this to say, I have far more important shit to get a handle on over my dating life.

Not that Quinton and I are dating by any means, even if it might feel like it right now. Because here I am, doing shit I'd be doing with a boyfriend—ice skating and Ferris wheel rides and deep, meaningful conversations—when all we are is fuck buddies.

Somewhere between the night in the frat house bathroom and right now, the lines got blurred. For me, at least. Because what we're doing doesn't make sense in my head anymore.

I'm helpless to stop it though.

"Where'd you just go on me?" he asks, cutting into my thoughts.

Busted. "Nowhere."

The look on his face tells me he's skeptical. "Oak, you might not know this about yourself…but you're a terrible liar."

"Just…it's a pretty great view. That's all."

His eyes move back to the skyline as we swing up for our third and final time. "It is. Say what you want about my parents, but I was lucky to grow up down here." Lifting his arm, he points to one of the high rises a few blocks away. "Right there. Penthouse apartment in downtown Chicago. More than most kids could ever dream of having, right?"

Nodding in agreement, I squeeze his hand. "So why does it feel like there's a *but* lingering in your head?"

His head shakes. "Not *but*. I never wanted for anything. Not when it came to all the things necessary for me to survive. I had a roof over my head and was always fed—usually some five-course meal our chef would make—and made it to my fancy prep school on time every day, thanks to my personal driver." He pauses, then repeats, "I never wanted for anything."

Except, from the way he says it, there's one thing he did want. Desperately, it seems.

Love.

And it breaks my fucking heart to pieces.

TWENTY-TWO

Quinton

"**W**here are we?" Oakley asks as I pull into the parking garage of the high-rise I grew up in. Turning into the spot reserved for my vehicle, I kill the engine and look over at him.

"You ask a lot of questions. You know that?"

He shoots me one of his death glares. "You're one to talk, Mr. Tell Me Something Real."

I let out a sharp laugh, his point valid. But I still leave his question unanswered, instead popping the trunk and pushing the driver's door open. Oakley follows me to the back of the car where I grab both our bags.

"Oh," Oakley says as I hand him his bag. "We're staying here for the night."

"Do you still think I'm planning to make you fish food or something?" I say, a smirk sitting on my lips.

He laughs. "We're well past that. If you were gonna kill me, you would've pushed me out the door of the damn Ferris wheel."

Another valid point. "I don't make it a habit to commit murder on the weekends. It's strictly a weeknight kind of thing."

His eyes roll. "He's got jokes, ladies and gentlemen. Too bad for him, they aren't very good."

"And I'm the comedian?" I laugh when he nods before grabbing hold of his hand. His fingers intertwine with mine, and together we cross the garage to where the elevator is.

"What hotel is this?"

Again with the twenty questions.

I arch a brow at him. "Who said anything about this being a hotel?"

A crease lines his forehead as his brows collide in the center. "Then where the hell are we?"

I don't answer, just keep leading him toward where the elevator leads to my parents' penthouse. But Oakley almost rips my arm from its socket for the second time tonight when he stops dead in his tracks.

"Jesus," I mutter, releasing his hand to roll my shoulder. "A little warning would be appreciated."

But when I look back to see why he stopped, I find him staring at me in abstract horror.

"Oh, my fucking God," he whispers on a sharp exhale. "We're at your parents', aren't we?"

I nod, pulling him to keep walking. "Sure are."

"And we're going up?" I try not to find the way his voice goes up half an octave endearing, but it's difficult. "Aren't your parents here?"

Giving him a reassuring smile, I shake my head before hitting the call button for the elevator. "They're out of town this week. I made sure before bringing you."

It's not that I'm wanting to keep Oakley hidden from my parents. It's more than I'd rather save him from their judgment, especially when I know that's all they'll give him. And not just because of his choice to also follow a career path into the NHL.

Plus, after all the shit I told him while on the Centennial Wheel, I don't think meeting either one of my parents is high on his priority list.

And even if it was, what would I even introduce him as anyway?

Yeah, we're kind of friends now. But calling him a friend doesn't feel right, yet neither does an enemy. He's just...Oakley now. The guy I like to taste and touch and turn on at any given moment.

Information that would go over wonderfully with my parents if they overheard the extracurriculars I have planned for us in my bed tonight.

When the elevator reaches the top floor, the doors open straight into the front foyer.

"Holy shit," he whispers, peeking through them before shifting his attention to me.

"Yeah, it's a lot."

I haven't brought anyone here in a long time, but it's the same reaction I've gotten from everyone who has visited Casa de Haas. Hayes included, and his family has just as much money as mine.

Per Oakley's request, I give him a quick tour of the lower level, starting with the living room. But even though the place is massive, there's not a whole lot to see. How could there be when it's more of a museum than a home?

But I introduce him to Marta, who we accidentally scare half to death as she's prepping meals for the week in the kitchen. Though the interaction was brief, from the way her eyes crinkled at the corners when Oakley was asking her about the chili recipe she was making, I could tell she liked him.

Which made me feel infinitely better about giving him yet another hidden piece of me. A piece I haven't shown anyone in a really long time.

"She seems really nice," he whispers as we climb the stairs to the second level of the penthouse, occupied by all the bedrooms besides the master.

"She's...amazing," I supply, though the word doesn't seem adequate to describe Marta in the slightest. Not when she's been more of a parent than either of mine have been for almost twenty-two years.

Oak nods and offers me a smile before grabbing my hand, giving it a gentle squeeze.

I keep hold of him as I drag him up the stairs, the heaviness in my chest quickly subsiding as we near the only place I care about bringing him.

My bedroom.

Pushing the door open, I lead him into my only sanctuary as a kid; complete with twelve-foot ceilings, wall-to-wall windows, and a massive, king-size bed in the center of the room.

"*This* is your room?" he says slowly, eyes taking in the space.

And yeah, it's nice. Big and spacious, lots of light during the day.

But it's cold. No photos or memorabilia anywhere in sight. It's been that way since I left for college. My parents had Marta clear out the room, box up all the things I didn't take, and shove it in the corner of the walk-in closet off to the left of the en-suite.

Now it's just another one of their five guest rooms, any traces of my existence wiped clean from the space.

Oakley's expression gives little away as he looks around the room, but from the set of his spine, stiff and rigid, I can tell he's thinking the same thing. But rather than mentioning it, he crosses the room back to me, a seductive smirk on those sinful lips, and wraps his arms around my waist.

"Are you planning to let me do dirty, despicable things to you in your childhood bedroom?"

My teeth scrape over my bottom lip. "I might just take you up on that offer."

One hand shifts up to the back of my neck, pulling me in until our lips are a breath apart. "Good, because I think I'm ready to claim my prize from our race."

He doesn't give me time to think, his mouth slamming to mine with a ferocity like no other. His tongue prods at the seam of my lips before sliding through to find mine. They twist and mate together while his fingers anchor into my hair, and he uses his grip to tilt my head, gaining better access to pillage my mouth as he sees fit.

He holds me so tight against him, I can barely breathe.

Or maybe he's stolen all the oxygen in the room.

He breaks our kiss far too soon for my liking, and I try to reel him in for more, but he shakes his head.

"Strip," he murmurs against my mouth.

I'm almost ashamed by how quickly I rip my body from his and shed my clothes. Within a blink of an eye, I'm down to only my underwear. Oakley's not far behind, naked from the waist up and already working his belt open.

After shucking my last remaining layer of decency, my hands are on him. Unbuckling the damn belt, I shove his pants and underwear down in a single fell swoop. I go with them, my knees crashing to the floor, about ready to take his thick cock in my mouth when he wraps his palm around it, effectively keeping me from getting a taste.

"What the—"

"Not happening," he scolds, pulling me back to my feet with his free hand. "It's my prize, remember? Now get on the bed."

Fucking hell. Leave it to him to wanna claim that shit at the most inopportune time.

And if this is gonna go anything like the shower did, I doubt I'm gonna survive it.

He practically throws me onto the giant mattress, sending pillows flying from impact before he covers my body with his own.

And then, with absolutely zero dexterity or self-control, we maul each other.

Oakley's lips trail down my throat, biting and nipping along the way. My hands anchor in his hair, his grab me by the hips, and we grind our bodies together. The ache in my balls is already present, and I know it'll be too much to bear soon.

I capture his lips again, spearing between them to take needy pulls of his tongue. He meets me with his own carnal lust, dragging moans and pants from deep within my chest as his hips rock against mine.

I'm enamored by him. Touch, taste, scent. All of it.

Every part of me craves every piece of him.

Shifting again, he positions his cock between my cheeks and slowly ruts against my skin and the silken sheets below. A slight flutter of panic races through me when his crown brushes against my hole. But still, the want and desire are there.

Oakley's not small by any means, and how in the hell he's gonna fit inside me is...well, it just doesn't seem possible. Just the first few inches the day in the shower felt like I might be split apart, even when I finally relaxed enough for it to feel good.

But it's the pleasure I *know* he can give me that has me saying what I do next.

"Fuck me."

"Quinn—" he starts, but I shake my head and cut him off with a kiss. It's urgent and needy and downright desperate, but I don't care. I don't fucking care if we're crossing all kinds of lines we shouldn't. It's like he said, fuck the rules. Fuck every damn one of them.

I just wanna know how it feels to be owned by him, even if it's just once.

"I want you," I whisper, like a secret in the night. "I want you so much, I can't stand it."

Tormented doesn't even describe the expression etched into his face as he looks down at me, two brown eyes watching and searching for…I don't know what.

"Are you sure?"

Rather than answering, I haul him in for another tantalizing kiss. I have no words of reassurance for him because…I should be freaking out right about now.

No, not should.

Am.

I actually kind of am flipping my fucking lid, fear and adrenaline and anxiety all mixing together in a potent, reckless concoction I know I should stay far, far away from. But I take it anyway, the desperate need for him inside me stronger than that for oxygen.

"My bag. Side pocket," I mutter, shoving him away from me to grab the lube.

He's gone for barely ten seconds before he's sliding his body between my thighs again, peppering kisses across my skin. Any piece of it he can find. My hips, my stomach. Pecs, throat, lips, taking his time to explore every line and muscle like it's the only thing in the world he wants to do.

All sorts of nerves twist and knot my stomach, the mixture of anticipation and a little fear sending my pulse skyrocketing as he pops the bottle of lube open, applying a generous amount to his fingers. Watching him only heightens the torrid emotions rippling through me, goosebumps breaking out over my skin.

The second a cool, lubricated finger slides up my crease, my senses go into hyperdrive. Every ounce of anxiety is gone, only need and desire left in its wake as he prepares me.

He massages my rim with deft fingers, ones far more skilled than with just holding a stick, dragging out moan after tortured moan while he does. I gasp when the first one breaches me, the long digit sinking inside me. The way he touches me and fucks me with his hand has my heart ricocheting against my ribs so hard, I think they might crack.

When another finger slips past the puckered ring of muscle, my need intensifies with the burn. I welcome it. Crave it, even.

My lips part on a gasp as he continues to stretch me, and when he curls his fingers against my prostate, I see every star in the galaxy.

"Shit, shit, shit, shit," I hiss, my ass bearing down on his hand.

It's a feeling I can't describe. Of being so full, I might burst at the seams, but also the desperate need for even more. And God, I want more.

I don't want to stop until I know what it's like to be shattered by him. Dismantled piece by piece until I'm just a messy heap on the floor only he can put back together.

His mouth descends over my aching length then, the dual sensation of it and his fingers setting all my senses on high alert. Every nerve ending in my body is hyperaware of where he's touching me, fucking me, owning me.

I lose myself in him, my head falling back against the pillow as he takes from me as much as he gives. But it's not long before even that's not enough, and I'm pushing him off my cock, desperate and ready to come.

And I refuse to let it happen until he's buried deep inside me.

Like he can read my mind, he adjusts his positioning and slathers his dick with lube. The ache in my balls intensifies at the sight, and only gets worse when he lines himself up against me, the red, angry crown of his cock nudging up against my ass.

And just like that, the nerves and anxiety come barreling back at break-neck speeds. Oakley must read it all over my face too, because his expression softens as he looks from where we're almost joined back to my face.

"Quinn…we don't have to."

"Yes, we do," I tell him. Because there's no other option. There's no other person I want to do this with. Who I want to give this part of me to.

He nods, as if reading my thoughts. Seeing what I so desperately need.

"If you tell me to stop, I will."

I know he will, just like I know he'll do everything in his power to make sure that doesn't have to happen. Even if it means sliding in one millimeter at a time.

His hips press forward in a gentle thrust, allowing the head of his cock to slip past the rim. And similar to when his fingers entered me, every nerve ending might as well be on fire. My ass throbs where he's penetrating me, barely lodged inside my body. Pulsing with an aching need only he can feed.

"Oh, Jesus fucking fuck," I mutter, my teeth sinking into my bottom lip.

"Can you take more?" he asks after a second.

I can tell he's doing his best to keep his own shit together right now. If the pinch of his brow and set of his jaw are anything to go off, he's barely hanging on from thrusting all the way in.

"Mhmm," I groan between gritted teeth, not trusting myself to form complete words. And for good reason, because all I can do is gasp when he flexes his hips forward, tunneling in another inch.

"Fuck, Quinn. Are you okay? I need you to say something."

I know he needs an answer, but I can't fucking breathe, let alone speak, so I just nod and dig my fingertips into his hips hard enough to bruise. A signal to keep going.

The look on his face is wary at best, but he continues his assault on my body by taking me another inch. Another excruciating but blissful inch.

"Breathe," he murmurs, brushing his lips against my jaw. "Relax for me, babe."

I do my best to listen, but damn, it's difficult. I feel like there's a damn hockey stick shoved up there, and he's not even completely inside me yet. Nowhere near close.

His hand wraps around my cock, the lube left on his fingers making it easy for it to glide up and down my length. The smooth strokes momentarily take hold of me, allowing my mind to focus on the pleasure shooting through me rather than the burning ache from where he's lodged inside me.

Oakley rains kiss after kiss down my neck, jacking me in long, languid strokes until I relax for real.

"I got you," he whispers against my ear, smooth as silk. "I got you, Quinn."

My brain immediately wants to read into his words and the unchecked emotion in them as he says my name, maybe find some double meaning. But that's just about the stupidest thing I could do, so instead, I wrap my legs around his ass and pull him toward me.

The movement causes him to tunnel in deeper, and I let out another tortured groan. One laced with both pleasure and pain.

"You're gonna fucking kill me with those noises," he pants, his voice more strained again.

"And you'll kill me if you don't start moving."

All talking ceases after that, Oakley's focus kept solely on sliding inside me deeper and deeper until he's completely seated inside.

And I'm delightfully surprised that once he is, the stinging burn has almost disappeared entirely. In its place is an aching, desperate need for—

"More," I moan, my hand squeezing his thigh. "Fuck, baby, give me more."

His forehead dips down, brushing mine as a bead of sweat drips from his cheek onto my lips. I'm quick to lick it away, the salt exploding on my tongue as the hand around my cock picks up the pace, jacking me in quick, hard succession.

His thrusts become harder and more punishing, and each time his head swipes my prostate, a tingling sensation works its way through my extremities. I can feel it take over, the impending sign of release, and I welcome it. I need it.

I feel wholly consumed by him.

Owned in a way I've never experienced before.

"Just like that, Quinn. That's it," he soothes, his hand anchoring on my hip as he impales me with his cock.

My body lights up like the city skyline, release barreling down my spine until I'm helpless to stop it. So I don't bother trying, instead letting it shoot me into outer space, going higher and higher as the stars behind my eyelids become blinding balls of light.

And I explode with them.

"Ohmifuckinggodyes." The sentence comes out as a single word of incoherent babbling while I lose myself in rapture. Transcending to a place I didn't know existed.

He works me through my orgasm with expertise, milking me for all I'm worth. Cum spills from my cock onto my stomach and chest, coating me with the white, sticky liquid as my ass clenches around him. Every pulse and squeeze brings him close to his climax until I finally drag him over the edge with me.

"Yes, Quinn. Yes," he rasps, sounding just as wrecked as I feel.

I feel his release jet out of him, each thrust he makes into my body filling me with more of his cum until he can't hold himself up any longer and collapses on top of me.

My arms weave their way around his back, and I cling to him like glue, no part of me willing to let go. The heart pounding in my chest syncs with his as we come down from our high. Exhausted, sated, and wrapped in each other.

We stay there, my fingers dancing along his spine as our breathing slows, for I don't know how long. Seconds. Minutes. Hours, maybe. But no part of me wants to move and risk popping the perfect little bubble we've fallen into.

He lifts his head from where it lay on my chest after a while, those brown eyes damn near unreadable as I stare into them. Lose myself in them and the depths they hide, like every canyon and crack in the Earth's surface.

And he stares at me too, like he's seeing me for the very first time.

He bridges the tiny pocket of space between our mouths, his lips brushing against mine in a feather-light kiss. One so soft, it's barely a kiss at all. And I sink into it. Into the pure innocence of it. Into the intimacy of it, until I'm unable to escape the hold it's got over me.

But I don't want to escape. Not now, not ever.

I want to bottle this entire moment up into a single heartbeat and cherish it in all its glory. Because come morning light, one of two things are bound to happen.

He'll wake up beside me and regret every moment of what just happened. Or he won't.

But either way, I need to save it. File it in my memory as something pure and perfect. Something to remain untouched, no matter what happens tomorrow.

And then pretend this doesn't change anything between us.

Even if I know it's a lie.

TWENTY-THREE

Quinton

February

Tonight is the first game since I brought Oakley to my parents' house and it's also the first game we're losing at the start of the final period. And I can't help but think it has everything to do with the fact that we've truly gone and fucked up this superstition beyond repair because we had sex.

Real, mind-blowing sex *outside* the limits of our superstition.

The worst part is our falling behind on the ice has nothing to do with the way we've been playing as a team. This might actually be the tightest game we've played as a whole all season. It's more like every time we score or catch some kind of lucky break, there's Wynnfield coming right back with one for themselves. Which is frustrating as hell on its own, but even more so when I have to believe this is partly our fault.

"What're you thinking right now?" Oak asks, skating up to my side as we make our way to center ice for the third period faceoff.

"That we can't lose this game," I mutter, my gaze colliding with his. But what I don't say is that even if we lose—and even if it is because of us—I don't regret the other night. Not by a long shot.

I just hope he can say the same, if it comes to that.

Oakley nods in understanding, but keeps silent as he moves into position on the opposite side of the circle.

Once the official drops the puck and the game is back in motion, every guy—teammate and opponent—slides into the zone with one singular task on their mind.

Get the puck in the net.

And by some streak of luck, we manage to with three minutes left in the game. All thanks to Oakley's keen eye, spotting I was open and allotting me the chance to score. Now with the goal tying us up at three apiece, I'm just grateful we've got a chance to take this to overtime at the very least.

Now the puck's live again, and we're about to do a change on the fly when Oakley skates up behind me, a massive smile screaming of pride and respect plastered on his face. "Nice shot, de Haas."

I'm aiming a returning grin at him, seconds away from thanking him for the assist, but I don't get the chance, thanks to one of the jackass defensemen, Jake Carter, from Wynnfield. Carter slams into me out of nowhere, the unexpected blow knocking me off my feet and sending me barreling straight into the boards headfirst.

It takes a second for me to catch my breath, the angle of the hit knocking the wind out of me. From the way my neck hurts, I can already tell I'll have major whiplash. Probably a killer headache for the next couple days too.

The way players from both teams surround me lets me know the play has been stopped—a whistle blown on Carter for an illegal hit—to check me for injury.

Oakley's in front of me a second later, arm outstretched to help to my feet. I reach for it, but I never get the chance to grab a hold because Oakley's shoved away by the defenseman who rammed into me.

"What the hell, man?" Oakley rights himself, a scowl marring his face as he glares at the asshole.

But this doucheface has no interest in talking, instead shoving Oakley again—crushing him against the glass too—before coming after me. His arm slams down over my throat, holding me against the boards that way. And when he leans in, his facemask colliding with mine, I recognize him as one of the many players I got handsy with last season after running my mouth for a little too long.

My damn mouth, always getting me in trouble.

"Not such a tough guy with your back against the boards, are you, de Haas?"

"Bite me, Carter," I snarl, teeth bared.

"Not really my kink. How 'bout I deck you instead?"

He's seething now as he jams me harder against the boards, the forearm locked over my throat grinding down against my Adam's apple painfully.

I can barely breathe, let alone speak, when Oakley grabs him out of nowhere just as he goes to rip my helmet from my head—probably to throw his fist into my face.

"Get off him," he snaps, shoving the defenseman away from me.

But it only makes the D-man even more pissed off.

He's after Oakley now, meanwhile pandemonium breaks out on the ice, all the players and officials doing their best to call off Carter's attack. It's no use though, because Carter is an animal on the hunt for blood.

Except as he rips Oakley's helmet from his head and raises his fist, I realize it's no longer my blood he wants.

He lands a blow on Oakley's cheekbone before bashing him back against the glass. And when I watch him crumple beneath the hold Carter has on his shoulder—his *bad fucking shoulder*—I see red.

And something inside me snaps.

The feral, carnal side of myself breaks free as I wrap my arms around Carter's waist, yanking him away from Oakley. I'm ready to give him a taste of his own medicine, the rage inside me about to be unleashed.

He can come after me all he wants if he's got a beef needing to be settled, but leave my teammates out of it. No one else needs to be injured because of me. Not again.

So if a fight with me is what he wants, a fight he's gonna fucking get.

Except I don't even have the chance to do a damn thing, because Oakley's right there to put an end to this squabble once and for all.

"Hey, stop. He's not worth it." His palm presses against my chest pads as two Wynnfield players work to separate me and Carter. But no amount of space or holding back can stop me from wanting to smash in this doucheknuckle's face.

And that's all I want right now, because how fucking *dare he*.

But Oakley presses fractionally harder.

"Quinn, he's not worth it," he says again, his tone soft yet firm.

The blood boiling in my veins demands release, but as I lean into Oakley's touch—even if I can't directly feel it through the pads and uniform—my rage tamps down. Cooling to a low simmer, and eventually, it's enough to remove my eyes from Carter to give Oakley my full attention.

A tiny amount of blood leaks from the cut below his eye, and I can tell from the way he's positioned, with his arm held up awkwardly toward his chest, this jackass somehow fucked with Oak's shoulder. It pisses me off more.

But still, Oakley's hand and imploring gaze are enough to ground me in the moment, keeping my rage from getting the better of me.

"You're right," I snarl, baring my teeth at Carter. "He's not."

And then I do something I've never done before during a confrontation on the ice.

I turn around, and I skate away.

I'm honestly surprised I was allowed to play the remaining few minutes, but since Carter was the one to clearly incite the violence instead of me, he was the only one tossed in the sin bin. Which was a weird experience for me, all things considered.

Things turn in our favor after the brawl on the ice, and thanks to the power play for the remaining time of the game, we pull a W out from all the chaos. Rossi, McGowan, and I are able to work together with Wynnfield down a man, sneaking a goal in with about thirty seconds left.

My third goal of the night, giving me a hat trick to end the game along with the win.

But the celebrations are cut short in the locker room when the team trainer pulls Oakley into a separate room to take a look at his shoulder before he even has the chance to shower.

Coach benched him the rest of the game after the incident with Carter, wanting to have it looked at before the game ended. But Oakley wasn't having it and said it could wait until the clock zeroed out, much to Coach's and my displeasure.

However, the way he was wincing at the slightest movement only proves pulling him off the ice was the right call.

Some of the guys are still milling about, but more than half the team has long since showered and gone home. I'm about ready to leave too, when Oakley appears at his stall, tossing his pads into the opening before stripping down and wrapping a towel around his waist.

The skin on his back where his shoulder blade protrudes is red and inflamed, probably due to the trainer's exam, but otherwise he seems to be moving it better than he was on the ice. But the butterfly bandage on his face to help close the cut on his cheek almost sends me over the edge into another ragey downward spiral.

My fingers twitch with both anger and compassion. With the urge to brush my thumb across Oakley's cheek, but to also bash Carter's skull in for daring to touch him.

In the end, I do neither, balling my fists and keeping them at my sides as I continue to give Oakley a once-over from across the room.

"I can feel you staring at me," he murmurs before shifting his focus to me.

There are so many things I could say, so many things I want to ask, but I know this isn't the time or place. So instead, I settle for the one piece of information I need right now.

"Are you okay?"

He gives me a tiny smile, but it quickly turns into a wince when he goes to hang his pads. "Yeah, I think it's just sore. But the trainer's confident it's not another break or tear or anything serious. Just a tweak. Some ice and rest for a couple days should make me good as new."

Somehow, that doesn't make me feel any better.

"Okay," is all I can say as guilt sweeps through me.

After all, if it wasn't for my shit-talking these past few years, Carter wouldn't have come after me, let alone bring Oakley into the mix. Fuck, if it weren't for me, Oakley wouldn't have been injured in the game against Waylon last season either.

As if reading my mind, Oakley cuts through my thoughts. "It's not on you."

It sure as hell feels like it is.

"Okay," I say again, because I don't have it in me to argue with him. All I really want is to crawl into bed and forget this day happened. Alone, because I can't handle any company tonight. "Just take care of it. Please."

He nods. "Of course."

I can't stay in here without making it completely obvious to the few guys still milling about that I'm hanging around for him. Which would probably set off some alarms in their heads, therefore going against the stupid fucking *no one can know* rule I've grown to loathe.

So I grab my bag and haul it over my shoulder to head home for the night.

I'm about to exit through the back door of the locker room when my name is called out from behind me.

"Quinn."

I turn to find Oakley watching me with that penetrating gaze of his. The one that makes my skin tingle with pinpricks whenever I feel it aimed at me.

"Yeah?"

He licks his lips, a small smile forming on them before he says four words I never thought I'd hear out of his mouth. "I'm proud of you."

From the way he says it, I know he doesn't mean for scoring the game-winning goal, keeping our winning streak—and the superstition—alive. It's because I did something I've never done before.

I walked away from a fight.

My heart ratchets in my chest, the damn thing pounding against my ribs a little harder at his approval. It's something I'd never thought I'd get from him, and now knowing how it feels to earn it, there's nothing else I want.

I want to keep making him proud. Always.

My lips lift at the corner as I smile at him. "I'm proud of me too."

TWENTY-FOUR

Oakley

The guys at home have been catching on.

Not about Quinton and I specifically, thank fucking God. It's more like I've been distracted lately. If I'm even home, which doesn't happen a whole lot lately either. And though they might not know why, apparently they've taken notice, the fact becoming crystal clear when I shove the front door open after the game against Wynnfield, only to be met with four sets of eyes locked on me from the sectional.

Waiting for me, like an intervention or something.

Slowly, I let my duffle slide off my good shoulder, my gaze flicking from face to face in an attempt to get a read on the situation.

"Someone die?"

"Yeah," Holden says, crossing his arms over his chest and leaning back against the cushions.

His seriousness paired with the quiet tension in the air, hanging there like a storm cloud, causes my stomach to roll with dread. "Who?"

A long sigh comes from him before he says, "Our friendship."

The rest of the guys chuckle as relief floods through me. My eyes narrow on my best friend, then the rest of them.

"That's not funny in the slightest."

"Yeah, well, neither is you being fucking MIA since classes started back up." Concern lines his features, and he shakes his head. "Where the hell are you lately, man?"

My brows furrow, and I try to play dumb. I play dumb like my fucking life depends on it, because it very well might if these guys discover what I've been doing lately. Or who I've been doing it with.

"In class or at practice most of the time. Sometimes the gym. And when I'm not at any of those places, I'm usually at the library. You know, studying? Because we're in college and supposed to be learning things?"

Though I do my best to keep the defensiveness out of my voice, I'm not sure I succeeded, because Holden's eyes harden on me, and I can tell he's well on the way to sniffing out my lies.

"Okay, then where the hell are you sleeping? Because it sure as hell isn't here."

What the fuck?

"I've been here pretty much every night this week?" I tell him, though it sounds more like a question because I'm not sure where he's getting this idea from. The *only* night I wasn't here was earlier this week, when I stayed with Quinn at his parents' place, and that's not something I thought anyone would notice.

"Pretty much?"

I gape at him, nearly at a loss for words. "Are you actually about to sit here and treat me like a teenager by asking me where I've been past my curfew?" A scoff escapes me, and I shake my head. "Did you body swap with my parents or something?"

"You wanna talk about body swapping?" he counters, brow arched. "Because getting into a fight on the ice sounds a lot like something de Haas would do, Oakley. Not you."

"News travels fast, I see." My focus flicks to Camden and Braxton, wondering which one of them opened their fucking mouth first about what happened tonight. "But I'm assuming you didn't hear the part where I *stopped* the fight."

"Yet the gash below your eye tells a different story."

You've got to be fucking kidding me.

"Give it a rest, Hold," Cam pipes in. "He's right. He was trying to stop it when he got decked. Can't blame him for that."

"I'm just concerned for my best friend." He motions to the other guys on the couch, his eyes locked on me. "We all are. I'm just the only one willing to fucking say something."

A twinge of guilt smacks me in the chest, no matter how unwarranted it might be. And it's at that moment, I almost tell them. Break the last and final rule Quinn and I put into place.

But I just can't.

Even if I wanted to, even if Quinn and I agreed to cutting out this final rule altogether, I still fucking can't. Not with the way Holden snarled his name at me moments ago. None of these guys have any love for Quinton, especially with the way we've acted toward each other the past few years. They've all been around to see it.

There's no way they'd ever understand this thing happening between the two of us.

"Earth to Oakley?" Holden's voice cuts into my thoughts.

I realize he must've said something I missed while I got lost in my thoughts, and I shake free from the fog. "Sorry, what?"

There's venom laced in his laugh. "See, this is exactly what I'm talking about. Even when you're here, you're not *here*. So where the fuck are you, man?"

His tone sets me more on edge than finding the four of them sitting here waiting for me like some goddamn intervention.

I drop my bag to the floor and toss my arms out to the side, doing my best to ignore the pain lancing through the shoulder I really need to get some ice on. But if Holden wants to start shit instead, fine.

Like he was quick to point out, this isn't the first fight I've been in tonight.

"I'm busy, Hold. I have a life outside of this house. One involving school and practice and studying and friends other than you."

Braxton lets out a low whistle. "Mom and Dad are fighting."

"Oh, fuck off, Braxton," Holden snaps. But when his eyes shift to me, I see the hurt in them. Hell, I can *feel* it radiating off him in waves.

I know what I said was harsh, but goddamn. It needed to be said.

Just because everyone in this house are good friends doesn't mean we need to know where everyone is at all times, and more importantly, who they're with. That's fucking insane.

Holden's lip curls back. "You don't have to be a dick about it."

Oh, but I think I do. Because I'm a grown-ass man, and there's no reason I should need to explain myself, let alone check in with any of them like they're my goddamn babysitter or something.

"Fine," I say, dropping into one of the empty spaces on the sectional. "You wanna have a little house meeting about when we're allowed to go somewhere or not? Maybe we need to make it a rule where everyone's schedule should be posted on the fridge. Then we know when everyone is coming and going. Does that sound good?"

All four of them keep silent at my ridiculous suggestions. And yeah, they are ridiculous, like this entire conversation has been from the start. But I'm on a roll, and I just keep going.

"Or better yet, maybe we sit around and braid each other's hair while talking about the people we're sleeping with?" I don't wait for a response, nodding my head over to Braxton. "Let's start with you. What twisted sister are you fucking these days?"

Braxton looks unperturbed by being put on the spot, a bored expression painted on his face when he mutters, "Kinsley."

"Shocking turn of events," I muse, my voice tainted with sarcasm as my attention shifts to Theo. "And what about you? Anyone special in your life that's been eating up your time?"

He arches a brow. "You think I have time to be fucking someone? I'm already going on no sleep between my parents and my course load. I don't have time to add another human to this shit."

Yeah, that's true. His parents have been going through an awfully messy divorce, dragging him through the middle of it, and now with the season about to start for him, I wouldn't doubt he goes with only a few hours of sleep at a time.

"Fair enough," I say, continuing down the line to my goalie. "And what about you, Cam? What's the name of your current flavor of the week?"

"This is fucking stupid."

You're telling me, man.

"Too shy to share? You know that's not gonna do for Holden."

Tongue in cheek, he sighs and offers up a name. "Her name's Rachel.

Wanna know her favorite position too?"

A small smirk plays on my lips at his snarkiness—not something that comes from him often—but I'm quick to hide it before turning to Holden.

"Well, Hold? Do we need to hear what Rachel's favorite position is while Cam fucks her into next week?"

"Okay, you're making your point," Holden says, shaking his head.

"No, no. I don't think I am. And don't think you're getting out of this without fessing up to your own shit," I snap, almost seething. "So tell me, how're things going? You and Kason still sucking each other off in the locker room after practice?"

It's a low blow and I know it, especially considering all the filthy shit I've done with Quinn in our own locker room. But I need to drive this home for him, let him see how absurd he's being, and finally put a rest to this shit.

"Kason and I are done."

Just like that, another pang of guilt hits me. Because even though I haven't been around, I still know Holden. I know he's not the monogamous type, at least not long term. But he and Kason were seeing each other more than I've ever seen him with any previous hook-ups, and I'm talking months longer.

So it's no surprise my stomach drops when I hear him say that. And now, of all times.

"What happened?" I ask slowly, my temper and irritation with him immediately subsiding into concern. "I thought you guys were good."

"We were," Holden mutters before blowing out a long breath. "But I fucked it up, just like I always do. Nothing new there."

A scoff comes from Braxton as he looks between us. "Yeah, I'm not sticking around for this. Y'all have fun braiding your hair and shit, but I'm out."

With that, he rises from the couch and heads up the stairs.

My eyes fall to Camden and Theo before I arch a brow at them. "You in or you out?"

"No, don't come in here acting like you give a shit now, Oak. It doesn't fucking work that way," Holden says, sinking back into the couch.

But I do give a shit.

Yeah, maybe I haven't been around. And yeah, maybe I've been a shitty best friend to Holden the past few months, not keeping up or checking in the way I probably should've been. Still doesn't change that he's my number one, and if he needs me to be here for him, that's exactly what I'm gonna do.

"Except I do care, and I'm sorry I made you feel like I didn't."

Holden shakes his head, but there's a smile hinting at the corner of his mouth when he says, "Fucking dick."

"Aw, look at that. Mom and Dad made up," Camden points out with a laugh, playing off Braxton's earlier dig.

"Which one of them is Mom?" Theo asks, his attention flicking between me and Holden.

Before anyone can jump on that debate—because we all know it's Holden—I turn us back to the topic at hand.

"So what happened?"

The smile that was working its way onto Holden's face quickly disappears. "Like I said, I fucked up. All there really is to it."

"But how?"

"Does this have anything to do with what's going on with Phoenix and Kason?" Theo chimes in. "Because those two are thick as thieves, and they haven't spoken in weeks."

I recognize Phoenix as one of Theo's teammates—maybe their center fielder—but I honestly can't be sure. Keeping track of my own is hard enough, let alone everyone on the football and baseball teams too.

Holden's head drops to his hands, shoulders slumping in defeat at Theo's comment, repeating himself again. "Like I said. I. Fucked. Up."

"Well, now I'm intrigued," Cam says, leaning back into the cushion like he's settling in to binge watch his favorite television show. "Theo, go grab the popcorn. We might be here a while."

Rolling his eyes, Theo rises and heads to the kitchen where I hear him digging through the pantry. Which is kind of hilarious, minus the part where Holden still looks like he'd rather lick a rusty pair of scissors than talk about this.

"Guys, seriously," he tries reasoning. "It's a saga, and not a good one."

"But Theo's already getting the popcorn," Cam counters. "And besides, I've got some time to kill, so might as well get it off your chest."

Holden's head drops back against the couch before he turns it toward me. "How much time you got?"

I lift my good shoulder with a shrug. "However much time it takes."

"You sure you don't need to go hang out with your other friends?" he teases before giving me a playful shove. Which, of course, is to the same shoulder that's been throbbing all night from Carter being a dickweed on the ice.

Holden's eyes become saucers when he realizes what he did, and I can't help but laugh through the pain shooting down my arm.

"Now you're lucky if I'll listen at all."

"So fucking dramatic tonight. You're definitely the Mom," Holden gripes before turning and calling over the couch. "Theo! Bring an ice pack while you're at it!"

TWENTY-FIVE

Oakley

Why in God's name I thought it would be a good idea to take another freaking philosophy class for an elective this semester is beyond me. It was meant to be a quick, easy A with everything I learned last term, but I end up studying this shit more often than I do anything else. And while it makes sense in theory, when the professor asks me to *put it in my own words* in an essay, it becomes a lot fucking harder.

Doesn't help that Kant, Hume, and all the rest of them blur together into one jumbled mess inside my brain after staring endlessly at my textbook, trying to figure out where I want to start. Which is what I've been doing since nine this morning, when I arrived at the library.

Eight fucking hours ago.

I'm about two seconds away from ripping my damn hair out when I notice a lone figure weaving their way through the dimly lit stacks toward me.

At first I think I might be hallucinating from staring at the computer screen for too long. Because there's no way in hell *Quinn* is at the library. On a Sunday…or probably any other day of the week.

But I'd recognize that smirk and saunter just about anywhere. They're the only things getting my blood heated these days—whether it be out of lust or anger.

He looks good. Damn near edible in his LU Hockey hoodie and sweats. None of which should be attractive in their own right, but Quinn makes it work for him just as much as he does leather and jeans.

Then again, maybe it's those fucking glasses getting to me instead.

"Stalking me, de Haas?"

He stops across the table from me, his damn smirk growing when his eyes lock with mine before shoving his hands into the pockets of his sweats. "Stalking? No way in hell. This little meet-cute is one hundred percent consequential."

I squint at him. "You mean coincidental?"

"Tomato, potato," he says, brushing me off. "The point is, it's not stalking."

"Oh, really?" My brow raises. "Because I know there's absolutely no chance in hell you just *happened* to stroll onto the fifth floor of the library. First or second, maybe. Highly unlikely, but I'll give you the benefit of the doubt. But up here? Absolutely not."

All I get is a non-committal shrug. "I know, it's weird. But I was just up here browsing the stacks in search of a good book and there you were. Must've been fate."

"Destiny," I deadpan. "Especially when the only *books* up here are actually research articles and dissertations."

He rounds the table, coming up beside me and placing one hand on the smooth wood, the other on the back of my chair. The light brush of his fingers sears me through my shirt, instantly making my stomach roll with anticipation.

There's nothing shook up in his stare down at me, blue eyes flaming and a quirk on those sinful lips. And it's infuriating to know the damn guy doesn't even have the decency to look sheepish when he's caught red-handed in a blatant lie.

"Give it up, Quinn. How'd you find me?"

"Sent out an APB, obviously."

I roll my eyes. "And the real answer, jackass?"

"Oh, calm down, baby." His deep laugh, a low baritone, floats over my skin and sends a rush of lust and adrenaline coursing through me. Or maybe it was the pet name that…I could get used to hearing more.

God, I'm so fucked for this guy.

My brow lifts some more as I wait for his answer. Which comes as he circles around me, both hands brushing my shoulders and his breath hot on the side of my neck as he speaks into my ear.

"I asked Cam."

I turn to face him, my mouth only inches from his. "Seriously? And that isn't going to be a dead giveaway to something being up with us?"

After all the crap that went down last week, the last thing I need are my roommates asking even more questions.

"He's none the wiser, I'm sure of it," he practically purrs. "I told him I had a book for you. *Leadership for Dummies.* He laughed and said you've been here all day. And since I know you have an essay due tomorrow, I figured you'd go where it's the quietest. With the least people around to… distract you."

Part of me wants to laugh at how clever, and insanely ridiculous, his excuse is, but my body is too keyed up from his proximity.

Thankfully, he leans away, giving me some much-needed distance as he pulls out the chair beside me at the table. Too bad it's not nearly enough, because my attention is still hyper fixated on his body only a foot away.

How in the ever-loving fuck this guy gets me worked up with his presence alone is so far outside my IQ range, it's laughable. Then again, it could also be the warm palm landing on my thigh beneath the table, just above my knee.

"And now you're here to fuck it all up, aren't you?" I murmur, gaze locking on his. When he nods, I can't help the soft scoff falling free from my lips. "Why am I not surprised?"

"Because whether or not you want to admit it," he whispers, fingers inching closer and closer to my dick. "I'm your favorite kind of distraction."

He's right, he's become my favorite distraction. And he's also correct in assuming there's no way in hell I'd ever own up to it.

Too bad he must read it all over my face, because the sinful grin on his lips only grows—like my fucking dick. Another thing he doesn't fail to notice, if the way his finger grazes against it, teasing along the head, is any indication.

"And honestly?" he murmurs, arching a brow. "You look like you could use a little bit of a…stress break."

My eyes leave him, checking around the dimly lit fifth floor. There's a handful of people in study cubes or strewn about at tables across the open areas…and the closest person is still a good thirty feet away.

Taking my silence as a go ahead, Quinn strokes me over my own pair of sweats. My hand darts beneath the table on instinct, gripping his wrist tight enough to hurt.

"Not here," I hiss, releasing my hold on him. "Last aisle on the left.

Go all the way to the back. I'll be there in a minute."

He smirks, pulling his hand back and rising from the table. "Don't keep me waiting, or I'll have to start without you."

I watch as he disappears from sight in the stacks, all the while willing my dick under control so I can go find him without waving a flag at anyone I might pass by on the way there. But when ninety seconds pass and I'm still harder than stone, impatience wins out.

"Fuck it," I mutter, tucking the damn thing in my waistband and pushing out of my seat.

Leaving my books and bag on the table, I follow in the direction I sent Quinn to wait for me. An empty table with a bunch of belongings on it might cause suspicion if left alone long enough, but it's a chance I'm willing to take.

The only thing I care about is getting my hands on the sexiest, most infuriating teammate I've ever had.

Except…the last aisle is empty when I get there.

I head through the stacks, all the way to the back, about to be really fucking pissed if he left me hard up in the library, of all places. Out of nowhere, an arm reaches out and grabs me by my hoodie, hauling me into a hard, masculine body.

"Took you long enough," he growls, pressing me into one of the wooden shelves before crashing his mouth to mine.

Tongues fight for dominance as hands frantically search for bare skin. The ends of his fingers dig into my hips while mine anchor into his hair, and we devour each other until we're both a panting mess, ripping at clothing like two wild animals.

I don't think I'll ever tire of this. Of the battle we have between us before he eventually caves, becoming putty in my hands.

Twenty-four hours are all the time that's passed since I've been inside him last, but I'm still starving for him. I didn't realize how much until now.

My fingers leave his hair and dig into the hard muscles of his shoulder, shoving him to his knees at the same time he pushes my sweats to the floor. It's agonizing how the seconds ticking by feel like years before he's finally pushing my underwear down to pull me free. But it's worth it the moment he flicks his wicked tongue across my slit, lapping at the precum like it's the best thing he's ever tasted.

My eyes close in rapture, head falling back against the shelf behind me, and I silently thank my lucky stars there's no real books on them to topple over with what's about to happen.

"Make it sloppy, Quinn," I rasp, hand cupping the back of his head as I thrust into his mouth. "I want inside that ass before I come."

He takes everything I give him, and I swear to God, he asks for more too. Every pump of my hips, he tries to take my length further, until I'm lodged deep down his throat.

When I lift my lids and look down at him, I find his gaze already locked on my face. Watching me. Taking in every ounce of pleasure written on my face. Pleasure *he's* giving me.

His nostrils flare, the heat in his eyes searing me, spurring me on more as I continue fucking into his mouth.

That mouth was made to destroy me.

But his mouth isn't enough. I want all of him. I want to *see* all of him. "Lose the pants," I order.

A wicked grin curls his lips when he releases me. "You want me to put on a show for you, baby?" He doesn't even bother giving me a second to respond. Instead, his sweats slide down over his thighs, revealing his cock. Long and hard and thick, a bead of pre-cum sitting on the tip making my mouth water.

And I notice, once again, he's commando.

"No underwear," I muse, locking gazes with him again. "You knew exactly what you wanted when you came here."

He grins, leaning in for me again. "I had my hopes."

Seems I'm not the only one who's been insatiable for this since the first time.

My eyes heat when his lips find their way back to my dick at the same time he wraps a fist around himself, giving his length a slow tug.

Yes.

"Lemme see how hard you get from me fucking your face."

He smirks again, around my cock this time, and makes a show of jacking himself while he blows me. It's a filthy, erotic sight, and soon enough, all my senses are quickly overstimulated in the best way.

A way bringing me closer and closer to release.

Using my free hand, I grip his wrist and drag his arm upward. His eyes flash to mine, a silent question in their blue depths as he continues to work me over with his mouth. Rather than give him an answer, I smirk and lick his index and middle fingers before dragging them past my lips. He groans around my length as my tongue swirls around the digits, getting them nice and wet for what I have planned.

Once I'm done and release him, I don't even have to tell him what I want to do. He's already reaching his arm behind him, sinking his fingers inside. I can tell the moment they breach past the rim, another sinful moan vibrating around my length, muffled it deep down his throat.

"That's it, Quinn. Work yourself open for me," I demand, my voice a gruff whisper as I piston my hips forward.

I'm caught between wanting to let my head fall back, truly letting the pleasure take over my senses, and keeping watch, all the while memorizing every single detail of this encounter for later. Sear it into my brain so I'll never possibly forget it.

Pleasure wins out in the end.

How can't it when everything he does makes me feel this good?

It doesn't matter that he's making me as rash and reckless as he's known for being. But fuck, if it doesn't make me feel more alive than I've ever felt before. And if we're gonna be reckless? If we're going to fuck around in public, we're actually going to *fuck*.

I wasn't kidding when I said I wanted inside him before this was over.

Pulling from his mouth, I yank him to his feet and spin him around to face the stacks. There's only so much time before someone's bound to walk through here, and I want him full of my cum well before that happens.

Spitting in my palm, I mix my saliva with his on my cock before lining up with his hole, pleased to find him already pressing back for more.

"Hold on to the shelf," I command softly, to which he quickly obeys. "And do your best to keep quiet."

Once I know he can steady himself, I press my hips forward just enough to crown him. I had planned to ease him into it, especially without any lube, but he pushes back on my second shallow thrust, and I slide all the way home.

"Oh, my. Fuck, fuck, *fuck*," he groans, both hands digging into the wood hard enough to splinter it.

"Shh," I murmur into his ear, pulling back an inch before sinking back in. "If you can't be quiet, I'm gonna have to stop. Something neither of us want."

I know it's asking a lot of him, the mouthy, vocal fucker he is. But there's a fine line between a little reckless fun and getting arrested for public indecency. The latter is sure to happen if he can't shut up. Though, I can't say I blame him. The pressure around my cock is exquisite, the clenching making it nearly impossible from letting a chain of expletives spill from my own lips.

He remains silent when I give a tentative pump of my hips, so I go for another, each time sliding in until I'm seated all the way inside again. Tension lines his shoulders as he tries to keep quiet while I start moving quicker, my tempo increasing dramatically.

I reach around him, circling his cock with my fist, only to find it leaking with precum and begging for attention. Something like a whimper, or maybe a choked gasp, escapes him the moment I stroke him to the rhythm of my thrusts, and I catch him biting his fist to keep from shouting out.

"Good, Quinn," I murmur hotly against the back of his neck. "Now, just relax. I got you."

He loosens for me then, not just his shoulders, but his entire body. Becoming pliable for me, allowing me to drive us both up the mountain until we reach our peak, ready to jump off into a freefall together. But it's not enough for him to let me take over, and soon he's slamming his hips back into mine with unrelenting force. Impaling himself on my length impossibly deep and thrusting into my hand when I pull free.

Seeking, needing, aching for more of what I'm giving him.

The bookcase he's clutching rattles from his frenzied movements, and I think he's going to topple the thing over before this is all said and done.

Ripping his mouth from his fist, he pants out a soft moan. "Fuck, baby. More. I need more. Please."

I'm giving him everything I fucking have as I pound into him at a frantic pace. With each powerful snap of my hips, he keeps pressing back against me, creating a muffled slap when I bottom out inside him. The little mewling sounds from the back of his throat becoming louder and more frequent.

So needy. So responsive to everything I do.

But also so, *so* recklessly noisy.

"Oh, fuc—"

My free hand leaves where it was planted on his hips, clasping over his mouth to keep him quiet again.

"Every sound you make while I fuck you is so damn hot, but not if they get us caught," I growl, giving his cock a warning squeeze in my fist. "Bite me if you need to, but you have to shut up."

His mouth moves beneath my palm, teeth sinking into the fleshy muscle beneath my thumb as I push forward at a relentless pace. Even with his teeth digging into my skin, damn near hard enough to break the skin, I still catch all the muffled moans behind my hand.

The potent scent of sweat and sex fill the air around us, sending my lust into overdrive. Need turns into desperation as I piston into him, taking from him as much as I'm giving. More and more precum pools on his tip, and I spread down his shaft as I jack him from root to tip. The desire to taste it runs rampant through me, but so does the need to fill him.

Mark and claim him as mine with my cum.

My tongue darts out, licking a bullet of sweat dripping down his neck instead. The taste of salt and Quinn bursts on my tongue, and I nip at his throat for more, causing him to groan some more. The sound vibrates off my palm loud enough, I swear someone has to be hearing us.

But at this point, I don't even care about getting caught. Hell, nothing else matters right now except for me and Quinn and this and us.

His breathing comes in harsh gasps from beneath my palm, quickly turning into a muted cry of pleasure. And I know I must be hitting just the right spot inside him. The spot that makes him see stars for me, and me alone.

And it's enough to make my balls ache and throb for release.

"That's it, Quinn. Get there," I rasp, my voice coming out low and ragged. "Come for me."

Almost on command, he bears down on me, his climax sending me spiraling into my own. Cum spurts from me as I bury myself deep inside him and hold there. His ass might as well be a vise, milking my orgasm with every constricting clench and squeeze it makes around my length.

"Fuck," I mutter, his cum spreading through my fingers and dripping to the floor at his feet. "Fuck, that's it."

His teeth release their hold on my hand, and when I pull it back to look at it, I find a couple spots where he damn near broke skin.

"Sorry," he murmurs, forehead falling against the shelves in front of him. "It was that or shout out for the entire building to hear."

"Don't you fucking dare apologize. That was the hottest thing I've ever done."

"Better than the shower?"

The comparison causes me to pause, because the shower was sure as hell one of the hottest experiences of my life too. Edging at its finest.

But this wins. By a fucking landslide.

"Better than the shower," I confirm.

And I'm now realizing Quinn might've found some sort of hidden thrill-seeker hiding inside me. The possibility of being caught gets me off. Him too, apparently.

But even with a new kink unlocked, it's not true exhibitionism, and I definitely don't *want* to be caught. The orgasm I was chasing made it so I didn't care, but now with the high wearing off, it doesn't sound pleasant in any capacity. No matter how worth it the release was.

So even though I'm ready to collapse into a sweaty, cum soaked mess with him and not move for hours, I pull free from his body and start righting myself. He does too, clearly agreeing we've been risky enough for one day. No need to add any extra minutes to get caught.

Once we're both decent, cocks put away and sweatpants pulled up our hips, I crowd him back against the shelves and kiss him.

Soft and slow, like it's the only thing in the world I want to be doing.

And right now, it is.

When I pull away, once again gasping for air, there's a dopey, euphoric smile on his face. "We're so doing that again."

I chuckle and rest my forehead against his. "Maybe we should make sure we've escaped unnoticed this time before we plan another round?"

"You're probably right." He lets out a soft sigh, adding, "And why limit ourselves to just the library? We've already christened the locker room. There's plenty of other academic buildings for us to fornicate in."

I lean away to look at his face. "Did you seriously just say *fornicate*?"

A small smirk lifts the corner of his lips. "What can I say? Maybe you fucked me so hard into these shelves, some of the knowledge on them got inside me too."

"Wow," I murmur, shaking my head. "Unbelievable."

He laughs, leaning in to kiss me again, but I shove my hand in his face and push him away.

"I literally think I hate you sometimes."

Rather than allowing me to deny him, he grabs the back of my neck and hauls me in and takes what he wants. He kisses me hard, the kind that curls my toes, before whispering against my lips.

"I wouldn't have it any other way."

TWENTY-SIX

Oakley

Quinton and I are lounging across the couch in his living room, some sitcom on the television screen, on one of the first nights we've snagged together all week.

Our schedules are both hectic this semester, not even lining up enough to grab lunch or dinner together like we did last term. Besides practice, I haven't even seen him. We've been too busy to do much besides send a few flirty check-in texts, thanks to classes now being in full swing.

And if our little rendezvous in the library taught me anything, it's that even studying together might not be the safest option if we want to actually *study*.

But we took a break from cramming tonight, and I have to admit, I'm glad. Happy to exist in this little pocket of space with him where we can relax and just…be.

He laughs at something one of the characters says on the screen, the decadent sound going straight to the organ in my chest as his fingers trail up and down the exposed skin on my arm.

Lately, he's always touching me. Not sexually, but just seeking contact.

His thigh pressed against mine when we'd sit together on the bus to away games, or brushing against me in the locker room as we're coming and going.

Some piece of his body connected to mine whenever possible.

Touches I much prefer over the kind we used to have. Harsh bumps and angry shoves whenever the words we'd toss weren't enough. And then there's the time I decked him, which neither of us are soon to forget. Even if it was four years ago now.

The memory sweeping into my mind takes over, and I realize, while we might've hashed out some details from the altercation, I still don't entirely understand how it started.

"Can I ask you something?"

His hand pauses its dance over my skin as he looks at me, a crease lining his forehead from my tone of voice. "Okay."

"How much of that night—the one back in high school—do you remember?" I pause, choosing my words carefully. "Some of the shit you were saying…it sounded delusional. About my dad paying off the refs so we would win?"

He lets out a heavy sigh, sinking back into the leather cushions. "I know it probably seemed like I was having some sort of psychotic break right in front of you—"

"Understatement of the century." I smile and reach up to his face, my thumb smoothing out the frown lines. "But continue."

Teeth scrape over his bottom lip. "You have to understand…I come from a world where people lie and cheat and backstab for sport. They control everyone and everything around them, always have. Me included. And if I don't comply, then he threatens to cut me off."

"That's…"

I don't have words for what that is.

"Yep. And he let the hammer fall with that fucking ultimatum at Christmas." He drags in a deep breath through his nose before letting out a long, slow exhale. Something I've realized is a method of keeping calm. "So I have to go home every week for Monday night dinners under their premise of looking like decent parents when it's really an excuse for my father to grill me some more about giving up hockey, *or else*, and my mother to set me up with another high-society girl I can't stand. All so I can be a little carbon copy of him in another fifteen years."

My nose wrinkles, appalled by what he's saying. "Seriously?"

He lets out a long sigh and glances over at me. "I wish I was kidding."

I blow out a long breath and sink back into the couch, the gravity of his situation sinking in. I just can't believe he waited until now to tell me about his dad's threats.

I hate that he's been carrying the weight of it himself for almost two months now.

"What a bunch of bullshit."

His expression is thoughtful for a moment, a small little crease between his brows. "Look, I know I've told you a lot of awful shit about my parents, but I don't want what I say about them to shape your opinion of them. They're my parents at the end of the day, and…"

I get what he's trying to say, I do. But the things he's told me paired with the crap I overheard his father spewing at him after our game earlier this season, my opinions are already made. I don't need to afford them a chance to change my mind.

Because unlike Quinton's case, some books really can be judged by the cover.

"They're trying to mold you into something you're not. And to say he'll cut you off if you go against his wishes, it's…disgusting."

He shrugs, doing his best to act indifferent. "It is what it is though. Can't exactly change it."

No, he can't change who his parents are any more than I can. But wanting to change who people are at their core is different than wishing you had a different last name than them.

"That's not what my world is like." I shake my head, hatred for two people I've never met threatening to bubble to the surface. "I can see why you might think it, coming from how you grew up. But no matter how successful my father and Coach might've been in the NHL, my family… we're not those things. Cheating and stealing isn't who we are. Neither is forcing you to be someone you're not."

"I know that now." His eyes soften around the edges.

"Good, because I'd hate to have to deck you all over again."

Those little divots form deeper in his cheeks. "Duly noted."

He continues mindlessly coasting his fingers along my skin, attention drawn back to the television screen like he didn't just break a tiny piece of my heart all over again. The same way he did the day on the Ferris wheel, telling me the closest thing he's ever had to a parent his entire life is his fucking au pair.

That's not how it should be.

I want him to know what a real family is like. He deserves it.

He deserves a lot of things. Far more than he's been given.

"Quinn?"

His attention shifts again, and when he smiles at me, my stomach does a little cartwheel. "Yeah?"

"I don't wanna freak you out or anything…" I start, not completely certain if I should act on this impulse without running it by my family first. But the feeling in my chest outweighs the warning in my brain, and I push forward anyway. "I have dinner with my parents and brother tomorrow night, and I was wondering if you wanted to go?"

It's impossible to miss the way his spine stiffens.

"You want me to meet your parents? Your brother?"

He says it like it's the craziest thing he's ever heard. And then I realize the offer sounds a lot like something a boyfriend would do, not just a… whatever we are.

"Yeah," I say slowly. "Not in that way, or anything. It's just dinner."

The look on his face is still one of utter disbelief, now mixing with a hint of uncertainty. His eyes shift between mine, and I can tell he's trying to work through what brought this on. Why I'd throw yet another wrench into things, once again blurring the lines and the rules when they were working perfectly fine before.

And from the crease still etched in his forehead, he's not finding any answers.

A knot forms in my throat, and I wet my lips before looking away, suddenly feeling way too transparent for my liking. "It's probably a bad idea, right?"

"No, it's…" His words trail off.

"Just forget I said anything. Seriously."

He shakes his head. "Oak, no. I wanna go, I do. I'm just a little confused about how this'll work."

And now I'm the one who's confused. "What do you mean?"

"Your parents aren't blind like mine. They've seen us fight and bicker and come to blows for years. And you expect them to just sit down and have dinner with me?"

Understanding dawns on me, and while his worries are valid, there's one important thing he's seemed to forget.

"We're not those people anymore, Quinn."

"I know that, but do they?" He pauses, a sharp laugh coming from him. "And what, you'd be bringing me as…your superstitious fuck buddy? I'm sure your parents would love that."

I know he filled the end of his sentence with the most ridiculous option for a reason. So I'd correct him, letting me fill in the blank so he'd know exactly where I stand.

The problem is, I don't know where that is.

Or maybe the real issue is I do, but screwing with the status quo is the last thing we should do. Not now, when things between us are in a good place.

Maybe this is a bad idea after all.

But I don't listen to the thoughts worming their way into my head, and keep pushing forward.

"I can introduce you as whatever you want. My rival. My teammate. My friend." Blue eyes flash up to meet my gaze and he rolls his lip between his teeth. It's the most vulnerable I've ever seen him, but I refuse to let it deter me. "Just Quinn could work too."

He's silent, mulling the options over in his head. But when thirty seconds pass and he still hasn't said anything, a rush of anxiety courses through me.

"It's your family," he finally says. "It should be whatever you're comfortable with."

Again, leaving it open-ended, allowing me to fill the gaps. Keeping the control of this whole relationship squarely in my hands.

In the exact place—I'm starting to realize—I don't want it.

TWENTY-SEVEN

Quinton

"**W**hat are you doing?"

I glance from the mirror I was using to knot my tie over to where Oakley is standing in my doorway dressed in…jeans.

Well, God fucking damnit.

"Changing, clearly," I mutter, stripping the tie from around my neck and grabbing a pair of jeans and a thermal from my closet. The only thing worse than being underdressed for an occasion is being *over*dressed.

"Dress clothes just to go to dinner?" Oakley muses, stepping into my room and closing the door behind him.

"Did you forget the world I come from?" I arch a brow at him over my shoulder as I unbutton my shirt and return it to its hanger. "A suit and tie for dinner was my life growing up."

His nose wrinkles up in the way I love. "Sounds fucking terrible."

It wasn't so bad. Not the clothes part, anyway. Sometimes it's nice to dress to the nines. It was the company I could've done without.

"How'd you get in here anyway?" I ask, changing the subject as I strip back to my boxer briefs. I can feel Oakley's penetrating stare on every inch of visible skin, causing goosebumps to break out across my entire body.

"Hayes," is all he says, and when I look up, I find him crossing the room and taking a seat on my bed. There's a pensive look on his face before he adds, "He didn't look very surprised to see me, actually."

This right here is a moment I've been dreading—and it has nothing to do with the anxiety of meeting his family for dinner.

"Probably because…he knows."

Oakley's reaction isn't what I expected. I was almost certain he'd be pissed and call the whole thing off. Which is exactly the last thing in the world I want, hence my delay in telling him.

But he's not pissed. In fact, he smiles a little and shakes his head. "He figured it out, didn't he?"

I nod, slipping into a pair of dark wash jeans. "I never mentioned anything to him obviously, but he's seen you here a lot lately. I guess he put two and two together somehow. Said if we're going to keep fucking like wild animals at all hours of the night, we need to take the party to your place sometimes."

I leave out the part where Hayes *definitely* caught us kissing a few weeks ago, which was confirmed when he mentioned knowing about Oakley and I sleeping together. And the only reason he hadn't said anything was because he wanted me to say something about it to him first.

But then we kept him from getting decent sleep one too many times, and he couldn't keep quiet any longer.

A sharp, disbelieving laugh comes from Oak. "Damn."

I shove my arms in a new shirt and yank it over my head. "You don't care if he knows?"

If I'm being honest with myself, I'm glad *someone* knows. Makes it a little more real. But I know how Oakley feels about this being kept private, just between us.

Which is why the shake of his head catches me by surprise.

"We were kidding ourselves by thinking absolutely no one would find out. And if you trust him to keep it to himself, then it's fine by me." He pauses, fucking with the snapback resting backward on his head. "It's better than all my roommates finding out, you know?"

Yeah, I'm sure Braxton in particular would be thrilled to know his bestie is boning me seven ways to Sunday.

My fingers twitch as I fix my hair in the mirror again, a slight irritation rushing through me. Of course I'd have to change what I was wearing and ruin it when I'd just gotten it to lay just how I like it.

Come on.

"Are you nervous?" Oakley asks, pulling my focus to him instead.

He must be noting my actions as a nervous tick. And he'd be right. Because, yeah, I'm nervous. Really fucking nervous, and not just because Oakley's dad was an all-star forward in the NHL for years. It's because they're his family, and I'm realizing their first impression means a lot to me. A lot more than it probably should, all things considered.

My lack of answer must give me away if the way Oakley's gaze softens is any indication.

Rising from his place on the bed, he closes the distance between us. His hand smooths the errant strand of hair I was fucking with before moving to cup the back of my neck. "It's just dinner, Quinn. Don't worry."

I swallow and plaster on a smile. "I'm not nervous."

His brows furrow, and he releases the hold he had on the back of my neck. "Cut the shit right now."

"What are you talking about?"

"This," he says, lifting his hand and brushing his thumb over my lips. "The fake, plastic smile you use when you're pissed or uncomfortable or lying."

My mouth drops slightly, floored he's picked up on something…I didn't even realize I did.

His lips form a tight line and he pulls his phone from his back pocket. "We're gonna cancel and order in pizza instead."

Pizza and the night with Oakley in my room sounds fucking heavenly, actually, but cancelling last minute on people rarely leaves a good first impression. The very thing I desperately want.

"Absolutely not." I grab his phone before he can finish whatever text he was typing, pocketing it in my jeans. "We're going tonight, come hell or high water."

Oakley's lips quirk in an amused smirk. "Okay, well then you need to just relax. They're just people; my dad included."

"You say that, but…"

"But nothing, Quinn. They're gonna love you." He wraps his fingers around my wrist and tugs me into him before placing a kiss on my temple. "Now, c'mon. We're already running late."

My jaw locks with another round of nerves.

Fantastic.

Dinner isn't at a restaurant like I thought it would be. It's at his parent's house.

Oakley's *childhood home,* which happens to be the exact opposite of mine. It's a nice, large home out in the suburbs, about forty-five minutes from campus. It's basically the American dream home, complete with a two-car garage, big backyard for barbecues, and a covered front porch with rocking chairs on it.

Fucking *rocking chairs.*

They've got the two kids, and when I pointed out the only thing they were missing was a dog, Oakley corrected me, saying they had a dog at one point, but it turned out his brother is severely allergic, so they couldn't keep it.

"Oh no, an imperfection in your perfect little life," I mutter, rolling my eyes. Which only made Oakley laugh more.

And to make matters more domesticated, some fancy caterer or a housekeeper didn't make dinner for the five of us. Oakley's mom did it herself.

"I feel like I've been shot into an alternate reality," I murmur to Oakley as we sit down at the kitchen table beside one another. My gaze connects with his. "Am I in *The Matrix* right now or something?"

His lips twitch in a smile. "You're ridiculous."

It's on the tip of my tongue to say *but I'm yours,* except...I'm not actually his. Not really, anyway. Not in the way this whole coming home for dinner and meeting the parents thing makes it seem.

Or the way he places his hand on my thigh beneath the table makes it feel.

Which he promptly removes the second his parents enter the dining room.

Having never been the type of guy to go home and meet anyone's family—save for Hayes's, because he's my best friend—I expect this entire thing to go poorly. *Very* poorly. To the point where I assume I'll never be able to speak to Oakley again afterward.

Which is why I'm pleasantly surprised the three of them make me feel like I've belonged at this table my whole life.

Oakley's mom, Janet, asks me about school and where I grew up, and the weirdest part is, the questions don't seem hollow. Like the small talk you're supposed to make with dinner guests, knowing full well you won't remember a thing they said once they leave. She genuinely wants to know more about who I am, where I came from, and where I hope to go next. Things…I don't even think my own mother knows about me.

Even Logan engages in some of the conversation, chatting with me about anime, my motorcycle, and some other things us black sheep have in common. And Oakley's right, we get along pretty well.

And then there's Oakley's dad.

He's got the same penetrating stare both Oakley and Coach have, but with him, it's almost magnified. Like he can see right through my skull, finding each and every mistake or terrible thought I've ever had, only to flip through them like a goddamn magazine.

It's unnerving.

Which is why my stomach rolls when Janet leaves for the kitchen to put away the leftovers, leaving the four of us at the kitchen table to chat about hockey. And seeing as it's Logan's least favorite topic, he goes silent and pulls out his phone, leaving Oakley, his father, and I to talk about the one thing in the world he can't stand.

"The two of you are working together well on the ice this season. Considering the history you two carry, I was surprised when Travis mentioned putting you together on one line."

Wow, it's weird hearing someone call Coach by his real name.

"Yeah, we were pretty skeptical about it too," I say, glancing over at Oakley.

He gives me a small, private smirk. "Understatement of the year."

Trevor lets out a laugh. "That coach of yours must see something the rest of us didn't, because it's probably the best thing he could've done for the team. I mean, the two of you are unstoppable as a pair."

"I have to agree," I tell him, nodding. "I don't think we would've made it this far if it weren't for Oakley and I learning to, uh…work through our issues and get along. Both on and off the ice."

Oakley's hand squeezes my thigh beneath the table, making the little tilt of my lips grow into a grin that's impossible to hide.

"So I've realized," his dad says, eyes floating between us. "Not saying you're a bad kid by any means, I just never thought I'd see the two of you being civil, let alone Oakley bringing you home for dinner randomly."

"Believe me, sir, it's the last thing I thought would happen too."

"Guess Oakley finally listened to me, deciding to chase after another player at his level to help make him better."

My brows furrow, "I'm not sure I'm following. Oakley's level is so far above mine—"

"There's no need to be modest here, Quinton. Your stats this season are fantastic. Neck and neck with Oakley's, actually. Sure, your minutes in the penalty box could be lower," he says, giving me a knowing grin, "but overall, you're a tight, solid player. Any team in the league would be lucky to add you to their roster next year."

I gape at him, because…this is coming from a ten-time all-star who played in the NHL for *twelve years*. And he's sitting here telling me I have what it takes to wind up in the league too.

Granted, I've heard the same thing from Oakley and Coach too, along with plenty of other highly respected people in the community. But this is fucking Trevor Reed we're talking about.

"I, uh…thank you," I tell him, not sure what else to say.

"Don't thank me, you're the one who did all the hard work. It's difficult to hold onto an average of just under two points per game, but somehow, you are. Then there's the number of goals you've scored in general, not to mention the number of assists you've given both Oakley and Rossi this season…" He pauses, shaking his head. "Numbers don't lie, and if you continue putting these up for the rest of the season, you've got a great shot of going high in the draft this year. If you're planning to enter, of course."

I clear my throat and nod. "I do, yeah. So any tips would be… appreciated."

He leans back in his chair. "Do you have an agent lined up?"

"I don't," I say slowly, and I immediately know it's the wrong answer. Coach had mentioned something recently about a few agents being interested in speaking to me, but nothing ever came of it. And from the way Trevor is looking at me, it might be time to take the future into my own hands instead of waiting for it to come to me.

Especially if entering the draft cuts the cord between me and my parents for good.

"Well, it's still very impressive, I've got to say." His focus shifts from me to Oakley and back again. "I can see why Oakley thinks you'd be a good—"

A loud bang comes from beneath the table, the wooden surface shaking with impact, and Logan turns to glare at his brother.

"That was *me* you just kicked, jackass," he snarls.

"Logan," their mother warns from the kitchen.

"Sorry, Loge," Oakley murmurs absently. Only he's not looking at his brother when he says it. Instead, he's in a stare down with his father at the other end of the table.

My eyes ping-pong between the two of them, doing my best to decipher what the hell is being spoken silently in their stares. I think I catch a subtle shake of the head on Oakley's part before he breaks eye contact with his father, looking at me instead.

"We should probably get going soon," he murmurs before glancing out the bay window of the dining room. "It looks like it's started snowing, so I'd like to get back to campus before the roads are shit."

"Language, Oakley," his mother chides, poking her head in from the other room.

He winces beside me at her glare. "Sorry, Mom."

"You'd better be," she says, popping back in the kitchen. She returns a few moments later with two Tupperware containers of leftovers, handing one to each of us. "These are for the two of you. Pop them in the microwave for a couple minutes and it'll be ready to go." She pauses and looks at me, a hint of a sparkle in her brown eyes that reminds me an awful lot of Oakley's. "I personally think it tastes even better reheated."

"Thanks, Mom," Oakley says before pulling her into a hug.

She wraps her arms around his shoulders and squeezes. "Of course, sweetie. We'll see you after the game this weekend."

"Yeah, sounds good."

The sight of their embrace forms a knot in my throat, and suddenly, I feel like an interloper on a private moment between them. But the feeling doesn't last long, because when Oakley's mom is done with him, she turns and hauls me in for an embrace of my own.

One making me feel more at home than I've ever felt before.

After she releases me, I give Oakley's father a handshake goodbye and wave to Logan, the normal Midwestern pleasantries exchanged before we leave. Meanwhile, Oakley pulls his dad in for a quick hug before going over to his brother and bopping him on the head like he's Little Bunny Foo Foo.

The entire thing is so foreign—the whole night has been, actually. But it's also something I could see myself getting used to very easily.

"That was…" I trail off, shaking my head in awe as we walk down the snow-covered sidewalk to where Oakley's car is parked on the road.

I don't have words to describe it. I just know I want more of it.

Of feeling like I belong somewhere.

"Was it okay?" he asks, rubbing the back of his neck. "I'm sorry for Dad putting you on the spot like that, but I promise he meant well and—"

I cut him off with a bruising kiss, because there's nothing else to say here. Nothing else to think or do other than kiss him more. Pin him against the door of his car and kiss him harder. Deeper. With as much passion and gratitude as humanly possible.

Leave him breathless, the same way he does me.

Constantly, and at every turn.

TWENTY-EIGHT

Oakley

Two firm hands grip my waist as I attempt to unlock the front door to the townhouse, causing all the nerves in my body to stand at attention. Including the ones in charge of my dick, because paired with the way I can feel Quinn's pressed against my ass, I'm sporting a full-fledged erection.

I have been all night, seeing as this guy is the biggest cock-tease I've ever met.

Ever since practice ended, I've been anticipating getting him home, naked, and under me more than I'm dying to hold that Frozen Four trophy at the end of the season. But he threw a massive wrench in my plans by asking to grab a late dinner instead of letting me have *him* as the main course. But sustenance is a good thing, and when he mentioned a hole-in-the-wall Mexican place I'd heard has the absolute best el pastor in the

Chicago metro area, I was sold.

Too bad I could barely enjoy my meal with him right there in front of me, close enough to smell his musky body wash, but too far away to touch him. All I could do was stare at him across the table. Which he felt necessary to mention. More than once.

Not being one to take his shit lying down, the second we paid and were in my car, I practically hauled him into my lap for a make-out and dry-humping session. It only lasted about twenty minutes before I couldn't take it anymore and had to drive us home, otherwise I ran the risk of fucking him in the backseat of my car.

Which is why we're at my place rather than his like normal. Cutting ten minutes off the drive means getting inside him ten minutes sooner.

He's dismantled ninety-five percent of my self-control. And I'm ready to devour him because of it.

If only I could get the fucking door open.

"Jesus fuck," I curse under my breath as I fumble some more with the lock and key. "You're making this far harder than it should be."

"Mmm," he hums seductively as his tongue flicks out over the junction of my jaw and throat. "But isn't that the entire point?"

To drive his reasonings home, he reaches around to cup my already aching cock through my jeans. I've been rock hard since we left dinner thanks to his teasing, and the pressure in my balls is becoming a matter of life and death.

Not kidding, if I don't come in the next twenty minutes, I might actually die.

Thankfully, I'm finally able to slide the key into the lock and gently push the door open, finding a quiet darkness in the living room of the house. As it should be, seeing as it's almost one in the morning on a weeknight.

The only one of my roommates that would even think about being awake at this hour is Theo, but thankfully he's two floors apart from my room.

Quinn continues to rub my length through the denim, and I let out a low groan before turning into him. One hand wraps around the back of his neck, and I spin him before planting the other firmly against the doorframe. I back him into the wood slowly, my body pressed the entire length of his, and he drops his duffle to the porch step.

"You're trying to kill me," I murmur, more a statement than a question. Because there's no way I can stand much more of the tormenting he's unleashing.

"Believe me," he whispers back, "that's not the intended goal."

He grabs my chin with his hand, pulling me in for a searing kiss, his tongue flicking against mine as it parts my lips. My heart does this weird thing in my chest as he tilts my jaw, fingers skittering along the skin there. A sort of pulsing squeeze, like a fist is wrapped around it as it struggles to find a steady beat.

The sensation has happened more than once now, the first few times after break. But the damn slab of muscle has been doing it a lot more lately, especially since introducing him to my parents, which was almost two weeks ago now.

I'm not sure how I feel about it, or why the fuck it's happening in the first place. Though I'm sure it has something to do with how easily he's wormed his way into my everyday existence.

Not just in the obvious ways, like with hockey.

I mean the way he's the first person I look for a text from in the morning, or how much my anticipation grows as I set foot into the arena, knowing I'm about to see him for the next hour or two.

He's become the high I'm constantly looking to chase, and with that, he's integrated himself into my life almost seamlessly.

But as flawless as he might fit into my life, we still haven't done one thing.

Not a goddamn soul on this planet—besides Hayes—knows about us hooking up. But as I stand here at my front door aching for him in every way possible, I also don't think there's any reason to keep it silent anymore. I'm sick of hiding this and sneaking around. It's gotten stale, and more importantly, feels pointless since we've foregone every other rule set out since the beginning. Keeping it on the DL is the only rule that's actually stuck this entire time.

And I think it's time for it to go too...though maybe it can wait until morning when the guys aren't all dead asleep. The last thing they'll want to wake up to is me mauling the guy who's supposed to be my enemy as we fumble our way to my bedroom.

"You gonna invite me in?" He laughs softly against my neck. "Or are you planning to let me freeze out here all night after mauling me on the doorstep?"

"Now there's a thought," I utter before grabbing his bag from where he dropped it. "But no, I have other plans for you that don't involve inducing hypothermia."

A sinful expression appears on his face, teeth scraping over his bottom lip as he takes his bag from me. "Then lead the way."

I do just that, taking his hand and dragging him through the front door until we're both enveloped in darkness. The door clicks shut silently behind us, and I release my hold on him to lock up for the night. All's going well, and just as I think we're in the clear from waking anyone, Quinn knocks a set of keys off the entry table with his duffle.

"Shh!" I whisper-shout. "It's like you want us to get caught."

A disembodied *sorry* is whispered through the darkness, and I follow the sound until the faint form of his silhouette appears before me.

Quickly flipping on my phone's flashlight, I grab Quinn's hand again and haul him toward the stairs. "Follow me. And try not to knock anything else over."

"I don't know why you didn't just put the flashlight on in the first place."

"Because I know this house like the back of my hand, and I don't need it," I tell him as we reach my door. Quickly, I push it open to avoid the loud creak it sometimes makes, and shove him through into the safety of my room.

I cross the space in darkness to the bedside table, my hand slipping beneath the lamp shade there and flicking the bulb to life. It casts a soft glow over my bedroom, illuminating Quinn as he drops his bag to the floor beside my desk.

A smile inches its way on my face as he digs through the duffle, not stopping until his puck is in hand. He meets my smile with one of his own when he catches me watching him, his more shy in nature.

It's probably the most innocent I've ever seen him.

He takes a moment to slip the puck beneath a pillow, and when he's done, I grab his waist and drag him to me.

"One superstition down," I murmur, my lips trailing down the column of his throat.

"Two more to go."

Quinn's dimpled smile flashes at me in the dim light before sealing my mouth to his in a toe-curling kiss. The kind that does all sorts of stupid things to my heart. Like ache and yearn for things it has no business wanting.

Mouth glued to mine, he backs me toward the bed, only breaking the kiss to slip my shirt over my head. He takes his time stripping every article of clothing from my body and tracing the newly exposed skin with the pads of his fingers.

The feather-light touch has my every nerve-ending on fire, burning for him.

When the backs of my knees hit the edge of the bed, he pushes me down. I fall onto the mattress alone with him still standing over me, still completely clothed.

"Well, this isn't exactly fair," I say, adjusting to the center of the bed.

A wicked grin takes over his face as he slowly peels off the hoodie he's wearing, revealing a tight six pack and miles of artwork inked into his skin. "Since when does fair have anything to do with it?"

His pants go next, his underwear quick to follow, and then he's bare. The sight of him—hard and waiting for me—is something that's ingrained into the very recesses of my brain by now. But it doesn't stop him from stealing my breath regardless.

One hand wraps around his shaft, and he takes long, slow pulls while he stares down at me, sprawled and at his mercy.

"Okay, this really isn't fair," I complain, my eyes latching onto where his palm is stroking that gorgeous cock. One I'd like to get my hands or mouth on before this is all over.

A flash of his tongue appears as he wets his bottom lip, and he continues to jack himself in leisurely strokes.

"Oh, baby," he murmurs, sex and desire dripping from his voice as he layers his body over mine. "You know all's fair in hate and hockey."

There's no denying the truth in his statement, but there's one thing I disagree with.

I don't hate him. And with the way things have shifted between us—so quickly and easily—I'm wondering if I actually did in the first place.

Nothing about him screams *enemy*.

Not anymore.

His mouth lands on mine again as he grinds his pelvis down. Our cocks rub and bump against each other, all smooth skin and blissful friction as he kisses and licks his way across my jaw and down my throat to my chest.

"Aren't you the least bit concerned about them hearing us?" His lips trail down some more, from my pecs to my abs, on a clear path to my cock. "I mean, assuming that's the reason we never come here."

"I figured Hayes could use a break from all your incoherent babbling while I fuck you," I say with a laugh, my abs bunching under his tongue as he traces the indents.

"And all of them hearing it is so much better?"

"They can press their ears to the door and listen in for all I care; it's nothing I don't hear through their walls too."

"The things I didn't need to know," he bemuses, and when I look down, I find his nose wrinkled in disgust. "I guess it's another reason I should be grateful Hayes doesn't usually have guests."

"You really wanna keep talking about our roommates' sex lives right now?" I counter, my hand anchoring in the back of his hair. "Because I'd much rather you be an active, *vocal* participant in ours."

A devilish grin breaks out over his face and he goes back to the task at hand: driving me absolutely mad with that sinful mouth of his.

He continues his path down my body, biting and licking and kissing a path to my cock, only to take a detour around it until he's trailing them down my inner thigh. I'm arching off the bed, desperate and needy for his mouth, his hand, fucking something. Anything would be better than this torture he's putting me through right now.

But he doesn't budge.

Which is why he hasn't even had the chance to wrap his lips around my cock before I've had enough of his games.

"We're not doing this anymore," I growl, gripping his shoulders and shoving him off me. He's stomach down on the bed when I flip around and slide between his legs behind him. My hand presses down on his spine, keeping his ass up as I tease my finger down his crease.

"Someone's getting impatient," he teases, but there's nothing funny about the torture he's going to receive as payback.

He's one to talk with the way he's arching into my touch when the pad of my finger swirls around his rim.

"You really don't wanna play games with me right now, babe," I murmur, leaning down to press a kiss to one cheek, then the other. "That's one thing I can promise you."

He lets out a sharp laugh that quickly turns into a gasp when I surprise him by burying my face between his cheeks, lapping at the sensitive bud. My tongue spears through the rim without preamble, and his body bucks off the bed, a guttural groan ripping from his throat. It spurs me on more, knowing he's enjoying what I'm doing.

My left hand grips his hip, holding him in place as I continue my torment. Slipping the right between his thighs, I take his cock and give him long, slow jacks as I nip and bite at his ass.

Harsh, ragged breaths leave him as my tongue prods his rim before backing off again, never giving him quite enough for his liking while I devour him.

"FuckingholyJesusGod," he moans, ass pressing back against my face.

"I told you that you didn't want to play games with me right now," I growl, my teeth sinking into one cheek before my palm cracks against the smooth skin. He jolts again, and I feel the telltale pulse of his cock in my fist.

He's loving this.

My mouth covers him again, licking at his puckered rim until saliva slides down his crack and drips onto the bed. His hips rut forward, seeking the friction my hand provides before pressing back against my tongue some more.

"Oh, God. Just like that, baby," he pants, taking me from both ends.

I love when he isn't shy about taking what he needs from me to feel good. I love a lot of things about Quinn, actually, but it's gotta be one of my favorites.

My train of thought causes me to falter for a split second, my movements stuttering before returning to normal again.

A throbbing ache weighs down my balls, and I realize this is turning me on just as much as it is him. I'm all kinds of keyed up, and the need to be inside him is dire.

Ripping my body away from him, I grab for the lube in my bedside table and quickly coat my cock with it. He watches me over his shoulder, ass still in the air and a sinful, lusty look in his eyes, only making me want him more.

With absolutely zero finesse, I line myself up with his hole, slipping through the rim with ease, and tunnel home until I'm bottomed out inside him.

A soft groan comes from Quinn at the same moment I let out a sigh of relief.

As great as sex is with him, all hot and explosive, one of my favorite parts is the first time I enter him completely. The sighs that come from him, the way his ass grips and clenches around me as he adjusts to my size. There's nothing like it.

Sometimes, I almost want to be on the receiving end of it.

And there it is again, another thought causing my movements to stumble, only this time, I power through, thrusting into him like it's the last thing I might ever do.

"Yes, yes, yes," Quinton chants as I pound into him, my pelvis colliding with his ass as I impale him with my cock. The slap of our bodies meeting merged with his moans and my pants create the perfect, filthy mixtape that I want to play on a loop in my head.

I can tell he's almost there, ready to explode, with the way he bears down on my length when the crown brushes over his prostate. He's this close to shoving me off the edge with him.

"Fuck, babe. Keep squeezing me like that and this won't last much longer."

"I'm counting on it," he says with another groan, fingers digging into the comforter beneath him. "Fill me with your cum, baby. I want every last drop."

Fucking hell.

I love that damn mouth of his almost as much as I love him.

Realization slams into me like a freight train, flipping my entire world on axis. Enough to have me skidding to a stop mid thrust, lodged halfway inside Quinn's quaking body so I can rewind to the last few words that almost zipped through my thoughts unnoticed.

I love him.

Three words, as simple as they might be, complicate everything the second my brain thinks them. Because now that I've made this realization…I can't *un*know it. I can't pretend all the secrets and stolen moments don't mean anything to me anymore.

As problematic as it is, they mean fucking everything.

And instantly, everything snaps into place.

"What are you *doing?*" he practically screeches, eyes flaring with anger from being pulled back right from the edge of release.

But I had to stop us if there's any chance of this going how I want to tonight. Which is something I didn't know I even wanted until right now.

Epiphanies are a funny thing.

"We're stopping," I pant, swiping the bead of sweat rolling down my cheek with the back of my hand.

"I can see that," he says through gritted teeth, baring them a little at me. "The question is why?"

I pull out of him and urge him to flip onto his back beneath me.

He must think I'm wanting to change positions from the lusty grin crossing his face, but when I pull away as he goes to reach for my cock, his brows draw together again.

"What's going on, Oak?"

I take a deep breath and utter a sentence I never thought I'd speak.

"I want you to fuck me."

TWENTY-NINE

Quinton

"W hat?" I ask, not sure if I heard him right. Because I swear to God, Oakley, who might be the most *top* guy I've ever met, just asked me to—

"Fuck me, Quinn."

Yeah, that.

Holy mother of shit.

I gape at him from my place on the bed, unclear how to respond when this has never been on the table for him. It's not something we've ever discussed, and honestly, I've been fine with keeping it the way we have.

But apparently the guy who loves nothing more than following the rules is looking to throw every fucking one of them out tonight, leaving me stunned silent.

He doesn't wait for me to respond, grabbing the lube from the other side of the bed and dousing my cock with it. A soft sigh leaves me as he strokes me from root to tip, getting me impossibly hard before climbing over me and straddling my waist.

And just like that, I'm brought back to reality. Nervous energy floods me, and I grab his jaw, forcing him to meet my gaze.

"Have you ever—"

"Once," is all he says before he reaches behind him with one hand, the other resting on my chest for balance. A brief flicker of pain crosses his face when he must slip a finger or two past his rim. My chest aches at the sight of it. But soon enough, pleasure takes over his features before he abruptly stops to position my cock at his entrance

I can tell from the set of his jaw, he's about to sink down on me without a second thought, but I stop him before he does. My hands latch onto his waist, holding him in a hover over me.

"Shouldn't we talk about this?"

He shakes his head. "No talking, Quinn. I promise, I want this."

Something in his expression is unreadable, but there's one thing I can tell with absolute certainty. He's telling the truth.

This is something he wants. Something he wants *from me*.

And I'll be damned if I can deny him a fucking thing anymore.

"Okay," I whisper, releasing my hold on his hips.

He takes it as permission to proceed, and without another moment to second guess his decision, he drops down onto my cock, impaling himself with half the length on the first go. And he makes no sign of stopping until I'm fully seated inside him.

"Shit," he hisses through clenched teeth. The hand resting on my chest balls into a fist as he pauses all movement, adjusting to my intrusion.

"You good?" I ask, though I'm not sure why. I'm barely holding it together myself down here, the tight sheath of his ass gripping and clamping around my cock making it nearly impossible not to come on the spot.

A sharp exhale leaves him and he nods. Shifting his pelvis, he rises up before sinking back down on me all over again.

"Oh, my fuck," I murmur. "You're gonna kill me by the end of this."

His tongue darts out over his bottom lip, a lusty, potent look in his eyes. "Now you know how it feels every time I'm inside you."

Do I fucking ever. It's like dying and going straight to my own filthy heaven.

He finds a rhythm quickly, every rise and drop of his hips drawing out more pleasure from me until I can't possibly take any more.

"Fuck, baby, look at you. You take my cock so well," I murmur, watching as he impales himself on my length. The sight alone is so erotic, it'll probably live rent-free in my head for the rest of my damn life.

A sensual grin crosses his face when I roll my fist over the head of his cock, and his head drops back like he's staring up at the stars. Except the only ones he's seeing right now are behind his eyelids as I drive up into him at the same time he drops down onto me.

"Do that again," he demands, arching his hips forward to seek more of my touch.

I do as he asks, twisting my wrist around the crown of his cock, lavishing it with attention as he quickens his pace.

"Trying to top from the bottom there, Oak?" I pant, lost in the way he's moving over me. Completely enthralled by him.

Another grin appears on his lips, this one more playful. "Technically that's what you're doing."

Well, we can't have that, can we?

One hand moves to behind his neck, the other latching tighter on his hip before I flip us without warning, all while keeping my dick buried deep inside him. His back hits the mattress below us with a thud, and a low groan rumbles from deep within his chest.

"Good?"

I pull back to search his face for signs of pain, but he offers me a nod of assurance as he grips my bicep for dear life.

"Holy shit, yes. Fucking perfect," he whispers as I roll my hips into him again.

My hips piston into him again, the new position not letting me go as deep, but it must peg his prostate just right from the euphoric expression on his face. All lips parted and hazy-eyed, like he's dick drunk on my cock.

"Good. Then fuck your fist, baby. I'm not gonna last much longer."

His fingers curl around his shaft at my command, stroking his length in time with every thrust. I watch his face as he takes himself higher, edging closer to the promise of release. Soft pants leave him with every pump of my hips, turning into full out gasps when the head of my cock brushes against his prostate some more, lighting him up from the inside out.

It's intoxicating, seeing him like this.

My hand wraps around the top of the headboard as I drive into him, grabbing his waist with the other hand. I anchor him in place as I take everything he has to give, and he doesn't fight me on it. Doesn't protest as I take control from him. And it's crazy to see the guy who loves to have a hold over every situation, with his rules and regulations, hand the reins to me without a second thought.

It's trust and respect, and earning those things from him is a feeling like no other.

"God, I can't wait to feel you clenching around me when you come," I growl, my hips snapping up into his harder as I find my rhythm. "It's gonna be fucking amazing."

It already is amazing. Everything about this moment is utter perfection, and while I'm growing more and more desperate for release, I also never want it to end.

I could stay here, just like this, wrapped up in him forever.

"Oh, fuck. Right there," he utters as I swipe over his prostate again. His teeth sink into his bottom lip as I continue brushing against it, the pace of his fist moving over his cock becoming more hasty and erratic.

He's wrecked beneath me. Ruined in a way I never thought I'd see.

And he's never been more perfect.

The need to kiss him becomes overwhelming, and I close the gap between us, taking his lips in the same way I'm taking his body. Methodically. Thoroughly. Leaving no part untouched.

"Come for me, baby," I coax, my lips a whisper against his. "Come."

Oakley's mouth crashes back into mine at my command, once again fighting for dominance, while still relinquishing his control. A sharp twinge of pain sends a bolt of lust straight to my cock when his teeth sink into my bottom lip until he draws blood.

It's ruthless and carnal, yes.

But it's also us.

My tongue flicks over the wound, the coppery tang flooding my mouth as his own dives past my lips for another taste. He invades my every sense as we grind and thrust and fight and fuck. I might be the one inside him, but he might as well be the one exploring every single inch of me.

"Fuck," he utters on a tortured breath, his head thudding back against the pillow as he reaches the point of no return. Baring his teeth, he strokes faster and harder until cum jets from his cock, covering his hand and stomach. He works himself through the orgasm, his ass constricting around me, sending me into a spiral of my own. Heading into freefall, the tension at the base of my spine builds and builds until it can't possibly anymore.

And then I shatter.

Break.

Completely fall apart as I lose myself inside him.

My orgasm slams into me at full speed, my cock almost bursting at the seams as I fill him with my cum. He clenches around me, drawing out my climax until I'm left a panting, breathless mess above him.

Exhaustion takes hold of me, and I collapse over his body. Too high on my orgasm and him to hold myself up any longer. His release spreads where our torsos connect, mixing with the sheen of sweat coating our bodies.

I kiss him once. Twice. Three times before dropping my forehead to rest against his, our breaths mixing in the sliver of space between our lips as we float back to Earth.

"You've just given me keys to a goddamn kingdom," I whisper against his lips. "You know that, right?"

A husky laugh comes from him. "Don't be getting any ideas."

Oh, but I'm full of ideas now. After that, how can't I be?

But with all these ideas comes errant thoughts. Ones I know I shouldn't be having. Not post-sex, not ever. Not when it comes to the way I feel about Oakley. Because I shouldn't be feeling *anything* for him. Certainly not the emotion currently cycling through my bloodstream like a drug.

Three naughty words sit on the tip of my tongue, begging to be said. Waiting for me to breathe life into them by letting them break free from the solitude of my brain.

But I can't do it.

Falling in love wasn't part of the deal. Hell, *I* was the one who went and told him not to fall in love with *me*, yet here I am doing exactly that. Catching feels in a fuck-buddy relationship, like a goddamn amateur.

And while we might've tossed out rules left and right, I doubt this is something we can overlook. Not for long, or I'll risk shattering my own heart for a few minutes of temporary bliss.

So I keep those naughty, errant thoughts locked up tight and do my best to throw away the key before they ever see the light of day.

I place a soft, lingering kiss to his lips before pulling free. It takes an obscene amount of effort to peel my body off the bed and away from him, but somehow, I manage. He's quick to follow, rising off the bed in search of a towel to clean up.

And I have to admit, the view of my cum leaking from him, dripping down his leg as he wipes off his stomach is...fucking unreal.

"Are you planning to force me into cuddling?" he asks.

When I don't answer right away, he turns, only to find me staring at his ass. It takes a minute for me to remove my gaze from the creamy white liquid marking his skin, giving him my full attention.

"Absolutely," I tell him, slipping back into my underwear like I wasn't caught ogling my handiwork. "There's no way you're getting out of it after that."

He just smirks and rolls his eyes as he continues wiping himself down.

I continue preparing for bed, piling my clothes together and shoving them into my bag before peeling back the covers. The action causes the bottle of lube still sitting on the bed to fly to the floor, and I snag it. The nightstand where he grabbed it from earlier is still partially open, and I'm about to drop it back where it belongs when I notice something inside the drawer.

A pill bottle.

The golden yellow prescription kind, with maybe one or two tablets left inside.

My hand shakes as I lift it from the drawer to read the label.

I find all the usual information on it, Oakley's name, his doctor's name—the team doctor, actually—and the name of the drug.

Vicodin.

Which I happen to know is…an opioid.

THIRTY

Quinton

My stomach rolls as I read over the label on the bottle once, twice, fifty fucking times. And each time I read the word, the gut-wrenching fear shifts more and more into anger. Swirling and rolling until finally, I can't keep quiet anymore.

"What the fuck are these?"

Oakley spins around, brows furrowed in confusion when he sees me holding the bottle of pills. And then, for the briefest moment, his face falls. He rights it quickly, almost fast enough for me to not notice the falter in his expression at all. Hell, if I didn't know him as well as I do now, I probably would've missed it.

But I caught it.

I caught *him*.

"What the fuck *are these?*" I ask again, more forcefully this time. My grip around the bottle causes the plastic cap to dig into my skin painfully, the same way this discovery is embedding a knife in my heart.

Or in this case, my back.

He crosses the room to where I'm standing and grabs the bottle from my grasp. Swallowing, he reads the label before meeting my gaze. "They're from when I broke my collarbone. Remember? In the game against Waylon last season?"

Ignoring his question, I ask one of my own. "Why do you still have them?"

"I guess I just never threw them away."

I guess I just never threw them away.

How fucking convenient.

"Or maybe you're still using them." I murmur, the pieces of the puzzle coming together in my head. "And the day of the drug test, you swapped the samples. Yours for mine, so you'd pass and I wouldn't."

"What are you *talking about?*" he asks, his head tilting to the side. "You didn't even test positive for narcotics. It was steroids."

"No," I growl, my teeth grinding as I grab the bottle from him again. "I just let you think it was because I didn't see the point in arguing with you about something like which drug they popped me for." I hold the bottle up between us, showing him the label. "This drug. Which I didn't fucking use, by the way. I was always clean, always fucking will be."

Oakley's mouth drops open slightly as his brows furrow, and I can see the wheels spinning in his head. "So wait…you tested positive for narcotics instead?"

"Stop acting like you didn't know!" I shout and throw the bottle across the room, where it hits the wall before clattering to the floor. "I saw the look on your face when I found those. You fucking knew. You had to have known."

He stares at me like he's seen a ghost, his head shaking back and forth at a snail's pace. I don't know if it's part of his denial, or maybe he's trying to process what's happening, but either way, it does nothing for me. It gives me no answers.

"Look me in the eye and tell me you didn't know," I demand slowly. "If you're gonna lie, then you can lie to my fucking face."

"Quinn, please—"

"Just answer the question," I snarl, cutting off whatever plea he was about to make. "Did you know? That's the only information I want."

Oakley's eyes sink closed, and there's a faint crack in my chest. Because the look on his face…it's answer enough. To the point where I could just leave and save myself the trouble.

But even if the words aren't necessary to know, I still need to hear them.

From his lying fucking mouth, I need the truth.

"I knew something was up. Braxton was talking all weird, and I asked him straight up if he did something, but all he said was *I was looking out for you* or some shit. I didn't…" He trails off, rubbing the back of his neck as he shakes his head. "I had no idea he *actually* did it."

"But you had suspicions."

"Yeah, but—"

"But *nothing!*" I shout. "What the actual fuck were you thinking, Oakley? How could you not say something if you thought he—"

"Because he's one of my best friends, and I didn't know anything for sure!"

And then it all falls into place. It makes sense. And more than anything, I'm pissed at myself for not seeing it sooner.

Not realizing I was being played for a fucking fool this entire time.

"He's your best friend…and I'm your rival. Your enemy. The only thing standing in your way of being captain. The pain in your ass teammate you can't stand to be around."

I roll my tongue along the inside of my cheek and silently beg my temper to stay under control. Beg for a break in the anger so I can breathe through the pain shattering my entire body from his betrayal.

But that's the thing. It wasn't a betrayal to him.

It was all part of a plan.

"What, was he in on all of it?" I ask, allowing the lies and deceit to sink in deeper. "Is he the reason you changed your mind about this whole fucking thing—you, me, the hook-ups?"

Is he the reason I made the mistake of falling in love with you?

"No, Quinn. I wouldn't ever..." He trails off, shaking his head frantically. "Just no. I kept my word with the rules. No one knows."

"Kept your word," I repeat with a scoff. "Well, I'm glad to know some things are sacred at least. Just not hockey, apparently. Which is hilarious, all things considered."

I bare my teeth at him, the agony ripping me apart from the inside out. It cuts and slices through me, making it nearly impossible to breathe, until I'm left suffocating and bleeding out on the floor at his feet.

"But then again, you wanted to set yourself apart from Coach and your dad, right? Well, congratulations. You did it, Oak," I snarl, ice dripping from my words. "Because neither of them would've ever dreamed of pulling the shit you have. You should be proud of yourself."

The words crack and shatter as they leave my lips right along with my heart while I spew venom and hatred at him, desperately trying to hurt him the same way he's hurt me. Dig blades into his heart, knives into his soul, and watch him bleed like I am.

But the problem about loving the very thing you hate is it destroys you to hurt it in return.

And as my words sink in past his armor, I feel every slash and wound like it's my own skin they're seeping into.

"I can't believe I was actually allowing myself to fa—" I cut the words off when they start to crack with more truths. Ones he doesn't deserve to hear.

Calamity stains my voice until it no longer sounds like my own, and the words rip from my throat with palpable amounts of anguish.

"But that's just it, right? Keep your friends close and your enemies closer."

His eyes sink closed. "I'm sorry, Quinn. Please, just hear me out. I'm so sorry."

That's all he keeps saying. Those two words—*I'm sorry*—like they have any fucking meaning anymore.

My teeth sink into the fleshy inside of my cheek until I taste copper, all the while counting backward from ten.

Then twenty.

Then fifty.

Because as pissed as I am right now, I have no interest in decking him for this. I'd rather him have to live with the repercussions, wishing I'd beat him to a pulp for it instead.

And it works. A cool, calm wave washes over me, if only for the briefest moment. Enough for self-preservation to kick in, forcing my body to move on autopilot. I turn my back to him, grabbing my jeans where they lay on the floor and shoving my legs through them.

"What are you doing?"

"What does it look like?" I bite back at him, finding my socks and shirt next. But it's damn hard when my heart is struggling to beat in my chest, thanks to him shredding it to pieces.

"I don't want you to leave."

A sardonic laugh slips past my lips as I slip into my shoes and socks. "What you want isn't really high on my priority list right now, Oak. Not anymore."

He remains silent, thank God, as he watches me continue to redress, throwing my shirt and hoodie over my head. His eyes burn me, even through the clothes, it takes everything in me not to look at him. Because I know the moment I do, there's a very real possibility my resolve might slip, and I might hear him out.

But I'm not in the mood to listen to any more of his lies.

"You know, I thought the golden boy was supposed to be perfect. Never do anything wrong," I tell him through gritted teeth. "It's about time your true colors show."

"Quinton, please—"

"No. *Fuck* you." I seethe, crossing the room until I'm standing right in front of him. My nose brushes his, and those two lying, deceitful lips are a hair's breadth away. "I trusted you. I handed over pieces of who I am on a silver fucking platter to you, and this is what I have to show for it. A knife in the fucking back and lies piled higher than that fucking Ferris wheel."

The sorrow in his brown eyes should be enough to stop me, but I can't hear anymore. I can't look at him, because all I see when I do is everything I've been missing in my life being snatched away from me with one, thoughtless choice.

I move to push away, to garner the space I so desperately need, when Oakley does the one thing we both know he shouldn't, even when it's the very thing we both crave.

He wraps his palm around the back of my neck and slams his mouth to mine.

His tongue seeks mine, coaxing it to life as he spins us, backing me up until we crash against the closest surface. A desk he lifts me onto before crushing the entire length of his body to mine. As if that's all it will take to keep me here.

Every emotion rippling through my body seeps into this kiss.

Anger, hurt, betrayal.

Hope, love.

Hate.

Each one of them flows from me as his mouth devours mine, once again taking things that don't belong to him. Pleading with me to stop and think and listen to the things his heart speaks to mine.

But it's not enough.

It'll never be enough.

And so I break my mouth from his and shove him away. I'm off the desk, wheeling around it to grab my bag from where I'd tossed it on the floor. Bolting for an escape before he can speak. Or worse, try to stop me once again.

But I failed to consider one thing as I let the door to his room crash open against the wall. Something that's now glaringly obvious as I'm greeted with four sets of wide, but sleepy, eyes on the other side.

We're not alone.

And from the looks on his roommates' faces, they heard more than enough of what just happened behind that door.

"Fucking fantastic," I mutter under my breath before glancing over my shoulder at Oakley. He looks like a deer caught in headlights, eyes darting between me and his roommates on the other side of the threshold.

Part of me almost feels bad for him—that his friends found out this way—but honestly, I'm too fucking pissed off to grant any sympathy right now.

My attention drifts back to the crowd gathered in the hallway, effectively blocking my escape route.

"Show's over, guys. Don't bother sticking around for an encore. There won't be one."

I expect them to move, scatter, do fucking something other than stay perfectly still, just…staring at me. Like some kind of caged animal at a zoo, ready to lunge at anyone who gets too close to the glass.

Doesn't matter.

They want to gawk? Fine.

I'll just plow my way through them.

The same way their roommate did my heart.

THIRTY-ONE

Oakley

"Quinn!" I shout, ready to shove through the guys and run after him. But I don't make it much further than through the door, because Holden presses his palm against my chest to stop me.

"It's better to just let him go," he mutters, sorrow written on his face. "Trust me on this one, Oak."

I push back against his palm, only to have another hand clamp on my shoulder. This one belongs to Camden. He spins me away from Holden and presses me against the wall with a painful grip.

"Look, I know you're used to being the one who always knows best and is always right, but right now, you're not. Going after him is only going to make things way worse." He ducks his head, forcing me to meet his gaze. "You know how he gets when he's pissed. You don't want to be on the receiving end of his fists when we've got a game to play tomorrow."

The game tomorrow is the last thing on my mind. My one and only thought is circling around getting to Quinn as quickly as possible. Maybe figure out how to explain this so it makes sense.

If it's even possible.

"Don't even think about it," Holden says, almost reading my thoughts as he stares at me.

Camden must pick up on it too, because his eyes narrow on my face. "Where are your keys?"

Goddamnit.

"Downstairs table."

Cam glances at Theo, who simply nods and sets off down the stairs to get them without a word, retrieving my keys and probably hiding them somewhere I'll never be able to find them.

Doesn't matter. I could always walk to Quinn's once they're all asleep.

"Are you going to make me camp outside your door all night to make sure you don't make a run for it?" Holden asks, cocking his head. "Because I will. I'm not above it one fucking bit if it means keeping your face nice and pretty and in one piece."

"We could put a bell on his door," Cam adds. "Make it easier to wake us."

Theo chooses that moment to reappear. "Are we planning to put bars on the windows too, or is that reaching extreme limits?"

The four of them get a good laugh out of his joke, but while they might find this entire conversation hilarious, I sure as fuck don't.

"You all fucking suck," I mutter, attempting to free myself from Cam's hold. Except Holden's right there when I fight back, and his hand presses against my other shoulder, keeping me firmly locked in place.

I'm being held there, powerless to the situation I've found myself in, and no idea where to go from here.

And while it scares the shit out of me, it also makes me angry. Irrationally so, and it's this moment when I realize why it's so easy for Quinn to let his snap.

Being backed into a corner, utterly helpless, is the worst feeling in the world.

My glare moves from Holden to Camden, and finally to Braxton. He's the only one not saying anything. In fact, he's not doing anything other than leaning against the opposite wall, arms crossed over his chest, and staring at me.

Like he doesn't even recognize me.

"Fine," I bite, sick of being the star of this Jerry Springer-esque showdown. "You win. I'll stay here. You can all go."

Not wanting to stick around long enough for them to ask any other questions, I shove free from Cam and Holden's grasps and barge my way through them until I'm inside the safe haven of my room. The door slams closed behind me, my back colliding with it, and I sink down until my ass hits the wooden floor. It's cool against my skin, and it's at that moment I realize…I'm still in only my underwear.

Great.

My fingers weave their way through my hair, and I grip the strands hard enough to rip them clean from my head. But the pain lancing through my scalp as I pull and tug has nothing on the fucking agony coursing through my veins, heading straight for my heart.

The gravity of this situation is suffocating, and it's all I can do to breathe through the panic.

I can still hear the murmurings of Cam and Holden's voices from the other side of the door, but it's low enough to where I can't make out the exact conversation. But I'm sure I catch the phrase *sleeping together* more than once, and it's more than enough to get me up from my spot on the floor.

The last thing I want right now is to hear their opinions on me sleeping with Quinn when they don't know a goddamn thing about it.

Crossing the room, I grab a pair of sweats and drag them up my thighs. I'm shoving my arms through the sleeves of my hockey hoodie just as a knock comes from the other side of my door.

A low growl works its way from my throat, and I don't care which of them it is. I'm not fucking doing this right now. "Go away. I'm not in the mood."

The sound of the door swinging open lets me know whoever it is doesn't care, and Braxton comes into view when I'm done pulling the hoodie over my head.

"What?" I snap again, irritation settling low in my stomach.

He steps into my room and slams the door closed behind him.

"Those guys might not have the balls to ask questions right now, but I'm not leaving until you tell me what the fuck is going on."

"You're asking *me* what the fuck is going on?" I hiss, pacing the room. "You're the one who has the explaining to do here. And I'm not doing this bullshit *don't ask, don't tell* crap anymore."

Too bad Braxton doesn't hear me, instead tossing accusations right back in my face.

"What do I need to explain to you?" he asks, incredulous. "You're the one who's been fucking de Haas behind all our backs. And even if the rest of them don't give a shit, I sure do."

Quinn's name from his lips lands a blow straight to my chest, damn near knocking the wind out of me. But I breathe through the pain, my gaze colliding with his.

"What does it matter to you who I'm sleeping with?"

"It matters when you're literally fucking the guy we tried to take out earlier this season." He shakes his head, tossing his arms out to the side. "I'm honestly surprised this didn't blow up in your face sooner."

"That's fucking rich coming from the guy who set this whole mess into motion."

"*Me*? You're the one who gave me the fucking idea in the first place, Oakley! So don't be coming after me just because you can't—"

"It was *my idea*?" I wheel on his, eyes wide and temper blazing. "Please tell me when I've ever said 'hey, let's fuck with someone else's drug test just because we don't like them and see what happens?'"

"No, but you *are* the one who brought up high school and were all 'too bad we can't slip weed or booze in his locker.'"

I blink at him, trying to see how he made the logical leap from that singular comment to…to— "So the next natural thought you had was to *drug him* without him knowing?"

He frowns, confusion etched into his brow. "I didn't drug him."

Slamming my eyes closed, I pinch the bridge of my nose. All these non-answers are starting to give me a headache, and I'm fucking over it.

"If you didn't drug him, then how the fuck do you explain the positive test then?"

"Shhh," he hisses, glaring at me as he crosses the room. "Look, just keep it down, all right? Holden and Theo might be all the way downstairs, but Cam's room is right next door, and the last thing we need is him hearing—"

He's actually worried about that right now?

"Oh, fuck off, Braxton. Just say what you need to say, because this entire fucking situation can't possibly get any worse."

He gives me a dubious look before shaking his head. "Well, it started when Holden—"

"Jesus Christ, you pulled Holden into this too?"

Braxton glares at me, a clear sign to shut the fuck up, before continuing. "Holden found out about the testing from one of his buddies on Blackmore's football team after a bunch of those guys failed theirs. I'd overheard him talking about when Leighton was planning to test us, and I figured…what better way to get de Haas out than that? So since I knew you had some leftover pills, I—"

Oh my God.

I drop my head back and slam my eyes closed.

"Stop."

He cuts his words off mid sentence, then asks, "Do you want this fucking story or not?"

I do. I really fucking do, but as it's unraveling before me, I can't stomach to hear much more. Because I know what he's gonna say. It all makes sense now, all the pieces fitting together.

He knew I had leftover pills from my injury because I rarely used them as it was. So he took them and framed Quinn for using them. Probably banking on a suspension, or worse, since he wouldn't have a medical exception filed with the NCAA.

Goddamnit.

"So how did you manage this if you didn't drug him?"

The next sentence he says damn near knocks me off my feet.

"I just took them."

My eyes snap back open. "What?"

He shrugs in one of those *what can you do* ways. "I wanted to slip them to him directly, but I couldn't figure out a way to without him noticing, so

I just took them. And when the time came, the label with our names was on the lids of the sample cups, so I just…swapped the lids." He shrugs again. "Made the whole thing a lot easier than having to swap the samples the way I thought I'd have to. Playing with piss is—"

"You really don't need to finish that sentence," I tell him, wrinkling my nose in disgust.

Fuck me running.

I can't unknow what happened now. And like Braxton alluded when this whole thing started, I don't *want* to know it in the first place.

Because now…I have to figure out what to do with it.

My fingers rake though my hair before I lock my hands on the back of my head. "This is really fucking bad."

He waves me off. "You really think de Haas is gonna do anything about it this close to the tournament? There's no way."

I blink at him, floored by the sheer audacity he has. "No, Brax. I don't think he will. But I'm sure gonna."

His eyes bug out of his head like in those old cartoons. "Why the fuck would you do that?"

Again, I'm stunned into damn near silence. Staring at him like…he's a complete stranger all of a sudden. "You're really asking that question right now?"

"You're really gonna sell me out when I did this shit for you?"

"I never asked you to!" I shout, tossing my arms out in front of me. "There was no time I ever asked you to do something like this."

"You didn't have to! This is what friends do for each other, Oakley. Or did burying your dick inside de Haas make you forget *we* are friends? You and me, not you and him."

Oh, but he's wrong.

Braxton and I…we're not friends. Maybe we were at one point a few years ago. Hell, maybe even at the beginning of the season when all this shit started. But that ship has long since sailed with everything happening right now.

And then me and Quinn?

My eyes sink closed. A knot forms in my throat as the image of him with that pill bottle in hand comes barreling back into my mind.

During this season, he's gone from the person I despised most in the world to the person I never want to live without. The one who makes me laugh harder than anyone else. The one who brings out my reckless side, because life shouldn't always be so serious.

He's the one I should've protected at all costs.

Not Braxton.

"No," I tell him, shaking my head.

"No?" he repeats, his dark eyes hardening. "Are you really gonna sit here and choose some good dick over me?"

"And that right there proves my point exactly." I scoff, my lips curling back into a snarl. I can barely look at him right now. "You might've thought you were doing me a favor with all this, but all you've actually accomplished is costing me the trust of the person who matters most to me."

Braxton shakes his head before waving me off. "Whatever, man. Give it a couple days and you'll be over it."

Yeah, considering the way I just tried to bolt after the guy in my underwear after letting him fuck the daylights out of me, I sincerely doubt that.

My eyes sink closed again, and I pray to whatever God exists for the strength to not lose my ever-loving shit on him.

"Get the fuck out, Braxton. It's over. We're done here."

"Are you really gonna—"

"OUT!" I snarl, grabbing him by the neck of his shirt and shoving him out the door. I don't think I breathe again until I slam it in his face and lock him on the other side.

Which only makes me realize one of my other roommates really did put a fucking bell on the door as a signal, because I can still hear the faint jingling of metal when I storm back over toward my bed.

Seeing as I'm not going anywhere with that wonderful little thing on my door, I strip back to my underwear and crawl into the bed, praying for sleep to take me quickly and end what might be the worst day of my life.

But instead of sleep granting me reprieve from reality, I only find more torment. Because my sheets still smell like him. Even after only setting foot in this room one time.

A knot forms in my throat, and I shove my arm beneath the pillow, attempting to get comfortable. But the second I make the movement, I brush against a familiar object.

One that makes the knot impossible to breathe around.

His puck.

I don't need to pull it out to confirm; the way my heart lurches, aching and throbbing in my chest with every painful beat it takes, is enough. My hand wraps around the damn thing, squeezing it so hard, the rounded edges actually dig into my palm.

He was so worried about getting the hell out of here, he left it.

His superstition. The piece of his history keeping him out on the ice every day.

All the things he's told me over the passing months come rushing to the forefront of my mind as my fingers coast over the smooth rubber disk. The hidden secrets and truths I would have never uncovered if I didn't change my mind about following through with this superstition. So many parts of himself he willingly handed over without looking back. Entrusted me to hold and safeguard, thinking I'd done the work to earn them.

Deserve them.

And God, how I want to be deserving of them.

But I'm not.

I don't think any amount of wishing and praying is going to change that.

THIRTY-TWO

Oakley

March

Outside of hockey, I've had zero interaction with Quinton in three weeks.

Three fucking weeks. Twenty-one days.

An obscene number of hours, minutes, and seconds ticking by without knowing where he is or what he's thinking.

Even with the team still winning despite our superstition coming to an abrupt halt, he's said nothing. Hasn't made a joke or jab or so much as looked at me in those three weeks.

He didn't even say anything the day after our blow out, when I'd left his lucky puck on the wooden shelf in his stall. I watched him pick it up. Turn it over in his hand when he thought I wasn't looking. I saw the way he swallowed as he squeezed it in his palm before putting it safely in his bag.

The sight tore me apart from the inside out.

Nor did he speak to me after Coach pulled him into his office before the game that same day, giving him back the title of captain, but also letting him know Braxton and I would be reprimanded for our involvement in tampering with his test and resulting suspension.

However, seeing as my role wasn't nearly as significant as Braxton's, I was let off fairly easily. A hearing with some committee put together by the university, which nothing came of. After all, an idea is just an idea until it's put into action, and since I didn't participate in messing with the test, they threw out the case pretty soon after.

Braxton, however, is no longer a member of Leighton University's hockey program. He was suspended at first, but soon after, he was booted altogether. Once that happened, it didn't take long for him to move out, letting the rest of us know he was transferring to another school for next year. Just as well, though. No one—on the team or at home—trusted him after hearing about what he did.

Hell, everyone is just now starting to trust *me* again.

Too bad the only person whose trust I actually want won't even look at me.

If it weren't for practice and games, being able to see his face and hear his voice, I think I'd have gone crazy by now. Even with those few moments, I still feel my sanity slipping. This silence is deafening, echoing through the gaping hole in my chest that only grows every day we don't speak.

Today, it's been unbearable. To the point where I do the one thing I swore I wouldn't do, not only to myself, but to Cam, Holden, and Theo the night everything blew up.

I go to him.

And as I knock on his door, a mixture of anticipation and anxiety rip me to shreds. Gripping and pulling me in opposite directions; between what I know I should do, and what my heart is aching for.

I just need to see him.

Outside of practice.

There, he's expected to be put together and on point with every move he makes. Zeroed in with focus, feelings and emotions flicked to autopilot.

No, I need to see him without the pads and skates he wears like an impenetrable suit of armor.

I need to know he's okay.

Too bad for me, Quinn isn't the one who answers the door a couple seconds later. Hayes does. And from the frown marring his face, he's not happy I'm here.

"Get lost, jackass. He doesn't wanna see you."

"Hayes—" I start, but he's already shut the door halfway on my face.

Shit, shit, shit.

"I don't wanna hear it either, Reed," he says, the door already swinging closed.

My hand darts out, stopping it before all hope I have of talking to Quinn disappears. "Please, Hayes. Let me talk to him. I need to see him, if it's only for a minute. I need to tell him—"

The door is suddenly ripped back open, leaving me off-balance to the point where I almost topple through the doorway and into the person on the other side.

And when I catch my balance enough to look up, I'm surprised to find it's Quinn.

My heart lurches at the sight of him, pounding against my chest with an unbearable ache. One that's been ever-present since the moment he walked out of my room—and life—weeks ago. And the ache grows into an agonizing throb as Quinn's icy blue gaze lands on me, only for me to find his eyes completely vacant.

No ounce of emotion in them at the sight of me.

His attention shifts away, falling on Hayes instead. "Thanks, man, but you don't have to."

"You sure, Q?" Hayes eyes me dubiously before looking back to Quinn. "I don't mind kicking his ass all the way back to his place."

He lets out a soft sigh and nods. "Yeah. It's fine. I'll take care of it."

As happy as I am to get to speak to him privately—which didn't look to be the case a minute ago when Hayes answered—I can't help but cringe internally at his word choice.

It.

Like I'm nothing more than a pile of trash that needs to be taken out, or a piece of gum to be scraped off the bottom of a shoe.

Then again, that's exactly what I feel like, so if the shoe fits, I guess I'll wear it.

Hayes leaves us, shuffling back into the apartment, but not without giving me a death glare first. One I'm willing to admit I deserve.

It's only once Quinton and I are finally left alone for the first time in weeks when he meets my gaze and speaks.

"What are you doing here, Oakley?"

I shake my head, because now that I've finally gotten a moment to speak to him, I'm not sure what to say. Not sure where to start. "I…don't know."

His brow arches, and he crosses his arms over his chest. "You're really gonna keep lying to me?"

Fair point.

I wouldn't blame him for not believing a thing to come out of my mouth ever again, so I might as well go all in with the truth. I've got nothing left to lose.

"I guess I was just worried."

"Why?"

"Because I saw you at practice today."

"You see me at practice every day," he counters.

"Yeah, but today was different. You were on autopilot and—"

He scoffs. "And you're worried it would translate into the games we've got coming up. Well, don't worry your pretty little head on it, Reed. I'll make sure I'm fully present when the time comes so you can win your stupid championship."

The way he calls me by my last name might as well be a knife to the heart, but not nearly as much as the accusation he's tossing at me.

"What? The championship? That's the furthest thing from what I care about right now."

"Then what *do* you care about?"

"You! I fucking care about you, or I wouldn't be here right now just to make sure you're okay."

He steps out into the hall, the door snicking closed behind him. "Tell me something, Oakley. Do I look okay?"

I take a second to look at him. *Really* look at him, and I hate what I see.

I noticed earlier this week he's dropped some weight, having watched him adjust the fit of his pads before practice. Not a lot of weight, but enough to see his chest and shoulders don't fill out his shirt the way they used to.

My gaze travels up, finding a vacant expression etched into his features, starting with his eyes. Ones that used to be full of light and fire, but now just look empty.

Hollow.

And I hate knowing I'm the reason. It cuts me to my core.

Which is why all I can do is shake my head.

"Well then, there you go. You got your answer. Now you can go," he says, tossing his hand toward the elevator.

Defeat slams into me like a tidal wave, and it's then I realize I might never get through to him. Might never have the chance to explain what he means to me, how much I care.

The extent I would go to make this right between us.

Which is why, though I know I should, I don't make a move to leave like he's telling me.

"I hope you know...I really am sorry. I didn't know Braxton would take things as far as he did. If I did, I would've—"

Quinton's fist slams against the wall behind him in frustration before he leans back against it. Two rows of perfect, white teeth gnaw at his bottom lip while he takes a deep breath, and I can tell he's trying to rein in his temper.

Something that hasn't taken control of him in quite some time now.

Then again, I've always been the person to make it burn the hottest.

Another deep, long sigh comes from him before he finally speaks. "Don't fucking lie to me again, Oakley. We both know you wouldn't. And the reason I know that is because you keep tossing Braxton's name at me like you're not equally at fault here. You might not have committed the crime, but you still knew. You could've cost me my future in hockey. And you didn't do a fucking thing to make it right, even after things with us..." He trails off with a shake of his head, eyes darting toward the floor. "You might not have held the gun, but you still helped pull the trigger. You're responsible for your choices. Now you have to live with them."

He's right. Every person on this planet has to live with the choices they make and suffer the consequences of them too.

The problem here is…I can't live with mine. Because it means living without *him*.

A somber cloud forms over both of us, twisting and coiling as it waits for the perfect moment to start a downpour of emotions. All the ones I've been doing my best to hold in over the past few weeks, if only to make it through the rest of the season.

But I feel it all coming to a head as tears well in those ice blue eyes I know better than my own.

Despite clearing his throat, his voice is grated, like it's been dragged over shards of shattered glass. And the sound of it pierces my heart.

But not nearly as much as the words he speaks.

"Just let me ask you this. Did the end justify the means?"

No.

And just like that, the storm swirling around us unleashes.

Shame and regret courses through me, because the answer came so quickly, it should've been obvious months ago. It shouldn't have taken me standing here, begging for him to see me or listen to what I have to say, to realize what I did was just…fucked up.

Even if I didn't act on it, I still planted a seed capable of ruining Quinn's career—his entire future in the NHL. And for what? To be *team captain* for one fucking season? To fulfill some role in a legacy I won't even be passing on to another generation of Reeds after me? To keep from having to play with him?

It's disgusting, and it's a bitter pill to swallow. I just can't believe I didn't make this realization sooner.

Nothing is worth ruining the hard work and determination of someone else.

It sure as hell isn't worth losing him.

I nod a couple times, swallowing harshly before meeting his gaze. "You're right. It wasn't justified. And sure, the me five months ago wouldn't have stopped him. But it doesn't change the fact that the me standing in front of you right now *would*. Yeah, sure," I say, tossing my arms out to my sides, "I wanted to be captain. I wanted to see you get knocked down a peg or two or ten, but it's no fucking reason for me to do what I did. I should have known and realized it, but I didn't. And I'm sorry for it. I really, truly am. But you have to understand I'm not the guy from *before*."

"Before?"

"Before I saw past the bullshit, Quinn." I lick my lips and step closer to him "When I got to see who you really were, it all started changing. Shifting, and no matter how many times I tried to make it stop, I was fucking helpless to it."

His nod is grim, matching the thin line his mouth creates. "Not a good place to be for someone who loves control, is it?"

I shake my head, a long sigh slipping past my lips.

Not at all, babe. Not at fucking all.

"I don't know…what you expect to come from all this." He rubs the back of his neck before dropping it to his side again. "What do you want?"

So many things. But the most important is…to not lose you.

"For you to forgive me," I whisper. "It doesn't need to be today or tomorrow or next week or in a month. But I want your forgiveness, however long it takes to get it."

Giving in to my urge to touch him, I close the couple feet of distance between us.

"Hit me. Hurt me. Get your payback. Your revenge. I don't care what you do or how you do it, but please, do something. Fucking anything is better than this." My throat feels raw and shredded from shards of glass as

I repeat the words he said the day he flipped my world on axis. "Fight me, baby. There's nothing I want more."

His eyes sink closed; only pure anguish etched into his features as his forehead connects with mine. "You really think I want that?"

From the tone of his voice, I can tell he doesn't. I can't say I blame him, either.

But I want him to fight me. Fight *with* me. Because if he does, there's still a chance. For this to be fixed. That I didn't fuck this up forever.

To know we're still *worth* fighting for.

Because I think we are. I just hope he does too.

It's only when his eyes open, gaze colliding with mine again, I find the courage to answer as honestly as I dare.

"I don't know what you want."

He shakes his head, throat working to swallow. "Well, that makes two of us. I can tell you I don't want revenge or payback or any of the petty bullshit you just offered me. It's not worth shit, after all. Something *you* taught me."

"Quinn…"

He shakes his head again, eyes darting off to the side as he speaks. "I can tell you what I used to want. Someone who understood my love for hockey. Who liked me for me, not my money or my name. Who would stand up for me. Who was on my side, even if it was just us against the rest of the world. All of which were completely obvious before you." He licks his lips, and lets out a sharp sigh. "But once this all started between us, I also realized I wanted someone who would laugh at me. Or with me, it didn't matter which. Someone to challenge me to be better. Who would drag me through the stacks and have his way with me. Who would tell me he couldn't stand me and then kiss me all in the same breath."

Every word leaving his lips breaks my heart more, and paired with the broken, raw way he says it, I'm surprised it's still beating in my chest at all.

Because all those things he said, I can do or I've already done. They're things we are or have together. They make *us*. And…it gives me hope.

Until he goes and quashes it altogether.

"But most of all," he utters, his voice shredded and raw, "I wanted someone who wouldn't fucking betray me."

His words are a knife slicing through skin, muscle, and bone, stabbing straight into my barely beating heart. But I can't even complain. Not when I dug one into his back first.

"I'm sorry, Quinn. I'm so sorry."

His teeth sink into his bottom lip, and he shakes his head again. "I don't wanna hear it, Oak. I'm sick of *I'm sorry*."

"Then let me prove it to you. Please. I swear on my parents, my brother, on hockey, on everything I love," I try reasoning. "Please believe me when I tell you I didn't know."

"You keep saying that, but you did, Oak. You told me you thought something was off, but you chose to sit on it."

"Yes, but I didn't know."

"You just said—"

"No, I didn't *know*, Quinn. I didn't know it would matter to me when all was said and done. I didn't know that I would care about what Braxton did or didn't do because I didn't know I would fall in love with you."

The words fly from my mouth, and honestly, I don't care if their presence destroys things more. I might've kept a massive secret from him about this whole shit with Braxton and his drug test, but to hell if I'm gonna keep how I feel about him to myself.

He's in every beat of my heart. And he deserves to know that.

I blow out a breath, and scrub my hand over my face, a sense of irony hitting me right between the eyes. And I can't help the sad, pathetic laugh breaking free when it does.

"That's the most fucked up part of it all, though. There you were, from the beginning, telling me not to fall in love with you. But I did anyway. And if I'd listened to you, this wouldn't hurt nearly as much. Because it does hurt, knowing you don't trust me. Knowing I don't *deserve* your trust anymore."

Every bottled up word and emotion comes spewing from my mouth in what can only be classified as word vomit, but I don't care. I let it flow free, giving him all the little pieces I've been too busy keeping to myself when I should have been handing them over all along.

But I can see now, it's too little, too late.

Quinn's jaw ticks, blue eyes flaring behind his glasses. I've learned him well enough to know he's holding something back. Keeping words to himself when I'd sell my soul to hear them. Ones I *need* to hear.

Even if it's rage or hate. Even if he tells me to go kick rocks and never come back. Fucking anything would be preferable over silence.

At least, that way, I'd know I've destroyed what we had beyond repair.

But all I get is…nothing.

So rather than keep fighting a losing battle, I walk away; tiny pieces of my heart left in my wake as he does nothing to stop me.

THIRTY-THREE

Quinton

We somehow scraped by with a victory tonight, the last game we needed to win to send us to the Frozen Four. I should be thrilled. Fucking ecstatic, seeing as I'm the one back in front of the team, leading them to victory.

Yet this win is more bittersweet than anything.

Obviously the competitive side of me—the piece of myself that has always wanted this—is thrilled to have made it this far. The entire team, myself included, has worked our asses off to achieve this, and I know we deserve it.

But we also brought home yet another victory without Oak and I hooking-up the night before. Which only makes me think what the two of us were doing was doomed from the start.

Too bad my heart doesn't care about those kinds of details, which is

336 | CE RICCI

the very reason it got itself all broken and shredded anyway.

I shower on autopilot, drifting and floating between my teammates laughing and jeering in celebration. As they should. Every single guy in here made tonight happen. Brought home this win. But there's a fine line between celebrating and being a complete idiot because you're on top of the world.

"I think the Kappas are planning a party tonight," I hear McGowan mention to my left.

"Oh, hell yes," Weston says, excitement evident in his voice.

"Just don't get too rowdy tonight, guys," I say. "We've still got a long way to go before bringing home that trophy. Starting with a morning skate tomorrow. Don't be late."

It's ironic, having these kinds of things come out of my mouth now, especially considering where I was not even a year ago. But a lot can change in a short amount of time.

My attention automatically drifts toward Oakley at that thought, finding him undressing for his shower. He must feel my eyes on him, because his head lifts and he meets my gaze.

A small smile curves the corner of his lips, one barely noticeable to anyone but me, and I swear I can read every thought going through his head right now.

Good job tonight.

You played amazing.

I'm so fucking proud of you.

Or maybe those are the thoughts running through *my own* head.

The stupid slab of muscle in my chest crawls its way into my throat, forming a knot there. One nearly impossible to breathe around. It's suffocating, the same way it is to be in his presence, but not be able to do the things I want to.

Like go to him. Talk to him. Fucking celebrate with him, because he's the only one I want to share this moment with.

I know the ball's in my court. He said all the things he needed to say the other night, and it's up to me to forgive him and move forward. But his betrayal cut deep, leaving a gaping chasm behind. One I'm not sure how to bridge yet, no matter how much my heart might want to.

"De Haas," Coach's disembodied voice echoes through the locker room, and just like that, all chatter ceases to the point where you could hear a pin drop.

I let out a long-winded sigh, still holding eye contact with Oakley while calling back, "Yeah?"

"Finish up getting changed and meet me out in the hall."

My brows furrow, wondering why the hell Coach would want to meet with me outside in the hallway rather than in his office. Then again, the last few times I've been called into Coach's office have caused major issues in my life, so I should probably be thankful.

I break away from Oakley's gaze and pull my shirt over my head. His eyes are still on me as I slip my shoes on, and they continue to sear my back until the moment I exit the locker room.

I miss the heat of his gaze the second it's gone, and more than anything, I hate how pathetic that makes me.

Shoving thoughts of Oakley to the side, I turn the corner and find Coach down the hall with another gentleman dressed in a suit, who motions for me to come join them.

My blood races, invisible pins and needles pricking across my skin as I close the distance, wondering who the hell this other guy is. As I get closer, I can make out salt and pepper hair, putting him maybe into his fifties. He's tall, probably about my height and is still fit. But I don't think I've seen him before. Not that I can recall.

Is he the team lawyer? Someone from administration? A representative from the NCAA?

Have they suspended Oakley after all?

I might be fucking pissed about everything that went down, but the last thing I want is to put the team's welfare in jeopardy during the most important part of the season. All I want out of the whole fucking thing is for it to be done and over with.

A thousand thoughts rush through my head, and none are good. By the time I reach the two men, I feel like I've walked into my own funeral.

"Coach," I say warily. "You wanted to see me?"

He nods, the corners of his eyes creased in a rare smile. "I did. There's someone who wants to meet you, and I thought this was the right time to make it happen."

Ah, fuck. Here it comes.

The man steps forward, holding his hand out for me to shake, which I take, albeit a little reluctantly. His grip is firm and intimidating, which only makes my intestines twist and knot themselves more.

"Quinton, I've been following you for some time, and would like to formally introduce myself," he says, glancing between me and Coach. "My name's Louis Spaulding."

I release his hand like it was a hot iron, my eyes widening slightly as recognition sets in.

"Like, the NHL agent, Louis Spaulding?"

Coach lets out a bark of laughter, and a grin appears on Louis's face, popping a small dimple below the left corner of his mouth. "I happen to represent a couple other athletes in the baseball world, but yes. One and the same."

Holy motherfucking shit.

"I…It's nice to meet you, sir," I say, slightly dumbstruck as I fumble for more words.

Coach laughs again, this time more of a bellow, and he claps me on the shoulder before speaking to Louis. "I think this is my cue to let the two of you speak in private. Besides, gotta make sure the guys aren't throwing a kegger in the locker room after that win." He looks down at me then. "You played one helluva game tonight, de Haas. Keep it up."

All I can do is nod after him as he makes his way back down the hallway, my mind still struggling to keep up with the fact that I'm speaking to Louis freaking Spaulding. Who also happens to be one of the top agents in the industry.

And he…wants to talk…to me.

"He's right. You played a damn good game tonight," Louis confirms, pulling my attention back to him. "You're quick and agile, with more untapped potential in that stick than I think you know what to do with. Something your boyfriend in there" —he nods over my shoulder toward the locker room— "wasn't kidding about. Or your coach, for that matter."

I swallow, a twinge of sadness hitting me. "I'm not…Oakley and I aren't…" I trail off, not sure how to broach this subject without making it far too personal. So I just pivot instead. "I, uh…thank you. Again, sir."

He lets out a chuckle. "You don't need to thank me. It's a matter of fact. Your talent will take you places in the NHL, especially with the right representation."

Representation?

"I'm…not sure I'm following, sir."

Or maybe I am, but with the lack of good happening in my life as of late, it's a little hard to believe.

He waves me off. "Enough with the *sir* crap. Call me Louis. It's what all my clients call me." A quick pause. "That is, if you decide to sign with me."

My heartbeat is in my ears as I stare at him, realizing…

"You're being serious."

Another chuckle leaves him. "As a heart attack. I'd be honored to represent you."

My mouth might as well be on the floor as I gape at him, flabbergasted this is happening right now.

"I'm sorry," I tell him, shaking my head in awe. "You're gonna have to give me a minute to just…process this."

Louis's hand lands on my shoulder, giving a reassuring squeeze. "Take all the time you need, Quinton. I'm here to answer any questions you might have before making a decision."

"Thank you, sir."

"Again with the *sir*." He shakes his head. "Of course, you don't need to decide on anything right now. Take the night, the week. Talk with your parents or Coach. Do whatever you need, and let me know what you decide."

I'm about to tell him I don't need any time when a burning sensation hits my back, making my spine go rigid and halting any words in the back of my throat. I don't even have to turn around to know Oakley's staring at me from outside the locker room door.

Which is only confirmed when Louis's attention moves back over my shoulder, giving a brief nod before returning to me once more.

"You know, I used to represent the Reed brothers back in their NHL days." He eyes me quizzically. "I wanted to represent the trifecta of Reed boys, but this last one wouldn't sign with me. Says if I'm only taking on one NHL prospect this year, there's someone far more deserving on his team who I should be looking at instead."

And if I thought I was flabbergasted before, it's got nothing on how floored I am right now. At a complete loss for words as what Louis just said registers in my brain.

Of course, Oakley has the pedigree that would make it easy for him to find another agent. But…having Louis is a piece of his legacy. One far bigger than becoming captain would ever mean to him.

So why the fuck would he be willing to give the chance up, only for me to take it instead?

"When did you have this conversation with him?"

Another quizzical look. "A couple months ago. I stopped by his parents' just after the New Year to speak with him."

My heart drops to my stomach, and without thinking, I turn to find Oakley. He's still there, right outside the locker room door, like I knew he'd be. And though he's far enough away that I can't make out his features, I can tell he's smiling.

I can't explain it, I just fucking know it.

I spin back to Louis. "He wants you to sign me even though you're like…Louis Spaulding. Even though you're a piece of his family's legacy. Even though you're only taking on one hockey player."

He nods, a small smile tilting the corner of his mouth. "It sure seems that way, doesn't it?"

"And you had this conversation months ago?"

"He was crystal clear about it, and your coach reaffirmed it with me before you got out here." Louis must tell I'm trying to grapple with my thoughts, because he offers another squeeze of my shoulder before releasing his grip. "You've got a lot to think about, so I'm going to leave you to it. But this offer is genuine, de Haas. I'd love nothing more than to represent you."

I can think about it all I want, but one thing is certain. None of this makes any sense, no matter how many times I try to work through it in my head.

This is Oakley's entire future we're talking about here. A legacy he's following, building into his own. It's everything he's spent his entire life working for, and he's just gonna…what? Give it up so I can have a chance instead?

But then our conversation from the other night comes reeling back into my mind until I latch on three fucking words I'd never expected to come out of Oakley's mouth. Ones that spilled from his lips so easily, I can't believe they'd be anything but the truth.

Words…I know I feel too.

And that's all it takes to understand why he'd give up having Louis as his agent so I could. He believes in me, maybe even more than I believe in myself.

Due to a single reason, so complicated, but so fucking simple at the same time.

Love.

Louis is already stepping away, back down the hall, and I blurt out an answer before I think any better of it.

"I'm in."

He pauses, giving me a look. "You're sure? The offer still stands if you need time. There's no need to feel—"

"I don't need time, I know this is what I want," I tell him, a surge of confidence in me like I've never felt before. "But I think I have one condition."

He grins, and it's the kind that tells me he already knows what I'm going to say.

"I'm all ears."

THIRTY-FOUR

Quinton

April

"This is it, guys." I glance between my teammates huddled around me, hanging on my every word before we head out on the ice. "This is what we've been working for all season. A chance to bring a Frozen Four victory back to Leighton."

Nervous energy radiates from every single person in the room, Coach included as he watches me talk to the team. It's been hanging in the air around all of us since we got on the team bus to make the trip from Chicago down to Indianapolis, only growing in intensity as game time came nearer.

Now, it's vibrating the entire room, along with everything—and everyone—in it.

Myself included.

Though, when my gaze collides with Oakley's from across the huddle,

I realize the buzzing through my veins isn't just from the impending game.

"We're solid as long as we remember we are a team. We play as one, we lose as one. This isn't the time for showboating or theatrics. I know scouts and agents are probably here, and you might want to make an impression, but they don't matter right now. Only this moment does."

Nods and murmurs float through the space, all in agreement.

"It's time to put it all on the line. Play your hearts out, but most of all, play smart." That gets a few of my teammates sharing dubious looks among themselves, and I let out a soft chuckle. "I know it's rich coming from me. But if we play hard and play smart, there's no reason we won't go home with that trophy. I believe in us, and you should too."

It's true. I have faith, as long as we're smart, the championship title is as good as ours. It doesn't matter that we're the underdogs in this battle, or that this is the biggest test we'll face this season as a team. Nothing feels impossible right now, including taking home this win.

Sure, I tend to be an optimist by nature as it is, but it's more than just that. It's a feeling, seated deep in the marrow of my bones. One that's been shot up on steroids ever since signing with Louis a couple weeks ago. A belief in this team, and more importantly, myself.

And the guys…they're feeding off it. Roaring around me, clapping and chanting and cheering to pump themselves up as we prepare to exit the locker room for the rink. A few of my teammates even jostle me around, smacking my pads and shaking me so I get as hyped as they are.

It works, even if I don't need the adrenaline, I'm ready to bore full-steam ahead, not stopping until the Frozen Four trophy is held over our heads.

When Coach calls out for us to hit the ice, I choose not to lead the charge out, instead staying back to allow myself one second to just…breathe.

Apparently I'm not the only one with that idea, because once most of the guys shuttle out to the rink, I notice Oakley still lingering off to the left of the doors.

"Nice speech, Captain."

The guy I was six months ago would've heard only venom and sarcasm laced in those words, even if there wasn't any to begin with. But I see them at face value now, and they're genuine.

"What can I say? I spoke from the heart."

I close the distance between us, his fixated gaze causing my pulse to thrum beneath my skin. I expect him to stop me when I reach the doors, but instead he just holds it open and falls in step beside me on our way to the ice.

"This is really it, huh? The last time we have to play together?"

His observation causes me to stutter a step, because until he said it, the thought hadn't even crossed my mind. I've only been thinking about the team, not myself.

Wow. Maybe I really was cut out for this leadership crap.

"I guess so," I murmur, the weight of the realization hitting me like a sack of bricks.

"Well, then let's make it count and go out kicking some ass?" He smiles. "And try not to take that too literally."

And there it is.

But the thing I've realized about Oakley's little jabs since this whole thing started between us? I don't actually mind them. They don't get under my skin or light my insides on fire the way they used to.

They usually make me smile or laugh right along with him.

And this one's no different.

The first fifty minutes of the game fly by in what seems like a single second, and as I hit the ice for another line rotation, the entire arena seems to buzz with unchecked excitement.

It's been a Frozen Four match-up for the record books, two teams putting it all on the line as we go head-to-head for the championship. And boy, have the guys from Ransom University put us through our paces for the past two and a half periods, barely giving an inch no matter how many times we push for more.

Their goalie, Henderson, has played a stellar game, blocking shot after shot on goal. Both Oakley and I have managed to sneak one by him, but it seems every time the lamp lights up for us, they come right back and do the same thing.

Like right now, when their star forward, O'Rourke, comes out of nowhere and sends the puck sailing past Cam, straight into the net.

Damnit.

The score's all tied up at two a piece now, and we're all desperate looking for a break in Ransom's game. O'Rourke, especially, since he's scored both of their goals. But Cam's still been killing it in the net, stopping far, *far* more than he's dared let in. I don't think he's made as many saves in a single game this season as he has tonight.

He rips off his helmet, sweat-soaked hair sticking to his forehead. I skate to a stop beside him, grabbing his water bottle from the top of the net and handing it to him.

"The dude's a beast," he mutters, eyes trained on O'Rourke as he takes a swig from the bottle. "I'm surprised I've stopped half the shots he's taken on me."

"Because you're a beast too," I tell him. "You got this, man. Shake it off."

His blue eyes shift to me, face completely stoic. "Do me a favor?

Check him a little harder into the boards next time. Rattle him a bit. Give me an edge."

I push away from the net, a smirk plastered on my face. "Remember what I said about playing a clean game?"

He scowls, calling out, "This really isn't the time to be turning over a new leaf, de Haas!"

Weston and McGowan have already joined Rossi at center ice for a face-off, and I slide up on the left of the circle to get in position. Oakley's across from me, already zoned in and waiting for the puck to drop.

The second it does, Rossi sweeps it out from Ransom's center, flicking it over to me for a breakaway. The puck changes hands rapidly after that, going from me to Oakley and back to Rossi and finally back to me for a shot on goal.

Blocked by Henderson.

Fuck.

Coach calls for a line change, and I saddle up between Oakley and McGowan as we wait for our turn in the rotation. It's painful though—watching and waiting—especially in circumstances like these. Every shift I spend off the ice feels like an eternity, and when I glance over at Oakley, I can tell he's feeling the same. For him, I'd assume it's even worse, what with his control issues.

But I get it. When I'm not out there actively playing, stuck behind the boards waiting my turn, I feel anxious as hell.

Thankfully we'll have one more turn on the ice, and when the time comes, the five of us on our line barrel out of the team box for the puck.

Ransom has possession, a defenseman slapping the puck past McGowan to O'Rourke, who just checked Weston into the boards before heading straight for Cam and the net. Dread fills my stomach as I skate after him, Oakley right along with me, but it doesn't matter. There's no way we'll catch him in time.

My breath catches in my throat as O'Rourke takes a shot on goal, the puck barreling straight toward our net…

And Cam blocks it.

Relief floods through me as I skate around the net, waiting for Cam to toss the puck back into play. He does to Rossi, who skates down the ice toward the net like a bat outta hell.

The two Ransom defensemen team up on Rossi, corralling him against the boards near center ice until McGowan and Oakley help break the puck free. Once they manage to, it goes flying to the other side of the ice, straight into O'Rourke's grubby little hands.

I swipe the puck from him, checking him straight into the boards in the process. It's a clean hit—I made sure—and the lack of a penalty whistle proves it. But at least I paid up on Cam's favor a little bit.

Quickly passing the puck off to Oakley, I glance up at the clock.

Twenty seconds.

I'd really like to keep this from going to sudden death, but we need to find a way around Henderson.

McGowan blocks one of the Ransom forwards, allowing Oakley to slip by and skate down the ice on a breakaway. I'm right there with him, adrenaline pumping my heart faster, and my legs push me to keep up.

Ten seconds.

Two Ransom players converge on Oakley, effectively blocking his path to the net.

I'm open, I'm open, I chant silently.

As if reading my mind, Oakley passes the puck to me, and it all falls into place. A quick snap from me over to Rossi as he finishes circling around the back side of the net gives us the opening we need.

He takes the shot and the lamp lights up…with the final buzzer going off a moment later.

The sound echoes, loud and glorious, making the crowd go absolutely haywire. The arena is overtaken with screaming and cheering in a roar so deafening, I can't even hear my own breathing. My heart races in my chest, amplified by the cadence of applause and ricocheting off my ribs at a hundred miles per hour.

I find Oakley on the other side of Rossi and Cam, all their helmets, sticks, and gloves tossed on the ice as they celebrate the victory. As if feeling my stare, his eyes find me, and I toss my own gear before closing the distance between us. The second I'm within two feet, I launch myself at him, only to have two strong arms hold me to his chest. Anchoring me there as best as he can with all these fucking pads in the way.

"We did it." My hand wraps around the back of his neck, and I pull his sweat-soaked forehead against mine. "We actually fucking did it."

He nods, his nose bumping mine when he does. "You were…amazing, Quinn."

I hug him more, tighter and closer than I have in weeks. And it's the first time in those weeks I've actually felt…whole.

What the fuck is that except—

"I love you too," I say, bringing my mouth to his ear. "I love you so fucking much."

He pulls back, dark brown eyes lighting up in ways I haven't seen in far too long. And I've missed it more than I realized.

"You're sure it's not the high of victory talking?"

"After all the shit you pulled?" I laugh. "Absolutely not. It's all me, baby."

His palm cups the side of my face as he examines my face like a blind man seeing for the first time. Slowly and thoroughly, memorizing every inch. And despite the pandemonium happening around us, like I'm the only thing that exists.

A flash of his tongue peeks out at the corner of his lips, and his eyes take on a sorrowful sheen. "I know you're probably sick of hearing me say I'm so sorry, but—"

"You're right. I am." My fingers wrap around his pads and I give him a wicked grin. "So you better make this last one worth it."

The playfulness in my tone must be enough to make him relax and even get a small smile forming. "Just know…it'll be a long time before I ever forgive myself for—"

I shake my head and cut him off again, this time by crushing my mouth to his.

My tongue spears between his lips, my arms wrap around his neck, and I kiss him the way I've never kissed him before: freely and out in the open, where the entire fucking world can see.

And if possible, the roar of the crowd gets even louder.

Then again, it's not every day you see two hockey players making out on the ice after winning the Frozen Four.

Breaking for some air, I rest my forehead against his again, needing some part of my body touching his at all times. Grounding me in a moment seemingly too perfect to possibly be real.

"Did you just kiss me on national television?" he whispers against my lips.

I nod. "You were still trying to apologize. I had to shut you up."

And then I kiss him again.

"Ah, jeez! Get a room, you two!" Rossi shouts, causing the two of us to break apart.

"Yeah, but preferably at Quinton's," Camden cuts in. I look up in time to see Rossi give him a *what the fuck* look, and Cam gestures toward me, sheepishly adding, "What? He's a noisy fucker. Quite literally, and I don't feel like having to sleep with earplugs tonight."

Oakley chuckles, pressing a kiss behind my ear. "Mmm, just the way I like it."

"Good to know." I grin, a different kind of adrenaline heating my blood. "Because celebrations are in order, and once we're back to campus, I know exactly how we can kick them off."

THIRTY-FIVE

Oakley

The bus arrives back to campus late. Way later than any of us thought it would, and by that time, most of the team's celebration high has worn off. Actually, half the team—Quinn included—is dead asleep when the bus rolls to a stop outside our home arena.

Not me, though.

I'm too busy reliving what might well be the best night of my life, and not just because of the trophy sitting in the front of the bus beside Coach. It's got a lot to do with it, but the guy fast asleep with his head against my shoulder is the main reason.

Just as well that he's getting some rest. He played his ass off tonight, and I have plans to keep him up for the rest of it once we're locked in a bedroom.

Who it belongs to and whoever else overhears, I don't fucking care.

Of course, we still have a lot to talk about, even if he doesn't want me continuously apologizing to him for the next twenty years for everything Braxton and I did to cause his suspension. But I'm hoping it can happen *after* we celebrate a little.

Our driver flicks the lights, illuminating the interior of the bus, and a series of groans follow.

I glance down in time to catch Quinn's nose wrinkle up, his eyes clenching closed to keep the light out before burrowing deeper into my shoulder. Which only makes his glasses fall clear off his face and into his lap.

I've never once in my life thought the word *adorable* while looking at him, but I'll be damned if the sight doesn't make my heart twist into knots.

"We're here," I murmur, brushing a kiss on the top of his head.

Two gorgeous blue eyes peel open, blinking rapidly before he repositions his glasses on the bridge of his nose. "What time is it?"

"Just after two."

Another wrinkle of the nose. "Ugh, we should have just stayed at the hotel another night."

He's definitely not wrong, but I'll never say no to sleeping—or fucking—in my own bed. Or Quinn's bed. I don't care which.

Coach rises at the front of the bus, looking us all over from the aisle.

"I'm proud of every single one of you for the way you played tonight. Like Quinton said, you won as a team tonight. No one player is more important than another." He nods toward Quinn, who gives a subtle nod in return. "We've still got work to do, as you know. But take the rest of the weekend to refresh and recharge. Get your celebrating out and come back Monday morning ready to hit the weights."

A few stray hoots and hollers come from my teammates at the mentions of celebrating the win, and I think I hear a couple younger D-men in front of us mention a party the Deltas are throwing in honor of the big win.

By now I've realized the frats at Leighton are just looking for an excuse to throw a rager. And this happens to be a perfect one.

Coach hushes us, waving his hands in a downward motion before continuing. "Please be careful tonight, whether you go out or just go home. But for those of you going out, make good choices. Don't do anything that will land you in jail or—"

"Your office," a chorus of us finish for him.

He smirks and taps the back of the seat. "Seems you know the drill. Now, off you get."

Quinn and I wait for most of the bus to clear out before climbing out of our seats. Our bags are already unloaded and waiting for us by the time we're off, Coach waiting with the trophy in hand beside them.

I grab Quinn's bag and hand it to him before shouldering my own. "Looks pretty good in your hands."

"It certainly does, but it'll look even better inside." Coach looks between us. "Figured the team captain should be the one to carry it in, though. But I'll leave you two to fight over who that is. Just…don't break it. And bring the key back on Monday."

Instead of handing it to one of us, he sets it on the ground with the key to the trophy case and heads to his SUV in the player lot.

Six months ago, I have no doubt the two of us would've gotten in a scuffle over the damn thing. But now we just stare at it, then each other, like we're afraid to even touch it.

"You should bring it in," he says first, breaking the silence. I lift my gaze to collide with his, and he continues, "You were captain for most of the season, not me."

"You should have been the entire season if I hadn't…" I trail off.

He grabs it from the ground and holds it out to me. "Okay, but if it wasn't for your injury last year, the spot would've been yours in the first place and we both know it."

What?

"That's got nothing to do with this. It wasn't even your fault," I say, pushing it back toward him.

"He was aiming for me, you just got in the way." Then he jams the trophy right back in my arms, and I realize we're about to play the most backward game of tug-o-war with this fucking thing.

"Still doesn't count." *Press.*

"Well, then you should take it because it's your legacy." *Push.*

"Maybe, but you earned it." *Thrust.*

"Quinn—"

My words are cut off when he shoves it against my chest and steps back, leaving him out of arm's reach. "Just take the stupid thing, Oakley, before I use it to bash your skull in instead."

I laugh, holding it out in front of me to examine for any damage. "Well, that'd be one helluva way to end the night."

Key in hand, Quinn starts for the entrance, and I fall in step beside him. "And would go exactly against Coach's wishes for us to stay out of jail."

"Eh, I'd make bail."

I scoff, opening the door to let him through. "I know you've got money and an army of lawyers, but I don't think you'd make bail on a murder charge."

"That's where you're wrong," he says as we make our way down the hall toward the trophy case. "I don't have either of those things."

His words cause me to stutter-step as a pained smile crosses his face. And I don't even need to ask what he means. The answer, as much as I hate it, is glaringly obvious.

His dad cut him off. Just like he threatened to over break.

"Quinn—"

"I knew it was coming," he cuts in, his eyes taking on a slight sheen. "It was only a matter of time."

The hatred I have for these two disgusting people rises to an all-time high.

"Do you want to talk about it?"

"Not right now." Quinn clears his throat and makes an attempt to lighten the mood again. "But now you know why I wouldn't murder you, just severely injure."

My heart aches for him in my chest, especially knowing this must've been weighing on him for a while. But if he wants to keep the heavy shit for a later day, that's okay. We have plenty of time to talk about it.

The rest of our damn lives, if I have anything to say about it.

"Well, I'm flattered you only want to maim me."

"It's a far step above wanting to kill you a few weeks ago," he points out, bending to unlock the case before sliding the glass door out of the way.

I know he meant nothing by the comment, but I can't help but feel the twinge of guilt rushing through me.

My teeth roll over my bottom lip while I push one of the other trophies over to make room for ours, and then set it in the empty space. "I'm not complaining at all, but can I ask what made you…"

Glancing up, I find his brow arched as he waits for me to continue. When I don't, he supplies, "Forgive you?"

I wince at the casual way he says it. "Yeah. That."

A noncommittal shrug lifts his shoulders as he slides the glass back in place and locks it. "I got your present."

My brows crash together, confusion setting in as I wrack my brain for anything I might've gotten him, only to come up blank. "Your…present?"

The grin appearing on his face is mischievous as hell when he says one word.

A name, actually.

"Louis."

I burst out laughing. "Louis isn't a present. He's going to be your own personal pain in the ass if you sign with him. Just ask Coach or my dad."

"I thought I was supposed to be the pain in the ass and he would be the one to clean up all my messes and fuck ups? Isn't that the entire purpose of an agent?"

"Yes." I chuckle. "But he's also going to harp you to death about training and food regimens, being *on time* to the arena."

"Hey, I haven't been late to practice or a game in *months*," he counters, to which I raise my hands.

"I know, I'm just saying that's what he's there for."

"Mhmm. You just thought I needed a babysitter next year since you won't be around to do it."

The thought of not playing with Quinn next year or even seeing him every day makes my stomach sink, and once again, the reality of tonight being the last time we might ever play together sets in. And it's sobering.

"I wanted you to have someone on your side to find the best place for your talent and skill to not just fit, but shine. Because with how hard you've worked, I know they deserve to."

He smiles at me like I hung the goddamn moon for him.

"Way to get sappy on me, Reed."

"And way to ruin a moment, de Haas," I say, giving him a playful shove. "But I need you to know Louis wasn't some sort of apology gift to make up for what happened. I talked to him long before you found out—"

"I know. He told me you spoke to him over winter break." He lets out an ironic laugh. "I got you crazy socks for Christmas, and you got me a fucking all-star agent. Way to be a one-upper, even if it was a couple months late."

"Well, I *am* the best boyfriend you'll ever have."

"Willing to place bets on that, Reed? Maybe you need to put your money where your mouth is."

A grin spreads across my face, his taunt taking me back to a similar one he made in a different hallway. One full of drunken college kids and pounding dance music instead of hockey memorabilia.

I go to grab for him, but he's quick, darting out of reach and running toward the exit before I have the chance to regain my balance. But the door causes an obstacle, making it easy enough to catch up.

My arms wrap around his waist seconds after we burst through the doors, and I haul him against me before he can make another break for it. We're chest to chest as I walk him backward, pinning him against the exterior wall of the arena.

"You caught me," he pants, breathless. "Now what are you gonna do with me?"

"Always fucking testing me," I growl before fusing my mouth to his.

I feel like I've been shot up full of uppers, because I'm on top of the fucking world as our tongues tangle and battle. His hair slides through my fingers as I try to reel him in more, needing to take as much he's willing to give. Which isn't much. The jackass that he is, he fights it. Until I roll my thickening cock against his.

Then he lets out a soft moan and rocks against me too.

I could devour him where I stand, no amount of fucks given about indecent exposure. I'm high on the win. On life. On him.

Everything about this moment is pure ecstasy.

My hands grip his hard, firm backside. One I fully intend to sink my teeth into as soon as humanly possible.

"You're trying to get us arrested or something?" he pants into my mouth before diving in for more.

"It's fine," I murmur, biting at his lip. "No one's dicks are out. And it's almost three in the morning."

"Maybe, but we're still bound to be putting on a show for anyone who might—"

A throat clears behind me, effectively cutting Quinn off mid-sentence. But I'm pleased to find the rush of dread doesn't flow through me at the thought of someone catching me with him. Though, I'd be lying if there isn't a slight amount of embarrassment at being caught with a raging boner in public. Especially if it's my uncle.

Which, thank God, it isn't. But it's not exactly who I was hoping for, either.

"You have a minute, Reed?" Louis Spaulding asks.

I glance between Quinn and Louis, not sure what he needs that couldn't wait until tomorrow. "Yeah, what's up?"

"Got something for you."

He hands me a manila folder with a stack of papers inside, and I frown. "What's all this?"

"Your contract. The one I was hoping to give to you in front of your parents in Indy, but you were on the bus and gone before I had the chance," he says matter-of-factly before sharing a knowing smirk with Quinn. "You're not the only one who knows how to work a deal."

Flipping the folder open, I glance over the top document to see it's definitely a contract with my name listed as the represented party.

Well, I'll be damned.

"I thought he signed you?" I murmur to Quinn. "And Louis was only taking one more client this year."

"I only signed on the condition he represented you too," Quinn says, peeking over my shoulder at the document. "I know it might not help us get drafted to the same team or anything, but I thought at the very least...I don't know...you'd still have that piece of your legacy intact."

Closing the folder, I tuck it under my arm and stare at him. At this amazing, beautiful man who loves with every inch of himself.

Who loves *me* with every fiber of his being.

"Have I told you I love you today?"

He scrunches his face a little, making a show of thinking before answering with, "Maybe once or twice."

"Uh-huh."

"You two are going to be a pain in the ass, aren't you?"

"Only Oakley," Quinton chirps, a megawatt smile on his face. "I'm a reformed pain in the ass these days. No more fighting here. But this one here" —he motions to me— "has a rebellious streak for days."

I give him an incredulous look. "You literally threatened to bash my skull in with a trophy twenty minutes ago."

"Yeah, but the difference between us is I don't act on the stupid shit I say."

Oh, he's definitely gonna be paying for that one later. And the glare I aim at him lets him know it too.

"And on that note, I'm heading home for the night." Louis nods at the folder beneath my arm. "You know what to do with it. Just get it back to me when you can."

We both offer a goodnight to Louis and a wave as he gets in his sedan to drive away.

The second we're alone again, I turn on Quinn.

"*You*," I say through gritted teeth, spinning him in a circle before setting him back on his feet, "are in so much fucking trouble."

Planting my hands on either side of his face, I dive in for another kiss, ready to pick things up where we left off.

Too bad he breaks away far too soon, and I'm left trailing a path down his throat.

"Am I? I hadn't noticed."

"Mhmm. Sure are, you mouthy little fucker," I murmur, kissing his throat again before returning to his lips.

God, I'd never stop kissing him, but for some unknown reason, he keeps pulling away from me. Yet another thing he'll be paying for soon enough.

But when he pulls away this time, his devious grins lets me know his mind has gone in the same wonderfully filthy direction mine has.

"Care to show me just how much?"

Nodding, I meet his wicked grin with one of my own.

"Whose roommates are we keeping up tonight?"

EPILOGUE

Oakley

4 Months Later — August

"Are you sure you're up for this?"

I glance up to Quinton where he's standing across from me, leaning against the handlebars of his Indian Scout. He looks sexy as ever in a white tee and jeans, the lines and patterns of his tattoos popping out from beneath the sleeves. It makes it hard to concentrate on what I'm doing.

Which is learning to drive the fucking motorcycle currently between my thighs.

It's never been an item on my bucket list, but I still remember the day he mentioned teaching me to drive it after one of our countless hook-ups, and more importantly, the spark in Quinn's eyes at the thought of teaching me about something he loves.

It's a light I never want to see go out. Ever.

So when he mentioned going for a ride today in passing, I thought… what better time than the present? Except, now that I'm straddling the damn thing, anxiety has set in, and I'm starting to regret my line of thinking altogether.

Still, I swallow down my unease and give a firm nod. "Yeah, let's do this."

One dark brow arches, but he just nods toward the bike. "Then start her up."

Doing as he says, I turn the ignition switch he showed me earlier to the right.

"Okay, now flip the switch on the right-hand grip. That engages the electrical system." When I do, he nods again and places his right hand over my left and gives a gentle squeeze. "Perfect, now pull in the clutch and push the start button."

My finger hovers over the start button on the right handle for a moment as I stare into his icy blue eyes, and he gives me an easy, reassuring smile.

"You got this, baby. Let her roar."

The engine purrs to life beneath me a moment later, and in that moment, I understand why he loves this as much as he does. The thrill it shoots through me is unreal. Only pure power and adrenaline.

I look up from the bike to him grinning down at me.

"You getting on?"

A look of amusement on his ridiculously handsome face. "You want me to ride bitch on my own bike?"

Now it's my turn to be amused. "As if you don't love every chance you get to rub up against me from behind?"

His lips purse for a moment before he nods. "Maybe, but you're not naked right now." Another brief pause, and then, "Wait, is that something we can—"

"Absolutely not," I say with a laugh, but I'd be lying if the thought didn't sound semi-appealing…as long as it was off and the kickstand was down. Or maybe him bent over it…

Damn. Spending all this time with him must really be rubbing off on me.

I shake the dirty thoughts free as best I can and motion with my head to the seat on the back. "C'mon. You know you want to."

His lips purse for a moment, forming into a tight, thin line as he debates if he has complete trust in me not to destroy one of his most prized possessions…only to round the bike and climb behind me with ease.

Probably a wise decision, if I'm being honest.

Quinn's torso presses against my back, making it even harder to concentrate than when I could see him. His heat radiating through my shirt sends shivers down my spine as he peeks over my shoulder and continues instructing me with reassurance.

"Okay, you got this. Push your left toe down to put it in first gear. You'll use your heel to go into second once we start moving. Okay, and then release the clutch slowly while rolling the throttle with your right hand." He pauses, and I feel the nod of his chin against my shoulder as I do what he says. "That's it, baby. A little more gas and—"

The bike jerks beneath us, and Quinn's hands latch onto the handle bars outside of mine, clamping down the clutch and handbrake.

"A little less than that. We don't need it flying out from under us." He laughs before pressing a kiss to the back of my neck. "C'mon. Try again. You got this."

He releases his hold on the handle bars, and I repeat the steps he told me, a little gentler on the gas this time. And like he said, we're moving across the empty parking lot.

Once we're going, Quinn's arms wrap around my waist the way mine have done to him countless times before while we fly down the pavement at what must be a hundred miles an hour, my heart pounding in my ears with the roar of the engine.

And again, I understand why he loves this so much.

The freedom of this moment here with him is unmatched, and I'm basking in it.

Until I realize we're quickly running out of room, and I have no idea which brake I'm supposed to use in order to stop this thing.

Quinn must realize this too, because he immediately takes control of the bike from behind me, both feet kicking mine out of the way on the footboards before clasping the handlebars too. Don't ask me how it happens so quickly and easily, but he somehow brings us to a complete stop twenty yards from the end of the parking lot.

Once we're no longer moving, Quinn kills the engine, and a stark silence falls over us.

He presses a kiss to the side of my throat right where my pulse is still racing beneath my skin, adrenaline coursing through my veins.

"Guess I should have mentioned more about braking *before* I let you ride off into the sunset." He laughs, wrapping his arms around my waist again and squeezing me. "We'll work on that the next go around."

I ignore him completely, still high on the mini adrenaline rush from driving the thing on my own. "Okay, but you just saw me do that, right?"

A low chuckle leaves him and he presses another kiss to the side of my throat before leaning away. "I did. Nice job, hotshot. Maybe next time we can go above twenty."

I turn and glare over my shoulder the best I can when he's almost plastered against my back. "We were going faster than that." Then I think about it, and... "Wait, we went faster than that, right?"

A shake of his head is all I get in answer, his lips rolling in to fight a smile.

Jackass.

He's my jackass, though, even after all the shit I put him through last year, and that's what's important. There are times I don't think I deserve the second chance he granted me, and when he looks at me the way he is right now is one of those times. With so much fucking pride and love, I could easily be consumed in it.

I'm proud of him too, having seen the work he's put into becoming the person he is now, and it's a damn shame his parents are still too fucking stubborn to see it. To want to know the brilliant, kind, charismatic man he is, rather than the shell of the person they wanted him to be.

But their loss…is my gain.

And I've gained the greatest teammate I could've ever asked for. On the ice, sure, there's no one better. But it's off the ice when it counts most, something he's shown me every single day since we left Chicago for New Jersey.

I know, not the place I imagined myself living once making it to the NHL. But Windsor is almost dead center between Philly and New York City, so it held a lot of appeal after we were both drafted this summer.

Him to New York, and me to Philadelphia.

Playing for different teams again is something I'm not fond of, especially with knowing how great we can be on the ice together. A true dynamic duo that could be unstoppable, if given the chance to shine. But at least we're on two different teams within a couple hours of each other, making living together a possibility during the off-season and when our home schedules match up.

It's better than nothing.

And I'd also be lying if I said I wasn't slightly butthurt over the fact that he got New York when they had been my team for *years* growing up.

Philly isn't bad though. Plus it gives me a little barb to toss at him, seeing as they drafted me five picks before New York got him.

Whatever little wins I can get in this never-ending competition with him, I'm gonna take.

"I'm still proud of you," he says, ice blue eyes darting between mine. "You did a lot better than I did the first time I drove one."

"I severely doubt that."

"Well, considering you didn't tip it, I'd say yes."

My mouth drops open slightly. "You're kidding."

Another shake of the head. "Hand on heart, I don't think I made it more than twenty yards before I toppled over. Granted, I was sixteen, but still."

Laughter erupts between us, and he reaches up, thumb caressing my cheek where I'm smiling. I fight the urge to lean into it, but it's almost impossible.

His touch still manages to light my skin on fire the same way that dimpled grin sends my heart into a tailspin. The same way his eyes tell me he loves me, even if the words don't leave his lips.

My phone rings, cutting through our silence, and a quick glance at it reveals Louis's name on the screen.

"Always ruining a moment," Quinn mutters, pressing a chaste kiss to my lips. "But you should probably take it."

I know I should. Louis never calls us unless it's something important— usually concerning our contracts or some other legal crap—which is exactly why I answer the damn thing as quickly as possible.

"Louis," I say in a way of greeting.

"Oakley," Louis's voice comes from through the speaker. "You got a minute?"

"Wouldn't have answered if I didn't."

He sighs on the other end of the line. "I see that boyfriend of yours is a wonderful influence on your attitude," he notes, exasperation clear in his tone. "I'll make it quick. Do you want the good news or bad news first?"

My stomach might as well have dropped off the edge of the Empire State Building. "Bad news. Always."

Quinn's brows furrow, clearly picking up on my panicked and slightly agitated state. Which only gets worse when Louis says the three words I was dreading most.

"You've been traded."

Instantly, my entire world tilts on its axis, my heart making its way into my throat. I suffocate on it as I gape over my shoulder at Quinn, completely at a loss for words.

He's off the bike in an instant, eyes checking me over as if the news Louis just told me caused physical damage.

"What's going on?" he whispers.

"I was traded," I murmur more to myself than anyone else, shock taking over and making me just...numb.

"What?" Quinn asks, and I can see a small amount of anger setting a crease in his brow. "How is that possible? I thought Philly drafting you locked you into a contract?"

"I thought so too." I'm at a complete loss, my stomach rolling and twisting, ready to revolt. "Louis, how is this even possible? Is there some clause or something that—"

"Would the two of you shut up so I can tell you the rest of the information?" Louis snaps, breaking through our conversation. "Jesus, I should have known not to sign the two of you together. Now you're gonna be even more of a pain in my ass than normal after this news breaks."

"What the hell are you talking about?" Quinn asks before I have the chance to.

Louis ignores him. "How do you feel about New York?"

That's enough to snap me out of my stupor. "It's fucking great, but you're about to send me off to some far end of the continent so I don't understand why you'd sit here and rub in the fact that—"

"Oakley. With all due respect, shut up."

My mouth drops open, then snaps back closed while Quinn chokes back a laugh.

"Great. Now ask me where you're going."

The urge to vomit is real when I whisper, "Where am I going?"

I wait for the words *California* or *Denver* or heaven forbid somewhere in fucking Canada to come barreling out of his mouth.

"New York."

I didn't hear him right, because I swear to God I heard him say—

"New York?" I repeat, my gaze locking with Quinton's. The second the words leave my lips, his eyes might as well bug out of his head, and he grabs the phone out of my hand, switching Louis to speaker.

"Surely you're joking," comes from Quinn, whose eyes haven't left mine. "And if you are, you're fucking fired because that shit isn't funny."

"Well, hello to you too, Quinton," Louis says, and I can almost see the smirk on his face at Quinn's threat. If there's anyone else on this planet who can handle my boyfriend's temperamental side, it's Louis.

"Cut the shit. Is this real?"

"You know I can't be discussing another player's contract—"

"Louis." Quinton seethes into the receiver. "Is. This. Real?"

"Quinton—"

"Just answer the question, Louis. Please," I snap, my temper wearing thin.

Another chuckle comes from him. "Yes, it's real. You've been traded to New York, effective immediately."

Quinn and I are both rattled from his bombshell as we gape at each other. Somehow, I find my voice through the shock. "How is this possible?"

A disembodied scoff comes from the phone, floating into the space between Quinn and I. "I'm going to pretend you didn't say that. I'm one of the best in the business, and when I have two NHL bound prospects who'd like to end up on the same team, I'm gonna do everything in my power to make it happen."

"But my contract with Philly—"

"There's a trade clause in it," he reassures me. "It's legal, and it's happening. As of today, you're officially a player for the New York Knights."

Quinton lets out a loud whoop, the sound of it echoing off the pavement of the empty parking lot. Then he jumps up and down, almost pumping himself up before squatting in front of me. Excitement and joy dance in those blue eyes as he reels me in for a long, slow kiss that draws a moan out from the back of my throat.

"I, uh…I take it you're no longer available to talk, Oakley. So just call me tomorrow and we can sort through the paperwork." I hear him pause before adding, "Congratulations. Both of you."

The phone beeps, notifying us of the call ending before we could say anything else, but it doesn't matter. Quinton's too busy stealing all the oxygen straight from my lungs. Something he's gonna be able to do a whole lot more now that we're on the same schedule.

Playing for the same damn team.

I finally break our kiss, resting my forehead against Quinton's to catch my breath.

"I didn't think I'd learn to drive a motorcycle *and* get traded when I woke up this morning." I blow out another long breath. "It's almost too much adrenaline for one day."

"Aw, c'mon," Quinn chides, a giant grin on his face. "I think this calls for a celebration. A really fucking big one."

And with that, my boyfriend drops from where he was squatting in front of me to a kneeling position. Specifically on *one* knee.

My heart leaps in my throat as I gawk at him, completely at a loss for words now. But somehow, I find them when I notice him digging in the front pocket of his jeans.

"Quinn, I love you, but—"

"Not exactly the word a guy wants to hear after *I love you*, Oak."

True. "But we've only been dating—"

"Relax, it's not what you think," he says, glancing at me briefly.

But it's so soon.

"Okay, but Quinn—"

"Baby, can you just shut up?"

I clamp my mouth shut as I watch him, waiting silently until he produces…a pair of socks. All rolled up in the tightest little bundle he could manage.

Not a ring.

I breathe a silent sigh of relief when he takes my hand, grabs the top end of the socks and lets them unravel right into my palm.

My jaw drops back open.

They're a pair of unofficial team socks for the New York Knights. Striped horizontally in hunter green, black, and white, complete with my name and #33 stitched into the material.

I look down at the pair of socks in my hands and back up at him, only to find him grinning at me like a goddamn fool. Dimples and all.

"Oakley Reed, will you be my teammate again?"

It's by far the corniest, cheesiest thing he's ever done, but fuck, if I don't love him even more for it. But then something dawns at me as I stare down at the socks a little more.

"You knew?"

He rises to full height with a laugh. "Of course I knew."

"But…how? Louis—"

"Accidentally attached the wrong contract to an email to me. Your contract," he finishes. "Which could have been really bad, yes. But thankfully it was to me and not someone else."

"So you knew before he called just now."

He nods. "I told him I wanted to surprise you with it, since I got to be the one to find out first. So I had the socks made and express-shipped to the apartment. They just got here this morning, so I let Louis know today was the day."

I blink at him, not sure if I'm in awe or completely pissed. "Just how long have you two been sitting on this?"

This time, I get an off-handed shrug. "Like three days?"

Yeah, definitely pissed. "You knew for *days* and didn't say anything?"

"I had to wait for the socks to get in," he says in defense. "And Louis wanted me to tell you he's sorry for accidentally breaching confidentiality and he hopes you don't fire him."

I scoff. "You two are unbelievable."

"No, what's unbelievable is the fact that you don't wanna marry me," he counters, brow arched playfully. "Care to explain that one, Oak?"

I bite my bottom lip because, yeah, it wasn't my finest moment. Not by a long shot.

"It's just too soon."

He nods. "I agree, but I can tell from your reaction, I'm gonna be ready a helluva lot sooner than you will. So just take your time, and you can ask when you're ready."

"*I* can ask?"

"I was the one who chased in the beginning. It's your turn now, baby." He steps between my thighs and gazes down at me, arms wrapping around the back of my neck. "But are you gonna answer me or not? Every minute you keep me waiting, I'm gonna double when it's your turn to get on one knee."

My brows furrow, and then I realize…

"I don't think I have a choice in being your teammate when contracts are involved."

"Good," he says, a lilt of laughter in his voice. "Just means you're stuck with me."

And with that, he pulls my head against his chest in an embrace that has me thinking I might be okay with it. After all, there's worse people in the world for me to be stuck with.

"I still can't believe you knew and you just pretended the entire time you didn't."

"It was pretty easy, seeing as I learned from the best."

The smile in his voice is obvious to anyone with ears, and I pull back to glare at him in disbelief that he actually went there.

But he did. It's Quinn, and he loves nothing more than to push all my buttons.

"You know, I really fucking hate you sometimes."

He laughs that smooth, satin laugh of his, squeezing me against his chest even tighter than he was moments ago.

"I know, baby. I love you too."

THE END

Acknowledgments

This book…I'm torn between calling it my longest project and my quickest. All in all, I wrote a good 75% of it in a two-week period, but it also took almost a freaking year to actually come to fruition.

First, I want to thank all my wonderful readers who have stuck by me during this extremely trying year. Every. Single. One of you.

There were times I didn't think I'd ever find my way back to writing again after the year I've had, but with each one of you waiting and championing for new work, continuing to read my work, write to me, check on me…I found my way through one of the darkest times of my life. I found my muse again. And I couldn't have done that without all of you.

To Abby, my PA. Thank you for your never-ending support, guidance, and love. This journey never would have happened without you.

To Nichol for checking on me every hour on the damn hour while I was deep in the writing cave. This book literally would have never seen the light of day if it weren't for you.

To Emily, for this cover. You slay, always, and I can't wait to continue working with you on the rest of this series.

To my alphas/betas, Amy, Emily, Jackie, and Meredith, for making sure this book wasn't a complete pile of garbage before going out in the world. And for checking me on all the hockey crap to ensure it was as realistic and accurate as possible. You're the real MVPs here.

To Marley, for kicking my ass into writing again and for withholding our project until I literally got my life in order. You're one of the best people I could ask for.

To Z and Amanda, for continuing to whip my books into tip-top shape and making them the cleanest manuscripts on the damn planet.

To my Enclave and my Legacies. Thank you for your dedication and love. For supporting me, promoting me, and cheering me on. You guys are the reason I've made it this far. I cannot thank you enough.

Thank you for being here. Thank you for reading my work.

Thank you, thank you, thank you.

— CE Ricci

About the Author

CE Ricci is an international best-selling author who enjoys plenty of things in her free time, but writing about herself in the third person isn't one of them. She believes home isn't a place, but a feeling, and it's one she gets when she's chilling lakeside or on hiking trails with her dogs, camera in hand. She's addicted to all things photography, plants, peaks, puppies, and paperbacks, though not necessarily in that order. Music is her love language, and traveling the country (and world) is the way she chooses to find most of her inspiration for whatever epic love story she will tell next!

CE Ricci is represented by Two Daisy Media.
For all subsidiary rights, please contact:
Savannah Greenwell — info@twodaisy.com